THE OTHER DETECTIVE

The mystery of a murder in a torn city

JAMES DAVIDSON

THE BOOK FOLKS

Published by The Book Folks

London, 2024

This book is a work of fiction. Names, characters, businesses, organizations, places and events are either the product of the author's imagination or are used fictitiously. Any resemblance to actual persons, living or dead, events or locales is entirely coincidental. The spelling is British English.

ISBN 978-1-80462-218-6

www.thebookfolks.com

1

Gdańsk, Polish People's Republic

1961

The First Rune

The tree writhed in a circle of headlights. Something hung there where its antlered branches vanished in the fog. Sleepless, the detective climbed the ragged dirt track towards a huddle of shadows picked out by the ends of their cigarettes. The wind carried a whiff of the sea through the dull wasteland, a swirl of dead leaves, and snatched it away. Roman, the superintendent, emerged from the void.

'They woke you too, Nowak.' His breath steamed in the ghost light. 'At this hour, I don't know if it's tomorrow or yesterday.'

'It's tomorrow, Comrade.'

'Don't be so sure.'

Behind them, the pale tree loomed – an ash, lopsided and brittle, branches woven crazy like tentacles. A ladder was propped against the side of the trunk, where an officer took photographs. Anna's torch swept over the roots.

Roman tilted his head towards the tree. 'She's all yours, Detective.'

She wasn't anybody's. In the fraught electricity, a woman hung from the tree, head slumped forward behind long, lank hair. Her limbs swayed in the salt breeze.

'I hate heights.' Anna tested the ladder and climbed a few rungs.

The smell of the sea was strong up there, shellfish and mist, the rusting hulks of trawlers in the shroud. She flashed her torch over drab clothes, worker's gear; bare feet with curled toes turned purple. Too exposed in the headlights, Anna felt a wave of vertigo. The ladder creaked and shivered.

'Can someone hold this thing steady?' she called.

'I'll do it.' Roman threw down his cigarette and stamped on the butt. He plodded over in his weary way and took hold of the bottom of the ladder. 'She's been here all night, they reckon. The rain washed her clean.'

Anna climbed a few rungs higher and checked the top of the woman's head, flashing the torch over a neat parting between fine strands of hair clumped together. She wiped the damp fringe out of the woman's face and tilted her head upwards. There was a rime of sand in her eyebrows. Smears of mascara and lipstick clung to dirty pores. The eyes were blue; they gazed empty into the beam. Caught by a swoon of gravity, Anna almost fell. The ladder rattled as she grabbed it. *Who are you?* She felt a thousand metres above the ground, closed her eyes, and clung to the ladder.

'Think she was a whore?' Roman said.

Anna breathed and opened her eyes. 'You say that every time it's a woman.'

'Yeah, well.'

'Does it make them seem less human to you?' She climbed down a few rungs. 'Does it make it easier to sleep after work?'

'Me? I sleep like a baby.'

'Of course you do.'

Roman was a prick, but he wasn't the worst in the Gdańsk Police. He'd been around forever and receded into the background like a familiar rock formation. Anna knew to ignore his crassness.

'Come on,' he said. 'Get down. Let's pack this up and go home.'

'Wait.' She peered behind the body, shining her torch through the gap. 'There's something there.'

'What?'

She pushed at the hanging corpse, but it was heavy. 'Grab her legs, budge her.'

She pushed at the woman's flank as Roman pulled, and the branch winced overhead. Behind the body, the light showed a rough symbol carved in the bark:

ᛃ

'What is that…?' Her torch cast grooves in the gnarled trunk.

'Shit,' Roman said.

'A rune of some kind?'

'Shut up.' He let go of the body and it swung back into place. The branch creaked. 'Not another word.'

'But…'

'Come with me. We need to talk.'

Flatfooted and dizzy on solid earth, Anna followed the superintendent into the black trees some yards away, out of the circle of headlights where the technicians smoked and muttered and loaded their gear into the van.

'That symbol…'

Roman lit another cigarette. 'Lower your voice.'

'I think it's fascist. They had an obsession with runes.'

He shook his head, breathed out smoke. 'There's no such thing as runes. Leave that carving – whatever it is – out of your report. Understand?'

'Why?'

'For my part, I'll make sure anyone who saw it, forgets they did. Forensics, technicians. If any photos turn up in the file, you burn them, got it? Or you'll be to blame.'

Through the smoke, his face was lined with anxiety. He rubbed his red eyes. 'This is all we need.'

'You think… is it… you think this is something to do with…' She looked around her then whispered, '…*Danzig*?'

'That name is forbidden, Comrade. The place never existed. Trust me; I'm old, I was there.'

'Right. So, I'll just–'

'You'll forget what you saw. Not a word. Get out to the docks and interview some whores. Find out if any working girls are missing. Dig something up. File her away neatly, or just file her away. We'll move on with our lives.'

'I don't think she was a prostitute.'

'Nowak, I'm warning you.'

There was no point arguing with him, she had learned. 'As you wish, Comrade.'

But as they walked back through the web of branches into the clearing where the old ash tree pierced the chill, the name *Danzig* persisted. Spoken aloud, an alternate history beckoned, concealed itself, mourned.

2

Danzig, the Free City

Three days before the start of WWII

It was late in Danzig. The nightshift was endless, but I didn't care. After dawn, the police station was peaceful. Loneliness suited me, I stuck to the dark and didn't need anyone. In my office with the curtains shut, I made peace with the end; this city was already dead.

The call came after 2am.

'Detective?'

'Who is this?' I asked.

'You're Tal? Johann Tal? It's about the murder. At the shipyards. They said it had to be you, nobody else. Come alone. Hurry.'

'What murder?'

'Go outside. Downstairs. You'll be picked up.'

'What are you–'

'Hurry. She's almost gone. There'll be nothing left.'

'She…?'

The line went dead. I gulped another coffee; there would be no sleep at the end of this shift. On the pavement, I paced in the shadow, avoiding the circle of streetlight. In my black coat and dark grey fedora, I let myself vanish. There might have been a moment caught there in the freezing Baltic wind that blows up the main street – time to prepare, to rehearse my death rituals – but the car arrived quickly. A black Volkswagen turned the corner, dark windows shiny in the lit street. It pulled up in front of me, and the window lowered.

Sleepless eyes looked out. 'You the detective?'

'That depends.'

'Get in.'

We drove through Danzig in limbo. I looked for the driver's eyes in the mirror, but it was crooked. He turned in his seat to glance back, blue eyes set in a brown tissue of insomnia, a gleam of malice and distorted pleasure.

'You look funny,' he said. 'Not Polish, are you?'

'I'm not anything.'

I leaned my forehead against the glass, hoping to discourage further conversation. But in the blur of streetlights, the inside of the car projected outwards into virtuality.

'No offence,' he said. 'You know how it is.'

They try to suck you into their world like this; subtle invitations to agree, hints at shared experience. I said nothing.

'Dragged a couple of Polish girls in here a few nights ago,' he continued. 'My mistake. Couldn't get the stink out of the car. Had to take if for a clean yesterday.'

I stared through the glass, letting the reflections slide off. Approaching the sea, the wind picked up, scattering litter and salt spray on the windscreen. The shipyards rose from the shadow, silhouetted cranes and warehouses picked out by lamplight.

'What's this job about?' the driver said.

'I have no idea.'

He shrugged. 'It's never a courtesy call, this time of night.'

The car pulled up outside a chain metal fence with a weathered sign, "DANGER". The headlights blinked out; I kept staring into the place where the outside had turned black.

'Come on. Let's get it over with.' The driver climbed out, slowly, heavily, as tired as I was.

A blast of wind caught through the open car door. The backdrop of the Baltic sky was blotted out, but I tasted it. I straightened into a freezing wind.

'This way.' The driver pushed open a gate in the fence that had been left unlocked.

I followed him through an overgrown lot, alongside a cliff of waste metal. Our footsteps rang and died among cavernous warehouses. Hidden walls loomed over hollow spaces, picked out by isolated lamps. A tang of seagull shit pricked the air of corrosion and crumbled bricks, but only just; the wind carried it away with everything else. A single bulb showed an open door hewn from nowhere. A man looked out, just like the driver, thickset, a rough brown suit, hate and lewdness in his blue eyes.

He nodded. 'The detective? In here.'

The metal door clanged shut behind us. A discoloured bulb fizzed in the ceiling, leaking stained light. I saw a metal staircase leading down and turned away. Anywhere but down.

The officer nodded; he blocked the way back. It wasn't too late to get out, but I knew I would follow this thread to the end. I wanted the end; let it come, I was tired of circling.

A metronome seemed to beat through the walls. I descended into a stone basement. I followed a scrap of light along a hall that throbbed with pipes and wires – industry that never stopped; even at night, the warehouses pulsed in a kind of living death. My chest fluttered with panic, being underground. A low-ceilinged corridor took shape as my eyes adjusted. A door opened up ahead, and the superintendent, Henrik, looked out.

'Tal. Thank God.'

I almost sighed with relief. Henrik had been my boss since I first made the Danzig Police Force. I knew he respected me; I'd proven myself over the years. I felt something release inside as I recognised a face down here, but the release was dangerous. Never let your guard down.

'What's this about?'

'Come in here. Shut the door.'

I found myself in a concrete side room off the basement. It might have been a janitor's office but there were no tools. A few thick pipes protruded from the wall, giving off heat. In the middle of the floor, a naked woman lay on her back in a patch of congealed blood, legs and arms spread out in an X. I saw stab wounds all over her torso. Blood was spattered in places on the wall and ceiling, which were otherwise pale grey, coated with dust.

Henrik stood back in the corner. In the sterile light, I saw how exhausted he was; he didn't belong down here either.

'Sorry to call you out like this, Tal. Truth is, we need your help.'

'You didn't need all the secrecy. It's my job to solve murders.' I took out my notepad and pen, but the superintendent stopped me.

'It's not that kind of case.'

'What do you mean?'

The ceiling was too low, it pressed down on us. The blood stank. I knelt over the body. There was a pile of clothes next to her, stained with gore.

'Early thirties. Indentation on her ring finger; she was married or divorced. Where's the ring?' I tilted her slack face towards me. Her eyes and mouth were open wide. I gritted my teeth and tried to see the real woman behind the trauma. 'Long skull, probably German.' I sniffed at her blonde hair. 'Expensive shampoo. She had money. Classy…'

'No, you're doing it wrong.'

Henrik squatted beside me. He pulled my hand from the dead woman's face, and she fell away. 'These people, they were important. It's dangerous.' He was speaking too fast; he didn't know how to mask his fear. 'Nobody knows about this room. The public can't find out. The Nazis are sending their own investigators from Berlin.'

'Berlin? But they can't… in the Free City… The Reich has no jurisdiction…'

'Tal, there's more.'

His breath was rancid – weariness and fear. He wasn't built for this life; he was a family man, the kind who gets up early in the morning and eats breakfast with his wife and kids. He didn't belong in an underground murder scene past two in the morning. I followed the whites of his eyes and noticed the dead man in the opposite corner. Sunk into shadow, he was partially hidden behind a pile of crates.

'Oh shit.' I crawled through the dust. Crouched by the body, I shone my torch over agonised folds. 'His eyes are sad, like he was crying. Who are these people?'

'It's better you don't know.'

The trembling ring of torchlight showed a dark suit with a swastika armband. 'A Nazi… and the woman, his wife?'

'Officially speaking, this room doesn't exist. This crime never happened. Tomorrow there'll be no trace of it. You won't mention what you've seen here to anybody. Least of all the press. God forbid if a journalist got hold of this.'

Henrik's wide eyes were bloodshot, buried in swollen creases; how old we had grown in this job.

'So, I'll just…' I let the sentence hang for him to complete, but it just hung. 'I'll check the body for cause of death…'

'Tal, there's a problem.' He didn't continue.

'What is that? On his wrist…' I picked up the dead man's arm; his jacket was stained inside the cuff. 'Looks like… what? Semen?'

'Tal, don't.'

I brought the cuff close to my face and sniffed at the material. 'Something sweet.'

'Tal…'

I licked the stain. 'Acidic. Milky… sour…'

'Stop it!' Henrik pulled me back. 'You're not here to investigate the bodies.'

'What then?'

'Look.' He drew me back to the dead woman and picked up the pile of loose clothes beside her. 'See?' He lifted a green-blue uniform to the light.

'What…' I took it from him. 'Danzig Police Force. Not her size, not his either. It's someone else's. A man's cut. The material is ripped here. And there's blood. Could be the victim's blood, could be someone else's.' I looked around. 'But these clothes aren't hers. Where are her things?'

'That's all that was in this room,' he said. 'Nothing was removed.'

I tried to think, in the heat and the welling paranoia. This had to be some kind of game. The way the woman was laid out, it was too obviously staged; nobody dies like that, limbs stretched in a star. They wanted to trick me. Was Henrik part of it? I grasped for a strategy, but the ceiling was too low, this room was strangling. Play along, I thought, play along.

'Alright,' I said. 'Do you want me to tell you that a Danzig police officer brought her here? He undressed her, took her clothes, and went out, leaving his own things behind?'

Henrik rubbed his eyes. 'If a Danzig police officer killed a Nazi… they'll shut us down. It could start a war.'

'There must be another explanation…'

'Listen, Detective, you take this uniform and find out whom it belongs to. You work alone, you don't talk to anybody. Nothing written down; no files.'

'And these… the woman…' I gestured at the corpses.

'That's not your affair. We'll handle them on the dayshift. Bernie will take care of it; he'll liaise with the Berlin police.'

'Bernie's one week from retirement.'

'Exactly.'

'I could–'

'You don't want to touch this case, Tal, trust me. You stay on the nightshift, out of sight. Take care of the uniform. Report directly to me, nobody else. Got it? If there's a killer in the police, you find them. Don't trust anybody.'

'And forensics?'

'No forensics. Gestapo are all over them. You're on your own. But, Tal, not a word to anyone. This room doesn't exist. What you saw tonight was just a dream.'

'Just a dream, sure.'

'There'll be chaos if this gets out. The public will panic. Germany will demand action. The Poles will respond. God knows, things are tense enough already. Pressure is unbearable. If people think there's some crazed police officer running around Danzig, naked, making scenes like this… Christ. They already don't trust us. If it's local police…'

I closed my eyes and let everything go still. The aftertaste of milk. 'There's a baby. Where's the baby?'

'What are you talking about?'

'These people, they were parents. They had a new-born child. That's vomit on the father's sleeve. The baby has colic, and threw up milk onto his arm while he rocked her.'

'Jesus Christ.' Henrik dug his fingertips into the raw skin beneath his eyes. 'You just find out who that uniform belongs to. Nothing else. There is no child, understand? There is no child.'

3

Outside, the driver was smoking. Needing to get my breath back, I sucked up the wind of seaweed and cranes.

'Get in,' the driver said.

'Nah. I'll walk. I need to think.' Snuggled into my armpit, I held the bloody uniform from the crime scene wrapped in my jacket.

The driver glanced at it but looked away. 'You have to get in. Orders from upstairs.'

'From upstairs, of course.'

We drove through frigid streets. For a moment there was something like peace in the old town, an empty square, flowerpots on a window ledge. I remember sometimes how I fell in love with Danzig, in youth, the narrow townhouses a blur of pastel shades; some woman's reverie at her window; the spectral melody of the carillons. But I could smell the heady scent of blood from the uniform tucked under my arm. We drove around a corner and came upon a group of men swarming in the street, howling.

I sat up straight to look through the windscreen. 'What are they doing?'

'None of our business.' The driver didn't slow.

We coasted past the scene; fifteen to twenty men were beating a few figures on the ground. They kicked and punched without rest. Absorbed in the carnival, they didn't notice us.

'Stop the car!' I banged on the window. 'Stop the car.'

'It's not our job.'

Through the glass we heard their hysterical joy, covering over the screams of whoever was lost from sight beneath stomping boots.

'Someone will die…' I swivelled to look out of the rear window as we carried on down the street. 'Hey! Stop! Let me out! I'm police… it's my duty…'

We drove around the corner, and the sight was annulled, replaced by a peaceful, empty stretch of road. Darkened windows reflected the streetlights; the angular roofs were still, the night sky swallowed up.

I sought the driver's face in his mirror. 'Didn't you see what they were doing?'

'You would have gone out there on your own, against all those men?' There was a trace of smile in his piercing eyes. 'It's true what they say about you.'

'What do they say?'

The smile went out. We drove on through the night.

* * *

Hours later I lay in bed, but this was only a game I played; there would be no sleep. Daria curled beside me, immersed in dream. I listened to her breathe and knew I didn't belong. Daria's cramped bedroom, with her scant possessions and the smell of her dark hair, the damp walls, her clothes drying on the rack. It was all too fragile. I felt frightened in a way I hadn't known since childhood. It was the bedroom mirror that haunted me. Dim streetlight through the curtains caught on the glass that hung on the wall opposite Daria's bed.

I got up, naked, shivering, and crossed the room. God, I was terrified. I took the mirror off the wall and laid it upside down on the dresser. The dread receded, but when I lay down again, I felt it pulse beneath the hidden mirror. I shouldn't have turned it over, that's how you let the fear in: I had given ground to it. To turn the mirror over was irrational, but when I asked myself if I could hang it back on the wall, I already knew the answer: let rationality wait until morning.

Somewhere in the sighing building, a baby's wail cut through the walls. I flinched in the bed and almost cried aloud. I needed to get away. I dressed quickly in the cold, but before I could sneak out, Daria opened her eyes.

'What is it?' she asked. 'Where are you going? Is it time already?'

'It's nothing. Go back to sleep.'

Her hands groped in the shadow and found the bedside clock. It was always dark in here. Lightbulbs could no longer be procured in Danzig, and we rarely met in daylight.

'Almost 5am.' Her voice was drowsy and soft. 'I have to get up soon. You should be asleep. What are you doing?'

Paralysed, half naked in the morning chill, I clutched my shoes. 'I don't know.'

That's how it worked between us: me on the nightshift; Daria with her early starts at the cafe. We crossed paths along brief in-between hours, in these premature autumn nights, we raked what rest we might find in each other's skin; and parted. I was a cop, she was a waitress; it might have worked out in some other city. My shift had ended, her day was about to start.

'Come back to bed.' Her voice coaxed, her hand beckoned in the shadow, but I couldn't move.

'I found a letter on my desk at the station. It said, "Quit the police before you drown in the dock." They signed off, "A Friendly Warning."'

Daria swore under her breath in Polish. 'It's a prank. Stop taking everything to heart. You're paranoid.'

'You don't know how bad things are. Listen, Daria, you should get out of Danzig. It's not safe. Not for Poles, not for anyone. There are rumours… Everyone says war is coming…'

'Hah! What, leave my job, my family? My mother who can't stand up? And go where? The economy's wrecked. There are no lightbulbs. Come back to bed. Sleep.'

'I can't. I can't.'

'What happened to you tonight?' In the dark, her eyes were like lamps. 'You're too sensitive for the job.' Her voice was soothing, like a mother's. 'The world's not ending. That's just a feeling. People always thought it was the end, but the world never ended.'

I buttoned my shirt and looked through the window blinds into the rain. 'I have to leave.'

'I see what this is. You're leaving me.' The tenderness drained from her voice, and I longed for it.

'What?'

'Be a man. If you want to leave me, do it right. Don't just sneak away in the dark.' She sat up with the sheet around her.

'Daria, I'm sorry, it's just…'

'Oh God.' She shook her head; I smelled her hair. 'What's wrong with me? My friends all warned me, never date a cop. I wouldn't listen. A German cop too…' She switched into Polish, muttering to herself, 'Germans and Poles, we're not supposed to mix.'

'Don't you start with that talk. There's enough at the station. I told you when we started: Poles and Germans, we're all Danzigers.'

'Creeping out in the night. Sneaking away. What, you got bored of me, and now you're moving on?'

'It's not that. It's just, I don't know, maybe the nightshift is making me crazy. I just… at the moment, with everything, I should be alone. It's better that way. Better for you, I mean. You need to get away from me. I'm bad news. There's war coming; we're on opposite sides. None of us can protect anyone else.'

'You know what, Detective? I pitied you because you were alone. I guess I thought I could help you. But you wanted to be alone, you always did.' She climbed out of bed. Naked in the frail light through the blinds, her gaunt frame was sickly. 'Go then. Be alone.'

She pushed me towards the door and opened it. I was outside. It was freezing in the hall.

'Wait…' I reached for her, but she skipped back, birdlike, into the dark.

The door closed.

4

At some lost hour I must have fallen asleep among sketches and notes while the first pale light filtered through the shuttered window. My mind wandered between dream and nightmare, seeking something. A memory of Daria's hair flicked and vanished in the dark. I awoke. The foundations breathed, footsteps in the halls and the stairway as workers rose and set out. Weak sunlight broke over Danzig. The carillon played from the tower of the town hall, its tuned bells intoned a strange, delicate melody – neither happy nor sad but nostalgic, though not for a history that passers-by might name as they stopped for a moment to listen in a pool of shade. Danzig's lullabies.

It seemed only a moment had elapsed. I woke with fright in the late afternoon. I felt ill. My limbs were heavy and stiff. After days of insomnia, I'd fallen too far into the well of sleep. This was not the time to rest, I needed to be on my feet. Our world was crumbling. Round-ups, arrests, mass expulsions, but this was only whispered about; the newspapers didn't dare report such things. The Polish army was massed along the border, they said. Who could tell what was true? Europe convulsed; Danzig lay at the centre of the ratcheting pressure. Independence was impossible, Germany or Poland would claim the Free City.

I was getting dressed when the landlady, Frau Grubach, knocked on my door, as she always did when I got up late. 'Just a minute…'

'Herr Tal,' she called through the keyhole. 'Daylight's almost spent. I don't mean to be a bother, you know I'm not that kind, but you really should get up before dark.'

'I know, I know.' I buttoned up my shirt. 'It was a long night. Working too hard.'

'I brought your coffee and your news.' She came bustling into the room with a tray and a pile of newspapers that she set by the gramophone.

'Have to let the light in.' Frau Grubach opened the shutters.

My heart braced for a flood of sunshine, bright afternoon, but there was only leaden sky outside.

'There,' she said. 'At least you didn't miss the whole day.' She couldn't hide the distaste on her face as she glanced around the disorder that the light revealed. She sniffed something. The bloody uniform from the crime scene lay on the floor where I'd sketched it in my notebook.

'Sorry about the mess… I've been busy.'

'You know I could clean it for you while you're out.'

'No. Thank you. I have my systems.'

'Ah, your systems, of course.' Would she never leave? 'But look at your uniform… it's filthy.'

'It was a messy job yesterday. Please, leave it…'

'I'll clean it for you.' She picked up the bloodstained uniform and held it to the dim glow of the window. 'Why, there's blood…'

I saw the dead woman laid out, her glassy eyes.

'No.' I snatched the uniform, too roughly.

Frau Grubach backed away, cheeks flushed.

'I'm sorry, Herr Tal. I don't mean to be a busybody. You know I'm not that kind of landlady. I always say, what my tenants get up to in their own time, that's their business. You're a good man. It's an impossible job nowadays, policing in Danzig. I'll leave you in peace.'

'Thanks for the newspapers.'

5

By the time I arrived downtown, Danzig was already darkening. Before going to my office, I stopped at forensics, across the street from the police station. I felt strangely guilty as I entered with the bloody uniform in a paper bag tucked under my armpit. At the front desk, Julia appeared asleep, head propped up on one hand, a closed book in the other. But as I was creeping past, afraid to wake her, she said, 'Tal. You're not supposed to be here.'

'I just wanted to talk to Esther. She in? Got a sample for her.'

'Who?' She rubbed her eyes. 'What are you wearing?'

I looked down and saw that I'd crossed the city in my house sandals. Like I was sleepwalking. 'Oh, my boots are dirty… I just… I don't know.'

'Get it together, man.'

'Is Esther upstairs? I needed to talk to her.'

'Didn't you hear?'

These were words that Danzigers had learned to dread. 'No…'

'Esther's gone.'

I looked for an escape route. The windows were black, the rest of the building was unlit behind the reception area; trying to cut energy bills, or just out of lightbulbs. Only the front desk was illuminated. Behind Julia's back, the corridor and the staircase receded into shadow.

'Gone. What do you mean?'

'You know what I mean.'

I parsed the communal understanding she implied; the confusion must have shown on my face.

'Tal, you're a good man. Everyone says that about you.'

'Because they don't know me.'

She checked over her shoulder but there was nobody in the shadow. Still, she lowered her voice. 'Esther, well, it was inevitable.'

'Inevitable?' These moments of communicative failure were becoming frequent. 'Esther's excellent at her job.'

'Yeah, well.' Julia looked around again.

The whole building felt deserted. Nothing moved but a tremor in the light fixture. I did understand of course, I only wanted to pretend, to play at innocence. Esther was Jewish.

'Remember when being good at your job made you valuable?' I said. 'People helped you.'

Julia picked up her book. The hints of mutual understanding were put away. She shrugged. 'Now we're all shit at our jobs; nobody imagines they'll be helped.'

'Who can I speak to instead of Esther? Who's around?'

'It doesn't work like that anymore. If you leave your sample with me, I'll give you a receipt. The lab will get back to you. But I have to clear everything "upstairs" first.'

I looked in the bag, smelled the encrusted blood. 'I'll come back later.'

As I turned to leave, she said, 'Tal. You're a good man. Stop all this. Stop trying so hard. It won't save you.'

6

I rubbed my eyes as I entered the police station. On the waiting benches, nervous visitors hunched, afraid to make a sound, glancing at the high ceiling, freezing in their coats and woollen hats. The waiting area was kept as cold as possible to deter people from coming in with their denunciations and complaints, their endless suspicions; or perhaps we just couldn't afford the heating bills anymore.

'Tal. What the hell are you wearing?' Markus looked up from the register at the front desk.

'What?' I looked down and remembered. 'Oh yeah, I... err... there was an accident.'

'Come on, man, get serious. There's war coming. Sandals at the police station, Jesus.'

The waiting visitors pretended not to watch our conversation. As I was passing the front desk, I almost collided with a tall man who emerged from the shadow. 'Excuse me...'

'Heil Hitler!' He snapped his heels together and saluted.

'Heil...' I almost dropped the paper bag as my arms got mixed up.

'Name?' The man had white hair and wore a black overcoat with a swastika armband.

I hesitated. 'Err...'

'That's just Tal,' Markus said. 'The detective. Don't mind him. He works the nightshift. We never see him usually. Tal, this is Inspector Wentz, he's over from Berlin to help with a case.'

'Help with a case?' I held out my hand, but he didn't shake it. 'This is neutral territory. Berlin has no jurisdiction.'

Wentz looked me up and down. 'Tal? Doesn't sound German. What kind of a name is that?'

'A short one.'

He stared a moment longer. 'We'll talk again.' He saluted and walked out of the building past all the startled faces along the waiting benches.

'Berlin?' I asked when he was gone.

'Gestapo,' Markus whispered. 'Everyone's on edge. They're watching us.'

I clutched the paper bag under my armpit as he eyed it. 'Is the chief in?'

'Henrik? You just missed him. But he wanted to speak to you. Said to find him.'

'That's what he always says.' Peering over the desk I saw a portable heater set up by Markus's feet. A crossword was nestled in the pages of the register. 'Busy shift?'

He shut the register. 'They went for drinks at the usual place. You'll find him there.'

'Strange. It's not like the superintendent. Henrik doesn't join in, he's not a drinker.'

'Tal, you dummy, it's the leaving drinks for Frank and Bastian. Everyone's gone down. I would too if I weren't stuck here, manning the last outpost of civilisation.'

'Leaving drinks? Nobody invited me.'

'Frank and Bastian got made redundant.'

'What?'

'Tal. You need to quit the nightshift, you're out of touch. You don't know what's going on.'

'Bastian leaving the force…? He's a good cop.'

'No point feeling sorry for him, we'll be next. Economy's gone to shit. It's the Poles. Their trade war killed the port. Everyone's out of work.'

'Yeah, well…'

'We'll be united with Germany soon. You'll see. The Poles will pay.'

I waited for him to finish. 'They have unemployment in Germany as well, you know,' I said. 'Inflation too.'

He stared. 'Did you want something? I'm busy.'

'I'm working on a case. If you…'

'Leave me out of it. I just got comfortable.'

'Anyone else around?'

'They've all gone for the drinks. The trainee kid's in the kitchen. I sent him to clean up.'

'I just need someone to check some files. Not difficult. You could do it from where you're sitting.' I took out my notes. 'It's about a police officer's uniform; I need to find the man it belongs to.'

He looked askance. 'What case is this? You're investigating police?'

'I can't discuss details. Official business. But look…' I took out the scrap of notepaper where I'd sketched out the measurements of the uniform. I checked it again and smoothed it out on the desk in front of Markus. 'Any idea who this might belong to? Around, I don't know, 165cm tall…'

'What the hell, Tal? Investigating the police, that's not good. Nobody likes a snitch, least of all these days.'

'No, it's not that kind of thing. It's just… look, there aren't so many officers in the Free City. You know everybody. "One-More-Round", they call you. Has anyone been missing lately? Any officer not turn up for work? Anybody acting strange?'

'You, for one.'

'Give me this.' I grabbed his register.

'Hey!'

I snatched the crossword and replaced it with my scrap of notepaper. 'See what you can dig up. Call me if you think of anything.'

'Fuck you, Tal.'

I passed reception and entered the echoing building. My house sandals clapped against the hard floors, and I felt ridiculous. A wanderer at night, I passed doorways into unlit offices where desks and chairs merged in the darkness, picked out in fluid outlines by the streetlights that pierced curtainless windows. It was peaceful. All the hidden sounds of blinking machinery came alive. I climbed the staircase, rising through the smell of disinfectant that haunted the landings.

Jo, one of the cleaners, was mopping when I came to the third floor. It was a relief to see him; I preferred talking to the non-police staff members.

'Evening.' I waved as I stepped carefully through the wet.

'Get off my floor!' he shouted. 'Just cleaned that.'

'Sorry, sorry.'

As I neared my office at the end of the hall, I saw the light was on. Through the open doorway I stopped and looked: there was nobody there. I was certain I hadn't left the light on yesterday, but who was I kidding? I wasn't certain of anything. I went in and shut the door behind me, sat down behind the desk and tried to find that old feeling of control I once felt there, with my documents, my systems, everything in its place. Next to the typewriter, a pile of papers remained to be typed up. There might be comfort in a bit of bureaucracy. I leafed through the printed lines and couldn't focus. An envelope dropped into my lap. Unmarked. Another note warning me to quit my job? I tore it open and pulled out a slip of rose-coloured paper.

> DEAR BELOVED,
> I CANNOT WAIT FOR US TO BE TOGETHER.
> DON'T FORGET ME, YOUR TRUE HEART.

Now I knew for sure, some trick *was* being played. They had sniffed out my paranoia and wanted to feed it. They would turn me insane. But, why? Was this real paranoia, or just pretend? Europe itself was crazy, Danzig was at its centre, caught between swelling technology and ranked masses of faceless men. Or perhaps it was only me, and everything was the same as ever in Danzig. A thousand years the port survived here on the edge of the Baltic; it would survive another thousand. I had to leave that room, leave the station altogether. I had to get rid of this case that didn't exist. I put the note in my jacket pocket and ran out, almost slipping in a patch of newly mopped disinfectant.

'Get off my floor!' Jo shouted.

* * *

Downstairs, a thin outline of light glowed at the end of the corridor where the kitchen door was half open. I hurried towards it, sandals sticking in the drying disinfectant. The trainee flinched when I looked inside and knocked.

'Hey, kid. You busy?'

'Shit. You frightened me. Thought everyone had gone.' Skinny, with red hair and glasses, maybe nineteen years old, he knelt in the cupboard with a toothbrush. All the cups and plates had been removed and piled next to him.

'What are you doing with that toothbrush?'

'Markus told me to give the kitchen a deep clean.'

'That's not your job. You're supposed to be learning police work.'

'Yeah well. Any time I ask, someone just sends me to clean a cupboard, scrub some boots. That kind of thing.'

'This place. If you need a job, come to me. I'll find something for you. If anyone tries to make you clean up, tell them you're running an errand for me. Come on. It's late. We need to get started.'

He gestured to the piled plates and cups. 'What about all this…?'

'Leave it. The cleaners will figure it out.'

We found an empty conference room down the hall. I set a pile of newspapers in front of him. 'Ready for some real police work?'

He watched doubtfully as I laid out the issues. 'I don't know.'

'This is the magic of the job. Investigation. It's addictive, trust me. I need you to look through these newspapers for a certain piece of information. When you've finished with these, go down to archives, you know where that is?'

'I dusted it last week.'

'What…? Never mind. Good. You go down there, and you get every newspaper you can find from this month and the previous month. You go through looking for news about a wealthy couple in Danzig with a baby. Ideally what we're looking for is a birth or a christening, that kind of thing. Or it might be a wedding or a divorce. Something to do with a family and a baby. We're looking for bankers, lawyers, business tycoons; rich folk. Plus, they're married. It's a husband and wife. Story could be about either one. Got it?'

'Err… do you think I could just clean the kitchen instead?'

I stopped. 'You want to be a police officer, don't you? Isn't that why you came here?'

'It was my dad who sent me. He got me on the Force through a friend of his. I tried to avoid it. It's because I told him I wanted to be an artist.'

'You wanted to be an artist? OK. Well, this is a kind of art. Find the information. Write down the edition of the newspaper and the page for every story you find that might be relevant. Anything at all about a wealthy couple with a baby, got it?'

'Write down…?'

'Don't you have a notepad? Jeez, kid, a police officer doesn't leave home without their notepad.'

7

At The Mermaid Tavern, a sign on the door read:

NO DOGS. NO POLES.
(POOR DOGS.)

I walked into a haze of brass and loud chatter, too warm after the gusts downtown. Swastika flags on the walls covered the usual pub fixtures. Several alcoholics glanced over their glasses as I passed. Although the bar was crowded with drinkers, it wasn't difficult to find the police officers as I followed the din of singing through a fog of cigarette smoke and sweat. Eight or nine cops were in full voice, chanting *The Watch on the Rhine.* To one side, the superintendent leaned back against the wall, eyes half-closed, cradling an empty mug of beer. He saw me and beckoned. The officers stopped singing when I entered the circle.

The nearest grabbed hold of me. 'Tal, shouldn't you be working your nightshift?'

'I needed to talk to Henrik.'

'Where are your boots?'

A few of them pulled at my jacket, a little too rough. 'You'll have a drink, won't you?'

I straightened my collar. 'Sorry, fellas, I'm on the clock. Just need to speak to the superintendent.'

But it was too loud to hear, or they were too drunk; they paid no heed. 'It's for Frank and Bastian. You heard what happened to them. Come on, Tal, police have to stick together. It's a brotherhood.'

'Sure, stick together all you like,' I said.

On the other side of the table, Bastian was leaning back against the wall, eyes bloodshot and mean. He drank and watched. I waved, but he ignored me.

Someone else shouted in my ear. 'Buy a round, Tal. Buy a round, everyone's bought one.'

'Another time. I'm busy,' I said. 'Got to work.' The smell of beer and tooth decay on his tired breath was nauseating.

'He's busy, he says. Looks out for number one, the detective. Let's his mates take care of themselves. Doesn't even buy a drink when they're made redundant.'

In the warm light with the smell of spilled beer, I felt dizzy. A horrible instinct of violence surprised me, I wanted to scratch and stab at these faces. The false smile dragged at my shoulders, burning resources. They were friendly, but I felt their hatred, the group hostility towards the one that doesn't fit. I tried to smile with my eyes. 'Excuse me…'

'Sing, Tal, come on, sing a verse.'

'Danzig's finest detective!' Frank grabbed me around the neck. He was completely drunk already. 'This is one man they'll never lay off. In the end, it'll be just Tal left on his own chasing all the criminals.'

'Maybe.' I tried to slip free, but he embraced me roughly.

'Have a gulp. Drink one schnapps with me. I have to go home to my wife tomorrow. What does she think of me now? I don't even have a job. I'm nothing. I'm trash. Have one schnapps with me.'

'I can't. I'm working.'

'Sit down, sit down. Christ, it's a special occasion. I've got my redundancy pay. Drinks are on me.'

'And your wife… she's pregnant, isn't she?'

'Fuck you, Tal.'

A new verse of the song started up, and they forgot me. I wasn't interesting after all. I'd known these binges along the harbour bars; nights when nobody wants to stop. The dim sense of some invisible door at the end of the morning, if we kept on drinking, we might pass through it. But the door didn't exist, and a sober detective didn't belong in that fantasy world. I managed to push through the singing men to where the superintendent was seated, heavy on his stool like a shipwreck. The bags under his eyes sagged. He looked like he hadn't slept in weeks.

'Henrik.'

'Tal, get me out of here. Let's go outside, it's too noisy.'

* * *

The rear courtyard was quieter, just a few lonely drinkers smoked and shivered in the cold. Filtered through the stained glass of the rear door, the singing and bustle inside was dulled, rendered obsolete.

'I need to go home,' Henrik said. 'My wife's waiting.'

'I could give you a lift.'

'What would the men say? They hate me, you know. They blame me for this. They don't know how hard I fought against the cuts.'

'They don't hate you, Henrik. Nobody does.'

'Worst thing is, this is just the beginning. They don't realise. We're down to the bones. The economy is rotting. There'll be more redundancies. I can't even protect my own job.'

'It's the alcohol makes you maudlin. You're a bad drinker, always were. Finish up and go home to your family. This place, you don't belong, trust me. There'll be stools and glasses thrown before closing time. There'll be a brawl.'

'You don't know me, Tal. I need the drink. I just like to pretend I'm a good husband and father.'

'We're all struggling. It's the economy. What can you do?' This was the question people asked nowadays. No answer was expected.

'Economy, my ass. We both know what's going on.'

His words were slurred, he was drunk as well. I needed to get away from him. I couldn't stand it, the smell of the beer on his breath, the slowness in his speech, the way he lost his grasp of space. He got too close, crowded me.

'What happened last night,' he said, 'I'm sorry about it. I don't like this business any more than you do. I was dragged out there in the middle of the morning. Jesus. My wife was frightened.'

'Yeah. About that…'

'You come up with any leads?' He glanced back at the window, the muted singing, as if he longed to return.

'I was thinking, this case isn't for me. Let someone else take it. I can't…'

'It has to be you, Tal.'

'Why?'

His glassy eyes slumped out of focus. 'It's just like that.'

'There's something else.' I took out the rose-coloured note from my jacket pocket. 'Do you know what this is? I found it on my desk.'

He glanced at the paper and shook his head. 'What the hell?' He read aloud, '"Dear beloved, I cannot wait for us to be together. Don't forget me, your true heart." I have no idea. Probably a prank. One of the other officers making fun of you. Be careful, Tal, you're not so popular down at the station.'

'Think I can't tell?'

'There's corruption in the police. It's worse than anyone imagined. That's why you have to do it; you're separate from the rest. I don't trust anyone, only you.'

'And the dead couple?'

'That's classified.' He drank from his glass. 'Ah shit. These people in charge. They're insane. I'm sorry you got pulled into it, Tal. Really. Some bigwigs high up in the Nazi party are upset. They have to protect their image with the public. They're secretive, masks and mirrors, for Christ's sake. I'm a simple man. I hate this.'

'So let me out.'

'I don't have the power. If only. Bernie's on the case, he's expendable, almost retired. He should've retired last year but he refused.'

'What do you mean, *expendable*?'

He shook his head. 'This case is nobody's business.'

'Where is Bernie? Isn't he here?'

'He's not a social drinker; he's the kind that likes to black out alone where nobody sees. It's why I like him.'

'Henrik, there's a baby missing. That man and woman, whoever they were, they had a baby. The child's out there somewhere.'

'There is no baby!' He had shouted and startled himself. He looked at the door with horror, but the dull background noise of singing and chatting didn't abate. Lowering his voice again, he pulled me closer. 'A baby? You're losing your mind. You're hallucinating.'

'Isn't that our job, if nothing else, to protect the innocent?'

'Tal, I'm warning you. Leave it alone. Find the officer that uniform belongs to and come to me. That's all. Forget the rest. Bernie will deal with the dead bodies. And, Tal, stay on the nightshift; the station is swarming with Gestapo by day.'

'I already met one of them.'

'That's bad. Oh. But I got one thing for you.' He took out a brown envelope and handed it over.

'What is it?' I was about to open it, but he grabbed my hand.

'I know you don't want to, Tal, but you have to. Sign this. Return it.'

'What…?'

'You know what it is. You know in your heart. It's time to join the Nazi Party. Everybody else did, everyone you know on the Force. You'll be the only outsider left.'

'No.'

'Tal… you're not seeing things straight. The time to be neutral is long gone. Nobody can be on their own now.

You're either with the Party, or against. Open your eyes. They control Danzig. It's only a "free city" in words. The League of Nations is useless. There are rumours of a coup. War's coming. We'll be united with Germany any day. Hitler already issued his ultimatum. And then...'

'And then...'

'They have no mercy for their enemies.' He glanced around the beer garden, pulled me further away from the door. 'You don't have to believe, Tal, really, in your heart. Do you imagine I like Hitler? The man's a psychopath. It's just, sometimes in life, you have to pretend.'

'I was never good at pretending.'

'Give it a try. It's easier than you think. It gets smoother with practice. Join now, before it's too late. I spoke to some people. Straightened things out. You're already accepted. You're a good German. Your record is spotless. They want you; you could be a real asset to them. They appreciate talent, these bastards. Just sign the paper, I'll take care of the rest.'

'I survived this long without it.'

'Fuck you, Tal.' Anger flashed in his haggard eyes. 'You're a fool. Worse, you're arrogant. You really think you survived by yourself? It was me. I was the one who looked after you, so did the others. We took care of you because we respect you. Everyone knows you're a good cop, and a good man. Even if you're an arrogant piece of shit. You love Danzig, that's what counts. I put my neck on the line for you, and I'm still doing it. You have no idea. Fuck you.'

'And Esther? Did you protect her? She was the best lab technician we had.'

'Esther?' He blinked and rubbed his face; he was drunker than I'd supposed. For a moment he seemed not to recognise the name.

'Esther. At forensics.'

'Oh, Esther, of course. She was Jewish.' He drained his glass. 'Jewish. Nobody knew. Her surname was German. She always seemed a good, loyal citizen.'

'Because she *was* a good, loyal citizen.'

'Someone denounced her. Anonymous letter. They must have dug up her family tree. Turns out her grandfather was an immigrant from some shtetl in Latvia. Changed the family name…'

'So what?'

He spluttered. 'I can't. Tal. I can't. It's not fair. I protected you this long, but I can't anymore. I can't even protect myself. Take these shitty forms and sign them. Hold your nose if it helps.'

I looked at the envelope. 'Let me think about it?'

'You have one day. After that, you're on your own. God help you.'

8

I drove to Esther's place, unsure if I'd be able to remember the address, or if she lived there anymore. Just a week ago, she'd been the best forensics technician in Danzig. Or had it been months? Guilt distorted the paths of memory where I followed her; I hadn't been a good colleague or a good friend, I hadn't helped, didn't even know for sure where she lived. Last time it had been out on the periphery of Langfuhr, the university district, but how long ago was that? The sleepless years got tangled. I drove and didn't care; it was a relief to be alone in the car after the drunken singing and thick smoke of the bar. The roll of the wheels over tarmac gave an illusion of freedom.

I turned on the radio and tried to find some music, but it was all state propaganda and news reports; tensions in the east, the Polish army was readying for war, they said.

I'd learned to read the news backwards: the German army, drastically limited by the Treaty of Versailles, was readying for war. Everybody knew it. When the war started, it would begin here.

Leaving the centre, I had to stop at a crossroads where the traffic was slowed by a mass of people screaming in the street. Just drive on, I thought, this isn't your problem. Drive on, drive all night until there's no fuel left to burn. I pulled up by the kerb and climbed out of the car. More than twenty young men, some of them just boys, were laying into each other with sticks and bottles, bricks, whatever came to hand, in a din of hatred and laughter. A crowd had grown around them, egging them on. To one side I recognised two police officers, Reiner and Lang, old-timers, veterans of the nightshift. They leaned against the bonnet of their squad car. Engaged in the view, pointing, commenting to each other like spectators at a sports event, they didn't notice me.

'Officers.' Approaching them, I was overcome with fatigue. Just the thought of the niceties, the policeman's etiquette.

They didn't smile. The din of the brawl was disturbing with its mixture of violence and pleasure. I strained to catch Reiner's words over the screams.

'Tal, this isn't your beat.'

'I'm on other business. Passing through. What's going on here?'

Lang shrugged. 'What else? Germans fighting Poles.'

'You fixing to do anything about it?'

They looked at each other, just a hint of amusement.

'It's best to let them fight it out,' Lang said. 'Get the energy out of their system.'

'I see.'

'You know what young men are like,' Reiner said. 'We were all young once.'

'Sure.'

He lit a cigarette. 'We'll let them beat the shit out of each other, then arrest the losers.'

'Unless the Poles win,' Lang said.

'Then we'll arrest the Poles.'

'Well, I guess you have the situation under control.' I stepped back. I needed to get away from them before I lost my temper and made a mistake. I'd be denounced like Esther in an anonymous letter. They already called me "Pole-lover" behind my back; someone must have found out about my relationship with Daria.

Lang exhaled smoke. 'What can you do? This city's gone to shit.'

* * *

It was true what everyone said: I needed to get off the nightshift. In shame and disgust, I found my way through the tangle of streets across town. As if Esther lay at the bottom of that melee of bodies, with her delicate lab equipment, all those fragile alembics and ampoules smashed and ground to dust. I pushed the pedal, drove as fast as I dared. There was a photograph in my mind: an old granite tenement painted mint green, with florid balconies, from the happier days when Danzig was a city of wealthy merchants, a prosperous port, "the jewel of the Baltic". These old townhouses with their terracotta roofs tossed like barnacled flotsam in the tide; my heart might break to see them burn.

I found the building I'd recalled among the boarded-up windows of a boulevard that had been opulent once. At least it might have been green; now, in the obscurity of night, lost in shadow, it was more of an underwater purple. The pavement was lined with sycamores and ornate wrought-iron streetlamps, but most of the bulbs had been smashed. Rubbish was piled up against the walls. Somebody had daubed the nearest door in red paint: "JEWS OUT". Crossing the street, I found a body face down in litter and a puddle of urine. I knelt beside him, holding my nose.

'Are you alright? Can you hear me?'

A window opened in the overlooking building; a woman shouted out, 'He sleeps there every night. Leave him in peace.'

'Can I–'

She slammed her window shut.

I checked the man's pulse, shook his shoulder, but he only groaned from within a dream. There was something soothing about him, the way he could sleep on the pavement, in a mulch of leaves, exposed to the wind. I was far from my bed. I couldn't remember why I was out here on the other side of town, instead of returning home. I got up and left the sleeper lying there.

The doorway of the purple-green tenement had been kicked inwards. I stepped through broken glass and splinters across the threshold. The place seemed abandoned. I checked the broken letterboxes and found Esther's surname, "Vogelsang", written above one slot. A beautiful word in the dark. With the uniform in the paper bag, I ran up to the third floor while the feeling of relief lasted. The doors were all shut along the corridors that I passed, and the landings smelled stale and dusty. Halfway up, a man coming down collided with me. I tried to get out of the way, but he brushed into me on purpose.

'Excuse me,' I mumbled.

He stopped. 'Who are you? You don't belong here.'

The light was broken in this section of the stairwell, the man was lit from below by the landing underneath, casting shadows upwards through the deep recesses of his eye sockets, a thickset figure, bald, wearing a vest.

'I'm looking for someone,' I said.

'That's not a good reason.' A blade flickered in his hand. 'You'd better leave, pal.'

He shoved me against the wall, but I was fast. I dropped the paper bag and knocked the knife from his hand. I flashed my badge. 'Danzig Police Force.'

His face transformed. 'My mistake. Forgive me, Officer. You understand, it's dangerous around here. Gangs taking over. Kids out of control. I just try to look after the building, keep the criminals out.'

'That's the job of the police. You call us if you need help.'

'Yeah, well.' He picked up his knife. 'Some say it's the police we need saving from. No offence.'

'Give me that.' I took the knife. 'If you need help, you call the station and ask for me. Tal, Chief Investigator. Everyone knows me. They'll pass your message on.'

'Tal. What kind of name is that?' He shook his head and carried on down the stairs, muttering to himself.

9

I banged on the door and straightened my collar, hearing dull movements inside. I felt somebody's eyes scrutinise my face through the peephole. Self-conscious, gripping the bloody uniform in a paper bag, I stepped back from the door. Bolts were pulled back inside, a key turned in the lock. Esther peered out with frightened eyes. Disbelief. Like some chance meeting of childhood friends at the end of the world.

'Tal. What the hell?'

'I'm sorry…' I held out the paper bag like a gift.

'But come in, come in.' She glanced over my shoulder into the dark hall. 'Quickly.'

I entered a stuffy living area, the smell of sweat and old clothes and something savoury cooking. I felt a shared intake of breath. Several figures dressed in black filled the dark corners of the room. Silently, they watched me. Three elderly ladies were seated on the settee, some old men occupied a few wooden chairs opposite. They wore suits that may have been expensive once but looked shabby now. Two children were cross-legged on the floor. It smelled like cabbage stew cooking through an open door behind them in the kitchen.

'A colleague,' Esther told them. She turned to me. 'This is my family. What's left of us.'

They stared with haunted expressions. Around them, suitcases and boxes were piled.

'I'm sorry. I shouldn't have intruded.'

'Why's he wearing sandals?' an old woman said.

'Tal, not at all.' Esther squeezed my wrist. 'Do you know, you're the only colleague who came to visit me since what happened. Nobody else did anything. They didn't even send a note.'

'Ah, well…'

One of the elderly gentlemen stood up and offered his chair. 'Sit down, sit down.'

'Thank you, but I can't. It's late. I can't stay. I only dropped by…'

'Nonsense.' One of the women got up. 'You're a guest. Drink something, you have to. You'll offend us.'

Somehow, I was seated in one of those old chairs. I held a glass of viscous, bitter liqueur. 'Thanks…' The word came out like a question.

Squatting beside me, Esther said, 'We're leaving Danzig.'

A strange, thrilling sentence. Sometimes I forgot that anywhere else existed. But she didn't sound happy, her face was distraught.

I looked around the staring eyes. 'What do you mean?'

'We've pooled our money. All our savings. We've been preparing for months. We got the documents through a friend at the civil service. We're leaving for Palestine. This is goodbye, Tal.'

'Oh.'

'Is he Jewish?' one of the grandmothers asked another. 'I don't think he's Polish.'

'Tal's just Tal,' Esther said.

I shook my head. 'Truth is, I don't know what I am.'

'Who does these days?'

'My mother was German, but my dad, he was a sailor. He never talked about his past, where he came from. He'd picked up languages at sea. He disappeared one day. We never talked about him after that. Tal was his name. God knows where he stole it from; some gravestone in the middle of nowhere.'

'That's alright. Here.' One of the grandfathers took the empty liqueur glass from my hand and gave me a new one.

'I shouldn't. I'm on duty… I work nightshifts.'

He patted me on the knee. 'Honour the widow, the orphan, and the stranger. The Torah tells us. It says, the Lord loves the stranger, gives him food and clothing.'

Unable to reply to that, I sipped at the liqueur and felt it seep through frenzied nerve endings.

'Can I help…?' I gestured at their suitcases. 'I've got my car.'

Esther almost smiled but caught herself. 'That's all taken care of. I'm glad you came by. It would feel wrong to leave Danzig without saying goodbye to one person at least, someone who stayed behind.'

I felt too sad to speak, and drank instead. A grandfather refilled my glass.

'What have you got in that bag? Stinks like an abattoir.'

'Oh. This. Sorry, Esther, truth is I didn't know you were leaving. I came to see if you could help me with something from work. But it doesn't matter. Forget it.'

'It's alright. I've got time to kill before morning.'

'No, you should make the most of this evening with your family. Forget about work. You've left that behind. I'm happy for you.'

'Tal, I love my work. God knows what I'll do in Palestine. If there's no lab jobs available… I might end up a seamstress or something worse. Who knows? Come on, let's talk in the kitchen. Like the old times.'

* * *

I laid out my notes on the counter, a sketch of the crime scene, every remembered detail jotted down, the dead woman drawn like a child's design. Esther leaned over the pages, humming to herself. Through the thin partition, the whispers of her family densified the shadows. I almost found again the old immersion of investigation, the absorption into a case while the outside world sloughs away. Countless hours I had stayed late in the forensics lab with Esther, drinking coffee, eating pickled eggs when we remembered how hungry we were, puzzling out the sins of our city.

'All this, it's like a dream. The woman. The missing baby. The clothes… I don't think it has an answer.' Her eyes were sharp, she hadn't changed.

'You think it's a setup; they're trying to get to me?'

'I have no idea.' She shuffled the papers together. 'If you'll take my advice, drop this case. Tell the superintendent you won't do it.'

'You're right. You're always right.'

'And this uniform?' She peeked in the bag I'd set to one side. 'What on earth?'

'That's all I have.'

'It's not much.' She took out the uniform, sniffed and grimaced, flipped it over, turned it to the light overhead. 'It's filthy, like it was dragged through every gutter in Danzig. Difficult to get a clean sample out of something like this.'

'Yeah… It's all I have.'

'We might be able to do something with it, but I've no equipment here.'

'Sorry, Esther, I've wasted your time with this. If I'd realised…'

'Not at all.' She folded the uniform in her meticulous way and put it back in the bag. 'Listen. If you're determined to carry on… There's a guy at the University. He's not police. He's a research student, did some field work with us for his dissertation. He's bright. They're researching blood types, new developments in criminology. They have equipment on the campus.'

'You think he'd help?'

'He owes me a favour. Probably too late for him to pay it back. I'll write a note.' She ripped off a sheet of paper and scribbled out a message. 'Show this to him. He'll understand. Tell him we're quits now.' She folded the paper and stuck it into my jacket pocket.

'Thanks.'

'Don't get your hopes up. It's just a dirty uniform. And this killing, I don't think it's meant to be solved.'

'That's the kind they give me.'

She laughed and seemed to surprise herself. The worry lines returned, renewed. 'Tal, you should get out of Danzig too. Nobody's safe. It's not just Jews. What's happening here, it's a collective hallucination. It spreads, it won't stop until everyone's infected. You think you're safe, you're not Jewish, but it's everyone. Once they're finished with us, who'll be next?'

'Believe me, I don't feel safe at all.'

'Escape while you can. Perhaps you could get to Palestine one day. They're building a new society over there. They say you can pluck pomegranates from the trees by the roadside. It's hot. The sea is warm and clear, it's nothing like the Baltic.'

'I'm glad for you, Esther. I'm glad to know one good person is getting away.'

'It's not so easy…' She leaned in close and dropped her voice to a whisper. 'The voyage is risky. My family, in there, they're brave, but they're fragile. My great aunt is ninety. One of the boys has tuberculosis. I spoke to a doctor; the others don't know…' She stared at the shut kitchen door as if the future pressed against the other side. 'He may not survive the journey. But it has to be now. There's no other way. Nobody's taking Jews. If something goes wrong… Tal, you know what's happening to Jews in the Reich… Danzig can't stay independent any longer. It could be any day now…'

I held her hand. 'You'll be alright. You'll find a way. You'll get there. You already did the hard part. You got the tickets, you got all the papers. In this world, if you have the paperwork, you can do anything.'

She squeezed my hand. 'Come to Palestine, Tal. You won't last here. Danzig will join the Reich… But in Palestine, I could vouch for you, help you find work. I could even marry you, maybe, if they need that.' A soft smile, sad, ridiculous.

It was too late. We'd had our chance for love, and let it go. Somewhere around the bend of a corridor at night, the blinking lights of the lab, the disorder of papers, our eyes might have met, and understood; alternate worlds receded on the tide and left this darkened kitchen counter where nothing had happened. It was my fault; I'd always been afraid of love.

'Esther, it's a long way to Palestine. Even if I took a ship… How would I find you?'

'You're a detective. It's what you do.'

10

I found Bernie drinking alone in the corner of a dark, underground bar close to the harbour, his usual haunt. Fishing nets hung from the ceiling like spiderweb, among the broken timbers and the wooden wheel of some old ship. It was a place where sailors drank, sawdust and venereal disease, and cheap vodka. I liked it; there were no swastikas on the walls. Communists came here, trade unionists, anarchists, all kinds of ideas washed up on the tides, messages from distant ports. It wasn't permitted to discuss such things aloud since the Danzig branch of the Nazi Party took control of the local council, but anarchists and communists and outsiders still need a place to drink.

The bar was quiet tonight; the harbour was dying, few merchant vessels stopped in Danzig since the trade war with Poland. Just a few solitary drinkers perched on their stools or slunk back in the shadowy corners. Bernie didn't look up when I pulled out the chair opposite him at a table soaked with spilled alcohol. Three small glasses, filled to the brim with clear liquid, were lined up in front of him.

'Time to go home,' I said. 'Your shift is over.'

His sunken gaze studied the glasses as if they were candles. 'Get out of here, Tal. This is my sanctuary. It's sacred ground.'

'I want to help you.'

He closed his eyes. For a moment I thought he had fallen asleep, he leaned forwards as if to pass out on my shoulder. His breath was heady with homebrewed alcohol, the kind that blinds. He whispered in my ear, 'See that guy under the sextant?'

I shifted on my seat, glancing over my left shoulder. The dusty brass of the sextant glimmered in the dull light. Beneath, a silhouetted form was barely visible against the wall.

'Gestapo,' Bernie whispered.

'I…'

'Shush.' He pulled away to rest his head against the bare brick wall. Eyes closed, he seemed to drift, but one hand groped and found the first glass. It trembled in his hand as he lifted it, sloshing vodka on the table. It caught a fragment of light and shone. Despite the shaking in his arm, Bernie found his mouth in one smooth, practised motion, and slammed the glass back on the table. He let out a groan of pleasure. A sheen of peace in his grimy face, so that I almost envied him, but it vanished as his breath ran out.

'Let me drive you home,' I said. 'You've had enough.'

He didn't reply, just raised a hand, eyes closed, found the second glass, and pushed it to me.

'I can't, I'm on duty.'

'Have a fucking drink if you're going to come in here. This place is holy, you can't just stick your nose in. Have some respect.'

'Alright, fine.'

I reached for the glass, and his hand caught mine, spilling vodka into the growing puddle. He pulled me close and whispered, so low in his choked, dead man's voice, I had to strain to hear. 'It's dangerous. You should leave.'

'No.'

He took a slow breath and I sensed for a moment the effort it cost him to concentrate, as his mind found a pool of clarity in the slump. 'Fuck you, Tal.'

'That's what everyone says.'

He took the glass, which was half spilled, and downed it with that quick, practised technique. He wiped his mouth with the back of his hand. 'Alright, you bastard, go to the bar, tell Ewa to put the record on, she knows which one. And send another round over.'

'Bernie, really, you should go home. It's late…'

'Put the fucking music on.'

I went over to the bar, which was made from the planks of an old vessel that had been named, to judge from the fading, upside-down letters in black paint, "NADZIEJA"; the Polish word for "hope".

The barmaid ignored me until I called her name and offered a chivalrous greeting in Polish. Contempt rose to her face; she didn't bother to conceal it as she came to me. I didn't belong in this place, just like I didn't belong in The Mermaid Tavern. I didn't belong anywhere.

'Ewa… forgive me, I'm a friend of Bernie.'

I felt the Gestapo agent sit up in his chair behind me, listening.

Ewa scoffed. 'A friend would take him home.'

'That's my quest. He humbly asks for a song and one more drink before he leaves.'

'He never humbly asks for anything. Go on and rouse him, I'll put his record on if you promise to get him out of here.'

'You have my word as a Danziger.'

She showed derision at that and turned to a gramophone that I noticed now sat at the rear corner of the bar. On the way back to the table, I risked a glance over into the corner. Eyes adjusted to the gloom, I saw a large man in a black overcoat, wearing oval glasses. His hair was slick with pomade. He caught my eyes and I looked away too quickly. Back at the table, Bernie had emptied his final glass. He lay with his face resting on his crossed arms, careless as the spilled vodka seeped into his sleeves.

'Wake up.' I shook his shoulder.

He didn't respond. This was a waste of time. What the hell was I doing there? But the music started. Crackling, a rich, baritone voice broke the dense sawdust air of whispers. I recognised the melody of the *Mingulay Boat Song*, a Scottish sea shanty. My father used to sing it. He knew the languages of all seafaring peoples, or so he used to boast as he held me steady on his knee and taught me how to greet a woman in Swedish; and I felt safe in his muscular care, at the confluence of horizons, all the seas he had known, and the furthest islands.

'You.' Bernie sat up straight. Before I could speak, he leaned close, eyes bright, a figment of sobriety, in a fog of stupor. 'The song lasts two minutes. Speak while you can.'

'The case, Bernie. I need to know.'

He glanced over at the Gestapo agent in the corner, before he muttered, almost inaudible beneath the music, 'Two dead Nazis. Good riddance to them.'

'But who were they? Give me a name. Just one name. I'll figure out the rest myself.'

'It's evil, this case. It stinks to hell.'

'Bernie, I can help. This is a big job, don't you–?'

'Stay away, Tal. I'm warning you. You're a good man, one of the few good ones left in the city. Don't touch this case, it'll swallow you.'

'But Bernie, there's a child.'

'What are you talking about?'

'The murdered couple, they had a kid. Where is it?'

He shook his head. 'Find a killer, I was told, and I will. There's no shortage. I'll be on my way. Gestapo are all over me, they're watching my home. I don't intend to stick my neck out.'

'But the child, if she's been taken–'

'She?' Something changed in his face.

'Or he. I don't know. Just a feeling.'

He leaned closer, his lips moist with vodka brushed my ear. 'I'll tell you one thing. It's strange. Those people went willingly to die. There was no break-in at their home. No violence. I searched every corner. Their dinner is still laid out on the table, half eaten. There's a fork with a whole chunk of ham stuck on the end. They just broke off the meal, got up, and went out into the evening without a struggle.'

I whispered in return, 'The killer was dressed as a police officer. He must have called at the house and told them some story, convinced them to go with him.'

'Tal, listen…'

The music stopped. Bernie's mouth hung open, disclosing all his decayed teeth, the thick brown-white fuzz of his tongue. 'Go home, Tal. This isn't a place for you.'

'But…'

He laid his head down on the table. 'I'm tired. Let me rest. It's late, it's so late.'

11

Back at the station, the waiting benches were full. The reception desk never closes; victims of crime just keep coming in at all hours with their complaints. Against the far wall, a group of young men, bloodied, bedraggled, were seated quietly, resting their heads against the benches or on each other's shoulders. Some of them appeared to be asleep. To one side, Lang was preparing some forms.

'The Poles lost the brawl?' I said.

He shrugged. 'They always lose.'

I looked for Markus at the desk, but Bertha had taken his place.

'Tal! Where you been?'

'Oh, hey Granma. I can't tell you. State secrets.'

Everyone on the Force called her "Granma"; I'd never observed anything grandmotherly about her.

'Hah.' She put down her cigarette in a cup that was full of butts. After a fit of coughing, she said, 'Tal. You look like shit.'

'Nice to see you too, Granma. Where's Markus? He was working here before.'

'"One-More-Round"? Where did you think? He joined the others down at The Mermaid.' She stared through her thick-lensed glasses. 'Why are you wearing sandals?'

'Long story. Markus was working on something for me. Did he tell you? Maybe he–'

'No one tells me shit.'

'Can I…?' I took the register from in front of her, and flicked through the pages, but there was no sign of the notes I'd entrusted to Markus, not even a crossword. 'He just left without…'

'It's a goodbye party. Redundancies and such. Don't feel sad; nobody invited me either.' She chuckled to herself. 'Markus asked me to cover for him. I got nothing better to do anyway.'

'I wonder if…' I went around the back of the counter and knelt, knocking over Granma's walking stick. 'Sorry.'

'What the hell are you doing?'

'Just need to check…' I found the wastepaper basket, pulled it out into the light and upturned it.

As I sifted through the crumpled papers, I heard the brawlers on the benches arguing about something. Lang shouted at them to shut up.

'Here it is.' The torn pieces of my notepaper with the police officer's uniform measurements; Markus must have thrown it in the bin. 'Son of a bitch.'

Granma chuckled. 'Never ask Markus for help. Unless it's something you don't want done.'

'The bastard. It wasn't even a big job.'

'What was?'

'I'm trying to find a police officer. Average height, male…'

Granma relit her cigarette. 'Think I see why he tore it up.'

'Has anyone been off the Force recently? I don't know, sick. Stayed off work… something…'

'No chance. Do you think we all want to be made redundant?'

'Still, somebody lost their uniform.' I tapped my fingers on the desk. 'It can't be so hard… there aren't that many officers in the Free City.'

She exhaled smoke and coughed. 'Well…' She wafted the fumes that curled in the dry, dusty light. 'Gerhard's been on leave.'

'Gerhard…?'

'Not sure why. I was asking yesterday where he was. "On leave", they said. That's all anyone knows. Poor bastard'll be collecting his redundancy pay if he's not careful.'

On the benches behind us, one of the beaten youths started to sing in Polish. In a croaky voice, untalented, just a guttural meowling at first, then a deformed melody took shape.

'Shut up!' Lang cuffed him over the head.

But the others took up the theme.

'Shut up, I said. All of you.'

The song grew in confidence, the chorus veered, careless of false notes and disharmony. I felt the twinge of their puffy, swollen faces as they strained.

'Shut up! Shut up, dogs.' But Lang's orders were drowned out by singing, he gave up.

'All I need,' Granma said, 'with this headache. Don't know why he brings them in here. It's just more paperwork for everyone. What the hell are they droning about?'

I translated. 'Poland will be married to the sea.'

'What's that supposed to mean?'

'They'll reclaim Danzig one day, and all of us Germans will be washed away.'

She blew out smoke. 'You speak Polish?'

'I speak many languages; my dad was a sailor, he–'

'So, you talk to them. Ask them if they want my boot in their mouth.'

'How tall is Gerhard?'

'What?'

The singing was louder, a half scream. I had to lean close into Granma's cloud of cigarette smoke. 'Gerhard, is he tall?'

'I'm 145cm. Everyone's tall to me.'

Behind my back, a gunshot burst the night. I threw myself down. Powdered cement rained from the ceiling where Lang's bullet had lodged. In the numb, ringing silence, I lay and checked I wasn't dead.

'What on earth...?' Granma hadn't moved from her seat. She exhaled a slow cloud of cigarette smoke. 'Have to fill out a form for that.'

'Jesus...' I crawled to my feet, legs wobbling.

Lang holstered his weapon. 'In this station, if you want to sing, you sing in German.'

The Poles on the benches hugged each other, stunned faces; a fine layer of pale dust covered their hair and shoulders. One of them managed to stutter, 'You can't...'

Lang called over, 'Tal, you're a witness. You'll back me up. These thugs attacked me. I acted in self-defence.'

'I'm busy.' I turned to Granma. 'Gerhard. Where does he live?'

'What am I, the encyclopaedia? I don't know.'

'There's a contacts book, where is it?'

She pointed with the end of her cigarette, scattering ash, to a drawer against the wall. 'With my arthritis, once I sit down, I don't get up again. Especially at night.'

I followed where she pointed. As I was pulling out a drawer filled with ledgers and binders, Lang came up behind me.

'Tal...'

'Leave me alone. I'm busy.' I scanned through the documents in the drawer and pulled out the staff address book.

'You've got my back, right? Officers have to stick together. It's a brotherhood, this job.'

'You shot the ceiling. Excuse me.' I pushed past him and carried the book over to the phone. 'What's Gerhard's surname?'

'Give it to me.' Granma took the book and flipped through. She found the page and smoothed it, brushing cigarette ash from the paper. 'Here he is. That's across town... you'll have to drive.'

'Does he have a phone?'

'Tal.' Lang tugged at my elbow.

I swallowed my disgust and faced him. 'Send those kids home. Get a ladder, pull the bullet out of the ceiling. Nobody needs to know this happened. Granma…'

She coughed. 'Leave me out of it. I don't care what you do, so long as I stay in my seat.'

'Alright.' Lang took a step away. 'Hey, Tal, a favour's a favour. If you ever need something…'

'Let those kids go home.' I turned my back.

'Right.' He muttered to himself as he walked away. 'Fuck me. What a shift. Jeez. This city. This job.'

'Welcome to Danzig.' Granma slid the address book over. 'Doesn't say anything about a phone.'

Behind our backs, the young men, dusted with plaster and cement, shuffled out of the station, blaspheming in their own language. A few other stunned visitors and homeless men got up and stumbled out as well, ushered by Lang. 'Go home. Get lost. Come back tomorrow. We're closed for repairs.'

I took out my notepad and jotted down Gerhard's address.

'It's late,' Granma said. 'What do you want Gerhard for, in the middle of the night? To return his uniform? You're strange.'

'I just need to check…'

'Tal, if you think there's trouble, take somebody with you. Not me, mind you. With my arthritis…'

'I'll go alone. Everyone's drunk at The Mermaid. I'm not taking Lang.'

'Take the trainee kid. He's in the basement, I sent him to clean the toilets,' she said.

'What? I gave him a job to do… never mind.'

12

'You're driving too fast.' The trainee kid surprised me; he hadn't spoken since we set off.

'Why do you care?'

'I don't care.' The kid stared out of the window with hollow eyes, dejected.

I noticed he wore a swastika badge on his lapel. How had I missed that before? I felt a wave of nausea followed by hollowness.

'Cheer up,' I tried, and heard myself sound pathetic.

He ignored me. I regretted bringing him along. If I'd thought he might like me for finding him work, for getting him involved, I'd only shown myself to be a fool, like always. I turned on the radio and scanned the news reports and interference for some music he might like. Beneath the tissue of acne, his skin was fresh. I felt a desire to help him, to guide him; to spare him what was to come. But I knew he'd only hate me.

Instead, I heard myself say, 'Kid, you need to stick up for yourself. Can't believe they had you scrubbing toilets.'

He shrugged, looking away. 'What difference does it make?'

'In the downstairs men's room, a lot.'

'We're all dead, aren't we? My dad says it could be any day. The war. The Reich can't wait any longer. Everything will be annihilated.'

'You're too young to think like that.' My fingers twiddled on the radio knob, finding nothing. I turned it off.

'How else can you think?'

'There's also springtime.'

'Springtime.' He guffawed to himself. I felt like he was the adult, and I was the child.

'When I was your age, spring was all I cared about.'

He didn't seem to hear. 'I read a report in the newspaper. Over the border, the Poles are rounding up Germans and castrating them.'

'Don't believe everything you read.'

'Why would they lie? The Poles hate us. They've killed Danzig with their trade war. My dad says so, he works on the harbour board.'

I took a breath and tried to teach him something. 'We need Poland, and they need us. We've got the port, they have the trade. We're in the mouth of the river, they own the river itself. It leads all the way down through Warsaw, for God's sake. That's how things work.'

'You're weird.'

'I could write you up for talking back to a senior officer.' I glanced over, but he didn't meet my eye.

'My dad says people who talk like you are traitors.'

'Yeah well, I'd like to see him work the nightshift.'

'No.' He shook his head, his voice deadened. 'It's peaceful on the nightshift. You can pretend the next day might not come. As if we could just stay like this, driving, waiting.'

'I used to think like that. I don't anymore. The morning always comes. Try to sleep while you can.'

He gave a sound like a thin, threadbare laugh. 'Sure.'

I pointed at the swastika badge on his lapel. 'You know what that is, that symbol?'

He didn't look at it. 'Everyone knows. You see it everywhere.'

'But do you know where it comes from? It's a kind of rune. You know what runes are? They're symbols that have magic powers. In ancient times, they'd carve the rune into a tree or a rock, and it would cast a spell.'

'There's no such thing as magic. How old do you think I am? I'm not a baby. I'm a grown-up.'

I rambled on. 'The swastika comes from ancient Sanskrit tradition. It represents the sun. Those symmetrical lines show the rays of sunlight. Daytime. Illumination. But our German swastika is backwards. The lines point the wrong way. That rune is like an inverse sun, it pours out dark matter instead of light.'

He didn't respond. It was just as well; I could get killed for what I'd said. We drove in silence. The streets were deserted, but I felt watching eyes behind the shuttered windows that overlooked the narrow passages.

I'd almost forgotten the kid was there when he spoke. 'It's not true, what I told you earlier.'

'About what?'

'About wanting to be an artist.'

'Oh.' I tried to remember that detail.

'I just don't want to do anything. I'm lazy. Dad's right about me. I'm useless.'

'Alright.' I braked too quickly. The tyres screeched as the car jerked to a halt by the side of the road. 'Want to get out?'

'What?' He stared back, flustered in the dazzling net of a streetlamp that stuck up just outside the window.

'Do what you want. I don't care.' I leaned across him and opened his door. 'Go on, get out. Go home and sleep or find your friends and beat up some homeless guy. Whatever young people do nowadays. I don't care. I'll sign your form and say you finished the shift with me.'

A draught of wind came through the open door. I supposed he must be calculating, but his eyes were empty, no life stirred in his face as he shivered.

'I don't know.' He faced the cold air, a breath of the sea.

'Go on. Get out. Give me a break. I've got my own problems. I'm busy.'

A gust ruffled his red hair. 'No. I'll stay with you. I'll do the job.'

'Nobody's forcing you.'

He closed the door. 'I said I'll do it.'

'Alright then. Forget art. Artists don't know real life like we do. Nobody knows it, until they do this shift.'

13

I pulled up outside Gerhard's tenement. Not a single window was lit. The kid started to get out of the car, but I stopped him. 'Stay in here.'

'Why?'

'Don't let anyone steal the wheels. Wheels are like currency in Danzig.'

'Do I need a gun? I'm not trained…'

'No.'

I climbed out, exhausted, relieved to be alone. Now that I'd reached its destination, the journey seemed absurd. Granma was right; this was a waste of time. But the front entrance to the building was open, like it wanted me to go inside. I glanced back over my shoulder but couldn't see the kid through the reflection of streetlight on the car windows. A smell of urine filled the entrance hall. The light switch didn't work. I flicked on my torch and the beam sent a rat scurrying through piled binbags. A sign on the lift said, "OUT OF ORDER. STOP PISSING IN HERE." I went up to the second floor. The Baltic night blew through a broken window with a sigh of withered leaves.

On the second floor, I moved through the dark, flashing my light over a few closed doors, stepping over rubbish, until I found 26B. I knocked. The sound was hollow, too violent in the density of sleeping residents. I felt a trace of movement behind the walls around me, the rows of closed doors, like a dreamer turning at an echo of the outside world. I knocked again. At the foot of the door, my torch showed the protruding edges of a few letters and leaflets;

nobody had come in or out for days. I tugged one of the leaflets from under the door: a Nazi rally held last week.

Behind my back, a door creaked open. 'What are you doing out there? It's night.'

I saw a crooked man with a few wisps of white hair. He covered his eyes and cowered back behind the edge of his door when I shone my torch over his stained vest.

'Police. Can I ask you a question?'

He slammed the door shut. Feet shuffled away behind the thin wall.

'Fair enough.' I faced Gerhard's silent door and found no answers. Even the 26B had been removed, a pale outline in the red paint remained where the digits used to show.

I tried to think but could no longer remember what I was doing out here, so far from the quiet bedroom where my totems were laid out: the gramophone, Mozart records, the picture of my mother, the mirror turned upside down. The way back home was locked behind this panel of wood that hadn't opened in too long. I could try and kick the thing down; I could look for the janitor and see if there was a spare key, I could pick the lock with the hairpin I kept in my wallet, I could come back in the morning and talk to the neighbours. I could forget this whole case, like Esther told me to do. Perhaps I really could leave Danzig, find a ship in the harbour, sail to Palestine.

I tried the door handle, absently, and felt it give. There's always a simpler solution. The door edged open inwards, discharging a smell of must and vinegar. Excrement. Blood. I took one step into the piled letters and leaflets inside, and hesitated. Back along the corridor, nothing moved. The building breathed hoarsely in its sleep. I tried the light switch inside the doorway. Broken. Something scurried as I cast the beam of my torch along the hall. A rat or cockroach disappeared into the wall.

I drew my revolver and moved slowly, swinging the torchlight that was too narrow to find purchase in the withdrawing space. The stink was vile, with both hands occupied I couldn't cover my nose and had to hold my breath. The flat seemed to expand into the surrounding darkness.

I came to an open door at the end of a short entranceway. Something rotted through there. I stopped and listened: a sound like a humming device, a motor running – after-echoes of the shipyards, underground tombs, the sleepless industry. I took another step, jerking the torchlight too quickly, my grasp trembling; I had to grip it with both hands. Another step forward, the beam swept and found what it was looking for. Not a machine at all, not an engine; this was a shifting, restless, factory of flies at work. I recoiled.

Empty space rushed in as the torch dropped from my hand. It might have been a bedroom. My fingers found a light switch on the inner wall and flicked it. The light from the bare bulb was blinding. Flies burst into the dazzled air and swarmed around me. I swatted them back. With the gun held over my eyes, I steeled myself to look. A man lay, naked, stretched out, covered in stab wounds.

I held my breath and took a step closer. From the smell, and the mottled flesh, he might have lain there a week, but I didn't trust my instincts; I didn't trust anything. Flies luxuriated all over Gerhard's form like a layer of intoxication. From the doorway behind me, someone screamed. I ducked down and raised my gun. The trainee kid cowered back against the wall.

'No…' He stumbled, tried to get away, and slipped on some loose paper, spraying vomit up the wall as he fell.

'Don't you dare puke in my crime scene.'

He tried to speak but could only moan. As he slid down the wall, he struggled to catch his own vomit, and cupped it, leaking, in both hands. That was the best I could ask for, under the circumstances.

'Good. Stay back there. Don't come any closer. If you see any neighbours stick their nose in, you chase them away.'

Holding my breath, I crept closer to the body. Gerhard's face was turned away as if ashamed. I looked in the pool of blood and shit that seeped outwards from the corpse, and there it was, too easy, as if my own imagination put it there: a pile of clothing.

Gerhard might have just undressed and thrown his things down. I put on my gloves and probed the material: a white vest, a pair of rough blue overalls like dockworkers wear, some socks with holes in the heel. These garments didn't belong to the dead woman, too large, and hardly her style. She was classy. It was disturbing, I already seemed to feel like I knew her. Where might her clothes be? It had felt wrong to leave her lying naked, alone. I'd tried to find them, but I'd only succeeded in digging up a new body, a new nakedness, a new set of clothes. The two murder scenes were identical, the pattern was exaggerated, but their logic faded into the dark. A baby cried somewhere.

14

Gdańsk, Polish People's Republic

1961

The Second Rune

It was early in Gdańsk. Anna Nowak stepped into a freezing wind. It wasn't light yet, but the trams were already crowded as the day's labour got underway. In the workers' cafes, rags were sloshed across tables and wrung out, chairs set up, floors mopped. Red banners fluttered over scaffolding and cranes, ruined buildings, war debris, new tarmac. The moon still hung in the sky, but nobody noticed. The police station was a work in progress, like everything in Gdańsk, patched up and papered over. Anna squeezed around a ladder as she entered the building. The reception area was busy, tired eyes, sleepless faces; the nightshift ended, and the dayshift began. A man on a ladder was painting the ceiling. She stopped and closed her eyes and smelled the paint.

At the front desk, Darek said, 'You look lost, Nowak.'

'I need to see Roman, is he in?'

'The superintendent?' Darek glanced at the wall, where one clock was labelled "Warsaw", and a larger one, "Moscow". 'I'd wait, if I were you. He doesn't like to talk before 7am.'

'Yeah well, I have to give a lecture. Stayed up all night preparing. I need to see him now.'

'Look at that!' The worker at the top of the ladder shouted. He held something out in his paint-stained fingers. 'There was a bullet in the ceiling. How long has that been stuck in there?'

Anna hurried along the corridor and sucked in the smell of new paint like it was a drug. This place was a maze, corridors shifted from week to week as they dug up hidden rooms. Some doors opened onto nothing. It used to be the old German police HQ, during the War. Some of the officers in the canteen said there was buried Nazi treasure under here, but all kinds of things were said in the canteen. She crossed a bridge of scaffolding to the other side of the landing and ran up to the top floor.

The superintendent had fallen asleep with a cup of tea in his hand. He flinched in his seat when she knocked and went inside. Displeasure showed just for a moment as he blinked and rubbed his eyes. His thinning hairs were dishevelled, his scarred face hidden behind white stubble.

'Sorry to disturb you, Comrade.'

'What?' He stared as if he didn't recognise her. 'Oh, it's you. Don't you ever start the day slow, Nowak? Sometimes it's nice to ease your way in.'

'I'm in a rush. It's my turn to speak. Are you coming?'

'Err… Is that today?'

'First, I need to talk to you about the case… The woman in the tree. Is the autopsy report…?'

'Not yet.' He waved his hand. 'It's too early for the morgue. Freezing down there. We'll get the results this afternoon. Don't get your hopes up…'

'I was thinking about the symbol in the tree. We should look into a German angle.'

Roman sat up straight in his chair and pointed. 'I warned you.'

'It's like a signature left by the killer. I think there'll be another.'

Something banged the wall to one side. Roman looked afraid. 'Nowak, it's not 7am. Just slow down for a second. Give us all a chance to wake up, will you? Take a minute, read the newspapers, join in with a bit of chat in the canteen. It's good for morale.'

'I know you don't want to talk about the rune, Comrade. I understand, it's dangerous. The public mustn't find out. It's just that, if another killing happened, it could get worse. The best course of action, in my opinion, would be to take prophylactic measures now, before it happens again. I think–'

'"Prophylactic". Where do you get these words?'

'If we stop the killer now, there won't be another.'

He gouged his fingers into the flabby skin of his cheeks and breathed out hoarsely. 'They warned me not to appoint a woman. I thought I was being progressive. You're a curse.'

'You said it was because the men never came home from war.'

'That as well. You're young. My generation are all either dead or gone crazy. It's a youthful country; a lot of innocence, no experience.' He stared out of the window as if he saw the past there.

'I care about Gdańsk same as you do. I want to keep her safe.'

'Gdańsk is a "she" now?'

'It wouldn't do any harm to check, would it?' she said.

'Check what?'

'I'll go through the archives and look for crimes that match. The rune. I was thinking, what if there's a German connection? If we check the records from the War and before–'

'Those records don't exist. After the War, the German police force was disbanded. The Germans all went away.' He glanced about nervously, but they were alone in the room. 'The topic is prohibited.'

'But there must be records. The old German police had records. This is the same building. Their files must be stored somewhere. We could check…'

'The security service took all the archives.'

'So, they do exist. You have influence, Superintendent. If you talk to them, they might let us–'

'Nowak, stop. Just stop. You know who works in the room next to this one? My double. His job is to follow everything I do. Every decision I make. Every form I fill in. He watches out for every tiny mistake. You see? Leave me in peace. You'll get the autopsy report later. Go do your lecture, and make sure it's a good one.'

'The lecture…' Anna glanced at the clocks on the wall. 'I can't even remember what it's supposed to be about. Don't you think we should postpone, under the circumstances? A homicide case like this… The lecture doesn't seem so important.'

Roman stared at the wall. 'On the contrary, it's the most important.'

15

Anna stared at her notes and could hardly read them. Her colleagues around the room slumped in their chairs, stared at the floor, out of the window or into empty space. In the back row, Zielinski's eyes were closed; on the front row, Sebastian watched nervously. A smell of new paint wafted in from the corridor. The paper trembled in her hand as she read aloud.

'Karl Marx writes, "The bureaucracy is the imaginary state alongside the real state; it is the spiritualism of the state."'

What did that mean? She couldn't remember. The dusty room creaked as her listeners fidgeted, scraped their chairs. She glanced into the corner where one of the party observers was taking notes. His pen scratched. What had he noted? She smelled paint and kept reading.

'Marx continues, "The bureaucracy holds the state, the spiritual essence of society, in thrall, as its private property. The universal spirit of bureaucracy is secrecy…"'

Anna turned the page and found an empty sheet of paper. Not quite empty; the rune was drawn in the centre.

ᛃ

Her hand must have copied it there last night, only she couldn't remember. Submerged in work as the night turned to dusk, poring through volumes of Marx and Engels for quotes, her mind had wandered inwards. She stared at it now. Purity. A sign divested of all the wearying, sleepless activity, reduced to form, lines and angles, symmetry. A muffled snore broke the dry air. In the back row, Zielinski had fallen asleep in his seat. Glancing around in panic, she caught the stifled grins in her comrades' faces as they tried not to react. The Party observer showed no sign of noticing, but he made another note. The rune had vanished; she held an empty sheet of paper.

* * *

After the lecture, she hurried out of the station before anyone could stop her. It was a relief to breathe in the wind. She crossed through the Green Gate onto the island and skirted through the ruins of an old grain warehouse. She found the metal door and knocked. The sound echoed inside.

'Come on,' she muttered, 'come on, open.' She knocked again.

The door groaned on its rusted hinges. Pirate looked out. Drowsy, he squinted into the daylight and adjusted his dressing gown. 'What the hell, Nowak? You trying to get me killed? Turning up here in daylight…'

'I need your help.'

'I knew I should've stayed in bed.' He glanced over her shoulder. 'You're alone?'

'Of course.'

'Come in then, before somebody spots you.' He withdrew, and Anna followed him through a leaking corridor lined with crates and barrels.

'It's just a small thing I need.'

'They all say that.' Pirate's sandals crunched through bits of broken glass. 'I already did more than enough for you. It's only on your dad's account I ever helped. But you're no different to the other cops. Breaking down doors, stealing merchandise. Your lot are worse than the gangsters.'

They passed through a hole in the wall into a courtyard overlooked by smashed windows and huddled pigeons. The smell of bird shit was intense. Pirate rubbed his freezing hands together. He was a man who could get things, not in a legal sense, but then not much was available legally. Poland had been left in ruins after the War. The communist government struggled to create a new society, while the people queued overnight for basic food items.

Pirate lit the butt of a cigarette. 'Business is tight. It's getting harder to move from place to place. You might help us, with those connections of yours.'

'I don't have any connections.'

'Half my goods are sat in a police warehouse. Get it out for me. Who'd miss it? The amount of crap that's confiscated all over the city. I don't know what they want with it all. They have a mania for warehousing.'

'I told you about that before, I'll see what I can do. It's–'

'Yeah, yeah. Paperwork, I know. We're all bureaucrats now. This is what happens when you teach people to read, who got no business reading.' He sucked on the last remnant of the butt as it burnt down to his fingertips.

'It's a book I need.'

'A what?'

'I need you to find a book for me.' She watched as he pocketed the last shreds of his cigarette, loss in his eyes. 'It shouldn't be difficult. I know you've got a whole library stashed back there.'

'A book?' He whistled silently. 'Books are dangerous, Comrade. Drugs would be easier.'

'I'll get your merchandise back from the depot. Just be patient.'

He glanced about the litter of broken glass as if somebody might be hidden there and leaned closer to whisper. 'What book are you looking for? I've got a special offer on Bibles.'

'Anything about German runes. The Nazis were–'

'What?' He raised his hands. 'You're insane. Is this a sting? You're trying to catch me out. I'm not stupid, just because my name's Pirate.'

'No. It's not anything political I'm looking for. More like a history book. Like German mythology. Specifically, I need something about runes. There must be a book…'

'German mythology. Runes. You're crazy. I'm not listening to any more of this.' He started to walk away through the glass.

'You can forget your impounded merchandise then.'

He stopped. The wind blew up the edges of his dressing gown. 'Your dad would weep to see how his daughter grew up.'

'There are worse things to weep about.'

'Alright. Maybe I can do something. Maybe, and only on account of your dad.'

'"Maybe" isn't enough.'

He shook his head. 'Get my stuff back today. I'll have something for you later. Maybe.'

In the quiet, the wind sang through so many cracks in the ruined walls. Anna looked over Pirate's shoulder towards the main storage building. 'How many packs of cigarettes have you got hidden back there?'

'What cigarettes?'

'Don't play stupid. A shipment was lifted from the docks two days ago. Right under the harbour master's nose.'

'First I heard about it.'

'I'm talking as a smoker here, not a cop.'

'As a smoker, huh.'

She took out a banknote. 'I'll take ten packs. The real stuff. None of that filtered shit.'

16

In the morgue, Roman wore earmuffs and a woolly hat. 'It's like Antarctica down here, let's make this quick.'

'Don't blame me,' the pathologist, Weber, said. 'We apply for heaters, but the paperwork just goes around in circles.'

Weber led them across chill, aquamarine tiles to where the dead woman's body lay on a plinth against the wall.

'What did you find out?' Anna wrinkled her nose. The chemical smell down here was nauseating.

'It wasn't hanging that killed her.' Weber's fingers were purple when she took off her surgical gloves.

'What?' Roman leaned over the corpse, holding his breath. 'Looks like a hanging to me.'

The dead woman's neck was dark with welters where the rope had been tied. Roman brushed the bruised skin with his mittens.

'How did she die?' Anna said.

'Drowned.'

Roman stepped back from the corpse. 'You're shitting me.'

'And look at this.' The pathologist held up a test tube filled with dark liquid.

'What is that? Looks like ink.'

'I pumped this out of her lungs. Whatever it is, she swallowed a skinful.'

'Can I see?' Anna took the test tube and held it to the light. Against the green shimmer down here, the black substance was dense, opaque.

Roman leaned over her shoulder. 'Is it oil?'

'I've sent a sample to Warsaw for analysis,' Weber said. 'It seems to have a high carbon content. Tar or coal, peat.'

'Where could she drink something like that?' Roman said. 'In the docks? Could it be pollution?'

'Could be.'

'Alright, that's settled.' He turned to Anna. 'It's the shipyards, like I told you already. She must have been a working girl. She drowned in the dirty water there.'

'I'm not sure–' Anna began.

'I'm pairing you with Zielinski.'

'Zielinski? He snored through my talk on Marx. Loudly.'

'He's a slob. I know. He's not the smartest, but he's strong. It's dangerous at the shipyards, they don't like police.'

'I'd be better alone. I know the shipyards; I grew up there. My parents–'

'Nobody gets to work alone, Comrade. We all have our doubles to watch us, like we watch them. That's what keeps the system fair and clear.'

'I think we should be focusing on the rune.'

'Rune?' Weber pulled a sheet over the dead woman. 'What rune?'

Roman's face was dark red with cold or anger. 'There is no rune,' he shouted. 'All we have is a dead woman and a test tube filled with pollution. Those are the only clues. The *only* clues. I don't want to hear about anything else. Leave me in peace. Go to the shipyards. With Zielinski.'

Anna sighed. 'Respectfully, Comrade, I don't think the victim was a prostitute.'

'Respectfully, Comrade, you'll go to the shipyards, with Zielinski, and play nice; smile at his old-timer stories, laugh at his dumb jokes. Keep him away from the underground bars over there.'

'If that's your order.'

'Let's get out of here. I can't feel my toes.'

* * *

In the parking lot, Zielinski slept in the passenger seat of an unmarked car, his head resting against the glass.

Anna knocked on the pane. 'Get up.'

'Just resting my eyes, Comrade.'

She climbed in the driver's seat of the beat-up car. 'Shit. Where did they dredge up this thing? Does it even start?'

Zielinski closed his eyes and laid his head back against the window. 'You must have fucked up, Comrade. Partnered with me, looking for a hooker… that's what they call "a dead shift" in the canteen.' His breath stank of stale smoke. 'I enjoyed your lecture, by the way.'

'You snored through the whole thing.'

'Really?' He chuckled to himself.

The car started at the third attempt, and Anna steered out of the parking lot. She glanced across at her partner as they coasted down the main road, Zielinski was unshaved, unwashed. Cigarette smoke soaked into the fibres of his clothes, his sparse, greasy hair, the pores of his skin. She hoped he would fall asleep again, but he rubbed his eyes and yawned.

'You must have offended someone,' he said. 'Someone important. Who could it have been?'

'Let's not overthink things. It's just a job.'

'Nah. A high-flyer like you? Everyone knows, you're the keenest. You've actually read all those big books by Marx and Engels, haven't you?'

'The development of class consciousness demands that we educate each other.'

Zielinski laughed. '"Class consciousness".'

'What would you know?' His grin chafed her, she couldn't stop herself. 'I grew up on the shipyards. I saw how the workers were treated. They slaved until they died, while the owners of the shipping lines lived in luxury. The workers weren't allowed unions. They had no protection; had to work without gloves or goggles or safety gear. They were illiterate, they didn't even know what they didn't know. My dad died in an accident; his mates had to work the next morning. They didn't know any better. How could they? They didn't understand the economic structure of class conflict. But we do.'

Zielinski shrugged. 'The workers still slave till they drop, looks like that to me. And there's no bread to eat. Nah, you messed up, Comrade. With your big books and your fancy words. "Class consciousness", is that really a thing? You shouldn't be in this beat-up old car with me. Didn't anybody tell you? The bosses only put me on a case they don't want solved. The rest of the time, I don't leave the office.'

'Maybe you're right.'

They drove around the corner into a flood of morning brightness that refracted through the windscreen, blinding them. With one hand, Anna took out a pair of aviator shades and put them on.

'Where'd you get those?' Zielinski looked at her differently. 'You look like a movie star.'

'Black market. There's loads of old war gear.'

'I'm starting to get a new idea about you.'

'Don't think too hard.'

The end of the street opened out onto a sky of cranes and circling seagulls. As the walls fell away, she felt a sway of childhood. She grew up with the ship workers, in the roar of machinery. Her parents worked here all their lives. Even after the accident, Anna kept coming back. Despite the efforts of the authorities who assigned her to orphanages and foster families, she would always run away and come back "home". The other workers, her parents' colleagues, they pitied her, perhaps they thought it was funny. They let her roam free. She wasn't the only ragamuffin kid running around. It never felt from her childish perspective that those labourers were at work in the cold, it was more like some mysterious, sacramental activity they engaged in for the joy of it. The moving assembly line and divided labour, a thousand mechanics, each with their own specialised role.

Her father's job was to tweak things. In fragments of memory, she saw him clearly. He tweaked bolts and screws and wires. The other workers told her, he had wonderful hands. To Anna they looked sort of rough and hairy, with broken fingernails. She watched him at work, with his screwdriver, making tiny adjustments, and believed that she could really see it, the tweaking. But work is work, it takes an adult to understand that. The shipping industry collapsed, everything fell into ruin, and her father was laid off. He got involved in union activity and died not long after.

'What's with you?' Zielinski peered at her.

‘Hey?’ She had stayed too long at the intersection, after the light changed to green. ‘Oh. Nothing. Just a memory. My dad used to work out here. He loved the shipyards.’

* * *

They parked outside the front gates that the workers used. Anna pulled out the bag of ten-cigarette packets that Pirate had given her. Zielinski leaned over and looked inside.

He whistled. ‘The good stuff. Where’d you get those?’

‘None of your business.’

‘Oh, I see. It’s like that.’ He sat back in his seat. ‘I get it; you’re not such a highflyer as you look. You’ve got your hand in the jar like everyone else. You just do it differently.’

‘It’s not–’

‘I mean it as a compliment.’

‘This is part of the investigation.’ Anna held his eyes.

‘Ten-packs of Russian cigarettes?’ He sat forward, curious. ‘How? Seriously, I’m trying to learn on the job here.’

‘You’ll see.’

‘Shit. Well, if it’s part of the job, we should probably try them, to be safe.’

Anna sighed. They tore open a packet and smoked. Nicotine fired in her fraught nerve endings; the outline of the rune danced behind her retinas.

Zielinski coughed on a fog of smoke. ‘Shit, these are the good ones. Think they actually contain tobacco.’ He opened the passenger seat window and wafted the grey cloud out as he spluttered and choked.

Anna climbed out of the car into a powerful wind. The tang of metal and sea was like a tunnel through a moment that had only just disappeared.

Zielinski got out the other side. ‘Hate this place. It’s too exposed. The wind never stops.’

If he tasted the air, if the horizon of cranes spiked any buried sense of beauty in him, it didn’t show; he hawked up a mouthful of dark phlegm and spat it out. She had to get away from him.

'Let's split up. It'll be quicker that way. And we can go home.'

'In a rush?' But he smiled; she had found the right button to press.

'Do what you want, just leave me in peace.' Anna stashed the contraband cigarettes in a backpack and shouldered it. 'I know the shipyards. I'll work better alone.'

'You should be careful, Comrade. You get ahead of yourself. Just because you read some books with fancy titles by Russian writers, you think you know best. But you don't understand the game. You're going to lose one day. Watch out.'

'What?' Her blonde hair blew crazy in the wind. She tied it back. 'You're the one who snored through the morning lecture. You should be careful. There was an observer.'

He grinned. 'You think snoring bothers them? It's what they want. Why else would socialism be so boring…? They want us all asleep. But you, you think too hard. One day you'll figure something out. They don't like that.'

'Figure out what?'

'You'll see.' He trudged away, up the wide path where tens of thousands of workers passed each morning, through the metal gates into the shipyards.

17

She was glad to be alone, but the shipyards were not the same. She used to be recognised and liked, the workers' "little sister" who grew up among the welding irons, but she didn't belong now. Workers in their rust-stained overalls crept into the shadows and corners as she passed.

Conversations broke off, voices shrank. She looked in every face for somebody she recognised, but they were all strangers.

A man wearing a helmet came out of a portable hut and shouted at her. 'Hey! You can't be in here. There's heavy machinery.'

'Relax.' She took out one of the packs of cigarettes and threw it to him. 'Where's Kostek?'

'Who the hell are you?' He turned the packet, tested the seal with his dirty thumbnail.

'Old friend of his.' The rejection was painful; this place was supposed to be her home.

'Kostek's busy.' The man tapped out a cigarette and lit it. Cautious acceptance.

She waited until he inhaled. 'Where is he?'

'Working at the furnace. You can't go in there without a safety helmet…'

'I grew up in the furnace. See this scar?' She held out her palm. 'Grabbed the wrong end of a hot pincer when I was ten years old.'

'You're police, aren't you?'

'How did you tell?'

'Listen, you seem alright. I'll give you some advice. It's not safe for police around here. We got our own world, there are rules.'

'I'm the good kind of police.'

'There's a good kind?'

'But listen, there's another cop. He's the bad kind. Stocky guy, stubble, greasy hair; can't miss him. Direct him to the empty warehouses where you put useless people. I don't want to run into him.'

* * *

The furnace was a wide chamber beneath a tall ceiling of red-brick and metal beams. Deafening noise. In childhood, the heat had awed her. In the dazzle of sparks, the pounding machinery, the swell of molten metal, she handed out two more packs of cigarettes, shouting to be heard, but Kostek wasn't there. The workers shook their heads and turned away, muttering words lost in the background rumble that cast vibrations through the floor. Somebody gave her a hardhat in return for smokes. She was running low, just five packs left.

The shipyards had changed. If she could just find Kostek. He was a union boss, in his sixties now, but still strong and energetic. Once a close friend of her dad's, he would talk to her. The backdoor out of the furnace used to lead to a room where smaller segments of the hull were assembled, but now it seemed to be just a kind of junk room. Relieved to get away from the noise of the machinery, she wandered between piles of old metal.

'Hey!' a man's voice cried out from the end of the warehouse.

She turned too quickly, banging a stack of metal doors. It wasn't Kostek. A young man in a vest eyed her from a back door.

'What the hell are you doing in here?' he shouted. 'You can't be in this room.'

'Oh, I was just…' She took out a pack of cigarettes, approaching him.

'Whores have to stay across the other side of the bridge,' he yelled, anger and spite in his face. 'What are you, stupid? Is this your first time?'

'No–' She stopped, still holding out the cigarettes. She had been about to correct him, but it was better to be taken for a prostitute than police. 'I mean, sure. Across the bridge.'

'Want me to show you?'

'I'll find it.'

She left the huddle of buildings around the furnace, glancing about for a sign of Zielinski, but he was nowhere to be seen. Good. She hurried along a connecting road with a set of tracks. It was a self-contained galaxy in the shipyards, with its own road network, its own traffic. She skirted around a slow-moving lorry, ignoring a few men in hard hats who whistled as she passed. Their skin gleamed with sweat despite the early breeze. All along the main drive, she passed doorways into industry, white noise, sparks. She leaned into the wind and hurried ahead.

Along the bank of a canal, wide space opened out where war damage had not been repaired. There used to be factories here, but it was just a wasteland now. Weeds pushed through the broken stones. She passed a little hut selling soup and realised she hadn't eaten yet.

The wind picked up along the side of the riverbend where the shipyards curved away in chimney stacks. The water was filled with old wrecks, rusted hulks. She held the railing and braced herself as spray blew in her face. Up ahead, the narrow bridge trembled across empty space, leaning out precariously to the opposite bank. It wasn't the same bridge that her father used to cross, carrying her on his shoulders so she could see all the ships on the skyline, but it was good enough. Hastily repaired after the end of the War, this was formed from two separated sections that could be raised up to allow ships to pass. A disused traffic light hung from a post, swaying in the breeze. Sometimes, if you got caught on the wrong side when a boat came through, you might wait an hour for the bridge to come down again.

A man in a booth by the entrance looked out. 'What business you got on the other side?'

'The private kind.' She threw a pack of cigarettes through his window, which he caught with surprise.

'You're a cop, aren't you?'

'Goddammit. We're not all bad on the Force.'

'I was almost a cop.' He took out a cigarette and lit it. 'I did an internship. That was just before the War. I wasn't cut out for it.'

'And that put you off police for life…'

'Actually no. There was one good officer, tried to help me. But I was young.'

'What happened to him?'

'Something bad. Go on, cross now before the bridge goes up.'

She ducked under the barrier and hurried over. The bridge wavered in the gusts. She felt nauseous. Halfway across, she had to stop and hold the railing. She breathed slowly and raised her head to look across the water at the crooked cranes and leaning blocks. The wind stung her eyes, icy with droplets of the murky river. She stared over the churn. Could this be the same water that was extracted from the dead woman's lungs? The surface of foam and slick oil shifted constantly.

She felt herself watched and noticed a pair of eyes looking out from a wrecked boat that was chained to the moorings on the opposite bank. She started walking quickly in that direction. The eyes disappeared. It was a relief to reach the other side, but she stepped onto the stone embankment with unease, knowing the bridge could be raised, stranding her on the island. She followed the railings around to the old ship, what had been a kind of tugboat with a blown-off chimney but was now just a hulk of scrap metal. A hole in the hull showed a cavity where the inner material had been stripped long ago by looters. She was looking over the edge of the railing, trying to find a gangplank or ladder, when a woman with red hair stuck her head out of a trapdoor in the deck.

'Comrade,' Anna called.

'What do you want, bitch?'

'A friendly chat, that's all.'

'Talk to somebody else. We only serve ship workers and sailors here.' Her frizzy hair blew in a cloud around her dirty face.

'I *am* a ship worker.'

'You're the most obvious police cunt I ever saw in my life.'

‘Please, I only–’

‘Think your job can protect you? You’re alone out here. This is no man’s land. They’ll put you in the incinerator and toss your badge in the sea. You wouldn’t be the first.’

‘It’s not what you think.’

‘You’ll see.’ The woman disappeared, slamming the trapdoor shut over her head.

‘For Christ’s sake.’

There had to be a way to get from the bank onto the boat, probably a ladder they retracted after use. She looked up and down the side of the walkway but there was nobody around over this side of the water. She ducked under the railing and felt the chains that secured the boat, rusted into a solid, immovable clump of metal. The deck of the boat was only five feet below. She jumped into the stream of the wind and hit the wooden beams of the deck with a creaking of rotten timber. She crumpled and rolled. She lay on her back and wiggled her toes and fingers to make sure nothing was broken.

The trapdoor opened, and the woman looked out. ‘What’s wrong with you?’

‘I don’t know.’

‘They’ll kill you. They’ll sink you so deep nobody’ll find you in a thousand years. Think I’m joking?’

Anna looked in her bag. The cigarette packets had been squashed by her heavy landing on the deck. She took one out and opened it. ‘Smoke with me?’

‘Get lost. They’d kill me too. My own fault for talking to you.’

‘A woman was found hung from a tree last night. They think she was a prostitute. Someone in Gdańsk is killing working women. That’s all I want to talk about. I don’t care about your day job or anything else.’

‘Shit on my life.’

Their eyes held a moment. The red-haired woman flinched and almost closed the trapdoor again, but she stopped.

'Alright, give me a stupid cigarette.'

'Here.' Anna tossed one through the hatch.

'This thing's bent.'

'I landed on top of them. Maybe I'm not as good at this as I thought.'

'Why would anyone kill a whore? We're the only ones that give what we have without complaining.'

Anna took out her notepad and flicked through the pages. 'Ever seen anything like this?' She knelt at the trapdoor opening and showed the symbol.

'What the fuck is that? Some religious shit?'

'It was found next to the body of the woman.'

'I never saw it before.'

Anna put her pad away. 'Any of the girls around here been missing in the last day or so?'

'Who could tell? They come and go. Drifters, waifs, the usual type. You don't wash up on the shipyards if things are going well in your life.'

'Seen any creepy guys hanging around? Strangers? Somebody dangerous?'

The woman laughed and coughed on her cigarette. 'I guess you never worked a nightshift like mine.'

'Alright, let's say, "more creepy than normal."'

'I don't even know what "normal" means. I didn't grow up in Gdańsk. I came over here from the East. I thought it might be nice to work by the sea, at least I could dream about leaving here. The Republic, I mean. Maybe try my luck in the West one day. You going to arrest me for saying that?'

'Relax. I'm not here to arrest anybody. I grew up on these shipyards, my whole family worked here one way or another. One thing you learn: nobody ever leaves on a ship except to come back.'

The woman squinted at her; she wafted cigarette smoke away from her face. 'Let me talk to the others a second.'

She disappeared through the hatch, which closed behind her. Anna looked up at the embankment and wondered how she was going to get off this boat. Seagulls circled in the opalescent sky that was streaked with darker formations of grey. Rain coming.

The trapdoor opened and the woman peeped out. 'Liza will talk to you. You'd better come down here. Straighten your cigarettes, you'll need them.'

18

Liza said she was eighteen, but she looked fifteen at most. In a rusted chamber at the back of the boat, where a mattress that reeked of semen was laid over rotting timbers, she smoked one of Anna's squashed cigarettes and couldn't meet her eye.

'I only saw him once. Never before. And he never came back. It was a week ago. He said he had a special request, and he'd pay extra.'

'What was the request?'

'He likes to hold a knife against your throat while he's… you know.' Liza looked at the floor like she was ashamed.

'It's alright, don't be afraid. Just tell me.'

'Am I in trouble?'

'No, of course not.'

'You think this man…'

'He might be a suspect in a case we're investigating. Maybe, maybe not. Tell me what happened.'

'Can I have another cigarette?'

'You haven't finished that one… Never mind.' Anna threw her another. 'Tell me what happened.'

'He said it was just pretend, the knife thing, he wouldn't hurt me. But then after we started, he got real intense. I could feel the blade cutting into my Adam's apple. I thought I should scream for help, to make it stop, but I was afraid if I made a sound his hand might slip, and he'd slice my throat. The blade was rusty, but it was sharp. Like a farmer uses for castrating sheep. I grew up on a farm.'

'And then what happened?'

'And then… then…'

'Go on.'

'He kept talking the whole time. Never knew such a talker. He was telling me everything he wanted to do. He was going to cut my jugular like a pig. He'd do it in the moment of, you know, the moment… And I had to surrender to it, he said. I'd be a sacrifice. If I just surrendered myself completely, everything would be perfect. And then, I don't know, the strange thing is, I started to believe him. He spoke so softly, he wasn't angry or wild, like some of them who come here. Maybe it's crazy, I felt like he hypnotised me. After a while, I could only hear his voice, and those things he was saying. It was like his voice was what violated me, not anything else. He was entering me, using me with words, and I felt myself opening like I never knew. And then, and then…'

'Go on.'

'I could tell he was getting close, you know, it was the moment, the moment was coming. He was going to… and then… I was ready for it. The knife. I wasn't even afraid of the pain. He told me that I wanted it, deep down, and I believed him. Dunno why. It seems insane now, but in the moment, I believed him, I really felt like I wanted my throat to be sliced in two. I was ready for it, I arched my neck. And then… and then…'

'Go on.'

'Nothing. He stopped, just stopped. He said I wasn't right. I wasn't the right one. It was no good. It didn't work.'

'What did he mean?'

'I have no idea. He just walked out. Ever since then, I've felt sick. I'm all twisted inside. I wanted him to come back, I wanted him to tell me I was the one. I'd do it right this time, I'd be the one he was looking for, and it would be perfect, like he wanted. But he never came back.'

Anna surfaced from the story as from a trance. She blinked her eyes.

Liza pulled the blanket tighter. 'Do you think…?'

'What did he look like?'

'I don't know.' She shook her dirty hair, the butts of two cigarettes in her mouth.

'What do you mean? You saw him, didn't you?'

'When he approached me, he was just normal, wearing overalls, a plain-looking guy like anyone else. Tall, I guess. But afterwards, down here, he told me to look away when he undressed. While we were doing it, he told me, don't look back at him, he'd cut my throat if I looked.'

'So, you didn't see anything?'

'I…' She closed her eyes, scanning the past. 'I caught a glimpse, but it was dark. He had tattoos on his chest, like marks.'

'What kind of marks?'

'I don't know, like I say, it was dark.'

'Hold on.' Anna flipped through her notepad to the sketch of the rune. 'Something like this?'

Liza's eyes widened. 'Could be. I don't know. Is that, is that what he…? What is that symbol? What does it mean?'

'It doesn't mean anything.'

'Where did you…? God, it's him, isn't it? He's the man you're looking for.' She stared at the door in terror.

'We don't know that. Every sailor has tattoos. And this sign, it could be nothing. Could just be a punctuation mark. A scar in the tree bark.'

'You found it in a tree?'

'Yeah.' Anna put her notepad away. 'Forget it. What happened is over. He won't come back. You're alright now.'

'A tree…' Liza's eyes narrowed. 'Have you seen the picture?'

'What picture?'

'It's on the side of the machine shed, across the way from here. You go left, then–'

'I know where the machine shed is.'

* * *

A group of four men were huddled on the walkway when she climbed up the rattling ladder from the boat. She tried to look like she wasn't afraid of being tipped into the polluted waters.

'She's new.' They turned to one another and did not smile.

'I'm not in the business.' Anna tried to push pass them, but they closed around her.

'What business is yours then?'

She considered saying "police" but thought better. 'It's a private matter.' She looked back down at the deck of the boat, but the trapdoor was closed, the women were hidden from view. 'I'm looking for Kostek. You seen him?'

A blonde man whistled. 'Kostek's lucky day.'

A shorter man with silver hair nodded at her. 'Come with me, I'll take you to him.'

'I'll find him myself.' She tried to walk around them, but they formed a new circle, blocking her path. She had left her last cigarettes on the boat.

'Let me pass,' she said.

'Or what?'

'Kostek will be angry with you.'

'Is that right?' The blonde man smiled, showing cruel incisors. 'Funny thing about that is, I don't think you ever met him.'

From behind them, a deep voice shouted. 'What's going on here?'

They looked back. 'Nothing, boss. Nothing.'

Kostek came striding along the embankment. 'Get back to work. I'll have your union cards.'

'We were just escorting this young lady.' The blonde man grinned. 'Shipyards are a dangerous place.'

'Of course you were. Leave her to me, I'll escort her myself.'

The men muttered among themselves as they drifted away.

Kostek took out a pipe. 'Christ, kid. What are you doing wandering around out here on your own?'

'I was looking for you.'

'So I heard.' He was a tall, broad man, completely bald, with a white beard. Through the gaps in his vest a chest tattoo of octopus tentacles showed through shaggy, grey hair. He wore a patch over his left eye. Her dad used to say he wore it just for show, sometimes he'd come in with it on the wrong eye. 'You should have called ahead. This is no place for police.'

'We're not your enemies. I want to help.'

He pulled closer, lowered his voice. 'Things aren't the same around here. It's not like when you were little. Workers are strained to the limit. They don't trust police.'

'Why? What's happened?'

'It's not safe to talk.' He glanced over his shoulder, but there was nobody around. The chains of the railing clinked in the wind. 'They're killing us here. We work till we die. Longer and longer shifts, and the money is worthless. Can't buy shit in Gdańsk.'

'We're all struggling. It's the economy.'

'They said socialism was for the labourers, but it's worse for us now than it was before.'

'Kostek, it's a work in progress. Give it time…'

'Go fuck yourself. Your dad would gnash his teeth to hear you.'

'I don't want to argue.' She tried to smile, mostly grimaced, but he didn't return the appeal.

He sucked on his pipe and breathed out aromatic smoke. 'Just tell me what this is about and get lost. It's not safe for either of us.'

'Show me the tree.'

'Tree? Trees don't grow here, you know that.'

'The picture on the wall.'

'Shit.' He stared and almost laughed, but he didn't smile. 'Is that what this is about? They got you investigating vandalism?'

'I'm investigating a murder.'

'Well then, you're just in time. I was about to have that thing cleaned off the wall. Follow me.'

They walked in silence along the embankment as their clothes buffeted in the wind. At a portable hut, they turned and went around the side of the machine shed. It was a relief to get out of the gusts.

'Happy now?' Kostek pointed.

At first, she couldn't see it. The outline was faint, a thin line of chalk sketched on the brick that disappeared in places where cracks showed in the wall. She took a step closer and traced the contour with one finger. Once you saw it, it was clear: the simple outline of a tree, a few crooked branches sticking out from a central trunk.

'What does it mean?' She took out her notepad and a pencil.

'Nothing,' Kostek said. 'It means nothing. Some fool messing about. Appeared out of nowhere last week. I'd have had it cleaned off already, but the men seem to like it for some reason.'

Anna took a step back and started sketching a copy of the image. 'Who did it?'

'No idea. Won't have been one of our workers. They're all too busy, and when they're not working, it's not trees they have on their mind.'

'But… a tree? Why a tree?'

'Anna, what is this? Why do you care? It's nothing.'

'Have you ever seen anything like this?' She showed him the picture of the rune.

ᛃ

He peered too close and pulled back, angry. 'Don't wave that shit around here. And keep it away from me.'

'Why? What is it? Do you know this symbol?'

'I don't know what it is, and I don't want to know.' He stepped back, fury in his old face. 'Don't play the fool, Anna. That's some old Nazi shit. That's the kind of thing that gets men killed. Runes, fascist symbols. This city burned down once before; I witnessed it. I won't have that shit around here.'

'Sorry.' She put the notepad away. 'Kostek, I didn't come here to argue. Really, I'm happy to see you. It's been years. I–'

'What happened to you, kid? Why did you choose the police? Always thought you'd be a ship worker.'

She tried to remember. Funny thing. 'I don't know.'

'Just get the fuck out of the way. And leave my men in peace. I'm sorry, Anna, I loved your parents, but you can't come back here no more.'

She retraced her steps back through the shipyard without being disturbed, but she felt sick. The workers kept their distance, they stared through her as if she were invisible, and fell silent if she ventured too close. There was no sign of Zielinski. He must be back at the car already. She passed back out the front gate, and something like loss stabbed at her ribs. She didn't belong. *You can't come back here no more.* The shipyards were the heart of the city; if you were exiled from the yards, you were lost from Gdańsk. She pulled her coat more tightly around her shoulders and hurried towards the car. Her partner should be… but she saw from ten yards away that he wasn't there.

'Christ.' She swore into the wind and couldn't hear herself. 'Where are you?'

Moving closer, she saw the passenger door was open, as if Zielinski had just climbed out. He must be nearby. But the road was deserted. Moss hung in the ravaged gaps of the surrounding ruins. She checked in the car, knowing herself it was absurd, as if he might be hiding under the seats. Nothing. Not even his musty smell, the wind had blown everything away. But glancing around she spotted something: a scrap of paper under the windscreen wipers that fluttered in the wind. She pulled it out and held it to the white sky. There was nothing there except a symbol in black ink:

ᚱ

19

Back at the station, there was no sign of Zielinski. The superintendent jumped up from his seat when she knocked at his office. Creases in his cheeks, he rubbed his eyes and yawned.

'Where's your partner?'

'I lost him,' Anna said.

'What do you mean, you "lost" him?'

'I don't know where he went. We were at the shipyards. We split up. When I got back to the car, he wasn't there.'

'He'll be in one of those secret drinking dens where the sailors go.'

'They don't serve police in those places.'

Dust motes hung in the slanting light through a tall window behind him that overlooked an empty space, rubble, the outlines of old foundations. A synagogue used to stand there but it had been demolished long ago, when the city had a different name, and different gods. Beyond, the towering basilica was scarred with scaffolding, endless rebuilding. Along the skyline, a few old church spires broke through the spiderweb of ruins. Gdańsk. Home.

Anna turned from the window with regret. 'I found another rune.'

'Are you trying to get me fired?'

'Someone left this under the windscreen wiper.' She took out the slip of paper and placed it on the desk.

ᚱ

'What am I supposed to do with this?' His face flushed red.

'That's two runes. There might be a pattern.'

'I don't want to know about it.'

'There's this as well.' She took out her notepad and flipped the pages to the sketch of the tree. 'This was drawn in chalk on the wall at the shipyards. Just appeared last week. Nobody there knows who did it. You think it could be an ash tree? Like the one from the crime scene…'

'A tree. So what?' He tore the page out of the notepad and ripped it in two.

'What are you doing?'

'Something's got into you, Anna. Is it because the victim was a woman? Are you too caught up in this? You're not thinking right.' He dropped the torn paper into the empty litter basket by the side of his desk.

'These are the only clues we have…'

'These aren't clues. Zielinski will be back later; he'll have dug something up. A dead prostitute. Some wretched day labourer got drunk and hit her too hard, threw her in the water. Things happen in the shipyards. You'll write up the report, we'll file it away. The sun will come up in the morning just like always.'

'Why would a drunk day labourer drag her out into the woods and hang her from a tree?'

'Anna, I'm warning you…' He rubbed his head, grimacing. 'I've got a migraine. I don't want to hear any more about this. When Zielinski turns up, you send him to me. You can go now.'

When she didn't leave, he groaned. 'Something else?'

'Comrade…' She strained to find the best words but could only see the rune's outline behind her eyes. 'You're older than me. You've been a cop forever, everyone says.'

'Don't listen to them.'

'You must've been around back then, I mean, when the Nazis took over. These runes…'

'You're close to the edge, Comrade. I'm warning you.' His face had turned dark scarlet. 'Get out, before I lose my temper.'

* * *

The afternoon passed, but Zielinski didn't turn up. Roman went home, complaining of headaches. Anna was glad to get him out of the way. Alone at her desk, she sketched out from memory the tree design that he'd torn up. At four o'clock, there was a radio broadcast that everybody had to listen to in the canteen. There weren't enough chairs to go around, so officers stood against the wall or leaned in the doorway. In the corner, the same Party observer made notes. Through the crackling radio, some minister or other talked forever. His voice, so slow, so monotonous, worked like hypnosis. Around the room, people swayed on their feet. The lucky ones, who were seated, rested their heads on the shoulders of their friends. At the back of the crowd, Anna ducked down behind some taller officers, and slipped out.

* * *

The shadows were lengthening across the street when she entered the storage depot. She found Basia asleep at the front desk. Behind her, a radio was playing the same broadcast. The speech would never finish. She was about to creep past, but Basia opened her eyes.

'It's alright,' Anna said. 'Don't mind me.'

'What do you want, Nowak? You look suspicious. I already told the others; the depot isn't a pharmacy.'

'I'm not looking for drugs. Just need to check some items. It's for a case.'

'You got the paperwork?'

Anna held her eyes. 'Remember that favour you owed me…?'

'Shit, Comrade. You're a pain in the ass.' She got out of her chair and looked up and down the corridor. It was quiet in the building; everyone was occupied with the radio broadcast. 'Go on then. I'll look away for five minutes, but after that…'

'Thanks, Basia. You're one of the good ones.' She slipped through the door into the cool shadow where rows of shelves yawned in the dust.

'Five minutes!' Basia called after her.

'I only need two.'

* * *

She drove by Zielinski's building and cursed him as she climbed to the top floor. The lift didn't work, and half the staircase had fallen inwards. Rats scurried in the broken walls. Nobody answered the door. She tried the neighbours on both sides and got no answer. Going back down the stairs, she ran into the janitor.

'Sorry, ma'am; I mean, Comrade.'

'Police.' She stopped him before he could hurry away.

'They have women police now?'

'I'm looking for a colleague of mine, lives on the top floor.'

'That would be Comrade Zielinski. I mean, we're not friends, but, well, I know everyone who lives here. It's been, what? Five years, at least, since the comrade moved in.'

'Stop saying "comrade". You sound sarcastic.'

'Sorry.' He looked at his dirty shoes.

'And Zielinski, you seen him today?'

'Went out early this morning, like always. He's a hard worker.'

'He been home since?'

The janitor scratched his face while he thought or pretended to think. 'Not that I saw. But I'm busy myself. In and out. That's my existence. People think it's easy to run a building like this, they have no idea.'

'Where does he go? A bar? A friend? A girlfriend?'

'Zielinski?' The janitor scratched his face again. Perhaps he was just itchy. 'Not much of a people person. Keeps to himself. There is a bar around the corner. I think I've seen him in there once or twice. But I wouldn't…'

'Thanks.' She started down the steps, turning back over her shoulder. 'If you see him, tell him to call the station.'

* * *

Pirate opened the bag, which was stuffed with contraband jazz records, and peeked inside. 'Is that all?'

'Best I could do. Take it or leave it.'

'What use is a contact on the police when they can't even–'

Anna snatched the bag. 'Give it back then.'

'Relax, Comrade. For you, I'll make an exception. Follow me.' The day had turned chill, but he still wore just a dressing gown, vest, and underpants.

They went through the courtyard, dipped in shadow now, into a kind of tool cupboard where a mop leaned against an antique armchair that must have been looted from some wrecked mansion.

Pirate cleared a space and sat down. 'Dangerous business, what you're looking for.'

'Did you get the book or not?'

He grinned. 'How's your German?'

'What do you mean?'

'*Sprichst du Deutsch? Oder nicht?*'

These words, lilting in his fluent tone and phrasing, surprised her. German was a ghost language that haunted the city, familiar like an old song, but rarely spoken aloud. It was dangerous.

'I'll take that contraband back.' She reached for the bag, but he held it to his chest.

'There are no books like you're looking for, not in Polish. You'd have to speak German.'

'I grew up on the shipyards; I speak every language. I just don't know which is which. Anyway, it's pictures I'm interested in.'

'Speaking foreign languages, tut, tut. Not thinking of defecting to the West, are you? That would be very undialectical.'

'I see.' She stepped away. 'You've got nothing, and you want to make fun of me. I need to sleep. It's been a long day. I lost my partner; he still hasn't turned up.'

'That's Gdańsk. People disappear. Where do they go? Nobody knows. You might try Argentina. New Zealand. This is a port city, after all.'

'Argentina, sure.' She walked out into the darkening courtyard.

Pirate jumped up. 'Where are you going? Don't you want to know what I got for you?'

'I'm not in the mood for games.'

'It's not a thing, strictly speaking, that I found. It's a man.'

'You're starting to annoy me.'

'A professor. He's a historian or some such, I'm not sure. Smart guy, wears glasses on a string. He comes to me for rare books. Nothing as dangerous as you're looking for, but he pays well. I saw him earlier, told him you'd pay a visit. He owes me a favour. Who doesn't?' He smiled. Pirate was a man who enjoyed his work.

'A professor?'

'Got the address here.' He took a scrap of paper out of his breast pocket. 'This guy knows plenty about, well, you know… the city that cannot be named. The things that happened. He's nervous though. Don't spook him. I told him you're not like other police, otherwise he would never help you. The guy's terrified of the authorities. Real paranoid. Like I said, he's smart…'

Anna took the paper and tried to make sense of the scribbled, almost illegible handwriting. 'And I should…?'

'Call there after dark. But I warn you, Comrade, don't frighten him. He's a loyal customer. Wouldn't want to lose such a man.'

* * *

Anna drove to the University, not far from the centre, in the district of Wrzeszcz. She parked along an avenue lined with poplars. A wide, red banner fluttered on the breeze outside the front wall as she hurried through, trying to orient herself. This place was huge, a sprawl of new blocks in the Soviet style, jumbled together inside the patched ruins of the older building. She passed beneath a temporary platform as the rain started to fall. The dust of red brick salted the air where what remained of the older section was covered with scaffolding. She showed her badge at the front desk and received a curious tilt of the head from the secretary.

'Is anybody in trouble, Detective?'

'No. It's nothing. Just a routine visit.'

'Do you need help? Is there anybody in particular you wanted to see…?'

'No. Thanks. I'll find my way.'

It might have been a hospital or a prison, bare walls, closed doors, only there were groups of students scattered about. She followed the smell of rain through dull corridors and climbed a staircase that echoed with students' feet on stone. Pirate's loyal customer had an office on the third floor. Prof. D. Kowalski. She found the nameplate and knocked. Nobody responded, but light showed beneath the door. She opened it and looked inside.

'Hello, Professor…?'

'What is it?' An ageing man with fluffy white hair looked up from a desk that was crowded with loose paper.

'I'm here about…' She stepped inside and closed the door behind her.

'Oh, you're the police officer. They didn't say it would be a woman.'

'Is that a problem?'

The look on his face was a failed smile. 'I just wasn't expecting it, that's all. But it's a new world. Things are like that now, of course.'

'Things are like what?'

'Please make this brief, Officer, I'm a busy man, as you see.'

Behind him, the curtains were closed over a window set between filing cabinets. A lamp cast sickly green light over bookshelves stuffed with volumes. A sense of manic labour, as if this man had carried on working here, bunkered down with his books and his paper through all the years of fire.

'Can I sit down?'

He sighed. 'As you wish. But, Officer, please, don't waste my time.'

'I was told you might be able to help me.'

'I won't ask how my name came up with your... informants. I only beg that you keep me out of whatever you're involved with. I have an academic reputation to maintain.' His eyes glared beneath pale, bushy eyebrows. Emotion flickered there, but it was more than fear.

'I only want to show you something.' She took out her notepad and placed the sketched symbols in front of him. 'Know what these are?'

ᛃ

ᚱ

The professor put his glasses on. Something screwed in his face. He shook his head and muttered some word to himself that she couldn't catch. It might have been German, the ghost language that haunted city corners where the street signs had been prised away from the walls and replaced with new names in Polish. He tossed the notepad back across the table.

'What's this about, Officer? Some trick?'

'Not at all.'

'We both know what this relates to. Old-timer stuff. Germanic gibberish. A man could ruin his life. I have no desire to.'

Was he acting, or serious? Intellectual types could be difficult to read, with so many layers on which they deceived themselves.

She studied his face as she said, 'I'll tell you the simple facts. This symbol, the first one, was found at a murder scene. I'm investigating the crime. I assure you, you're not under any suspicion or threat. I'm here in a totally unofficial capacity. I'd just like your help to know what the symbols mean. It could help solve a crime.'

'Why should I?' Behind the glasses, his small, grey eyes scurried across her face and couldn't find what they were looking for.

'With your assistance, we could bring a killer to justice, and we may be able to avert another killing.'

'You think they'd kill again?'

'Could be.'

Yes, there was something there that he couldn't hide, a hint in the cruel turn of his lip. Curiosity. He leaned forwards. 'Who was the victim? None of this was in the newspapers.'

'I can't discuss details. I'm only here to talk about the symbols. I was told you have some knowledge. You could provide a valuable service to the State.'

'Give me the pictures.'

He reached and snapped with his fingers, a patronising gesture. The students must really love this guy, Anna thought and handed the notepad over.

'This…' He started to speak, but stopped, and fixed her with one eyebrow raised. 'And this is off the record. Just between our four eyes. My name will be left out of any reports.'

'Of course, Professor.'

He pointed at the first symbol. 'This is the old Germanic rune for the harvest. It was thought to hold magical powers. It asked the gods for a good year, a fertile year, an abundant harvest.'

'A harvest. A harvest of what?'

'It's your job to figure that out, not mine.' He grinned, enjoying this.

'And the other one?'

'It's the rune representing a journey. A long, difficult journey is just starting out. But you only mentioned one murder. Where was the second rune?'

'As I mentioned, I can't discuss the details. There's another thing.' She flipped through the pages to her sketch of the tree design. 'Know what this is?'

He put his glasses on again. 'I won't say "a tree"; I guess that would be facetious.' He chuckled to himself. 'This killer has really got the Gdańsk Police in a spin.'

'Sure, it's a tree, but what do trees mean? Does it connect with the runes? Something to do with old German mythology?'

'Well, the ash tree is sacred in old Norse myth, and other systems. The god Odin was hung from an ash. He sacrificed himself.' The professor flipped the notepad back across the table. 'Now, if that's all, I've work to do.'

'Thank you. This has been helpful.' She stood up. 'It's possible that I may need to consult you again…'

'Please don't.'

'If…'

'If you discover more runes?' He opened a drawer behind his desk. 'I'll give you something.' He pulled out an old, leatherbound book. 'Take this. It contains everything you need, and more than I could ever tell you.'

'That's kind of you.' She reached for the book, but he pulled it away.

'There's one condition: don't come back here, and don't connect me to this book. Whoever owns it could get in trouble. It's yours now.'

'Of course. Thanks, Professor. Your identity is safe.' She grabbed the book before he could pull it away again. The pages smelled mildewy as she flicked through. 'It's in German.'

'You don't speak German?' The tone of disdain that this man's students must have come to despise.

'Well, some.' She felt like a stupid *kindergartener*. 'I picked some up. I grew up on the shipyards, every language was there. Problem is sometimes I don't know what's German and what's Dutch or Swedish or English…'

He laughed in her face. 'This country. No wonder nothing works. Here.' He strode over to the shelf and pulled down another book. 'German dictionary. You'll figure it out. Hope you came here in a car; this thing's heavy.'

* * *

Anna's flat was cramped, just one room separated off in the teeming building where countless families piled on top of each other. She shared a toilet with so many people, she'd given up trying to learn all their names. Her room must have been a kind of storeroom once, part of a larger flat with three bedrooms, a living room and a kitchen, but each room had been converted into a distinct flat of its own now. To move between them, she had to walk through connecting doors, around strangers' beds and tables. The thing she treasured about the cupboard room was that it was too small to be further subdivided; she didn't have to share it with anybody; and it didn't have a second door connecting it to another room. A measure of privacy in a world of spies.

Whoever owned the flat before her must have been a criminal, or some kind of deviant, or perhaps a detective: they'd left a cavity in the wall hidden behind a wardrobe. This wardrobe was her only piece of furniture, and one that she could hardly use as she had hardly any clothes, but it served a purpose, keeping the secret cavity hidden. Not even the landlady knew about the secret. Anna hadn't discovered it at first either. It was after she'd been living here a year, when she acquired some contraband during a raid on a black-market depot and was looking for somewhere to keep it safe. She'd pushed on the back panel of the wardrobe and felt something give. Gdańsk was like that.

She checked again that the curtains were sealed over her one small window, that nobody was lurking at the door, before she pulled out the back of the wardrobe and exhaled. She was safe, nobody had discovered her stash. Why did she keep all this stuff? Cigarettes and cognac. A little marijuana. Prohibited books published in the West, including the works of Trotsky, along with all kinds of odd bric-a-brac like maps and old coins. Truth be told, she had no idea why she'd amassed this collection. It started with the first raid, where she'd learned from the older, more experienced cops, that creaming off the take was more than just a perk of the job, it was a necessary symbol of their group identity. It showed they were all in it together.

Later, she had built up connections with the black market. The memory of her parents brought her credibility among those who knew. She gained sources of information about Gdańsk's underworld; people who could get things, find things out. In return, she'd tip them off when raids were coming, or retrieve their possessions held at overcrammed storage depots from where they'd never be missed by the police. She had shown herself to be discrete and reliable.

She started to understand what Karl Marx was talking about in his concept of "commodity fetishism": there was magic in objects. Her network of informants grew wider, she became known at the police station for having black-market connections, and underworld fixers. Her bosses didn't mind this, they even valued it, they let her carry on, so long as it helped to solve cases and bring suspects to justice. But the others didn't know about her growing love for the marijuana that came in via the port in Gdynia. With a glow of sin, she prepared a joint.

She sat against the wall and leafed through the pages of the professor's old book. The smell was heady. It was all in German, but the pictures were striking, the runes woke something inside her. Stark, striking, they touched at meaning and concealed it. She turned a page, smelled it, traced a finger over the symbol and shivered.

ᛞ

Underneath, in German, she read, "*Tag*". She knew enough to translate "Day". It was beautiful. With the joint resting between her lips, she grabbed her notepad and jotted the symbol down, next to its definition. Soon she had a page of runes sketched out. The night deepened; she sank into it and drifted. The tenement was textured with noise in the dark, through the interlocking, overcrowded spaces, flats within flats, the sounds of snoring, sleepwalking feet, whispers, and creaking furniture. A baby wailed somewhere in the density. Two floors above, the ageing landlady screamed out 'No!' in her sleep. The others had learned by now to ignore this terrifying shriek that happened every night.

Anna turned a new page. She should stop and go to bed, but she didn't want to. There was something in the lull, a sound of voices and movement. Some disturbance, but there were always disturbances. She traced another rune. Footsteps sounded louder, closer… There was a knock on the front door in the landing. Perhaps one of the old men had come home drunk and lost his keys. Feet knocked and butted against the walls. A discordant voice: she thought she heard her own name spoken. A shiver of fear, but she was insulated by rooms within rooms. There were three more doors to pass between the unseen intruders and her own shelter. They came closer. Somebody was saying her name out there. She froze. It was too late in the evening for a neighbourly request.

A voice shouted, 'Nowak! You in there? Wake up.'

She jumped up and for a moment was paralysed with the joint in one hand, the book in the other. The knocking sounded again.

'Nowak! Wake up. It's urgent.'

'OK, OK. Give me a minute.' She opened the window and threw the joint out, and just stood for a moment in regret and shock at what she had done, in a ghostly cloud of marijuana fumes.

'Nowak! Come on.'

She wafted the smoke out of the window, pushed the books under a blanket, closed the wardrobe over, then wafted the air again. She put on a dressing gown and opened the door.

'Who is it?'

In the dark, she recognised one of the nameless old guys from the police station who never went outside. He stared openly at her body beneath the gown. 'They found Zielinski…'

'Oh.' Her mind was floating in the aftertaste of the drug, she tried to focus.

'…drowned.'

'What?'

'They need you to come down right away.'

In the shadow behind him, old Mrs Lipinska shouted, 'Anna! What's this fuss? People are sleeping.'

She shook her head. 'I don't understand. What happened?'

'Drowned.'

'Zielinski? That's not possible.'

'In ink, they said. If you can imagine such a thing.'

20

Danzig, the Free City

Two days before the start of WWII

There was no sleep that night. I lay in bed in the dark, but my eyes still flashed with the lights of police cars and cameras. Voices, shaking heads merged in the shadow. One of our own was dead. Activity swirled around Gerhard's flat, as the crime scene was recorded, the body taken away. Disembodied hands touched me, squeezed my shoulder. A cup of tea appeared from nowhere. Cigarettes were passed around, and again. The trainee was mute. Seated in the back of my car, he hugged his arms over his chest, stained with vomit, and didn't respond. Hours passed in slow motion, explorers at the bottom of the ocean. Inspectors and deputies pulled drunk from The Mermaid, eyes glazed, mouths slack; we crossed in the landing and said nothing. It was understood, this was no ordinary killing; a cop had been murdered. Methodically, we measured the crime scene, photographed, and mapped it, recorded the details, and tidied it away.

Hours later, I lay in my tangled bedsheets, the mirror face-down on the dresser, I stared at the ceiling and probed the seabed, the stunned flashes of memory. I wasn't supposed to talk to anyone. Henrik had sworn and massaged his scalp and pulled me into the cold to mutter some secret words that didn't make sense. In the drying foam of adrenaline, I couldn't leave the murder scene. Even afterwards, standing outside the building in the freezing wind, the details all packed away into the back of a van, the paperwork signed and filed, the police cars pulled out, headlights fading into dark, two Gestapo agents observing from the shadow, and I couldn't leave the suffocating room in my mind.

Splayed on the mattress in dried sweat and fear, I gave up trying to sleep. There was no point wasting time, I may as well work. In wavering candlelight, my eyes chafed against the notes I'd taken. None of it was legible at this time of the morning, close to daybreak. I longed for a taste of the Baltic. I stuck my head out of the window and breathed. There was nobody in the courtyard outside, but it wasn't quiet; the wind swirled in a trap, caught between the leaning inner surfaces of the hollow quadrant. Something rattled. I squinted in the dark and thought I saw a cat dart out of sight.

'What am I doing?' I put on my dark coat, my grey fedora, and went downstairs.

All the way through the sleeping building, I crept like a stranger. Passing the courtyard, I looked for the black cat. Her green eyes held mine for a moment and disappeared into the shadow. Outside, the beige front of the narrow townhouse shone; the streetlamp was still lit, it never went out, this bland duration that nullified time, as if nothing ever changed, nothing ever would. Something creaked further back in the entrance corridor, and I was electrified with guilt, I felt myself a trespasser in my own home. I fingered the pliers and screwdriver in my jacket pocket, the electric torch, and hurried out before any sleepless eye might catch me.

My feet wandered grey roads, rotting autumn leaves, along the Amber Way, through the Green Gate. Railings clinked and moaned in the wind. The shipyards called me. Electric light mapped onto the silhouettes of industry. Machines heaved and groaned. Even in the dead places of night, the water didn't rest. Workers' shouts carried on the salt air; a boat, apparently deserted, drifted along the bend of the river. I passed raw eyes, machinists who didn't seem to notice, they let the world outside their work disappear and didn't mourn it.

I tried to find my way back to the murder scene at the shipyards. Away from the activity of cargo and freight, the sea's late shift, I returned to the disused warehouses where Danzig crumbled, slipping into the Baltic, gently, quietly, unnoticed. I found the chain metal fence. In the dark, my torch picked out the same enormous mound of waste metal behind it.

'Man, what are you doing? Go home. Go to bed. Stop talking to yourself.'

If I closed my eyes, I might fall asleep standing. Somehow it felt more restful there in the freezing wind than in my own room. I followed the fence back to the gate that said, "DANGER". It was locked with a chain. That's what the pliers were for.

I shook the metal and called into the night. 'Anybody there? Hello? Anybody?'

At the sound, a few seagulls took flight from crevices in the surrounding warehouses. I shone my torch through the links of the fence, seeking anybody. The place was submerged in mineral density, brick, and iron, it was impossible to believe any living being ever breathed this thick air. But I knew better. The chain lock on the fence was rusted, it left a red-brown stain on my fingers when I cut it loose. The air had changed, I felt it: daybreak in the east, still not visible but carried on the wind that blew in across the sea. There was no time; when the sun rose, I'd be caught here, and there'd be questions. I had no energy left to answer.

I let the chain clank to the floor, wiped the rust from my hand on the back of my pants, and regretted it. Frau Grubach would make a fuss. It was hard to believe out here at the end of the night that such a domestic being existed. My feet splashed through stagnant water, sent echoes up the looming brick surfaces. Metal gates shivered as I passed them.

Despite the anxiety, there was comfort in these moments of industrial decay; my father had been a seaman, still was, for all I knew. Sometimes when I couldn't sleep, I'd sift the alternate paths life might have taken, and there was strange consolation to imagine myself as a sailor, away at sea, far from murder scenes and office paperwork. Perhaps there might be time to join a ship, at the last moment, before all of this collapsed into the tides. But I knew, when Danzig falls, everyone will swarm to the sinking harbour to climb on any ship that might save them. The wharfs will be crushed by panicked crowds, there will be no escape.

I trudged through seagull shit in my house sandals – sandals, why? – and no longer worried about Frau Grubach's annoyance. I might as well return to the flat soaked in oil. I reached the warehouse and found the metal door in the shadow. The handle hardly turned; the lock seemed rusted into place. I started to doubt. Could I have come to the wrong building? All these warehouses looked alike, and in the dark, one pile of scrap metal was just like any other. I was running out of time. I smelled the bright chill of morning, the herring fleet returned, and I couldn't bear to go home without something to show for this journey through the tunnel of night into dawn. Sleep demanded a tribute. I banged on the metal door. A dull, hollow thud that raised little sound no matter how hard I struck with the side of my fist. A thread of rationality thinned in my head, and I was hammering with both hands on metal.

My voice became a scream. 'Let me in! Let me in! Let me in!'

Somebody coughed behind me. I swung around and was blinded by his torch.

'Stand back,' a voice shouted. 'I'll call the police.'

'I am the police.'

'Don't make me laugh. Some homeless lunatic wandering around in your sandals… You stink, man.'

I held out my badge into the glare of torchlight. 'Didn't you hear? We're all homeless lunatics now.'

He looked at the badge, turned on his heels, and ran. The dropped torch clattered against the floor.

'Hey!' I sprang after him. 'Hey! Come back! Don't be afraid. I just want to talk.'

He was quick. I was losing him, but as he came to the gate he tripped, sprinting too fast, he lost control and flew forwards with a cry. Seagulls along the wall broke loose. I jumped on him, pinned him with my knees, shone my torch in his face.

'Who are you?'

'Let me go! Let me go!'

'Why did you run away?'

'I thought you were crazy. You are crazy, aren't you? Please, please… don't arrest me. I've got a sick kid at home. And my wife with some kind of tropical disease. Can you believe that? It comes from Madagascar. A sailor on the harbour must have carried it. They bring back parrots and bananas, tarantulas… and this. She just lies there now, won't move or make a sound. The job is all I have…'

'Alright, shut up. I'm not going to hurt you.' I pulled him to his feet. 'What are you, a cleaner? Janitor?'

'I'm the overseer. It's not like it sounds; there's nothing to oversee.'

'You got a key to that warehouse?'

Tears in his eyes caught the torchlight. 'Ah shit. Can't you just let me go home? Can't we both go home? It's almost day. You must have a wife and kid too. You know what families are like; they get sick.'

'I don't have anyone. Open that door.'

'Why do you want to go in there? There's nothing. Honestly. All this is abandoned. Hasn't been used in years. Please, Herr, don't get me in trouble. I'm not supposed to let anybody in. You shouldn't even be in this yard. I could lose my job. God. I'm fucked, aren't I?'

I tried to soften my voice that was raw. 'Relax. I just want to look around one room, that's all. It'll take five minutes. I won't touch anything. You can come with me and watch. Just five minutes. I promise.'

In the gleam of his bloodshot eyes, I saw his anxious mind revolving. 'You need a permit, don't you? A warrant. I don't know. A piece of paper. You got anything like that?'

'I could get one. I'm a detective. Chief investigator.'

'So, no paper then?'

'Don't you want to go home? We'll be out here all day if you want paperwork.'

'I don't believe you. You're bluffing.'

'Shit. I don't have time for this.' I took out my wallet. There was one bill inside. It fluttered in the air when I pulled it out, almost blew away. My last resources. 'Take this, alright? For your sick kid. Or your wife. Whatever. Buy some medicine.'

He looked at the bill. 'I don't know.'

'Five minutes. Come with me. We'll look around and be out again. You'll never see me again.'

'This is a mistake.' He snatched the money from my hand. 'Shit. My wife always called me, "Him and his mistakes". Now she don't call me anything.'

* * *

We descended into the basement, and it was the same staircase, the same low-ceilinged passage, I was certain. But it was changed. The pipes were cold, the dust dry.

The overseer muttered to himself as we reached the bottom of the stairs, 'Now where?'

'There should be a door at the end of this passage.' My torchlight found the door, closed, in the dark. 'Here it is.'

The overseer tried the handle and it creaked inwards. 'You sure you've been here before? There's nothing down here.'

'Just open it. Alright. Now stand back, let me go first.'

'What kind of crime are you supposed to be investigating?'

'Shut up.' I stepped inside, suddenly terrified; I was glad of the miserable overseer's company. Keeping to the wall, I tried the light switch, but nothing happened. 'Shit.' I flicked the button uselessly.

'What did you expect? Told you, there's nothing here.'

I stepped deeper inside the chamber and felt the same pressure in my skull. Something throbbed in here. My torch criss-crossed the darkness finding nothing to catch onto. Empty surfaces, deeper shadow. Nothing. In the middle of the room, I knelt and brushed the floor of concrete with my fingertips. Dust and metal grit. She was gone. I looked closer, staring into a bright circle of torchlight. Perhaps there was something, a hint of discoloration. The floor was stained with patches of paint, chemicals, God knows what; blobs of red-brown, black, and green, that merged and faded in the grey. I sniffed at the ground: iron, concrete, dirt.

'What you looking for?' the overseer said.

I almost jumped at the sound of his voice. 'This floor.'

'Well, you found it.'

I scooped up a dust of dried waste, whatever these stains had been, and licked my finger.

'You some kind of property surveyor?'

Blood and metal taste alike. 'Yeah. A surveyor.' Shining my torch close to the ground, I followed the dulled specks where the earth was stained, just a grainy blur, disappearing in patches, but pricking up again, a dot of brown-red here, a clustered spatter further along. I crawled across the floor.

'There's nothing here,' the man said.

'Shut up.'

The trail, petering, disappeared beneath a pile of empty crates and pallets. 'Help me with these.' I pulled and pushed aside the bits of old wood in a flare of hope… and found nothing. Of course, the room had been cleaned, neatened out. They'd been thorough.

'Whatever you're looking for,' the man said, 'it's not supposed to be found.'

'Everything is supposed to be found. Why else would you hide it?'

I crouched in the empty space where the crates had been pulled aside and shone my torch over the ground. Dull concrete.

The man muttered to himself.

'Wait, what's that?' I traced the dust, marked with a few tiny spots, almost invisible.

'I don't see anything.'

On my hands and knees, I followed the last droplets of somebody's dried blood all the way to the wall where it ended. Solid brick, unpassable. 'Shit.' I banged against the surface, so thick, it absorbed sound. 'There has to be…'

With the torch between my teeth, I probed with my fingers into the crevices, felt the gaps and scars in the brickwork. Where the wall met the floor there was a seam filled with dust. I scraped with my nails. One part seemed thicker than the rest. The torch dropped from my mouth.

'What's this?' I dug into the dust and felt a hard, cold resistance.

'Found something?' The man leaned over me.

I pulled out a metal ring. Sliding against the wall, I held it into torchlight. 'I don't believe it.'

His eyes shone. 'Oh Christ, you were right. You were right.'

'Wedding ring, gold. Inlaid with amber.'

'Incredible. But why? How? What's it doing there? How did you know?'

I pictured the woman, laid out in an X. 'She put it there. She wanted to keep it safe.'

'She?'

21

I trudged home feeling more awake than ever, frenzied with victory. I longed for Daria, just to lie in the dark and tell her what I'd done; how the city, closed behind shutters and locked doors, had opened in the dark, revealing a secret. But Daria would never speak to me again. In the corner of the sky, a fine sliver of silver blue leaked into the clouds, staining their underside pale. Day came back around, despite everything. I might lie down in bed and rest at least, even if I couldn't dream. There was a long shift ahead: the death of a police officer would bring turmoil to the station, anger, suspicion, conflict. For an outsider like me, it would only make things worse.

Crossing the Long Market, my legs were like sludge. Danzig's polluted harbour water dripped in my veins. Back home, I leaned against the front door while I fished for my house keys, but the panel gave against my forehead; the door was open. Had I left it that way? Tal, you're losing your mind.

Climbing the stairs I heard a commotion through the spiral of banisters, two floors above. Footsteps stomped in the hall, a door banged shut, somebody screamed, and I was running. At the first floor, somebody peeked out, saw me, and slammed their door. I kept running, up to the second storey. The banister shook in my grip. Turning around the angle of the stairs, I found Frau Grubach, in her night dress, crying.

'Oh, Herr Tal. You have to do something. They'll kill him.'

'What? Who?'

Her words dissolved into sobs. I ran up to the next floor. Halfway between the storeys, I had a view from below of the open door at my neighbour's flat, the Binders. Wearing just a pair of underpants, Herr Binder lay on the ground while two men kicked and punched his prone form. Behind them, through the open door, Frau Binder screamed. Another man dragged her by the hair and shook her. The men wore black, their faces covered by socks with eyeholes cut out.

'Stop!' Rushing up, my foot caught on the top stair, I tripped and fell forwards with a clatter. The landing went still.

'Back away!' one of the men shouted. 'Stay out of this. Stay down, pal. It's none of your business.'

Herr Binder was rolled into a ball, he looked at me through one swollen eye, but when he opened his mouth, no sound came out. His ribcage might have broken under the kicks; the men wore steel-capped boots.

Behind them, Frau Binder screamed, 'Help! Help us, please!'

The man struck her in the face, and she stopped.

I climbed to my feet, wary, keeping distance. The men watched in the musty light of the hall, eyes livid in the holes of their masks.

'Go home,' the first man shouted. 'Go to bed. This is police work. It's none of your business. Just–'

'I *am* police.'

He stopped with the word unfinished in his mouth. 'What did you say?'

'Police.' I took out my badge.

The man stepped over Herr Binder's body and approached me slowly, his palms raised. 'Let's not have any misunderstandings…'

'All of you, get away from him. Let that woman go.'

The other two men didn't move. They looked at each other, eyes swivelling in the cut holes. The first man chuckled. 'You're up late, Detective. Shouldn't you be in bed?'

'I work nights.'

'You live here…?'

Frau Grubach came up the stairs behind me and poked her head over my shoulder. 'That's right. He does live here. You'd better clear off before you all rot in jail. Breaking in here, beating innocent people in their own home–'

'Nobody is innocent.' Behind the thin, black fabric of the sock, the man seemed to smile. His blue eyes scanned my face. 'Detective Tal…'

'Get out of here now,' I said, 'or I'll have you all taken in.'

'But, Detective, there's no need for that tone. We're all on the same side here.'

His two companions appeared at his shoulder; the three of them blocked the landing. Their eyes danced across my face, my hands, my jacket, they wondered if I had a gun. I fingered the pliers in my pocket.

'We're not on the same side,' I said.

'This man, your neighbour, he's a communist spy. He's in the pay of the Soviets.'

'Show me one piece of evidence for that.'

'Evidence? Ha. Your Herr Binder admits it himself; he's proud to be a socialist. He writes tracts and spreads them around town. Propaganda.' The man turned back and squatted over Binder. 'Isn't that true? Hey, I said, isn't that true? Tell the detective what you've been getting up to.'

Binder only groaned, a bloody glue of saliva leaked from his bruised lips.

'Look at this…' The man stomped back into the flat, pushing Frau Binder aside, and pulled out a handful of leaflets. 'Communist propaganda. Tonnes of the shit.'

I kept my voice low. 'Who are you? You're not police.'

'No.' The nearest man narrowed his eyes through the sock holes. 'We do the dirty work; the police don't dare. It should have been you in here. How long have you been neighbours with this traitor? And you never did nothing.'

The first man came back out of the flat, brandishing the leaflets. 'We could file a complaint about you. Judges might be interested to know what's going on in your building. They might get it into their heads you're part of this conspiracy.' He pushed the leaflets into my hands. 'Do your job. Arrest this scumbag. We're leaving now. Don't try to stop us.'

I stood aside. 'Get out. Don't come back here.'

'You tell them.' Frau Grubach kept close to my shoulder, snivelling.

The man snarled. 'We'll see you again, Tal.'

They walked past slowly, heads held up, snickering to themselves. One of them muttered, 'This fucking city.'

Through the long, narrow window over the stairwell, weak blue light fell across the quiet landing. The sun was pushing to be born in the east. A cold, fresh day was just beginning. I climbed into bed and let myself sink. Through the wall, I heard Frau Binder crying. The hours passed as I stared into my horror and found no rest.

* * *

And now I was driving. Was it a dream? I drove over to the old University of Technology, through streets shaded with poplars, divided with tramlines, bedecked with Nazi flags. A million runes. I should be in bed. Morning light revealed the sky of towers and spires, but barely. The early day was covered over with thick grey cloud. At some point, the black car following me was lost in traffic. I turned down a side road, parked up, and grabbed the brown paper bag I'd been carrying around for too long. The stink of old blood was getting worse. Keeping it hidden under my jacket, I skirted around clusters of students who stood about smoking and chatting. They didn't notice me at all; I was old, I didn't belong in their world. Other people's nostalgia haunted the corners of the quad, a youth I might have had, to wander among the poplars, in the shadow of the University buildings, imperious red and white brick, pointed arches, rows of narrow windows. A stone head of Medusa watched over the entranceway as I entered.

In the foyer I glanced around for a sign. Nobody asked if I was lost. Students chatted and laughed beneath a high, vaulted ceiling painted white. Did they imagine they were safe here? The gorgeous walls and the tall trees would all burn. Youth would be swept away.

I wandered through a maze of innocent eyes and banal conversation, and didn't belong, too used up to contemplate asking one of these strange young people for directions. It was daytime, and I was a trespasser from the realm of night. I knew that my eyes were like an owl's, they would recognise me as an outsider from faraway, they would hate me. A dead trace of ash in the air. I tried to pin it down and lost my way. In a wide rear courtyard, a group of students was building a bonfire.

'What are you doing?' I asked a few grinning young men.

They laughed and turned their backs as if I were invisible. The flames caught and grew in the piled kindling.

I found the biology faculty and climbed the stairs. How many sets of stairs have I climbed in this city? Everything leads upwards here, instead of outwards. The space is too cramped by the seafront, along the riverbanks; our city planners, centuries earlier, brought in Dutch architects to put up these tall, narrow buildings. Inner space created above the ground, where extension outwards was blocked. I followed a smell of chemicals, formaldehyde, poison, and came to the lab. Three students wearing goggles and aprons were hunched over some test tubes.

One of them looked up. 'You can't come in here.' He glanced at the paper bag in my hand.

'Lukasz Fabianski? I'm Tal, Chief Investigator, Danzig Police Force.'

The students looked at each other and shrugged, unimpressed at my credentials.

'What is it?' He took off his goggles. 'We're busy. If you want to do something useful, stop the barbarians running around campus. They break in here threatening students, damaging our work. Police don't do a damn thing about it. When we call the station, they just laugh at us.'

'Really? Is that…? That's not why I'm here.'

'Why are you here then?' Another student took off her googles and stared. 'They've ransacked the library. First, they burned all the Jewish authors. Now they just burn anything.'

'They burn books?'

'I tried to tell them,' she said. 'Thomas Mann isn't Jewish, but they don't listen. They don't care. They love to burn.'

'I'm sorry about that…' Here I was, apologising to some kids at least two decades younger than me. Youths who had never stared into the face of a murdered woman. I tried to remember what I was doing in their lab.

'Are you going to stand there all day?' Fabianski said.

'What's that smell?' The girl with the contemptuous stare wrinkled her nose.

I remembered and took out Esther's note. 'Esther sent me, she said you could help.'

'Who?'

'Esther. Esther Vogelsang.'

'Esther.' Fabianski groaned. 'Shit. I knew I'd regret taking that favour. What's this about?'

'Can we talk in private? Should only take a moment.'

He looked at the other students, who shook their heads. 'We don't work with police. I did it before, and I rued it.'

'I'm not normal police.'

'You would say that, wouldn't you?'

'Do you like Esther?'

'She helped me out in a pinch. Sure. But she's not police really, she's a scientist. You wouldn't understand that.'

Why did they hate me? I looked for a way to convince him. 'Esther's in trouble. She's Jewish, you know. I'm trying to help her. I'm her friend. This case...'

Fabianski stared, sniffed the air. 'What the hell have you got in that bag?'

* * *

It was dark and quiet in the little office off the lab, a bare room with no furniture other than an empty set of shelves and a desk.

'We're in the middle of a reshuffle,' Fabianski said.

I stared at the empty walls and the desk with longing. A solid surface of wood; if I laid my head down there, I might find rest. Few such uncluttered places remain in Danzig, this storehouse of the past, too much history; memories piled up, hoarded, and abandoned.

Fabianski took the bag from my hand. 'It stinks.'

'Oh.' The spell of peace was broken. 'I'd like you to run some tests for me.'

'That's what everybody says. "Run some tests." It's not magic, you know. I can't just snap my fingers and make the truth appear.'

'This police uniform.' I held it up. 'It was found at a murder scene. I'd like you to check it for me.'

'Why?'

'Just anything you can tell me about it. Anything at all might help.'

'You got your own forensics people, don't you?'

'Yeah, well, Esther recommended you. She says you're the best.'

'It's from a crime scene?' Perhaps the appeal to vanity softened him. He took the uniform and held it to the light, sniffing. 'Reeks. Somebody was murdered?'

'I can't discuss the details. Just call me if you find anything. Anything at all. Nothing is irrelevant or too trivial.'

'The thing is filthy. I doubt we'll get anything from it.'

'Just do your best. I believe in you.'

'Shit. I'm too good for this.' The look on his face was derisive. 'This fucking city.'

22

I drove back across town in a trance of refracted daylight, haunted by the smell of burning books. It was chilly in the morgue. Gerhard's body lay beneath a sheet, a dull mound, given vague human shape by the impression where his nose stuck up.

'Bad business, killing cops,' Henrik mumbled. Despite the chill of the basement, he wiped sweat from his brow.

'You can't be in here.' A short man came in through the side door, wearing a surgeon's mask and gloves.

'Who's he?' I pointed.

'This is Fitz,' Henrik said. 'Got in from Berlin this morning.'

'Berlin? Where are our people?'

'He's here to help.' Henrik wiped his brow again. Perhaps it was just a gesture he couldn't help making.

'Who are you?' Fitz said.

I couldn't answer. The fluorescent light played off the green tiles like some underwater grotto. Despite the artificial brightness, it was always night in this basement where the dead slept, you could forget the world above, sunlight, the open spaces.

'This is Tal, our best detective. He found the body.' Henrik turned to face me. 'It's a different kind of case now. Dead cop. A German one too. They brought in specialists from the Reich.'

'What, our people aren't good enough?' I asked.

Fitz shrugged. 'You tell me.'

'They fear corruption,' Henrik said. 'It's better for this to be handled externally.'

'It's not legal,' I said. 'The Reich has no jurisdiction in the Free City.'

Fitz might have smiled behind his surgeon's mask, his eyes tightened. 'There are rules, and then there's reality. Danzig is part of Germany, it always was. The League of Nations is like God; nobody believes in it anymore.'

'I want to see the body.' I took two strides through the blinking light, but Fitz blocked my path.

'Step back, Detective. The body hasn't been cleared yet. You'll receive my report. I'm almost finished in here, just need to type it up,' Fitz said.

'What did you find?'

Fitz tilted his head, measuring me, the way forensics people do. His brown eyes over the top of the mask were too bland, too innocent. 'You're the one who discovered the crime scene…'

'That's right.'

'And puked in it,' Fitz said.

'No, that wasn't me.'

'What?' Henrik said. 'Tal, what the hell?'

'It was the trainee kid. Where's the kid now? I need to talk to him.'

'I told him to stay at home. He's shaken up, poor little bastard,' Henrik said.

Fitz took off his gloves. 'Ought to be shot by firing squad. Puking all over a perfectly good crime scene. And why did you take an intern to a police homicide? Never mind, I don't want to know. Whatever you bumpkins are doing over here in Danzig, it won't be for much longer. You'll find the Reich has made advances in criminology. We lead the world in this field. Now, gentlemen, leave me in peace. I've work to do.' He turned his back and started wheeling the body towards the rear door.

I followed him. 'Wait.'

Henrik pulled at my arm. 'Tal…' But I shrugged him off.

Fitz picked up speed, almost running to the door as the trolley wheels quivered, but I kept pace. 'Wait a second.'

He stopped as the trolley slammed into the side of the doorframe. His eyes were furious when he spun around. 'What do you want?'

'Answer one question for me.'

'You'll get my report later, as I explained. Is this how you do things in Danzig? Superintendent, get your dog off me.'

Henrik patted my shoulder. 'Tal…'

I grabbed Fitz by the collar. 'Just tell me, what's the time of death? When did he die?'

'You'll receive my report later. This is a sealed zone. Let me work.'

'When did he die? Tell me and I'll let you go. Just tell me.'

Fitz backed against the closed door. 'Get off me! I'll have you reported. This city is barbaric. You're no better than Poles.'

'Tell me!'

Henrik tugged at my arm. 'Tal! Jesus. Let go. Let him go.'

For some reason, I shouted, 'Gerhard was one of ours!'

'Get off me, you animal.' Fitz wriggled in my grip.

I screamed in his face. 'Just tell me! When did he die?'

'A week ago. OK? At the most. Somewhere around six days ago.'

I released him and smoothed my shirt down, suddenly conscious of the freezing chamber, the green light. 'Thank you. I'll look forward to reading your report.'

Henrik spluttered, out of breath. 'Tal, for Christ's sake.'

* * *

We took the lift up to the ground floor. I was filled with a sense of dread as the metal doors clanged shut, and the gears began to grind. The thought of being trapped down here in a refrigerated mausoleum. Henrik couldn't stop wiping the sweat from his brow.

'Tal, you weren't supposed to talk to anyone about this case. I told you that. I was very clear. Now everyone knows. Gestapo are crawling all over the station.'

'If Gerhard died a week ago, that puts his death before the woman from the shipyard.'

'Everyone at the station… They're losing their minds. There's panic. There's talk of reprisals. Some of the guys want to go out and get revenge. And the press… if this gets out…'

'We can assume it was the same killer. This killer put on Gerhard's clothes to kill the woman. He must have posed as a police officer to get into their house. Then for some reason, he left the uniform at the crime scene but took her clothes away. Why?'

The metal walls shimmered with distorted reflections like a mirror that had melted. The dark mass of my jacket and hat merged with Henrik's brown coat to form one inky smudge.

'Shut up a minute,' Henrik said. 'Let me think. If Gerhard was killed, and his uniform was taken… that means the killer isn't police. They stole a dead officer's uniform. That's good, that's good. It rules out corruption. This might save my job.'

'There's still three corpses and a missing child.'

'What child? What are you talking about?'

I fingered the wedding ring in my pocket, inlaid with amber. Should I tell Henrik about that? But he'd hand it over to the Nazis. 'From the murder scene, there–'

'Listen, Tal, we've got a dead police officer on our hands.'

The lift stopped. The doors heaved open. We looked out in silence at a woman in a lab coat who was waiting to get in. She started to step forward but hesitated.

'Excuse us a moment.' Henrik stopped me as I went to leave. He pressed the button to close the doors.

'What are you doing?'

'We need to talk in private. Somewhere they're not listening.'

'Who's not listening?'

'This lift is as good as anywhere else.' He hit the button for the ground floor.

As the lift doors started to slide back over, I caught a look of astonishment on the woman's face. She opened her mouth, but the doors were already shut.

'Stop. No.' I banged on the "open" button. 'I hate lifts; you know I hate lifts.'

'Tal, calm down. What's got into you? Are you not sleeping?'

The machine jerked into life again, it shook as it descended. Hollow vibrations shivered through the shaft.

'Henrik, take this case off me. I don't want it. I refuse it. You can suspend me if you want, or punish me some other way.'

'You have no choice.'

'I'm the wrong man for the job. It's an internal investigation now. The others at the station already hate me…'

'Tal. Did you fill in that form I gave you?'

'Which form? Oh. The form… I forgot. With Gerhard, this case, Esther, everything…'

'Sign it man, quickly. And solve this case. It's the only thing that might save us.'

'But… why?'

He grabbed hold of me to whisper, even though we were alone in the lift. 'They don't know about the police uniform at the murder scene. They don't know the two cases are related. That might keep them off our back a while.'

'Wouldn't it make more sense to link the cases?'

'Can't risk it. In Germany, they're looking for an excuse to annex Danzig. That would mean war with Poland. And for us, the Danzig police would be swallowed up in the Nazi forces. We'd be on the frontlines of a new war.'

'I guess–'

'You stay on the nightshift. Keep your head down. Find Gerhard's killer, solve the case, neat and tidy. Don't cause any ripples. You're the only one I trust. Hopefully this will all turn out to be some random madman…'

'I need to talk to Bernie.'

'Leave him in peace; he's got his own problems. Don't we all?'

The lift landed heavily on the ground floor. The doors yawned apart. Fitz looked inside. I almost didn't recognise him without the surgeon's mask and was surprised at how ordinary he seemed.

He took a step forwards, quizzical. 'Did you forget something?'

'Sorry, Fitz' – the superintendent pressed the button to go up again – 'do me a favour, take the stairs.'

The doors closed over Fitz's stunned face. The lift started up again.

'Christ, Henrik, you'll break it. We'll be stuck inside for hours. It's happened before.'

'You're paranoid. I've told you before, you need to cut down on the caffeine. How much did you drink today?'

'It's this nightshift…'

'Listen. Go down to the station. Interview as many officers as you can. Find out what Gerhard was involved in. But keep it under wraps. Not a word about the dead couple at the docks. Leave that to Bernie. Nobody needs to know more than necessary. If the other cops ask questions, you tell them it's official business. Internal investigation. If you find anything out, you come to me before anyone else. We'll decide on the next step together.'

'But, Henrik, the others hate me. They won't talk to me.'

'They will. I'll make them. I'm going home now. It was a late night at The Mermaid. And everything after. I'm dog-tired. A dead cop, this is all I need. Berlin is itching to swallow us.'

'The whole city's exhausted.'

The lift came to a halt on the first floor. The doors slid open. The same woman in the lab coat looked inside and saw us.

'It's fine,' she said. 'I'll take the stairs.'

23

The station had disappeared. Where it usually opened into the night with its three floors of lit windows and its glowing foyer, I found a black hole sucking grey Danzig sky into nothingness. I groped in the dark and found the railing that led up three stone steps to the entrance. I pushed open the front door.

'We're closed,' Granma said.

'It's me.'

'Who?' Her thick-rimmed glasses reflected a tiny flicker of candlelight from the reception desk.

'What happened?' I left the security of the wall and crossed the shadow towards her.

'Oh, it's you. There's been a power cut,' she said.

'Who's that?' Markus shouted behind her, in the obscurity. A torch beam swung and missed me.

Metal shimmered in the darting light. I went around the desk and found him halfway up a ladder inspecting the wires that ran along the corner of the ceiling.

'Need a hand?' I asked.

'This fucking city. Power cuts, breakdowns. Nothing works,' Markus said.

'Yeah.'

'Mark my words: one day, and soon, we'll be reunited with the Reich. Then they'll pay, all of them,' he said.

I waited for him to finish. 'You know, they have power cuts in Germany too.'

'Fuck you, Tal.'

'Is the whole building in the dark?'

'What do you think?' he said.

From the dim tunnel of the corridor behind reception, three shadows emerged. Lang, Reiner, and Stolz. They squinted and shielded their eyes when my torch scanned their faces.

'Shit, that's blinding,' Lang said. 'Who is that?'

They had changed into civilian clothes, dark overcoats, and gloves. Reiner carried a toolbox.

I lowered my torch. 'Where are you going with that?'

'Leave it, Tal. We've finished our shift. We'll go where we want,' Lang said.

'Not planning trouble, are you?' I asked.

'What do you mean? We're just going to have a few drinks, in Gerhard's memory,' said Reiner.

Markus shouted from the top of the ladder, 'I'd join you, but I'm on nightshift again.'

My torch scanned their hands. 'What's in the toolbox?'

'Nothing,' Lang said.

'Not revenge, I hope.'

They hesitated.

'Would that be wrong?' Lang said. 'They killed one of our own, Tal. Shit. We can't do nothing.'

I lowered the torch beam. 'Problem is, nobody knows who killed him.'

'So, we'll find out. We'll ask around. You know, the usual spots, where the deadbeats drink. Someone will know. You can't kill a cop in Danzig without someone hearing about it.'

From the top of the ladder, Markus shouted down, 'The city's gone to shit. Police aren't respected. It's anarchy. We need to put on a show of force.'

'This is my case,' I said. 'The rest of you leave that to me. You'll muddy the tracks.'

Lang scoffed. 'You don't seem to be working hard at solving it. Shouldn't you be outside rounding up suspects? What are you doing standing around in here?'

'I need to talk to everyone at the station about Gerhard. Individually. I'll start with you three.'

'Ah, shit. Our shift finished already. This is down time,' Lang said.

I turned to Granma. 'Who else is in the station at the moment?'

She tutted. 'What am I, a bat? I can't see everyone who comes in and out in the dark.'

'You?' Reiner said. 'What gives you the right?'

'You think another cop did this?' Lang said.

'I'm running the investigation, not any of you. I need to interview everyone here who knew Gerhard. Superintendent's orders.'

'Shit,' Lang said.

'You can go first,' I told him. 'We'll use one of the conference rooms.'

'Me?'

'The day shift's ending for most people,' Granma said. 'Some of them are still upstairs. They're planning a drink in his memory. Problem is, they're all hungover already.'

'Gather the others,' I said. 'Markus, you help. Draw up a list, put them in order. I'll speak to everyone I can.'

'Can't it wait until tomorrow? The lights don't even work,' she said.

'We've got candles, don't we? Come on, hurry up. The sooner we get it done, the sooner you can have your drink.'

As I was about to push past the others into the darkness, Granma called after me. 'Oh, Tal, wait. Bernie was looking for you.'

'Bernie?'

'Said to call him.'

'Where did he go?'

'I'm not his minder. One minute he was here, next he was gone. He looked drunk, if you ask me. He needs to retire. He stood there in the foyer with his mouth hanging open like he didn't know where he was.'

* * *

Submerged in night, the old building was transformed. As if I'd never really known it, I wandered its empty corridors and found new dimensions; the halls were longer than I'd supposed, the stairways more complex. Spectral light shimmered in the curtainless windows but failed to brighten the hard surfaces inside. I hurried up the stairs to the third floor, passing long windows where nothing showed. No sky, no stars.

My torch swept the passageway and found the open door of my office. I was sure I'd closed it yesterday; I always closed it when I left. From the doorway, I tried the switch, knowing it wouldn't work. It clicked and did nothing. My torch crossed the room and bounced back at me, dazzling. I averted my eyes. What was that? I lowered the beam, and looked again: seated behind my desk, a man in a black suit was almost invisible, submerged in the gloom, but he held an oval mirror over his face where the light danced.

'Turn that thing off,' he said.

'Who are you?' I clicked the torch off, and darkness flooded in. The mirror was just a speck of light reflected from some hidden source in this transparent building where night played freely.

A low, gravelly voice, urbane. 'It's regarding your case.'

'Which one?'

'It was you who found the body.'

I stared into the dark as my eyes adjusted, a denser mass was just visible at my desk. 'Who are you?'

'We've taken interest in this affair. We'd like to see it solved as quickly as possible. We'd like to help.'

'I don't want help. I work alone. I work at night.'

'And yet, you do need a favour. Do you expect favours for free? Don't you know, in this world, we have to help each other. We do something for you, you do something for us.'

'What are you talking about? This love letter? You want it? Here, take it back.' I dug the note out of my pocket and threw it on the table.

He must have taken a torch out of his pocket; the note appeared in a narrow thread of white light, and the surrounding room was swallowed up in nothingness.

> DEAR BELOVED,
> I CANNOT WAIT FOR US TO BE TOGETHER.
> DON'T FORGET ME, YOUR TRUE HEART.

'What is this?' he said. 'A prank?'

'It was on my desk.'

'You imagine that I wrote it?'

'Who else? You're the one hiding in the dark.'

He pushed the note back across the table to me. The torch went out. 'I've never seen this before. You think it's connected to the case?'

He sounded sincere. Nothing to do, I picked the rose-coloured note up and put it back in my pocket; ridiculous.

'I don't know anything,' I said, 'and I don't want your help. Find some other fool.'

'Are you sure about that, Detective?'

'I'm not playing your games.'

'And yet, a favour from us is valuable.'

'What favour? What are you talking about?'

'Well, take for example the train that departed early this morning carrying a cargo of Jews towards the border. Beginning of a long journey to Palestine, they said. Some border guards found a discrepancy in their paperwork.'

'I don't follow…'

'But you do. Oh yes. You know how bureaucracy is in Danzig. Those passengers are in a cell now, awaiting review. Isn't it funny how a person's whole life can come down to a piece of paper? An X marked in a box, a signature on a dotted line.'

'What is this, bribery? Blackmail?' I turned on the torch to expose him, but the light only reflected back towards me in the mirror that hid his face. I recoiled and turned it off.

He chuckled to himself. 'You have one free dream at your disposal. Spend it wisely.'

In the darkness, echoes of the light, floating blobs of colour, rotated in front of my eyes.

'You'd let them leave for Palestine?'

'Do your job, Detective. If you're as good as everyone says, and as loyal, this won't be difficult for you. A killer will be brought to justice. Your friends will find their paperwork. And you, you can have whatever you desire. But what do you desire, Detective?'

In the silence, police boots tramped through the building. I couldn't answer, my mind toiled in the different threads, disconnected memories, pictures of corpses, X-shapes, open mouths in dead faces. Esther. I opened my eyes and the floating blobs had faded away.

Somewhere back down the corridor, a voice shouted. 'Tal! What are you doing? The conference room is set up. They're waiting for you.'

24

The station was in mourning, not to mention hungover, and dark. Somebody had set a jug of water on the table of the conference room, some cups, a few dry biscuits from the store cupboard. The day's work was ending for most of the station, and the officers came in one at a time as their shift ended. Lang was first.

'What is this, an interrogation?' he said.

'If it was an interrogation, we'd be downstairs in one of the interview rooms. I'd be recording our conversation.'

'What is it then?'

'An informal chat. Have a biscuit. Tell me about Gerhard, how well you knew him. How long. Anything at all you can think of, anything that might help.'

'Are you serious?' His face, lit by the candle below, showed disgust.

'You know how these chats work; you've interviewed people yourself.'

He blinked and rubbed his scalp. 'Ah shit. I'm too hungover for this.'

'That's what the water's for. Have a cup.'

'It's not that kind of hangover. Tal, how long's this going to take?'

'As long as you like. How well did you know Gerhard?'

'So, I can leave now?'

'If you wish. I'll let the superintendent know you chose not to cooperate.'

'Tell him he can eat my ass as well. I'm leaving, Tal. See you tomorrow.'

* * *

Next to come in and sit down was Officer Jakob Berman, a middle-aged bachelor who handled shipyard cases. He kneaded his red eyes, looked at me through the shield of one palm.

'You alright?' I said.

'That candle's too bright. Don't you know? It was late, very late. Most of us stayed out till the early morning with Bastian.'

'I heard.'

'You weren't there.'

'I was working. Drink some water. How well did you know Gerhard?' I picked up my pen and notepad.

'A little.'

'Could you elaborate?'

'Tal. They say you're the one who found him.'

'Me and the trainee kid.'

'And, what…? Did he…?'

'I can't divulge details. Not yet. First, we're just chatting to the others, see if anyone knows anything.'

'What about?' His metal chair scratched the floor as he sat back.

'About Gerhard. Whom he might have met. What might have happened to him, and why. You got any thoughts?'

'Is this an interrogation? Christ, Tal, I'm hungover to shit and I'm all, you know, grieving or whatever. My head's spinning.'

'Were you close to Gerhard?'

'We were colleagues. It's a brotherhood, this job, isn't that what they say?'

'I'm not sure I know what a brotherhood is.'

'No. You wouldn't.' He reached for a cup and poured himself some water. 'You think it was one of us? Someone on the Force killed him?'

'I don't think anything. That's why I'm asking.'

'They say you found him in his flat. What were you doing there? How did you know?'

'I was investigating a different case, which turned out to be the same case.'

'Convenient.' He swallowed the water down in one dry gulp.

'Tell me something. Anything. When did you last speak with Gerhard?'

'I'm obliged to answer?'

'By no means. This is a free exchange.'

'Tal, my head. I feel like a might puke. I need to lie down.'

'So, lie down. Make yourself at home.'

He glanced around the bare room. 'You're bringing the wrong people in here.'

'What do you mean?'

'It's Roman you want to speak to.'

'Why?'

'Ask him yourself.' He stared back across the table, his jaw set, but candlelight caught a note of regret in the corner of his eyes.

'Where is Roman? I haven't seen him around.'

'Working on something special. A secret operation, apparently. I don't know what.'

'OK. So…'

'Listen, Tal. I'm sorry I couldn't help. I'm going home now. If I think of anything that might be helpful, I'll call you.'

* * *

Officer Fiona Spielman looked like she'd been crying all day. She held a crumpled tissue in one hand and dabbed at the corners of her watery eyes.

'They probably told you already. I mean, you know, about Gerhard and me.'

I turned a new page in my notepad. 'Tell me anyway.'

She glanced at the door. 'I don't know…'

'It's alright. Nobody can hear us.'

'They bug these rooms, you know.' She stared wildly around the empty walls.

'No. They bug the downstairs rooms. These rooms are just for show. Tell me about Gerhard.'

'What is there to say? What's the point anyway? He's dead now.'

'Justice is the point.'

A tear trickled hotly down her cheek. 'I don't understand…'

'You're in shock. I'm sorry. We don't have to talk now. You know what, go home. Call me tomorrow if you feel up to it.'

'Thanks, Tal. You're alright. You're better than the others.'

'I'm nobody.'

'You really do think you can help, don't you? God. You're the kind of man I should have got involved with. I'm drawn to the wrong ones, I can't help it.'

'Gerhard, he was a "wrong one"?'

She dried her eyes. 'Forget it. Don't listen to me. I'm delirious. All this, it's like a nightmare.'

'When did things end between you and Gerhard?'

Something hardened in her eye. A mirror seemed to drop between us. 'Well, things never exactly began. It was on-off. Sometimes it was more on. Lately, not so much. But he changed.'

'Changed, how?'

'You're asking the wrong person.'

'You seem to me like the right person.'

She made a strange sound like a groan and a cackle, I never heard anything like it. But then, I've shielded myself from pain. I never get involved with anybody. This isn't the kind of world where you can risk attachments. Perhaps that's why nothing ever happened with Esther, despite those times we talked all night, and laughed, every time the conversation might have turned a certain way, we would lower our eyes, shrug, and get back to work. Or perhaps I'm just a coward.

'You're cute.' Her voice shifted again. From bereavement to a kind of tormented flirtation. 'You think because me and Gerhard banged, he used to tell me things. You think he used to share with me. It was never like that. That was the best thing about it. We didn't talk about anything. Really. Sometimes it was like Danzig didn't exist. In bed with Gerhard, that was the only place I ever managed to believe it.'

'But he changed, you said.' My pen hovered over the page and wrote nothing.

'He was mixed up in something. He turned serious. He used to laugh when we banged. Later, he only did it like he was angry. Like he had this painful grudge against the world.'

'And you never asked why.'

'Oh no. I liked it, I didn't want it to stop.'

The notepad dropped from my hand. I twiddled the pen like a fool. 'But do you know who might be able to tell me? Who could explain the change in him?'

'He never told me a thing. You'd be better asking anyone else than me, honestly.'

'What about Roman? Did you ever…?'

'*Roman*?' She said the name strangely. 'Roman doesn't look at me. He's hard-line; he thinks female cops are pointless.' She gave a sad smile.

'And Gerhard?'

'Who knows what Gerhard ever thought. He was a silent type. Maybe I loved him. Can I go now? I'm exhausted.'

'Alright. Get some rest. Grieve. If you think of anything…'

'I'll call you. Of course.' She stood up. At the door, she turned. 'And if you find out, do me a favour, Tal, don't tell me. I'd rather not know.'

* * *

In the hall outside the conference room, three others waited their turn on wooden chairs.

Granma saw me looking out. 'Tal. How long is this going to take?'

'I need a break. Give me five minutes. I'll just get a tea.'

'Ah shit. I knew this would be a waste of time,' she said.

I hurried down the darkened stairs. Approaching the staff kitchen, I saw a ghost of candlelight, and turned off my torch. Quiet voices muttered through the open door, but I couldn't hear what they said. Creeping closer, I made out three voices. They stopped dead when I reached the door.

'You're still here?' I said.

'Just leaving.' Jakob jumped up.

Fiona stood as well. A few revolvers and a rifle lay on the table. Reiner stuffed them in a duffel bag as I watched.

'What are those for?' I asked him.

'Nothing.'

'What are you doing down here?' Jakob said. 'Interviews finished?'

'Needed caffeine,' I said. 'You free, Reiner? I'd like to talk to you as well.'

He smiled. 'There's tea there. I'll drop in later. Got some things to take care of first.'

They went quickly out of the door. I listened as they crossed the hall, but not one of them spoke. Their footsteps rang on the hard floors. I was glad to be alone. The tea had gone cold and bitter. I drank a cup of it and felt worse. Crossing the landing, I saw that the door of the archives room was open; candlelight flickered in the dark. I poked my head in and found the intern kid seated at the table beside a stack of newspapers.

'What are you doing here? You were supposed to stay at home. It was a difficult night. Nobody forgets their first murder scene.'

'I don't want to stay home.' His lips were pale, his eyes wide as they scanned the page in front of him. His voice was toneless. 'There's nobody there. I can't be in an empty house. I feel safer in the station. There are people here. There are rules, it's safe.'

'Alright. Well, you can clean the kitchen if you'd prefer.'

He turned a page of the newspaper and didn't glance up at me. 'I like it in the archives. It's calm in here.'

I looked around the walls lined with filing cabinets and knew what he meant. Peaceful, like a library. If I could stay in there, in the quiet, I might find the answers in one of those documents stored in alphabetised drawers; this city might hold together a moment longer before it all collapses. But the kid looked traumatised.

'OK.' I wanted to help him, but there was nothing I could say. 'You'll be OK. The feeling passes. Just… you can talk to me if you need to.'

He shrugged. 'Nothing matters. I'll find the newspapers, like you wanted. I already checked a bunch. A rich couple with a baby. Look, here's one.'

He picked up one of the papers from a pile set aside and handed it over. The *Danziger Neueste Nachrichten,* the most popular newspaper in the Free City; a bourgeois publication, and not much use for anything since the Nazi-controlled council shut down free journalism. The edition was a week old. Page five. The taste of stale tea on my tongue, I smoothed down the folds of the sheet. The blotchy ink was almost illegible in this harsh light. A grainy monochrome photograph showed a mass of blobs that must be people. My fingers traced the outlines of faces that might have smiled. I tilted the torchlight and saw it more clearly: a woman, the white of her dress formed from absence, blank paper. Her man was a black density merged into the background.

ONE OF DANZIG'S OLDEST FAMILIES
ANNOUNCE BIRTH OF DAUGHTER

My eyes scanned through the text, struggling to focus on the meaning, but grasping at random words.

> Herr Schmidt, the celebrated jeweller and dealer of amber, together with his wife of one year, announced the birth of their first daughter, Anna… The happy family, prominent members of the Danzig branch of the Nazi Party, and key donors to its cause…

I grabbed the newspaper and held it to my eyes. Was it the same woman? The closer I looked, the less that blurred image pertained to any human form at all. Just a few scattered drops of black ink. And yet there was a hint of elegance in the crick of her elbow, her hair tied back, her dress minimalist, even severe.

'Is it right?' the kid said. 'Is it what you wanted?'

His voice made me jump. 'She, this woman… it could be. The picture's blurry. It's dark in here.'

'Tal?' Hermann shouted through the door. 'What are you doing? Reading the funnies?'

I stared at the picture until it was no longer a woman or a human being or anything, just an abstract shape. 'I don't know.'

'We're waiting for you upstairs. It's past home time.'

'Oh. Sorry.' I folded the newspaper and stuffed it in my pocket.

* * *

Markus blinked in the candlelight. His forehead was smudged with grease from somewhere.

'You know what this is about?' I said.

'What do you expect me to tell you? You already spoke to the others. Everyone knew Gerhard.'

'Funny thing is, nobody can tell me anything about him.'

He shook his head. 'Well, isn't it obvious?'

'What?'

'Does it really need to be stated?'

'Does what?'

The candle had burned halfway down, releasing a drowsy, churchlike smell of molten wax.

'We all know who killed him,' he said.

'Finally.' I took up my notepad. 'Who?'

His eyes narrowed at my pen that hung in the air above the pad. 'Well, I can't give you a name. But the general idea.'

'Which is?'

He stared at the pen. 'Do I really have to be the one to say it?'

'Apparently.'

'You can't trick me, Tal. I know you're not dumb. The others might fall for this act, the holy fool. You're wasting your time with me.'

'If I'm dumb, it's not a pretence. Who killed Gerhard? If you know, you can save all of us a lot of time.'

'It was the Poles, wasn't it? I don't know which one exactly. Probably there were a few. We'll find them. How hard can it be? We have spies among their organisations. We have informants. A dead cop is big news. With the rumour market in Danzig, the whole city should know. Christ, does it even matter which Pole in particular killed him? They're all the same. Dogs. We'll round up a bunch of them. If they won't give names, we'll punish them all. Send them a message.'

I dropped my pad. 'Do you actually know something? I can't tell if you're just racist, or paranoid, or both.'

He leaned forward. 'Gerhard was involved in some things. Don't act like you don't know.'

The candle flickered in his breath and almost went out. I stared as it wavered and steadied. 'I'm not acting. I wish I had such talent. I don't know anything. I wouldn't have wasted my time in here if I did. What was Gerhard involved with?'

'He was working for the Nazi Party in his spare time. They use certain trusted police for jobs. You know, at night. In an unofficial capacity.'

'How come I never heard about this?'

'Could they trust you?'

I held his stare. 'Could they trust *you*?'

'We're not here to talk about me.'

'So, Gerhard was doing night work for the Party. What kind of jobs?'

'I don't know, but I can guess. You know, dirty jobs.' He smiled at my confusion. 'Violent ones, perhaps. But I can't tell you any more than that.'

'Who can tell me?'

'I shouldn't say.'

'Why not?'

'We're a brotherhood, aren't we? We don't snitch.'

'A brotherhood, everyone says. Sounds like a cult to me. All I want is justice for Gerhard. Give me a name. They won't know it came from you.'

He stood up. 'I already said too much. This is your investigation, not mine. You figure it out.'

'Wait…'

'Or maybe the rest of us will figure it out ourselves.' He walked out of the room, a forced grin on his face.

* * *

Granma was next. She lit a cigarette off the candle that was almost burned down.

'I can't help you, honey. If I'm being honest, I just wanted to come in here because it's an excuse to talk and have someone listen. Nobody listens to me in this place. They just nod, their face goes all limp, then they find an excuse to walk away. I'm not deaf, you know, just because I'm a thousand years old. I hear what people say. They think I should've been retired years ago. They think I'm useless.'

'I never heard–'

'"Why was Bastian made redundant, instead of Granma?" That's the kind of thing they whisper. "She's half senile. She can't get up. Her cough gets on my nerves." They think I'm deaf, but I hear them. All day long. I hear it behind every door.'

'Well…'

'They want my job, that's what it is. A cushy job I have, they say, sitting at the desk instead of walking the street bashing Poles over the head. Maybe they're right. It's OK. I don't mind. I used to treat the elderly like shit as well. Poor old Granma, she's lost her mind. By the way, when did I ever agree to being called "Granma"? No one asked my opinion. They just call me that. They think I like it. I bet half of them don't know my real name. I bet you don't, do you?'

'I–'

'It's alright. I don't care anyway.'

'I'm sorry you feel like that.'

'Shut up, Tal.' She blew out a cloud of smoke. 'You're not bad. I don't mind you. You're an outsider too. They whisper about you behind your back. Lots of whispering in this place.'

'And what do they say about me?'

'I bet you'd love to know.'

The candle had burnt down almost to the bottom. I stared, fascinated as the flame dwindled. 'Alright. We're wasting time here. Let's wrap it up, *Bertha*.'

She grinned as she stubbed out her cigarette. 'I'll tell you one thing I heard through the walls. Gerhard was spending a lot of time with Roman. Maybe too much time, some people said.'

'Roman. Was he around the station today?'

'Nah. Hasn't been here in a while. He's working on some special operation. Or so I hear. Nobody tells me anything. I have to prick my ears up. Sounds to me like he's been busy, infiltrating Polish separatist groups–'

A knock on the door silenced her. We looked up as Markus stuck his head inside.

'Phone call for you, Tal. Downstairs.'

'Who?'

He yawned. 'How should I know?'

'You're on reception, it's your job…'

He had already gone.

* * *

Standing at the reception desk with the phone at my ear, I tried to block out the accusing eyes of the others as they lingered in the dark.

'Who is this?'

'Fabianski.' The voice was disdainful.

'Who?'

'The student. From the university. Jesus, do you want my help or not?' His voice was mocking. He took me for a buffoon, and he knew best. He was the student; I never had the chance to study at a university. I don't know anything. They say there's an outside world beyond Danzig, but I can only take that on trust.

'Fabianski. Oh, sure. Thanks for calling.'

'It's about the uniform.'

'Yeah. Hold on…' I sensed the curiosity of the other officers at the desk. Markus was staring into the register, but his ear was turned to me. I pulled the phone away as far as the cord would reach. 'And…?'

'There's not much. Thing's too dirty to run tests with the equipment we have here. Seems to have the blood of at least two people on it.'

'So, you didn't…'

'There's only one thing I can tell you. It's probably not helpful, sorry.'

'Just tell me.'

'The person who put it on was too big. That uniform was made for someone around 170cm tall, with a chest about 90cm. But from the tears in the seams, we can tell that the person who wore it was much bigger. I found some students with different sizes and had them try it on.

The length of the rips suggests a man around 189cm tall, with a chest at least 98cm.'

'A big guy. Hold on.' I jotted these numbers down, my mind blank, hardly aware of what I was writing. Markus glanced up, something like a grin on his face. I ignored him. 'Alright, carry on.'

'That's it. That's the best we could do. If we had more equipment, or more time… but I'm busy. Understand?'

'Sure. That's great, that's helpful. Thanks.'

'I'll leave the uniform in a clean sample bag in the lab. You can pick it up.'

'Thanks again, kid, I really–'

'Tell Esther, that's it. Finished. I don't want to hear from you police again. I'd ask you to do something about the bonfire of books in the quad, but I know I'd be wasting my time.'

'I…'

'What's going to happen when they run out of books?' He hung up.

25

I looked for Bernie at his usual bar by the harbour. The same barmaid, Ewa, was slumped on a stool behind the counter, her head resting in one hand. Without speaking or getting up, she set an empty glass in front of me and reached for a bottle.

'I'm not here to drink. I'm looking for Bernie.'

She poured out a measure of vodka. 'You want to talk in here, you drink. Nothing's for free.'

'I'm on duty.'

'So, go away and arrest some people. A gang of thugs dragged one of my best paying customers out of here, beat the shit out of him. Look for yourself.' She pointed at the floor behind me, where scuffed heel marks showed in a trail of dried blood along the dirty floorboards.

'Alright.' I took the shot and slugged it back.

'Your friend isn't here. He came in earlier, but he only drank one vodka. That's not like him.'

'Did he say anything?' I laid a few coins on the table and stopped her hand before she could refill my glass.

'No, but he was scared. I could tell, he was terrified about something. You should take care of him if he's your friend.'

'He's more like a colleague. I don't have friends.'

'He's a baby, that man. The drink made him that way. Innocence can't last in Danzig, they'll kill him, you'll see. Go find him.' She reached behind the counter but it wasn't a bottle she brought out; she held an umbrella towards me. 'He left this. He'll be soaking wet. You take it and give it to him. Nobody else will.'

* * *

I lost track of where the shift ended or started. Shadowy cloud stretched over Danzig and the rain descended like a veil. Wanderers ran from cover to cover beneath awnings in a grey evening. I sheltered for a moment outside the cafe where Daria worked. Through a window misted with condensation I watched her take the order from a table of sailors. Eyes vacant, absorbed in monotony, she tucked a loose strand of hair back behind one ear. She looked exhausted. Was her shift about to begin, or about to finish? There was nothing we might say to one another anyway, our muttered conversations, our world of blankets, shadow, and beaded sweat, had petered out. Her arms were skinny, she looked famished. I hurried away before she might glance and catch me in the rain.

I was saturated, and no longer cared. I wandered through the downpour to Bernie's apartment building, just a block away from the train station. I carried his umbrella but couldn't bring myself to open it. This used to be a busy place, railway tracks branching outwards to all the cities of Poland and Germany, but tonight the massive edifice was invisible in the background; all its lights were doused. I turned down a side road that was lit by a single working streetlight. Bernie's building was halfway along. I shone my torch through the opening to the tenement and called out, but if anybody heard, they shied away.

It was a relief to get out of the rain. I held the banister as I climbed the stairs, dripping water, into a dim green space where the night filtered through a stained-glass cupola over the stairwell. At the second landing, I turned the corner and felt a surge of déjà vu. I had to steady myself against the wall. It was just like the previous night when I discovered Gerhard's body. The same spiral motion upwards through the shadow, the same extension of silent, dark corridors disappearing. The building dense with sleep, and this detective a trespasser among their dreams, caught in a loop, doors opening upon doors opening upon doors.

At the end of the landing, a narrow window let in streetlight, disclosing mottled wallpaper, a filthy floor, all kinds of junk, bits of broken furniture, old bottles. I found Bernie's door and knocked. Nobody answered, nothing stirred inside. I banged and shouted.

'Bernie! Bernie! Open up.'

I tried the handle, but it didn't give. No light showed beneath the door.

'Bernie! It's me…'

Nothing. A door opened further back down the corridor. I heard the hinges creak, but couldn't see anything, deep in the shadow.

A frail voice said, 'What are you doing? It's late.'

'I'm police. I need to speak to the detective, it's urgent.'

'Is his car there?'

'What car?' I shone my torch over an old lady, bone white in the electricity, lurid wrinkles exposed; she might have been a hundred years old.

She cowered back. 'When he's home, his car is outside. It's a silver Volkswagen. He always parks it in the same space, under the lamppost opposite, the one that works.'

'Is it there?' I tried to remember. 'I don't know, I didn't see.'

'Most often it's not. When he drinks, he sleeps in his car, wherever he finds himself. You can see the street from the window at the end of the corridor.'

'Thank you, Frau…'

She closed her door. I heard a bolt click into place on the other side. It was late, too late for this. I felt ashamed, waking mothers and grandmothers at night. And for what? I crossed the hall and came to a grimy windowpane. There was the one lit lamppost across the street, a circle of stale, yellow light, and nothing inside it. Just a flutter of moth wings. No car. Bernie was gone.

'Where are you, you old drunk?'

* * *

Crossing the Long Market again, I passed Daria's cafe, but it was closed. I stared through the window at the empty tables, the piled chairs, until my breath steamed the pane. Back at the police station, a guard stood at the entrance with an automatic rifle, beneath the leaking gutter. Two members of the public, old guys in shabby jackets, were being frisked against the wall by another officer.

'What are you doing?' I asked the guards. 'Isn't this a bit extreme?'

They shrugged. 'There's a cop killer out there.'

Inside, Granma smoked and coughed and chuckled when I asked about Bernie. 'I told you before, he looked drunk when he came in. He'll be lost on another of his benders.'

'He's not drunk. He's working a special case.'

She stubbed out her cigarette. 'It won't stay special. You'll see.'

Nobody knew where Bernie was. Some of the officers in the station seemed to have never heard his name before. They shook their heads, eyeing me strangely. I ran up to Henrik's office, but he had gone home hours ago. In the canteen, something was different. I couldn't tell for a moment what had changed.

'Anybody know where Bernie is?' I asked the handful of officers who sat around smoking and sharing the pages of a newspaper they passed around.

'Didn't he retire?' Lukasz grinned.

I realised what was new: somebody had hung a portrait of Hitler over the side table. I pointed. 'Where did that come from?'

'You read the news, Tal?' Hermann held out a page from the paper. 'Poles are preparing to invade, says here. Tanks stationed along the border. What do you make of that?'

They stared at me.

'Why would Poland invade Danzig?' I said.

The others glanced at each other, raised eyebrows, smirking, like this was the stupidest thing they ever heard. I fingered the amber ring in my pocket.

'Anyway, if you see Bernie...'

I was about to walk out, but Hermann said, 'Oh, hey, Tal, you're the expert. Answer a question for us.'

'What?'

'Is it true what they say about Polish women? I'd ask someone else, but you're the only one around here who sleeps with dogs.' He could hardly finish speaking before his voice broke into laughter.

The others couldn't hold it in, they hid their faces and spluttered. I ran out before my hands might do something stupid.

26

Evil doesn't belong in a place like this. A cool driveway shaded by pines, a neatly tended front lawn. You forget what cut grass smells like, living downtown. This was a classy neighbourhood. I rarely got the chance to wander quiet suburban avenues at night, they don't murder here, or they keep it hidden.

My torch beam caught at the upstairs windows where white, lace curtains hung motionless. The amber dealer's house, where the newspaper photograph was taken. It was different at night. I checked the page again: "ONE OF DANZIG'S OLDEST FAMILIES ANNOUNCE BIRTH OF DAUGHTER". The monochrome image was like a dream version of this silent place. The house stood empty, black windows reflecting back nothingness. It was beautiful, pale walls, balconies overlooking a pretty garden.

It was Baltic amber that made them rich. Our city had thrived with its amber markets, the centre of a global trade. I'd never understood the appeal. Fossilised sap washed up on the shore, the memory of trees that died a hundred million years ago. That's what history looks like in the end. That's what we kill each other for; flotsam, shoreline detritus.

The front door of the house, at the end of a winding path, showed no sign of damage. A sign over the door said, "FOR SALE". There was no number to call. I had come too far to go home. It was peaceful in the garden; all the smells of the grass and leaves were opened at night, in the rain. I shone my torch through the windows and caught a sense of spaciousness within. I knocked on the door, but nobody answered. The sound of my fist banging was swallowed up. I crept around the side of the house, my skin prickling with fear, almost pleasurable. There was a wooden gate to one side of the building that was closed with a padlock.

'Ah shit.' I hoisted up my trouser legs, found a slippery foothold, and climbed over.

A night bird screamed and vanished in a sigh of leaves. I stopped, caught halfway over the gate. With my torch turned off I couldn't see anything. This was a mistake, of course. The wood was flimsy, it rattled as I half tumbled over to the other side, landing on a gravel path. I turned on the torch and lit up a growth of ivy that covered the side wall. The night was full of flowers. I stumbled around in the dark and found large glass doors looking out over darkness.

There was no sign of a break-in. I shone my torch over the glass. Through the vestibule doors, I made out the contours of a dining room with a high ceiling. Some cups and plates were laid out on the table, wine glasses half-drunk, food congealing; a sign of habitation in the stillness that reigned here. Somebody had got up and left their meal and never returned. Peering around the corners of the space, I sought their remains. The thin beam of my torch caught a baby's crib by the side of the settee, with a blanket and a doll inside.

Then I saw the pale face. Horrified eyes in the dark at the back of the drawing room held mine for a moment and vanished. The face was gone so quickly, I almost doubted I'd seen it, but there wasn't time to question my sanity. I sprinted around the side of the building and jumped back up the side gate. As I was straddling the top, I heard the front door open, and slam shut. Somebody went running down the driveway.

'Stop!' I called after them as I dropped down from the fence, too quickly, and landed awkwardly, almost rolling my ankle. 'Stop! Police!'

I just caught sight of the stranger running out of the front drive as I chased after them into the dark. 'Stop!'

Out on the road, the runner was just a silhouette weaving between the streetlamps, but they were slow, I gained ground.

'Stop! Stop there!'

Close now, I heard the man's ragged breathing. He must be elderly. I came up behind him and grabbed his shoulder. He spun around with his hands in the air. 'Don't hurt me! I'll scream.'

In the streetlight, he looked over seventy years old. I took hold of his wrists. 'Police. What were you doing in that house? Why did you run?'

Out of breath, he doubled over sucking up the air.

'You're under arrest.' I took out my handcuffs.

'No. Please.' He took another deep breath and straightened. 'I'm the butler. I have a key to the house. I'm not a thief. I didn't break in.'

'Why did you run then?'

'I thought you were an intruder. I've been afraid ever since… ever since…'

'The butler? I'm going to have to take you down to the station. I'll take your statement.'

'But I already gave a statement. Your colleague took it.'

'Which colleague?'

'I can't remember. Bernhard something or other, I think.' His face in the rain was drawn and fearful. He stuttered as he spoke.

His panic seemed genuine; I released his wrists.

'Alright, calm down. It was Bernie you spoke to?'

'Could be. Ask them yourself, they'll tell you, I cooperated fully. I told them everything I knew. I promised to call if I thought of anything else. But you… why were you sneaking in the garden at night? You almost gave me a heart attack.'

'It's the baby I'm interested in. I saw the crib.'

'Oh.' He wiped the rain from his brow.

There was a moment of silence filled with the patter of rain as we watched each other.

'You're referring to the rumours,' he said.

'Which rumours?'

'About the baby.' His face was blank with innocence or craft.

'Enlighten me.'

'Well, you know how rumours go. People whispered that it wasn't really hers. She never showed any sign. Just one day, there was a child, as if by magic. But that can happen sometimes. A woman can be pregnant and not show it.'

'The baby wasn't hers…' I thought back to the underground chamber where I'd seen the corpses. That woman's naked body, thin, sickly; there hadn't been any marks of pregnancy. 'And where is it now, this child?'

The old man wiped the rain away again. His teeth chattered in the cold. 'I don't know. I swear I don't know.'

'Alright. You should go home before you catch a chill. Here's my card. If you think of anything, you call.'

* * *

Back in the heart of Danzig, and soaking wet, I crossed the train station and returned to the street where Bernie lived. Incredible. His car was parked under the lamppost, just like the old lady said, a silver Volkswagen in the electric light. My heart jumped at the sight. With a burst of energy, I ran through the entrance of the building and hurried up the stairs, taking two steps at a time, almost stumbling upwards. What time was it? Surely, too late to be calling. I didn't care. I came to Bernie's landing and ran past the closed doors. Too tired and too electrified to slow down, to quieten my steps; I didn't care anymore, didn't even turn on my torch, just ran through the dark. I knocked on his door. Without waiting for a response, I rattled the handle and knocked again.

'Bernie! Open up! Open up, it's me.'

The locked door didn't budge. Now I was certain, it was the same night over again, and had to end the same way. This time, there wasn't even the intern kid; I was alone. I banged louder.

'Bernie! Are you in there? You have to open.'

I didn't hear the old lady until she was behind me. 'Why are you running around so late at night? You should go home and sleep.'

I turned on the torch and swung it around. 'Oh, it's you. Did I wake you? I'm sorry. Maybe I'm losing my mind.'

'You didn't wake me. I never sleep these days. Old-timers don't need it. But you should. Sleep is important. It's only now that I've lost it, I realise dreams were the best part of life.'

'I need to speak to my colleague. It's urgent.' Looking closer, I saw that her eyeballs were bloated, set in a leaking film of serum that left dark stains like tear tracks. The pupils had faded, discoloured, greying, until they were almost indistinguishable from the whites of the balls.

'He isn't home,' she said. 'I would've heard him. I lie awake every night and hear the neighbours. The walls are thin in here. I know them all by sound. Your friend comes home late, he's always the last one on the corridor. He tramps up the stairs, dead drunk. Unmistakeable. He's not here. I told you; his car would be outside.'

'But his car is there. I just saw it. It's parked under the lamppost like you said.'

'It is?' She backed away. 'Well then, I'm sorry. Pay me no heed. I'm just a crazy old lady. My brain's leaked away. The neighbours say that; I hear them through the walls.'

'Yeah, well.' I knocked on the door again. 'Bernie! Bernie!' No answer. 'Fuck it.' I took a run up and slammed into the door with my shoulder. It didn't budge, but I felt the vertebrae in my neck rattle.

'What are you doing?' the old lady said.

'I'm worried about him. A cop was killed the other night.' I took another run and crashed into the door. It rattled in the frame but didn't give.

‘Why didn’t you say?’ The old lady went away down the corridor towards her flat. ‘I’ve got a key.’

I rubbed my shoulder. ‘You’ve got a key?’

‘I take care of him sometimes. He has days where he can’t move. Just lies there like a corpse. Can’t speak, just moans.’

‘And you look after him?’ I followed her along the hall.

‘Who else? He doesn’t have anyone.’

She came back out with an old key and handed it over. I opened the door.

‘Stay out here,’ I warned her. ‘It could be a murder scene.’

She laughed at that, for some reason. ‘I’m going to bed. You do what you want. I’ll be glad to let someone else take care of your friend. He’s never grateful. A man like that, kindness makes him sad.’

I waited until she was gone before I shone my torch along the inner hall of Bernie’s flat and stepped inside. The stink of alcohol was like a fog. I closed the door behind me.

‘Bernie?’

Nothing. The first room was a small bedroom and study combined. An unmade bed lay open in the corner, giving off a reek of chemical sweat. I shone my torch around the corners of the room. Empty bottles lay on their side among a few books and some sheets of paper, piles of crumpled newspapers. I poked my head through the next door – a cramped, windowless bathroom, stinking of stale waste.

‘Bernie? Where are you?’

Only one door remained. I shone my torch around a basic kitchenette with a view of the street through a filthy window, a glimpse of the one functional lamppost like a lighthouse on the edge of the sea. The sink was empty. Nothing in the drawers and cupboards, no food anywhere. Apparently, Bernie didn’t eat. A few glasses stood on the counter, rimed with dregs. I sniffed at them: red wine, cheap stuff. He wasn't home. I went back through the flat looking for a door I must have missed, but there was nowhere.

'Bernie, for God's sake. What am I doing here?'

My torch flashed over a broken segment of mirror stuck to the wall of his bedroom, smeared with fingerprints. I sat on the edge of his filthy bed and let my torch beam float idly over the floor of bottles. I found a sheaf of paper at the foot of the mattress and snatched it up. A certificate of some kind. Bureaucratic, boring, I almost threw it down, but my eye caught a line of text:

DATE OF BIRTH: 1 July 1939.

Two months ago. I glanced through the rest of the document, typewritten, with a few illegible, florid signatures at the bottom. It was a copy of a birth certificate. I scanned through the document and found what seemed to be a name, "Anna". The same as the child whose birth was announced in the newspaper, the amber dealer's daughter.

'Bernie? Where have you been digging?'

Back in the kitchen I looked through the window and saw his silver car still parked in the empty street. He must have fallen asleep in there. I closed the front door behind me and ran down the stairs. I almost felt the presence of that frail old lady, tiny as a child, lying sleepless in her bed, those eyes that seemed unable to close, as if the lids had shrivelled away. She listened in the dark in some hidden corner to the echoes of my feet as I withdrew. The birth certificate was still in my hand, I folded it and stuffed it in my pocket.

Outside, the streetlamp was bright after the dimness of the building. I blinked and averted my face as I entered the light's circle, approaching the car. I shielded my brow as I crouched and looked inside. At first, I couldn't see anything, and couldn't understand why. I rubbed my eyes, grimaced, and looked again: the side window was blocked out as if painted from the inside. I skirted around the front of the vehicle, trying to see through the windscreen, but it reflected back the streetlamp's glare. On the other side of the car, I opened the passenger seat door and stuck my head into air dense as soil. I'd smelled it before, just one night ago. The other window hadn't been painted over at all; it was spattered from the inside with dark blood. Bernie lay prone in the driver's seat, a revolver in his hand. The side of his face was blown away. He slept at last.

27

Gdańsk, Polish People's Republic

1961

The Third Rune

Dark inside. Something dripped.

'Through there.' The woman with the handkerchief crushed against her face, pointed and cringed back. 'In the bathroom.'

'Can't see a damn thing.' Roman went to the window and opened the curtains.

Through the slanting, icy light, a narrow living room mouldered. Peeling brown wallpaper. Old furniture and stacks of newspapers formed a sediment in the putrid air of damp and decay. The light petered out as they reached the bathroom door. Roman pushed and it floated inwards. 'In here?'

The woman nodded.

'Don't go anywhere,' he told her.

She gave a kind of muffled laugh from behind her handkerchief and ran out of the flat.

'Hey! If you think you can avoid a signed deposition…'

'Let her go.' Anna put on gloves. 'Pretty sure she's senile anyway.' She poked in the refuse of a desk in the alcove that was covered in old paper. Damp, illegible detritus.

Roman peered into the bathroom. 'What is that smell?' He tried a switch. 'Lights are out.'

She sniffed. 'It's like an old farm.'

'Let's get this over with.' He went through the bathroom door into blackness.

Anna followed. It was chill inside. The light filtered brown through a small pane of green glass at the top of the wall above the toilet. Against the tiled wall, a stained bathtub was full of dark liquid behind the torn shower curtain.

'Come on, let's just…' The superintendent rolled up his sleeves. 'You take that end.'

Anna pulled the shower curtain back. 'What is this stuff?' The liquid was dark, she couldn't see below the surface. She dipped a finger and licked it. 'Is it tar?'

Dark water sloshed over the side of the tub as they reached inside, staining her trousers.

'Shit.' Her hand slipped against eel-like skin beneath the surface. 'Oh God.' She jerked backwards and for a moment lost balance on the slick floor, grabbing hold of Roman.

'What are you doing?'

Their arms meshed for a moment under the surface, and she plunged forwards, sending a wave of liquid over the edge. Zielinski's face broke the surface, pale skin with black ink running through features that were fixed in a scream.

'Come on, grab hold of him.' Roman thrashed in the water, trying to find purchase.

Anna couldn't move. Her eyes locked upon the dead mouth, a black orifice discharging non-space, it sank back beneath the dark water.

Roman let the apparition slip away. 'God help us. I never saw anything like this.'

* * *

Nobody wanted to talk. The room was sealed off with crime scene tape. A police officer standing guard outside looked nauseous. The slouching inhabitants of the building snuck down the stairs with frightened eyes and shook their heads when Anna tried to question them. She found the landlady who lived on the floor below, an octogenarian who wore the rags of a silk dressing gown and smoked a pipe.

'How long have you lived in this building?' Anna said.

'I don't know. Forever.' The woman's face was wretched. She cringed in the doorway, hollow eyes staring. 'Some bad things happened to me in the War. I don't look back far. It's like time split in two, I try to live in the second part, the new part. How long is that? Twenty years, I guess. Feels like one day.'

'Twenty years.' Anna jotted down the number, whatever it signified. 'And you say that room was empty?'

The landlady glanced up the creaking stairwell. 'It used to be owned by a Mr Borowski. He was a teacher, or so he believed. Never knew him to teach anything. A miser more like. Haven't seen him in months. He went away somewhere. Never came back. One of the neighbours said he poisoned himself to death. I don't ask.'

Anna noted down these meaningless details in a numb state. 'And who does ask?'

'You could try Karo. She lives on the top floor. She's the town gossip. She's the one who found the body.'

* * *

It was airy on the top floor, and Anna was glad to climb up into a pocket of freshness where Gdańsk wind blew through a smashed skylight. Karo's flat was overgrown with potted plants, vines fell in a curtain covering the mantelpiece, creepers sent tendrils over the window ledges and shelves.

'I'm sorry.' Karo dabbed at her eyes. 'I don't know what came over me. The door was open. I saw wet footprints coming out. I thought the teacher must be back. I knocked and called. God knows why. It's not like Mr Borowski was a talker. Nobody answered. I smelled something odd. I took a step inside; I know I shouldn't have. I'm sorry if that was wrong. I'm not in trouble, am I? You won't arrest me?'

Anna lowered her notepad. 'Just tell me what happened. Take your time.'

'You can ask anyone in the building, I've always been an honest woman. I'd never break a rule, not even a tiny one. I don't know why I went in there. It's like I felt something, it was a mystical thing, I just sensed it. Do you ever feel like that?'

The story dragged on like this. Hours later, when Anna read back through her notes, she couldn't remember recording them, her hands had transcribed the words through a fog of shock. All the inhabitants of the building were the same, stunned, quiet, and distracted. Weird. Nobody had seen or heard anything, nobody knew anything. Their eyes turned dull, memory fragmented, they forgot what happened just yesterday; they began to doubt that the damp, mouldering room was ever occupied.

Outside the building, a few officers smoked cigarettes in silence. They looked down at the pavement when Anna came outside.

'Comrades. Did anyone turn up? Anybody wanting to get in?'

They shook their heads.

'Not a soul,' one of them said. 'Did you find anything? Do you think… one of those people…?'

'I don't know,' Anna said. 'We don't know anything yet.'

It was like she couldn't leave the vile bathroom. She smelled black liquid on her clothes as she walked back along the Long Market to the station. Even the Baltic wind couldn't shift it. In the canteen, a few stunned officers asked if it were true. She craved solitude. Climbing the stairs up to her office on the third floor, her limbs were weighed down by slime and disgust. She closed the door behind her, and sniffed at her sleeves, her collar, her hair, trying to find the source of the stink, but it was everywhere. She opened the shutters and let daylight stream across her desk. She put her head out of the window and breathed in a cold gust of salt, edged with pollution.

She sat at her desk and started working through the day's pile of mail. If she could just find the most trivial, mindless task, she might be able to blot out Zielinski's face, vomiting tar like a message from an inverse reality where everything is lost. Eternal night. She tied her hair back and tried not to smell it. On top of the pile was a copy of *The Baltic Journal*, one of the main newspapers in the region, with a note attached. She tilted it to the daylight and read, "You're famous. Page 5. Roman".

With all that had happened, she'd forgotten the feature in the newspaper about women police officers in socialism. She had felt proud of the article, but now it was empty. Everything was worthless. She put the newspaper aside and skimmed through some other notes, bureaucratic odds and ends, nothing of interest. At the bottom of the pile was a plain envelope. She slid it open and pulled out a small piece of paper that was tinted rose. The message was brief and senseless, even after reading it over five times:

> DEAR BELOVED,
> I CANNOT WAIT FOR US TO BE TOGETHER.
> DON'T FORGET ME, YOUR TRUE HEART.

She checked the back and inside of the envelope, but there was nothing else. Some kind of joke, or worse, a real love interest. More likely it was meaningless. Her mind was too disturbed to think the permutations through. She crumpled the paper and the envelope and dropped them into the wastepaper basket, but a sense of unease remained.

She took up the newspaper, licked her finger, and turned the pages. She found herself, in a small square of ink.

> Deputy Chief Investigator Anna Nowak. Socialist criminology shows the value of women in the police force. Backward West decades behind.

She had hoped the piece would be inspiring, but now she started to read, it was just dull. The citations from Marx sounded formulaic and meaningless. Her face in the picture was unrecognisable. Hair tied back tightly, lips unsmiling. Cold eyes. Who was she? A stranger, unloved.

She flipped the pages looking for distraction. The news was boring as always: bureaucracy, legislation, economic forecasts, government plans, new buildings. The security minister warned that West Germany eyed Poland's western border; the capitalists desired to annex Gdańsk. The Kremlin pledged to support Warsaw against any foreign aggression. But these stories were common, there was nothing new reported.

She was about to give up reading when she turned a new page and found something different: a story about archaeology. The photograph showed workers at a dig somewhere outside the city. As her eyes skimmed the article, they caught the word "rune", and stopped.

'What?' she asked the morning. She started again.

> NEW DISCOVERY SHEDS LIGHT ON ANCIENT SLAVIC BURIAL SITES.
> An archaeological site… previously designated a Germanic burial ground… during the Nazi occupation of Poland… reassessed. Exciting discoveries… site much older than previously supposed…

She jumped up and carried the newspaper to the window. A strange light had broken over Gdańsk, the colour of spider threads, twining grey and white cloud in layers. She tilted the picture and looked more closely: three silhouetted figures posed in the frame, not touching, with their shovels in the earth against a pale background. Two men to the left, and on the right… a woman. Was it her? Anna closed her eyes and strained to bring back the hanging body that swayed in the breeze. She could only remember the ash tree.

* * *

Downstairs, Sebastian slumped back in his seat at the reception desk with his eyes closed, as if sleeping. She crept past.

'Nowak!' He sat up in his chair.

'I'm in a rush.'

'Where are you going?'

Something in the tone of his voice, too nervous for casual conversation, stopped her and brought her back to the desk. 'What do you care?'

He leaned forwards. 'Superintendent told me to keep track of you.'

'Why?'

'He didn't say. Just to let him know where you went.'

Roman was spying on her, but then, everyone spied on everyone else. *Don't get paranoid.*

She held his eyes. 'There was a weird note in my mail this morning. Any idea who might have…?'

'How should I know? Am I supposed to keep track of everything?'

'Do me a favour, give Roman the same answer when he asks where I went.'

'Is it true what they say?' Sebastian whispered.

'What?'

'Zielinski.' The emotion in his brown eyes was like excitement and fear and apathy mixed.

‘That’s still under investigation.’

‘They say you were the last one with him.’

‘They say a lot of things.’

‘He drowned in ink?’

‘That’s impossible.’

As she turned away again, he called after her. ‘Where are you going?’

‘Archaeological dig.’

‘A what?’

But at that moment, Roman appeared behind the reception area. ‘Nowak! There you are. Come on. They’ve brought the body in.’

28

Zielinski lay naked on a slab under the light bulb, his skin indigo, his belly swollen, his face bloated and confused. The thick white hairs of his chest were discoloured, purplish. Roman stamped his feet and rubbed his hands in the cold.

‘Cause of death is drowning.’ Weber held up a phial of black liquid to the light. ‘Same as the woman from the tree.’

‘Toxicology?’ Roman said.

‘Clean. Comrade Zielinski was sober.’

‘Can I?’ Anna took the phial, delicately, from the pathologist.

‘Knock yourself out. There’s a gallon of the stuff.’

She swirled the liquid in the glass and watched a galaxy of black particles dance beneath the frozen light. Slowly, they drifted and fell together into a sediment.

‘This is a mess.’ Roman blew on his fingers which had turned bright red. ‘They’re sending someone from Warsaw. Internal affairs. They’ll want to check everything out.’

'Secret police?' Anna couldn't take her eyes off the dark liquid. 'That's an overreaction. We'll solve this ourselves. Zielinski belonged to us.'

'It's a state matter now. We've got a dead cop. Shit on my life.' He nodded towards Weber. 'Comrade, leave us alone a minute.'

'Take your time.' The pathologist bowed as she retreated into a rear office.

Roman came over to the body. Without looking at it, he pulled the sheet over, hiding Zielinski's face. 'You were the last to see him, Anna.'

'That we know of.'

'How did he seem?'

'Like a shitty cop waiting for retirement. About normal.'

'Don't.' Roman flashed a look at her.

'Sorry. Shouldn't speak ill of the dead.'

'It's a shame he wasn't drunk. Would be easier to sell the story.'

The lights hummed in the silence. Roman's steaming breath formed patterns in the crystalline light.

'What story?' Anna said.

'The story of his accident.'

'I wasn't aware that was a story.'

Roman rubbed his hands and couldn't get warm. 'Don't play stupid. The situation's tense. We haven't been able to recover Zielinski's uniform, his badge, or his gun. There could be someone running around dressed like police. And in Gdańsk, of all places. Moscow's watching us. Warsaw's jittery.'

'So…'

'So, the best thing for everyone is to write this up as a neat and tidy accident. Drowned in the bath. File it away. Move on. Without Moscow breathing down our necks. Do we understand each other, Nowak?'

'Sure.'

'They'll want to interview you. You'll be a witness.'

'There's not a lot I can say. He was in the car last I saw him, outside the shipyards.'

'You can tell them he was depressed, talked about his dead wife, alcoholism. I don't care, just anything. He seemed desperate. He seemed crazy, out of his mind, whatever. Wild enough to take his clothes off and drown himself.'

'I should lie then.'

'It's not a lie. Zielinski was a mess, everyone at the station knew it. He had a drink problem.'

'Not according to toxicology.'

'The only reason he wasn't drunk yesterday was to spite me. The prick. He left me with a dead cop and no clues.'

'There is one clue.'

'What?'

'The rune.'

'Jesus, Nowak, I should have you fired. I'd kick you off the Force now, but it would make me look suspicious. Don't you dare, don't you mention a thing about runes. If the secret police find out about them, they'll connect the case to Germany. They'll put you in an interview cell, they'll try to crack you. They'll look for dirt on the station, on me. I'm in charge. I'm the one will take the fall. Don't you dare. Don't even think about it. No runes. Not a mention of Danzig… I mean, of Germany. Now get out and solve a crime. Do your job.'

29

Anna drove south through a gale of litter and seagulls. On the radio, the newsreader reported a speech made in the West German parliament. A group of prominent German community leaders "demanded" that Gdańsk and Wrocław be "returned" to their "rightful owners". She wondered which owners they referred to; there were no Germans in Gdańsk. And yet, in the hidden space behind her wardrobe, she'd found a torn scrap of yellowed newspaper in German. The broadcast dissolved into static as a powerful blast of wind shook the car. She turned the radio off. The thin metal skeleton of the vehicle rocked and whistled, she felt herself carried by raw forces. How long had she felt somebody following? The tickling sensation crept slowly into dread. She glanced in the rear-view mirror as a black car slowed and disappeared behind a corner. She accelerated away. Ten minutes later, the road behind was empty in the mirror.

She was getting paranoid. Somebody had killed Zielinski, while she was working practically at his side. He might have been grabbed just yards away while she was walking in the opposite direction. Her mind resisted but she had to face the fact: a cop had been killed. It could have been her. A turn of a path, a corner, a doorway, all that might have saved her condemned her partner. There would be another death; the runes proved it. Her eyes kept looking in the rear-view mirror, but the black car was gone. Desolate fields extended through the windows on either side of the car, stretching into a flat horizon. The wind died down as she left the coast further behind, entering the hinterland.

She had to stop from time to time to check the map spread out on the passenger seat. The name of the village was mentioned in the newspaper article, but on the map, it was just a dot surrounded by emptiness. There were no signposts. After an hour driving down winding, narrowing paths, as her fuel dwindled, she came to the village – five cottages set among fields where nothing grew. She parked outside a rickety outhouse overgrown with weeds. The sky crawled with grey clouds overhead. To one side, a footpath disappeared into a wood of scrawny trees. A few crows hung in the air. Nobody responded when she knocked at the first cottage. Black footprints muddied the earth between the buildings. At the second cottage, an old woman with no teeth stuck her head out of the window.

'Can you help…?' Anna showed her the picture from the newspaper. It almost blew out of her hands.

'What do you want? Another one of them journalists? I told the newspaper folks, there's nothing here for you. Find your own food and water.'

'I'm not a journalist. Police.'

'Shit. What now?' The woman vanished; the window clanged shut.

A set of dirty footprints led from the door and disappeared where the track thinned into just a groove in the overgrown grass.

'Hey!' Anna knocked on the window. 'Please, don't be frightened. I just need to know, where is the archaeological site?'

The woman's voice came from somewhere in the creaking interior. 'Follow the path!'

Anna followed the "path" as it faded through grey scrag, wove between ramshackle buildings, dead trees, and the rusted frames of old vehicles. At one point she lost the trail altogether but picked it up again some yards further ahead – or perhaps it was a different path that twisted around a cluster of charred tree trunks and blackened grass. A few crows pecked in the dirt. Fresh tyre tracks cut through the earth in places. On the other side of the trees, the landscape flattened into an expanse of marsh and choked vegetation. A forgotten place.

She stopped in despair; all this was a mistake. She should be in Gdańsk with the others; there was a murder to solve, a police officer had been killed. Something had gone wrong; she shouldn't be here.

She was about to turn back but she knew, she couldn't bear to leave here with nothing, a wasted trip. She hated to be wrong. The superintendent would be furious anyway. She carried on another ten yards and saw something up ahead, the remains of a fence, a few lopsided posts and some wretched loose ends of barbwire. Crows perched on the stumps where they stuck out.

She followed the broken perimeter until she reached the remains of a gate – two posts sunk into an overgrowth of nettles, and a wire entrance torn from its hinges that lay on the ground. Crows broke away as she approached. She examined the old gate and found a rusted, bent panel still attached, hanging askew from the wire links. She knelt and brushed a loose covering of earth to find a faded warning sign.

ACHTUNG

The letters were in red, and beneath, a simple design of skull and crossbones. Whatever was inside this fence, it wasn't intended for the public.

She crossed the collapsed entrance and looked around. An earthy undertone of sludge in the breeze. The ground was waterlogged, it oozed under her boots. Up ahead, the roofs of a few portable huts stuck up out of overgrown rushes and reeds. Beside them, a beat-up truck was parked away from the dirt track.

A voice from behind took her by surprise. 'Are you lost?'

She looked around to see an old man in filthy overalls, carrying a broom. 'Who are you?'

'I'm the engineer. I'm just cleaning up.' He took a step closer, and she backed away. 'You must be another one of them journalists.'

'Something like that.'

He was malnourished, scrawny, several teeth missing from his stinking mouth. Scraggly grey hairs fluttered around the dome of his head where a dent showed. He must have taken a vicious blow to the cranium some years ago. He wasn't dangerous; she could overpower him easily, but something about him was wrong, or maybe she was just going crazy.

‘I told your colleagues,’ he said, ‘there’s nothing here for you. Nothing to see. And it’s dangerous. Haunted place. You smell that?’ He took a breath that whistled audibly through a nose broken many times.

Despite herself, she sniffed the air. Damp earth, tar, rust. What else? Just a touch of something rotten.

‘You do, you do smell it.’ He grinned. With the wide gaps in his teeth, he looked insane.

‘Smell what?’

‘The dead.’ Just like that, the grin was gone, his face was transformed, almost priestlike.

‘What is this place?’

‘Not very good at your job, are you.’

He stepped closer, and she resisted the urge to back further away. She needed to make him talk.

‘Tell me anyway.’

‘All this’ – he pointed along the remains of the fence with a hand that trembled – ‘used to be a Nazi site. Secret place. Some farmer found an ancient burial ground. Nazis wanted to prove it was Germanic. Could justify their claims to Polish soil. Show the world that Germans were here first. They spent a lot of money and time on this dirt, brought all kinds of scientists.’

‘And what happened?’

‘I’m just an engineer.’ The grin returned to his face. ‘Whatever they were looking for, they didn’t find it. Before the War was over, they flooded the site, they didn’t want anyone else to have it.’

Anna took out her notepad. ‘You know what these symbols are?’ She showed him the runes.

He went rigid with the broom in his bony hands. ‘Where’d you find them?’

She studied his reaction, and his face had changed. Still insane, just in a different way. ‘Does it matter?’ she said.

‘Is that what you’re looking for here? Magic runes. Bring the dead to life, enchant the earth.’

‘I just need to ask a few questions. If I could…’

He backed away. Was that fear in the set of his jaw? 'You're talking to the wrong person. Go up there. You'll come to the bog. Go clockwise, you'll find some portable huts. The archaeologists work there. They're the experts. Ask them.'

'Thanks. All the same, could I take your name?'

'I'm busy.' He hurried away, dragging his broom.

There was a moment she could have gone after him, but she was stuck in place in the soggy earth.

He called back over his shoulder. 'Careful, Comrade, there's graves under your feet. Thousands of years old.'

He merged into the background of rusted metal wires and the skeletal ruins, the burned trees. Gone. Crows hung from the pale sky. A shiver wormed through her, she shook and turned and started in the other direction. Her mind was empty, her skin crawled. A darker fuzz of clouds showed in the north, they'd be gathering over the sea. She followed the man's directions and came to the bog, a wide expanse of dark liquid spotted with lily pads and floating algae. The earth was waterlogged here as well, her boots sank. It stunk like a dank cellar. She looked back just to reassure herself she could still return. The car was lost from view, but she saw the stumps of the fallen entrance gate.

That smell again, a hint of the stain from the crime scene where they'd found Zielinski. She came to the edge of the bog through an overgrowth of reeds and looked out over a vast black mirror, a lake of tar. It was too much, she dropped to her haunches and almost vomited, dizzy with the sense of something beneath the surface, Zielinski's face, longing for her. She shook it away. *Socialist criminology shows the value of women in the police force. Backward West decades behind.* She headed clockwise around the bog, pushing through tall rushes, and came to the huts. Portable cabins of thin panels. Swallowing panic, she pressed through the sinking mud towards them. As she approached the first hut, a man in a plaid shirt looked out. Their eyes held for a moment before he ducked back inside.

'Hey!' Anna called. 'Excuse me, Comrade.' She banged on the flimsy door. 'Open up. Police.'

'Police?' A voice came from behind her.

She spun around. 'Who…'

'You shouldn't be here.' A man in overalls, dripping with slime, emerged out of the reeds.

'Stay back.' For a moment she was mesmerised by the black liquid that coated his legs and waist. 'Gdańsk Police Force. Detective Anna Nowak.' She took out her badge. 'Who are you?'

'I'm Miro, I'm in charge of this dig. That man you scared away is my assistant, also called Miro. But you can call me Doc, to avoid confusion. I'd shake hands, but…' He raised his arm to show a rubber glove soaked in bog water.

'Just stay back.'

'What's this about, Detective?'

'I need to ask you some questions…'

'Excuse me a moment.' He walked past with a contrite smile and banged on the side of the hut. 'Miro! Come out. There's somebody who wants to talk to us.' He glanced back over his shoulder at Anna. 'Sorry about him, he's shy.'

Something rattled in the hut. The door opened and the man in plaid looked out. Around thirty years old, perhaps a decade younger than his companion, he was bald and wore glasses. The older Doc was a handsome man with a thick, dark beard that exaggerated his teeth when he smiled, as if they were too big for his mouth.

'I saw your picture in *The Baltic Journal*,' Anna said. 'That was you, wasn't it?'

The two men exchanged a glance. Doc smiled. 'I guess we're famous now, hey, Miro.'

Miro didn't smile. 'What's this about, Detective? We're busy here. Our work is being interrupted since the newspapers found out. All kinds of strangers popping up, sticking their nose in.'

'I wanted to ask you…' Anna took out the newspaper and turned the photograph towards them.

Miro peered through his glasses. 'Yeah, that's us. So what?'

'And the woman?' She pointed.

'Our colleague, Gosia.' He straightened his glasses and looked at Doc, who did not notice.

'Can I speak to her?'

'She's not here,' Doc said.

'Where is she?'

'Excuse me a second.' Doc pulled off his rubber gloves, scattering droplets of slime. 'Sorry.' He rolled down the top part of his soaked overalls to show a plain white shirt beneath. 'It's not as glamorous as it sounds, archaeology.'

Miro seemed angry about something, he clenched a fist and set his jaw. 'Gosia's busy. She had to err… She had to go back to Warsaw.'

'Why?'

He hesitated. 'I don't know. Does it matter?'

'She had some paperwork to take care of,' Doc said. 'A perfectly banal matter. The job is mostly bureaucracy nowadays. You might picture us digging up Roman amphitheatres, but it's just filling in forms.'

'When did she leave?' Anna folded the newspaper and put it back in her bag. She took out her notepad while the two men hesitated.

Doc blew out his cheeks. 'Gee, I'm not sure. Was it yesterday? Could have been the day before? I must apologise, Detective. We're a scatter-brained bunch in our profession. Too much time spent with the past.'

'Our jobs aren't so different.' She turned a new page and jotted down "Gosia". 'Yesterday, or the day before…'

'It was two days ago.' Miro couldn't hide his irritation. Was he angry with Doc, or with Anna? Or perhaps it was something else. 'I remember.'

'Two days ago, thank you. And was she driving a car?'

'A car? Err…' Miro frowned. 'I guess so.'

'You *guess* so?'

Doc gave his toothy smile. 'A car? Of course she was driving a car. How else? This place is a wasteland. There's no other way.'

'And do you know the licence plate?'

'Licence plate, licence plate… I'm afraid I don't. I was never one for numbers. Truth be told, that was more Gosia's field. Do you know the plate, Miro?'

'Why should I? Do you imagine I care about a stupid licence plate?'

Anna lowered her notepad. 'You two seem upset about something.'

Doc looked at Miro, a spark in the corner of his eye, a warning, an appeal, or just nothing. He turned to Anna. 'Detective, is Gosia alright?'

She took a breath. 'When did you last hear from her?'

The men glanced at each other and shook their heads. They seemed able to communicate without words, a silent conversation excluding her.

'It's a busy time for us,' Doc said.

'Do you have a phone number? Any way to contact her in Warsaw?'

Miro looked at Doc, who shrugged, but the act of calm was unconvincing; he was nervous.

'Sure,' Doc said. 'We could call the office.'

'You have a phone here?' She looked around.

'Our set-up is not as uncivilised as it looks. Across the way there's a temporary office. There's a phone in there. We even have a kitchen, if you can call it a kitchen. Speaking of which, perhaps a hot drink, Detective? It's a bitter wind.'

'Just call her. Show me your office.'

The men exchanged glances again.

'You go,' Miro said. 'I should get back to work.'

'Is that OK?' Doc asked.

Careful, Comrade, there's graves under your feet. Thousands of years old.

'Sure.'

* * *

She followed Doc around the edge of the bog. They passed several crates full of mud and dirt. The smell of putrefaction was intense. Through the rushes, a kind of bunker emerged, made of metal. Coming closer, she saw it was a simple cuboid like an industrial container.

'This is home,' Doc said.

'Everything alright here? Feels like there was an argument.'

He made a sound like a laugh that didn't quite catch. 'The life of an archaeologist. We argue all night, but in the morning we're friends again. Miro's not bad. He's got a chip on his shoulder. You know the type.'

'Maybe.'

'Here.' He opened the door to the container, revealing a cluttered space, clothes hanging off the back of a few chairs. A smell of damp washing. 'Sorry about the mess. We weren't expecting visitors.' He hurried to a low table and tidied a few loose bits of paper.

'You sleep in here?'

'Not every night. There's a small town about forty minutes away, we rent rooms there. But sometimes we have to work late at the dig site. We've got sleeping bags for that. It's not like the West. There's no money for our work in Poland. Let me just heat some water.' He cleared a space on the table and set a portable stove. 'I'll catch a chill. Been in the bog all day.'

She watched him light the stove and set a pan of water on top. 'What do you do in that bog?'

'There's a Bronze Age burial site under our feet. Part of it was preserved in tar. Amazingly preserved, it's like time stopped. The Nazis flooded the site during the War. But the water protected it. Otherwise, it might have burned up like everything else.'

His voice changed, turned lyrical when he spoke about the dig. It was beguiling to listen to, and the topic was fascinating. A different world, as if Gdańsk did not exist. Seated in a folding chair, she started to feel comfortable, curious. But the paranoid part of her mind said he was playing for time. Water bubbled on the stove. It might be nice to live a life like this, out in the wilderness, digging. She noticed a woman's skirt draped over the empty chair across the table from her. Pulled out of the spell, she wondered where the other Miro was, and a sliver of fear worked through the cold draught. She was alone out here, and nobody back at the station knew where she was. Why did she do that? A part of her must want to drown in the bog. She could have brought another officer with her, but she was somehow glad to be alone, she was free.

'Is that Gosia's skirt?'

'What?' Doc showed his oversized teeth as he set down two empty mugs. 'Would you like to see the bog, Detective?'

'Maybe later. Can you call Gosia now?'

'Oh, of course. I forgot. I'll just make the tea…'

'I'll make it.' She grabbed the cups. 'You call her.'

His smile vanished. 'Right away.'

At the back of the room, he picked up a phone and set it on an upturned box. Anna watched him dial a number and set the receiver to his ear. He looked back and smiled weakly. The metal walls shivered in a passing gust. She glanced back over her shoulder through the open door and saw the rushes sway.

The silence was broken by Doc speaking into the phone. 'Oh hello, Comrade. It's Doc. Yeah … Right … No, not exactly. Listen, I can't talk now, I'm trying to get hold of Gosia … She there? … You haven't? … OK, I'll wait.'

Still holding the receiver against his ear, he nodded at Anna. 'Someone's just going to look for her. It's the office in Warsaw. We're based at the University.' He turned away. 'Hello? … Yes, Comrade … No … No, she's not here.

She left here two days ago … Yeah, two days ago … What? … No. She drove … No. She was on her own … No, we haven't heard anything … She was supposed to go straight to the office. You didn't…? … Are you sure?'

Anna watched closely as he screwed his eyes shut and rubbed his brow with his free hand. Was he acting? He seemed surprised by what he heard, but the best actors always seemed genuine, that's how you could tell they were actors. Real people don't react so smoothly, they tend to go numb.

'Thank you, Comrade … Yes, I will, of course … Goodbye.' He hung up the phone.

'She's not there?' Anna said.

'Nobody's seen her. Do you know something? Please. Gosia's precious to us.'

'A woman was found dead in Gdańsk. We don't know for sure it was her. The body hasn't been identified. I've only seen one picture of Gosia, in the newspaper, and it was black and white. I can't be sure. Do you have any other photographs?'

Doc stumbled out of the container, knocking over a stool. He seemed to no longer hear her voice. If he was acting, he was pushing it; he hadn't even noticed that the water was boiling over in the pan. Anna turned off the stove.

Outside, Doc staggered over the putrid ground. 'But why?' he shouted. 'How did she end up in Gdańsk? I don't understand.'

'Nobody's saying it's her. I need a photograph. Don't you have anything?'

'I…' Doc gazed around the surrounding emptiness. 'I guess…'

He seemed lost.

'Shall I make this tea?' Anna turned to the water. When she looked back for affirmation, there was only an empty square of blank sky. 'Doc?'

She jumped up and ran outside as he disappeared into the reeds. 'Hey! Stop!'

She set off running and slipped on the wet earth. She went sliding down the slope towards the bog and caught hold of the fibrous leaves of the rushes. The sound of splashing feet faded.

'Doc! Stop!'

Only the cawing of birds. The rushes were tall. She crawled out through the thick mud and couldn't see him, but the frightened crows took flight, dozens of them flapped their wings above the dig site.

'Doc! Where are you?'

She headed towards the portable huts at the bog's edge. As she got closer, a breeze ruffled through the reeds. She stopped and took out her gun. 'Anybody there?'

Something clattered inside the hut. She raised her weapon. 'Police! Come out now! Hands in the air.'

Another clatter. She stepped closer. The reeds sighed as the wind fell dead. All the crows settled down on the ground.

'Come out! I'm warning you…'

The door opened. Miro edged out sideways, his palms held out. 'What is it?'

'Where's Doc?'

'How should I know? You were with him. I'm just working on some diagrams.'

'He ran away.' Anna held the gun to his chest, keeping a few feet of distance. 'He just ran off into the reeds.'

'What? Why?'

'We rang your office back in Warsaw. Nobody's seen Gosia in days.'

'Oh shit.' Miro dropped his hands, causing her to flinch, but he only knelt in the ground with his head in his hands. 'Something happened to her, didn't it? That's why you're here. Is she dead?'

'Put your hands behind your back.' Anna inched closer and rounded him.

'Why? Why would anyone…? What happened? What happened to her?'

She took out a pair of handcuffs. 'I'm going to have to put these on you.'

'Gosia… she was gentle. She wasn't… why would…?'

The man didn't seem dangerous, kneeling in the dirt, rubbing his face. Anna pocketed her gun. She snapped the first cuff onto his wrist.

'What are you doing?'

'Don't move.' She took his other arm, forcing it as he started to resist, and got the other cuff in place. 'You're now a suspect in this case.'

'Why? What did I…?'

'I don't know, but you and your friend were the last to see her alive, and the only other suspect just took off running.'

'You don't think…?' The look on his face, like he smelled something awful.

'Why did Doc run?' she said.

'I don't know. He loved Gosia. They were engaged. They would've got married already, only this has been such a big job. There wasn't time to think. We've all been in over our heads. It's a huge operation and we have no funds. You can't think… really, you can't… it's impossible.'

'Innocent men don't run. Come on, get up.' She pulled him to his feet. He was scrawny but she sensed strength in him; he might give her problems if he tried to get away.

'What are you doing?' he said.

'We're going back to the container. Come on, start walking.' She kept a tight grip on the cuffs as she pushed him forwards. 'We'll use your phone to call the station in Gdańsk. I need help here.'

'Is this really necessary?' he said.

'There's three of you, only one of me.'

'Three? Who's the third?'

'The old guy. The engineer. Where's he now?'

'What old guy? We don't have an engineer.'

'What did you say?' She tugged on the cuffs a little too hard and felt him wince. But it felt good to make clear who was in charge. 'The engineer. I just spoke to him before I found you and Doc.'

'I'm telling you, we don't have any engineer. The only people working on this site the last few months are me, Doc, and… well… and Gosia.'

'Stop playing games. You'll be in a cell in Gdańsk tonight. Don't fuck with me.'

'I'm not–'

'Keep moving.' She kneed him in the back. 'You think because I'm a woman you can mess around? I've dealt with bigger men than you before, turned them to jelly. What, you don't believe me?'

The toughness was just an act; horror had turned her blood into ice. She had spoken to that weird old man about the runes and let him go. She was losing it. She wasn't thinking straight, something was wrong with her.

'I believe… I believe you.' Miro picked up speed; he really was afraid. 'I'm a scientist, not a criminal. I'm just trying to understand, that's all. If someone killed her…'

'Who said someone killed her?'

'You did, didn't you?'

'No.'

'So, she's… she's alive then?'

'I don't know. Where could Doc have gone? Is there anywhere nearby he might have headed?'

'Let me out of these things, I'll help you look for him.'

'Don't be stupid.'

They walked back to the container and Anna pushed him down onto the folding chair. 'Sit there a minute. I'm going to use your phone. Do I have to dial something? Enter a code or something?'

'It's just a phone. Just a regular, normal phone.'

'Good.' She picked up the receiver and called the office.

Through the telephone wires lined with crows, Sebastian answered drowsily. 'Gdańsk police headquarters…'

She felt relief to hear a familiar voice.

'It's Nowak.'

'Nowak? Where the hell are you? The boss is looking for you. He's been screaming the place down.'

'Listen, I'm at an archaeological dig.'

'At a *what*?'

The phone line buzzed with electric currents, ghost voices. A crow cried out hoarsely in the reeds.

'A dig, an archaeological dig. Can you hear me? Are you still there?'

'An archaeological what?'

'A dig. It's an ancient burial site.' She glanced over at Miro, but he didn't look like a man plotting his escape; he stared at the floor with dead eyes. A tear on one cheek dried and went cold in the draught.

'What the hell are you doing there?' Sebastian shouted in her ear.

'It's connected to the case.'

'The case? Zielinski was there?'

'No, the dead woman, the one from the tree.'

Miro looked up at that, something changed in his eyes. Another mistake.

Anna lowered her voice. 'I'll explain later. Look, I need backup. I've got three potential suspects here, and I'm on my own.'

'I… err…'

'Tree?' Miro said. 'What tree?'

'Comrade,' Sebastian shouted, 'you need to get back to Gdańsk. There's a new development. I don't know what's going on with that pharmacological dig, whatever, but that's not where you should be right now.'

'Sebastian, please, I don't have time for this. Can you put the superintendent on the line?'

'You don't want to speak to him like this, he's not in a good mood.'

'Just put him on.'

'Alright, hold–' The receiver buzzed.

She glanced at Miro.

'What's happening?' he said. 'What tree?'

'Nothing. Just sit there. Don't move.'

The receiver buzzed again. Roman's voice burst into her ear. 'Nowak! Where are you?'

'I'm at an archaeological site. I–'

'Goddammit, Nowak. Get back to Gdańsk now. Immediately.'

'I'm headed back, but I've got three suspects here. I'm on my own.'

'Suspects? Is this connected to Zielinski?'

'Well… potentially, we need to–'

'Let them go, Nowak.'

'What?'

'Let them go. Get in your car. Drive back here, right now. It's important. We've got a new suspect.'

'But, Superintendent, I have suspects here–'

'Take their goddamn names and addresses. You can go get them another time.'

'But, Superintendent–'

'Get back here, now, Comrade, or you're fired.' He hung up.

Nowak sat with the receiver against her ear listening to the fuzz. Somewhere outside, a crow screamed. For the first time, she noticed the sketch of a rune among the scraps of paper on the desk:

ᚠ

'What is that?' she said. 'I recognise it…' She grabbed the paper and held it up for Miro to see.

'What? Oh that. We found it carved in a tree by the bog. Gosia made a copy of it. It's the old Germanic rune meaning "wealth". But the carving isn't old, it's not part of the site. Someone put it there recently. I don't know why. Probably it was Doc, playing a trick on us. He's like that, when you get to know him.'

30

She drove back north as quickly as she could, stopping for fuel at a dilapidated gas station along the way. She'd had to free Miro, stunned, rubbing his wrists where the cuffs left a raw imprint. He'd written down his name and address for her, along with contact details and information for Doc and Gosia. He swore he didn't know anything about the supposed engineer. Well, it was something to go on, if Roman let her do her job, it might not be too late to follow the trail. But the rune… Roman wouldn't like it. Perhaps this woman, Gosia, would turn up just fine in Warsaw; Doc would meet her there, and the two archaeologists would get married as they'd planned.

Miro told her one more thing as she was leaving. Perhaps he wanted to show himself cooperative, perhaps he really was innocent. He said that Gosia had been working on a new theory at the dig site, based on some statuettes and carvings they'd recovered from the bog. Supposedly, she posited the existence of an ancient matriarchal society that had ruled these lands back in the Stone Age, before Bronze Age warriors from a patriarchal culture wiped that away and imposed a new regime, overwriting feminine gods with masculine ones, women's roles with men's.

None of that meant anything to Anna, but Miro said she could view the findings, if she liked; they had recovered some curious statuettes of goddesses. He'd also added one more thing, that Doc didn't like his fiancée's new theories, they'd argued about it. The first falling-out between them in all the years they'd worked together. Why did Miro tell her that? Was he trying to exonerate himself? Casting a shadow of guilt over Doc, just the hint of a motive?

Anna drove. She let the oppressive presence of the bog recede, as she followed the new communist-built highway north towards the coast, but something of the tar's darkness remained at the back of her thoughts. The black depths, sludge, a hidden world beneath a surface, still as glass. Crows lined the telephone wires along the side of the road. She turned the radio on but couldn't find a station. She drifted into a tense daydream while she drove, with visions of the ash tree, the hung woman, floating over a dark mirror. She didn't notice the black car until it had been following her for a few minutes. Only when it came too close, she sat up in her seat and realised she'd been listening to a white noise of radio static. The cars almost touched fenders. She stared into the rear-view and caught the light off a tinted windscreen, a sky of thick cloud in tumult reflected.

She pressed the accelerator and pulled away. The car behind didn't pick up speed, it grew smaller in the back window until it was just a dot. Perhaps it was nothing. How many black cars existed in Poland? All at once, the radio burst into life: a marching band playing socialist music, one of the anthems of threshers at harvest that Stalin had loved. She felt her jaw go rigid. She didn't want to arrive in Gdańsk, she only wanted to drive and drive and disappear. There was no longer any car in the mirror. She turned the radio off.

* * *

An hour later, Anna pulled into the police station carpark. The afternoon was dying beneath a sky that writhed with cloud. It would rain soon; she already felt the breath of drizzle on her face. A sign on the front entrance of the HQ said: "CLOSED FOR MAINTENANCE". Downstairs, the reception area was empty; everybody must be out hunting for Zielinski's killer, or else mourning. Sebastian was seated at the front desk. He put down a newspaper, seeing her enter.

'Where have you been, Comrade?'

'I was chasing up that dead woman, from the tree.'

'But, Zielinski… he was your partner. Don't you think you should help with that?'

'The two cases are connected.'

He blinked. 'How?'

Behind him, Roman appeared at the rear doors leading into the building proper. 'Nowak. Where the hell…?'

'Superintendent. I was just telling Sebastian–'

'Come with me. They're waiting for you in the interview room.'

'Who?'

He disappeared into the shadow. She hurried after him.

* * *

In interview room 3, Anna sat on the other side of the table; usually she was the one asking the questions, now she had to answer. Opposite, the Inspector wore a silver-grey suit. She wasn't told his name.

'What's this about?' Anna said.

'Wait.' The Inspector was tall and thin, his skin stretched tight over high cheekbones. He set a briefcase on the table and took out some files, a pen and notepaper. He stated the date and location in a dry, factual voice.

'Where did you go today?' he said.

She stared at the blank page of his notepad, thoughts scattered and confused, until the Inspector repeated his question in the same level, neutral voice.

'I was at an archaeological dig, south of here. It was flooded during the War, but now…'

'I know the site.' He made a note. 'Why did you go there?'

'Am I under investigation?'

'Just answer the question.'

She peered at the file but only caught a glimpse of her name upside down before he picked it up and tilted the page towards him.

'I was looking into a murder case. A woman was found dead a few days ago, hanging from a tree outside the city. She–'

'I have that file as well.' He took another file out of the briefcase and opened it. 'A prostitute was found murdered. No identification. Body unclaimed. Case tagged for clearance and archiving.'

'I identified her.'

He looked up from the file. 'You were supposed to be working the Zielinski case.' His voice lost its neutral tone, something vindictive poked through, a higher pitch, nasal.

There were two kinds of person you might meet on the other side of the table in a room like this: the kind who were practical, to whom you might appeal; and the kind who were sticklers, inflexible, ruthless. This man was the latter. Nobody got to be an internal investigator of the police otherwise.

She tried. 'There was a certain resemblance between the two deaths, between the woman's and Zielinski's, that is.'

'A certain resemblance. Please specify.'

'A kind of symbol.'

He flicked through the file. 'There's no mention here of any symbol.'

She hesitated a fraction too long. 'It was felt to be tangential, not important enough to include in the file.'

'Who made that decision?'

She couldn't tell the truth; Roman would make a dangerous enemy. 'I did.'

The Inspector made a note. Whatever he'd written, it elicited a shake of the head and a tut. 'Tell me more…'

'It would be quicker and easier if I just explained about the dead woman.' She raised her voice and spoke quickly before he could interrupt. 'I identified her today. Her name was Gosia Svoboda. She was working on an archaeological dig–'

'And how did she end up hanging from a tree outside Gdańsk?'

'There are three suspects on the loose right now. I was forced to abandon pursuit and come back here for this interview. If we stop wasting time, we can catch up with them. If we leave it much longer, we might never see them again. They'll try to get to the West.'

'Detective, your judgement seems clouded by emotion.' The Inspector smiled, showing sharp incisors. He had won.

Anna's anger shrivelled. 'I only want to do my duty.'

'Your duty is to follow orders, not to go off running around the country by yourself. These men you speak of will be apprehended. Our borders are well guarded. They won't escape. Our security is tight, they'll be swept up. Do you have names and addresses?'

'Yes.' She reached into her pocket and took out the slip of paper where Miro had jotted down their contact details.

'Give it to me.' The Inspector reached out a bony hand of long fingers, stained with ink.

'This is my case. It's my responsibility to catch them.'

'Not anymore.' His beady eyes glittered.

She didn't resist when he rose in his chair and plucked the scrap of paper from her hand. He glanced at it and put it in his briefcase. 'These men will be apprehended immediately. We'll deal with it from here on. Don't worry, your case is being transferred to the best possible hands.'

'And what about me?'

He held her eyes as he shook his head. 'You'll be remanded into custody. You are now our number one suspect in this investigation.'

'What?' The words made no sense.

'Your behaviour has aroused suspicion. This isn't the first time, Detective. We've had an eye on you for a while. After reports of irregularities in this case came to light, we had no choice but to search your apartment. There, regrettably, we found a hidden space containing illegal drugs, prohibited literature, various contraband items. I won't list them, since you already know. All of this might have been explained away, but we also found something far more consequential.'

'But… I don't understand. My record on the police force, and in the Party, is impeccable. There was no justification–'

'We found this.' He put on a pair of gloves and set an evidence bag on the table. He pulled out the old book of runes.

'Oh. That's what this is about. I can explain–'

'How long have you been engaged in fascist ideology?'

'In what?'

'Detective Anna Nowak, you are accused of fostering a Nazi plan to bring about an uprising in Gdańsk, with a view to attaching the city to Germany. You killed your partner, Zielinski, when he found out about it.'

'That's laughable.'

'You are now under arrest and will be taken to a secure compound. This interrogation will be continued within the confines of a prison facility.'

He closed his file.

31

Danzig, the Free City

One day before the start of WWII

The forensics lab was locked. I stood in the rain and peered through the glass. Lights were on inside, but nobody came when I knocked. Bernie's autopsy would be taking place. I banged against the wet glass and screamed but it was like I didn't exist. When I looked down, the birth certificate was scrunched in my fist; proof that last night wasn't just a dream. A baby girl was lost somewhere in the city's pathways. The circular stain of a wine glass marked the corner like Bernie's last message to the world. I put it away and ran across the street. I needed to hand this over to Henrik and be divested of the responsibility before anyone else died. I'd done all I could. Let someone else bear the guilt.

The entrance to the police station was shut. A line of downtrodden citizens huddled under umbrellas against the wall outside.

'Excuse me.' I pushed through them. Overalls and dungarees, shabby suits that didn't fit, they smelled of herrings and stale beer.

'Why won't they open?' a woman said.

'If you'll let me through…' I reached the door to find it locked. 'This isn't normal.'

'Been knocking for an hour.' The old man held a small, frightened girl by the hand. 'Nobody answers. Came to see about my son. He was dragged into a police car last night. No explanation. Nobody will speak to me. You're police, are you? Help us.'

I banged on the door and shouted. 'Hey! Open up. It's Tal.'

'You're police?' A woman tugged at my elbow. 'It's about our janitor. Disappeared. Nobody's seen him in days.'

A slot in the door opened, and Granma looked out. 'Tal. What are you doing in the rain?'

'Let me in.'

She blew out cigarette smoke through the slot. 'I'm not supposed to.'

'Why? Come on. It's urgent.'

'And let all those tramps inside? We'll be swamped.'

Behind my back, the old man shouted. 'Where's my son? Is he in there? You can't keep us out forever.'

'And what about our janitor?' the woman yelled.

'I need to speak to Henrik.' I pulled at the door handle, but it rattled uselessly in my fist.

Barely audible over the shouts, Granma said, 'Henrik's gone.'

'What did you say?'

'He's been suspended. Schechter's in charge now.'

'I don't understand.'

The old man shouted right in my ear. 'Let me in! I want to talk to my son.'

Granma breathed out smoke. 'You should go home, Tal. This isn't your shift. You look like shit. Get some sleep.'

'Let me in a minute. It's pouring down out here.'

She took a drag and considered. 'They'll all rush in…'

'Too right we will.' An angry woman jostled me out of the way.

'Just open,' I said, 'it's urgent. I'll deal with these others.'

* * *

Upstairs, the briefing room was crowded, no space to sit down among the packed, tense officers. Sweat patches stuck to their armpits and the backs of their uniforms. The walls tightened. I leaned in the doorway and peered over the pressed shoulders of Lang and Reiner.

'What's going on?' I whispered.

Lang glanced back. 'Police work. Shut up.'

'Stop talking at the back.' Schechter, the deputy superintendent, stood in front of a map of Danzig and a blackboard covered in chalk scrawl. 'You've been called here for a reason. I know you're angry…'

'Where's Henrik?' I whispered.

'Gone,' Lang said.

'Shush!' Reiner gave me a shove. 'We're listening.'

Others glared back in my direction. Schechter stopped talking. The heat was unbearable. 'Tal. This isn't your shift.' Overweight in his tight black suit, he dabbed sweat from his wrinkled forehead.

'Yeah, I…' My voice cracked, the tight bodies, all those faces staring. I was singled out in the crowd. 'I just… I came in early to speak to Henrik. I saw everyone was in here…'

'Henrik's on leave,' Schechter said.

'Why?'

'Two cops dead in forty-eight hours. The Council wants answers. I've been put in charge. We'll do things my way now. Keep quiet back there or get out. Now, everybody, listen up…'

The others turned to face the front, and it was a relief to escape their gaze. All I wanted was to get out of there, the smell of boots, the grinding of their teeth. Fear and anger. Two cops dead. A hostile city. Downstairs, a mob of complaining citizens filled the waiting benches and shouted to be heard. I couldn't escape, I needed to see what would happen on that coloured map of the city.

'It's a new Force,' Schechter said. 'Unity is our watchword.'

'Unity's well and good,' Reiner shouted. 'Two officers are dead. What are you going to do about it?'

The others muttered. The air was dry, too many sets of lungs sucked the same oxygen. The windows shut, curtains drawn, I felt sweat condensing on the ceiling. This room was going to burst. The look on Schechter's face was hateful, but it was me he stared at, not the others who murmured and threw up their hands.

'Quiet down!' He banged on the table. 'We have a plan. Roman has been working these last months on an undercover operation. His team has pinpointed the main dissident groups in the city. He's the expert. He'll talk you through the targets.'

Schechter stepped back from the blackboard as the whispers died, and Roman came forward into the circle of eyes. I felt the strained muscles, taut necks, the veins of their temples, beaded with perspiration, the anxious faces that could not stop searching around the room.

'Brothers.' Roman rubbed his hands, encased in leather gloves. Tall and angular, a hooked nose and shining eyes. In the canteen they said he was handsome, but I never understood the canteen. 'Let's come together now. You want answers, and I'll give them to you.'

Nobody said anything. They waited for him to speak.

'We're being eaten from the inside. Look here.' He pointed on the map. 'There are four centres of dissident activity in Danzig. Polish nationalist groups are based around the harbour. Communist organisations work at the shipyards. Intellectual enemies hide in plain sight in the University and the surrounding district.' As he spoke, his gloved, pointing gestures moved quickly like stabs. Daria's cafe was right beneath his finger.

'There are other criminal elements in Old Scotland and the poorer, working-class districts,' he continued, 'but these are disorganised and mostly weak in ideology. The city is full to the brim with enemies. We're at the verge of collapse. For a long time now, I've been calling for a stronger hand. Finally, with Herr Schechter in charge, and a Nazi Party majority in the city council, we have the necessary leadership.'

'So what?' Lang said. 'What are you going to actually do?'

Roman restrained a grimace. 'I've drawn up four action groups. Each will take a segment on the map. You'll receive a list of internal enemies. We'll drag some suspects in here, show them the pictures of Gerhard and Bernie, see what they have to say.'

'They won't say anything,' Lang shouted. 'They never do.'

Roman grinned. 'It's a war footing now. Normal rules don't apply. If anybody gets hurt… so be it. Extreme measures are in place. Do what you have to do, just find the culprits.'

The room went silent as this idea fumed in the fraught air between us. Their eyes widened, seeing the possibilities, wondering. I couldn't listen to any more of it. The end – when it comes, it comes so fast. Nobody can be prepared, no matter how hard they try.

* * *

I ran upstairs to Henrik's office, but his room was empty. I glanced around the shelves and checked in a few drawers. Nothing. All of Henrik's things had been removed already. My last ally on the Force. The old brick building shuddered as Schechter's meeting broke up and the stairways clattered with boots. I closed Henrik's door quietly and crept across the landing to my office, fearful of meeting another person.

I found the number for Daria's cafe. It rang out several times before a woman answered in Polish. 'We're busy. Call back later.'

For a moment I was caught between languages, I couldn't find a word to say.

'Did you hear what I said?' She was about to hang up.

I managed to find the Polish word. 'Wait.'

'The rush is just starting. Have you any idea–'

'Is Daria there? I need to speak to her.'

'You never worked in a cafe, I'm guessing.'

'It's urgent. I'm police.'

She hesitated. 'Is that Herr Tal?'

'How did you know?'

'Daria told me before, if a policeman, a Herr Tal, ever called, she's busy.'

'I just need–'

'Sorry, pal. You missed your chance. Daria always wanted to have children, she can't have them with a man like you. If you care about her at all, leave her alone. Let her go.'

'She wanted to have children?' I shook the idea away. 'It's not about that. Listen, there's a police operation. They're sweeping through all the Polish centres. It isn't safe. Tell Daria, and anyone else who's Polish: stay home. Don't go outside.'

The woman's laughter played distorted down the wire. 'Stay off work? Are you crazy? In this economy? What are we supposed to eat?'

'Certain Polish writers frequent your cafe. It's in the line of fire. You should–'

The line went dead.

32

Downstairs, a growing crowd filled the waiting benches and blocked the front desk. They demanded to know where their children, janitors, and teachers were; who was going to pay for their ruined businesses, their smashed windows; who was going to clean up the mess.

'How did they all get in?' Lang said.

Granma shrugged. 'It was Tal. I tried to tell him.'

'Tal…?'

I pushed through the crowd and squeezed out of the station. The carpark was almost empty, most of the squad cars had been taken. They'd be coasting through the streets now, intent on violence. I climbed into my car and didn't notice anybody inside until I put the key in the ignition.

'Where'd everybody go?' The intern kid, skinny and withdrawn in the corner of the passenger seat, stared out of the window into the rain tracks.

'Jesus. You almost gave me a heart attack. What are you doing in here?'

He sighed but said nothing.

'Get out. You can't come with me.' I took my hand away from the key.

'I'll just sit quiet. I won't say anything.'

'I'm on a case. It's dangerous.'

'I'll stay in the car. I won't get in the way.' He didn't look at me, just stared through the rain that pattered on the passenger seat window. He seemed to have shrivelled overnight, becoming even younger, so that the blue-green police uniform hardly fit him.

'I'm sorry, kid. I'm sorry you got caught up in that crime scene. It's my fault, I should never have taken you. But I can't have you in the car. It's too dangerous. I can't look after anybody else. I can hardly take care of myself.'

'I don't want to stay in the station. They're all talking about murder. They want to find some Poles and hurt them.'

'I'll drive you home. You can stay indoors until this blows over.'

'I don't want to go home. I can't stand to be in the house on my own.'

'There's no other option.'

'I hate my dad.'

'That's what dads are for.'

He turned to look at me and his eyes were ancient in his fresh, youthful face. 'I'll just sit quiet in the car. You won't know I'm here. I won't do a thing. You don't have to worry about me or take care of me. Just drive.'

* * *

The kid was as good as his word; he didn't say a thing, just stared out of the window as I drove over to the newsroom of the *Danziger Neueste Nachrichten*. He was like a ghost in the car, I felt haunted. I found myself talking to him just to fill the silence.

'That newspaper you found was useful. You did good.'

He didn't respond or move. I kept talking, trying to encourage him, like an idiot. 'I'm going to see if those journalists can tell me anything about the amber dealer and his wife, their child.'

Nothing.

'One thing you'll learn on this job, relations with the press are complex. Over time, you come to know which journalists you can trust. Don't try to ignore them. That's a mistake some cops make; they think they don't need the newspapers. Actually, a good detective keeps a healthy, careful balance.'

I'd never been a father, never wanted to be one; I wouldn't inflict the failures on another child that my own father's absence worked on me. Yet here I was, talking to this hostile youth like some hopeless parent, offering advice and wisdom while he stared away and only resented.

'Journalists have sources and information. It's funny, sometimes they solve a crime quicker than police. Folks are more willing to talk to a journalist than to us. We're not trusted. But on the other hand, if you go to the press for help, you have to be careful, it cuts two ways. They expect favours. They want tips. If you make a mistake, let out one loose word, you can ruin a case. Once certain things get out into public knowledge, you never get them back.'

No response. The windscreen wiper flicked in the rain, and I kept on talking. 'I was in the newspaper myself, last week.'

Did I imagine I was going to impress him? He seemed to have fallen asleep against the window.

'But the journalist wrote the story all wrong. Stupid writer said I cracked "the case of the year". I told him not to put that in, it looks arrogant. This is the kind of thing that makes the others at the station despise me.'

The kid didn't speak, but he reached out to the radio. His shy eyes brushed mine – just a hint of asking for permission – then glanced away as he turned the dial. Static broke out, and a news report. He let it play. We drove the rest of the way without talking.

As soon as I turned the corner and saw the newspaper offices, I knew the poison had got there already. The front windows and entrance were smashed, the newspaper's name above the door was torn down. Groups of people stood in the rain, smoking, surveying the damage. Despair is like that; you stop taking care, you don't use an umbrella. In the end, you don't feel the rain at all.

'Stay in the car,' I told the kid.

He shrugged.

'Alright, good.' I jumped out into a downpour.

Under the torn awning, a woman and two men in raincoats smoked and stared with glassy eyes. Drops of water hung from the ends of their hair.

'What happened here?' I asked.

The woman exhaled smoke in my face. 'Oh great, another one.'

'We've nothing to say to police.' The man wore tinted glasses, his silver hair was receding. He was the subeditor; I'd spoken with him before, but he showed no sign of recognising me.

'Why not?'

They affected a laugh, but the sound was like hopelessness.

I wiped rain from my brow. 'Hey, you know me, remember? I was here just last week.'

He peered through his glasses. 'Oh, it's you.' He didn't sound glad.

'Tell me what happened.'

'See for yourself.'

I pushed past them and entered the building. It was shadowy, the lights were all smashed. Broken glass littered among spilled paper and ink, trashed fixtures, fittings pulled down and trampled. Further inside, the printing equipment lay ruined on the ground. I smelled blood. Some drunken hand had spelled out on the wall in red paint, "JEWS DIE". I couldn't look at it. A few lonely figures moved among the wreckage picking things up.

I approached a man on his knees brushing glass into a bucket. He wore a loose bandage over the side of his head.

'What happened?'

He didn't look up. 'They broke in here last night. Destroyed everything. Beat up anyone who got in their way.'

'Why?'

'Violence is violence, it doesn't stop to explain itself.'

'But who were they?'

He picked himself up. 'I know who you are. You're the detective. We published a story about you. You cracked "the case of the year".'

'Journalists exaggerate.'

The journalist wiped a tear from his cheek. 'What do you want? The police already came this morning, said there's nothing they can do. No evidence. No suspects. Maria reckons it was police who did it.'

'Did you get the names of the officers? I'll have better ones sent over.'

'Don't bother.' A woman's voice. 'There's no difference between law and crime now.'

I turned and recognised Maria, who took my picture for the stupid newspaper story, "the case of the year".

'You're the photographer–'

'*Was*. They smashed all the cameras too.'

'Maybe you can help me.' I took out the copy of the newspaper that had been folded and refolded so many times now sections of text were illegible along the creases. 'Did you take this picture?'

She glanced at it with disdain. 'That depends. Are you looking for trouble?'

'No trouble. I just need…' I took out the wedding ring with the inlaid amber. 'This ring. It was lost. Did the woman have one like this?'

She took the ring from me. 'Sure, it could be. I don't remember. It's a ring. Who cares? Look around. We have bigger problems.'

'You took the picture then–'

'I take a lot of pictures.'

'And the baby…?'

Maria's face changed. 'Oh, she was a sweetheart. Prettiest baby you ever saw, and never cried once. That's not normal. Try taking pictures of people's kids, they can't stay still. Wait.' She frowned. 'Did something happen? Are they OK? If anything happened to that baby…'

'I don't know. I'm looking for information.'

'They were rich folks, I'm poor; never figured I'd see them again.'

'And this…' I gestured across the wreckage, the splintered machinery, the shattered glass, loose paper everywhere. 'Why?'

She scoffed. 'Like you don't know. You're part of it, aren't you?'

'It's alright,' the journalist said. 'I heard about Tal. He's one of the good ones.'

She closed one eye and scanned my face, as if for a picture. 'The man who cracked the "case of the year". If you're so smart, how come you don't know anything?'

'Honestly,' I said, 'sometimes I feel like the dumbest man in Danzig.'

She studied my eyes and didn't find what she wanted. 'The days when the press and police could work together are over. You're part of the evil. You make me sick.'

It's not easy to be hated. I've grown used to it, my brain ceases to resist; I can no longer look in the mirror without seeing the root of hatred, and hating it myself.

'Please.' All I could do was beg. 'I want to help. Let me prove it to you.'

'Get out of here before I throw up.'

'Maria,' the journalist said, 'I think you should show him.'

'Shut your mouth.' The look on her face was poisonous.

'Show me what?'

'What else can we do with it?' he said. 'It's worthless now. We can't print it. Nobody else will touch it. There's nothing to do. Maybe Tal–'

'What is it?' I said. 'Let me help. I'll do anything in my power.'

She brushed a grit of glass from her sleeve. 'Whatever. Nothing matters anyway.'

I followed her down a set of stairs stained with blood into a basement. Open doors showed ruined machinery and paper everywhere. Quiet figures swept up the trash. At the end of the corridor, we entered a development room. Maria turned on the light, revealing shelves torn down, broken cameras. The tiles were slippery with spilled development fluid.

'Breaks my heart,' she said.

'I'm sorry about it.'

'Sure you are. Look.' She pulled out the bottom drawer of a filing cabinet on the floor. 'They didn't find everything.' She held a roll of film to the light. 'It's not much.'

As I watched, she unwound the spiral of negatives slowly beneath the bulb. I leaned closer, squinting. Every frame seemed the same: a man in a window. Dozens of images the same or similar flashed past as she unspooled the coil. A window. Over and over, a window. A man looked out through the glass. A man turned to talk to somebody inside. Was it the same man? Young, handsome, short hair. Sometimes he looked different, darker, taller. Sometimes there were two men or three in the window, but they all looked alike.

'I don't understand.'

'Keep looking.'

She kept unrolling the film, showing these same variations of man and window. But it wasn't quite the same: sometimes the window was different, this one was beneath a roof, this one was beside a tree. Sometimes it looked like a different building, sometimes a different day, as the angles of shadow shifted, but always a man or two men in the window.

'Who are they? Where...?'

'This is the Hotel Astoria. I photographed every window over the course of a week.'

'And?'

'Every window, Detective.'

All my life I've solved crimes, or so it feels, so lost in the job that I searched in my dreams for clues that didn't exist, groped after solutions to crimes that hadn't happened yet; but I couldn't understand what she wanted to show me.

Maria smiled at my confusion. 'Every room of that hotel is filled with these men.'

'But who… I don't…'

I closed my eyes. The darkness was permeated with the inky smell of development fluid. 'They're soldiers, aren't they?'

'A whole platoon of German soldiers just living in a hotel. They never leave. Nobody knows they're there.'

'Germany isn't allowed to have soldiers on Danzig territory…'

'There's more, but the rest of the photos were confiscated by your colleagues.'

'More hotels?'

'Not just hotels. There are ships in the harbour crammed with soldiers. They're waiting there. God knows how long they've been living in those boats. They never come out. It wasn't easy to get the pictures. I had to smuggle my camera into the harbour. I found a vantage point, hidden, where I could snap them. But somebody must've seen me. It doesn't matter anymore. They've destroyed everything.'

'Maybe I could help. I could find out where your pictures are being kept.'

'They'll be burnt up by now. Anyway, forget it. Even if we had them, the newspaper couldn't print them. Wouldn't dare. The owners and editors all received death threats. Not just for themselves, for their children as well. They are terrified to print anything.'

'You're saying there's a secret German army in the city, and nobody knows? You won't print it? That's the scoop of the century. Your paper would be legendary.'

'Our paper's dead.'

33

I climbed into the car and just sat motionless, silent. A drop of rainwater faded on my tongue. After a few moments, the intern kid turned from the window and noticed me.

'What's that?' He pointed to the roll of camera film in my fist.

'It's… It's… Nothing.'

He turned back to his window, apparently satisfied with this answer. I stuffed the film in my pocket and started the car.

'Where are we going?'

'None of your business.' I pulled out from the kerb and set off a little too fast, a little out of control, and was glad when he didn't ask anything else.

But when we turned onto the main road, he glanced back at me. 'Did you really believe it, about spring?'

'About spring?'

'What you said.'

'I don't know. What did I say?'

'How it comes around.' His voice was toneless, cheerless.

'Sure. That's what spring does.'

'But for us, I mean, not just for some other people.'

'Spring doesn't come around for anybody in particular. It comes around for itself, that's all. I admire that.'

'Oh.'

I waited for a follow-up question, but he didn't say anything. I felt his doubt. We drove through the rain.

* * *

Parked outside Henrik's house, I told the kid to wait in the car. He grunted. Good enough. I ran up the driveway and banged on Henrik's door. Rain streamed from the gutters.

'Please open. Please open.'

The water dripped down my face; I'd left the umbrella in the car.

The door opened and Henrik looked out. His eyes were bleary, hungover. 'Tal. What the hell? Didn't you hear? I'm not your boss anymore.'

From the hall behind him, Henrik's wife called, 'Who's that?'

'It's just Tal. Come to say goodbye.'

'Don't stand in the rain,' she shouted. I heard her footsteps recede along the old floorboards.

'What difference does it make?' Henrik growled. Unshaven, wearing a pair of crumpled pyjamas, I hardly recognised him.

'What happened to you?' I said.

He held up a finger and nodded back into the space where his wife's feet retreated. We waited for her to disappear. In the silence, the patter of the rain intensified.

'What happened to me? What else… Danzig.' He sighed and his breath stunk of vodka. 'I knew it would happen; I just didn't think it would come so fast. The new war is about to erupt. It could be tonight. It might have already started.'

I couldn't bear to smell him, to see him so dejected. Divested of his job and status, how quickly he became a slob, a kind of baby. He was pitiable. Looking over his shoulder, I saw a pile of suitcases in the landing. 'You going somewhere?'

'What? Oh, yeah. I'll try at least. Look.' He reached behind the door and pulled his wallet out of a coat pocket hanging back there. From a wad of bills and notes, he produced two slips of paper. 'These are the last tickets out of Danzig. The ship leaves tonight. It's the *Humboldt*.'

I glanced at the tickets. 'To New York. You're sailing to New York.'

'It's the last chance. Every berth on every boat leaving Danzig is fully booked. Tal, listen, you have to get out. They've got lists of internal enemies. Your name is written there, I saw it. When the war starts, they'll round up these people first. They want to make everything as smooth as possible for when Hitler arrives. For their victory parade.'

'I can't leave Danzig. Where would I go?'

'Anywhere. There's no alternative.'

'What if there was. What if there was an alternative?'

'Like what?'

I took out the roll of film. 'I got this from a journalist. The Nazis smashed up their presses, destroyed everything, but they didn't get this.'

'What the hell?' Henrik squinted at the roll as if he'd never seen such a thing.

'Henrik. This is hard evidence of a secret Nazi army hidden in Danzig. They've got soldiers stashed in hotels, hidden on boats in the harbour. They're just waiting for the signal.' I held the roll out to him. 'Take it. Look.'

He pushed my hand away. 'A secret army. All the more reason to keep your head down. Stay quiet. Get out as soon as you can.'

'You already knew.'

'I heard things, sure, but I stopped paying attention long ago.'

'Henrik. If we could get this to the League of Nations, they might be able to step in before it's too late. They could disarm these soldiers before the war starts.'

'There's no time. And who'd listen?'

'They'd listen to you. You have authority in this city, you still do. You've been superintendent for decades. They can't just push you out. If you take this to the League of Nations offices, or to the American embassy – I don't know, somewhere – they'd listen to you. They could take action now, avert a new world war before it starts.'

He stared at my trembling hand in the rain but made no move to take the film. 'I've got a ship to catch.'

'There's time. You can still catch your ship. Please, just take the film. Make some phone calls. Somebody you trust, an ambassador or some other foreign representative. Please, Henrik, I'm begging you. For the sake of this job, we spent our lives doing this; trying to keep Danzig safe. Wasn't that the point? Everything's going to burn. Everyone will die.'

He stared at the film through a curtain of rain. Blinked his eyes. His hand moved, hesitant, he took the film and just weighed it. His eyes were curious, he seemed to find it light. That such objects could exist… 'Tal, you're a pain in the ass. I'll make a phone call, but I won't promise anything.'

'Thank you, Henrik. Thank you.'

'It won't make any difference,' he said. 'Schechter's in charge now. Police are already out securing the city. Rounding up their enemies, dragging innocent people in. Nothing can stop them.'

'I can.'

'You?' A trace of the old Henrik showed in his face as he stared. 'And how?'

'I'll find the cop killer they're looking for. I'll solve the case. I'll calm everything down.'

From the hall, Henrik's wife called again. 'Why are you standing out there? Can't you see it's raining?'

'Goodbye, Tal. You served Danzig as best you could.' He slammed the door in my face.

34

Driving away from Henrik's house, the intern kid shifted in his seat. 'What happened to the superintendent? He looks homeless.'

'Politics. Danzig.'

'It's starting already, isn't it?'

'What's starting?' I rubbed the blur from my eyes, they'd drunk Henrik's bleary stupor. I tried to concentrate on driving.

'Do you really think you can stop it?'

'I'm going to find the cop killer. It might calm things down a little, at least for now.'

'But... where? How?' He sat up in his seat, showing interest for the first time. 'Is that where we're going?'

'There's something I have to take care of first.' My tone was cold; it was too late for him to find enthusiasm for this job. In a different city, perhaps I could've guided him, perhaps he could've really become a good policeman. Nothing turned out good anymore. It was too late for fresh starts.

* * *

I parked up across the street from Daria's cafe. The intern kid started to get out of the car, but I pushed down the lock on his door.

'You stay in here. Don't move. Don't make a sound.'

'But...'

'I'll only be a minute. Put the radio on if you want.'

The rain pattered on the roof of the car as I climbed out into a puddle by the kerb. The light dwindled in the west; candles were lit in the cafe. Tracks of rain distorted the window. I straightened my collar, brushed back my wet hair, and went inside. The door jingled into a dead silence. Wide eyes at every table stared and held me in the doorway beneath the bell. Roman stood in the middle of the room, flanked by Lang and Reiner. He stopped speaking. A half-finished sentence died in the strained hush. I looked around for Daria and spotted her pressed against the wall at the back of the cafe. All the things I'd dreamed of saying to her, and now I could only stare. Horror on her face. This was all wrong.

Roman stepped backwards. 'What are you doing here, Tal? Get out. This isn't your beat.'

'I was passing through. What's going on? Is there a problem?'

'You know what's going on. We're hunting a cop killer.' His leather boots creaked.

The glances of Lang and Reiner darted from my face to Roman's and wondered who was stronger. They hunched behind him.

'In here?' I glanced around the tables where the stunned customers still held knives and forks in their hands, afraid to make a sound. 'I know this cafe. It's a peaceful place.'

'Maybe you don't know it so well. Maybe you don't know Danzig like you think.'

'Roman, can we talk a moment? Outside. Let's all be calm. I've got a big lead in the case. If we work together, we can find the killer now. Today.'

'What lead?' His eyes darted around the space of paralysed faces, thinking, calculating the risks. But these folks were mostly elderly and malnourished, they ate tinned herring and drank tea.

I kept my voice calm, but it was too loud in the quiet. 'I'll show you. But not in here.'

'Funny thing about that, Tal, I don't think you have a lead. I think you're cooperating with the Poles; you want to distract us. You're trying to buy time.'

'Look at these people.' I gestured to the nearest table. 'This man's ninety years old if he's a day. He's no threat to anyone. Leave them in peace. Let's you and I go outside and put our heads together. We can solve this case. We'll have the culprit in custody before night.'

I glanced and tried to meet Daria's eye, to reassure her, but she wouldn't look at me. She thought I was part of this, she hated me, and she was right. To look away from Roman was a mistake, it showed weakness.

He grinned. 'You think I need your help? What, because you solved "the case of the year"? I've been just fine without you.'

'Even so.'

'Get out of here, Tal. I won't warn you again.'

'I can't do that.'

Doubt showed in Lang's face, behind Roman's shoulder. If I could hold out, the tension would drain away. But Roman's grin only faltered for a moment.

'Take a seat then, Tal, and watch. But stay out of this. If you make a move, I'll arrest you too. Police corruption, conspiring with dissidents.'

'What dissidents?' My voice faltered, I was losing the struggle.

The wonky table closest to me rattled against the floor as the old man quaked in his chair. I smelled vinegar – pickled onions on his plate. The embroidered tablecloth was like a relic from some folklore world, white with delicate red and green floral patterns.

'That's what I was about to find before you blundered in. I was just explaining to everybody assembled: I'm not leaving without a suspect. They can surrender the dissident to me, or I'll take someone else in their place.'

'That's laughable.'

'Shut your goddamn mouth, Tal.' He unholstered his pistol and raised it in the air. 'Enough games. Who's the dissident?'

Gasps broke the air that trembled with rain against the window. An old lady let out a scream through her fingers. At that sound, the spell was broken. The tables and cutlery shook – frightened faces, the patrons cowered back.

'Come on, Roman' – I raised my hands in a passive stance – 'put the gun down.'

He spun the pistol around to face me. 'Stay out of this. Final warning. You think you're safe because you're a cop, but there's a list with your name on it. Nobody will protect you.'

'There's no need for the gun. Put it down.'

'You two!' he shouted at Lang and Reiner who snapped to attention. 'Grab those men, at the corner table. They're Polish nationalists, anyone can tell. They're coming with us. If nobody wants to talk here, we'll make them. Nobody leaves this cafe until we have a name.'

Hardly aware of what I was doing, I pulled out my pistol and raised it to Roman's head. 'That's enough. Put your weapon down. Let's end this.'

'Finally.' He pressed the end of his gun into my chest, a wild smile on his face; this was what he wanted all along.

Customers ducked beneath the tables, somebody screamed, Daria and the other waitresses huddled together against the wall. She stared as if she'd never seen me before. The gun shivered in my hand; I needed all the force I had left just to hold it steady. Roman gripped his weapon in both hands, one eye closed, his sharp teeth gritted.

'Are we going all the way?' He might have been talking to himself.

Lang and Reiner drew their pistols as well, but kept them down, uncertain.

'If we must.'

'Back down!' Roman shouted. 'Back down!' The veins on his neck bulged like roots.

'No.'

'Back down.' The hard point of his gun pushed over my heart while I held his face in my sight and wouldn't blink.

'No.'

Silence stretched to breaking point and in that strangling despair, the door opened. The bell jingled, an absurd sound, trivial, innocent. Afraid to take my eyes away from Roman, I darted a glance over to see the intern kid standing in the rain at the open door.

'Please.' He trembled like he was freezing to death, arms hugged across his chest. He seemed to have shrunk even further so that the police uniform hung baggy from his limbs. His face was pale, his teeth chattered together, his eyes clouded with tears. For a moment, everybody stared at this apparition from some lost, mangled realm of childhood. 'Please, please stop it.'

Roman lowered his gun. 'Tal, you brought the kid here. Don't you know who his father is?'

'I wasn't intending…'

He went over and patted the intern on the head. 'Christ, kid, it's alright. Relax. I wasn't really going to shoot anyone. It's just an act. Sometimes in policework, you have to scare people a bit, you know, make them respect you. It's all part of the job.'

The intern didn't look at him. He couldn't stop trembling.

'Shit.' Roman put his gun away. He gestured to Lang and Reiner. 'Let's get out of here. All this is a waste of time.' He patted the kid on the head again. 'Relax, it's alright. It's alright.'

Lang and Reiner rubbed the kid on the damp shoulder of his uniform as they went out. In the doorway, before he left, Roman turned and pointed at me. 'Take him home. It's not safe. You shouldn't be bringing him around. This is a manhunt for a cop killer, for Christ's sake.'

The door jingled and closed. I found that I was still holding the gun in my shaking hands. I looked over to the waitresses who didn't dare leave the corner. 'Daria… I…'

'Get out!' she screamed. 'Get out!'

* * *

Back behind the wheel of the car I tried to remember anything that I'd ever believed. In the passenger seat, the kid shivered so violently the frame of the car shook.

'It's OK,' I told him. 'They're gone now.'

'Those people hate us.'

'Roman doesn't hate us, he's just full of poison.'

'Not Roman. The customers in the cafe. The Poles. The way they looked. They despise us, they'll kill us. When the war starts.'

'It's not true. I've got many Polish friends.'

'Who'll win the war? My dad says Germany is invincible, everyone believes it. They say we'll crush Poland like dust. But I don't know… what happens if we lose?'

'There isn't going to be a war. There's still time.'

'Where are we going next?' he asked the ghost in the rain's patterns on the windscreen.

'Not "we". I'm taking you home. Roman is right, it's not safe. You're not trained, you're not ready. And who is you father, by the way?'

'I don't care about that.'

'Too bad. You don't get a choice.'

'You can't force me.'

'Actually, I can.'

'I'm going to stay in this seat. You can try and drag me out of the car, but I'll fight.'

From the look on his face, he meant it. I asked myself if I had the strength left to argue, but I didn't even have the strength to think.

'Fine,' I said. 'Stay in the car. I'll walk.' I got out, slammed the door, and set off before he could argue. Halfway down the road, as the downpour soaked into my coat, I realised I'd left the umbrella behind. Too late now.

35

The maternity ward was too hot, overcrowded and pierced with the wailing of babies. I stopped at the front desk in a puddle of rainwater.

The receptionist didn't look up from her register. 'You a father or a son?'

'I'm police.'

She glanced over the top of her spectacles. 'Ah shit. Who's in trouble?'

I showed her the birth certificate I'd taken from Bernie's flat. 'I need to find out who signed this document. Can you help me? The signature's illegible.'

She squinted at the paper. 'Is that a wine stain?'

'It's evidence from a case I'm working. I need to talk to the person who signed it.'

She brought the signature close to her eyes and tutted. 'Doctors think they're too important to write slowly. Try doing my job for one day.' She gestured to the stacked files on the desk behind her. 'Maybe I can decipher it. This is a copy. Let me see if I can find the original.'

She went through a rear door. I glimpsed rows of shelves in a shaft of light from a slanted window. After five minutes, she hadn't returned. I called through the door, 'Hello?'

No answer. I climbed over the desk and went through into an office. 'Hello? Where…?'

'You're not allowed back here.' Her head popped up over the top of a filing cabinet. 'Please wait in the designated area with the other fathers.'

'I'm not a father.'

She rubbed her glasses. 'Oh, it's you. I've turned this place upside down. Your certificate isn't here. Where did you find it?'

'It's connected to a case.'

'A case. I see. Well, I can't help you.'

'But the doctor… who signed it?'

She held the certificate to the light. 'If I had to guess… it could be one of Dr Ludendorff's hieroglyphs.'

'Is he here? Can I speak with him?'

'You can try. Bottom of the corridor, on the left. But I warn you, he's not welcoming.'

* * *

'Go away!' Dr Ludendorff shouted when I knocked on his office. 'Busy.'

I opened the door. 'Sorry, Doctor, it's a police matter.'

Seeing no patient inside, I shut the door and went over to his desk. Gynaecological diagrams were stuck on the wall behind him, cruel-looking tools and implements laid out on a small table.

'Shit.' Ludendorff put away the crossword he was working on. 'Police? Not again. It's like a policeman's ball around here.'

'What do you mean?' I sat down opposite without being invited.

'Had one of your boys in here just the other day, digging.' Ludendorff took off his glasses. His face was young, but his hair was snow white, and his pale eyebrows were thick like two clouds above his blue eyes.

'A police officer? What was his name?'

'I was never very good with names.'

I showed him the birth certificate. 'Was it this he wanted?'

Ludendorff glanced at the document as if it were the most trivial thing in existence. 'Might have been.'

'Is this your signature?'

'Could be. It changes every time I sign something. Sort of defeats the point, I realise. But I'm busy. Women make babies in this city faster than we can pull them out. The Poles are Catholics, and poor. What can you do?'

'The original of this document is missing.'

'Yeah, well. You've seen the people who work here. Is that a wine stain?' He pushed the certificate back across the table. 'Are you alright?'

'What?' I realised I was staring at a poster on the wall by the window, a diagram of the uterus with all its parts labelled in Latin. Like seeing Danzig exposed in the cold, dissected, laid out open on a freezing slab.

'I said, Are you alright?'

The certificate shook in my hand. 'What happened to this baby, Doctor?'

'A difficult birth. Labour lasted three days, but the child was beautiful. Blue eyes like a lake, never seen anything like them. She seemed wise before she even knew her own name.'

'And the mother?'

He raised his bushy white eyebrows and stared. 'Whose side are you on, Detective?'

'The side of the baby. She's missing. Her parents are dead.'

'Oh, for God's sake. Dead. Already? People think they're ready for parenthood. The world today. It's impossible.'

'What happened with the kid? Why was my colleague in here digging up certificates?'

'Why don't you ask him yourself?'

'He's dead as well.'

He threw up his arms. 'This city. Well, there's your answer. Some things are best left alone. Look the other way, keep walking.'

'Even if a baby's been stolen?'

'I know your type, Detective. I bet your mother had a rough time squeezing you out.'

'I never asked her.'

'Children never do; they're selfish like that. Never crosses their mind that somebody almost split in two making them.'

'She's dead now.'

'Is everybody you know dead? I sense a pattern.'

'Doctor, please. I'm looking for a missing kid. You could help me.'

'I ask you again: which side are you on?'

I held his bright eyes. 'Your side, Doctor, your side.'

'And yet, here you are, asking the wrong questions. You don't know where to look. You don't know whom to ask.'

'Tell me, then.'

'And you'll leave? And never come back here? And never mention my name in any reports?'

'I swear it.'

'Not good enough.'

'What else can I do?'

'Tear up that copy of the certificate. It shouldn't exist. It already got one man killed. Tear it in pieces, drop it in my bin.'

'What are you talking about?'

He took hold of the litter bin by his feet, full of cigarette stubs, completed crosswords, and old teabags, and planted it between us. 'Tear that thing up. Throw it away. And I'll tell you what you want to know.'

'Why?'

He pulled the bin away. 'Forget it then. Please get out of my office, I'm a busy man.'

'I could take you down to the station, force you to talk.'

'Plenty of police are on my side, high up too. You might be surprised. They'd let me walk and you'll never find out what you need. It's time to decide, Detective.'

'Fine.' I folded the certificate and tore it in half. *Sorry, Bernie. I can't anymore.* I folded the torn halves and tore them again and dropped the pieces in the bin.

'Very good.' The doctor took out a notepad and scribbled something down. 'I'll write it neatly, so you can read it. Maybe. Go to this address. You'll find your answers. It's only for the baby's sake. She made a bloody mess coming out. Detective, I don't want to see your face again.'

36

The address, once deciphered, was a nondescript tenement across town, shaded by plane trees and swastika banners. Danzig rearranged itself, redeployed, there was always another staircase, always another door. A window in a photograph, a face in the window; always the same, always different. I climbed steps, crossed a corridor, knocked on a door. It's what I do. When nobody answered, I went inside. Bright electric light. A middle-aged couple, well dressed, were seated side by side on a bench by the wall. They waited for something, staring at the closed door opposite, in an otherwise empty room. It was calm, civilised. Potted plants in the corners, and a painting of the sea that hung on the wall in a gilt frame. Taken by surprise, I stood in the middle of the room and tried to think.

The woman smiled nervously. 'Are you here for the…?' She stopped.

Her husband frowned at her. 'Quiet, dear.'

I tried to look friendly. 'Yeah. Just waiting for my wife. You know.'

In the silence the room was altered: the potted plants were fake, the painting on the wall was kitsch, a buckle was broken on this woman's shoe. Footsteps moved back behind the closed corner door while we watched it.

'They say it's a simple process,' the woman said. She couldn't help herself, the awkwardness had to be addressed.

Her husband patted her knee. 'Leave the gentleman in peace, dear.'

'Oh, of course.' She smelled of starch and steam, a launderette somewhere.

I looked for something to say. 'Yes, I believe it is complicated. Do you–'

The inner door opened, and a man came out, head down, muttering to himself. He wore a suit.

'Herr Lahm…' Immersed in looking over a file, he didn't notice me, as he handed it over to the waiting visitors. 'You'll see here…'

I coughed.

He straightened and looked at me with shock. 'I'm sorry, Herr. I…'

'Don't mind me. Please, carry on.'

The man in the suit gave a bow. He smiled at the couple but failed to reassure. 'Excuse me a moment.' He bowed again and ran out through the back door. We heard a key turn in the lock on the other side.

'What in the world?' The woman jumped up. She looked at me with a mixture of confusion and anger. 'Who are you?'

Her husband grabbed her hand. 'Come on. We're leaving.' He pulled her out of the room.

'Wait! I'm police…' I called after them, but their feet already clattered down the staircase. 'I need to talk to you. Wait there. Wait!'

They ran so fast they almost fell. I watched their gloved hand on the banister that rattled as they descended. The sound of their panting receded. A door slammed downstairs.

'Alright, fine.' I went back into the room with the waiting bench, the potted plants and the painting of the sea, and knocked on the inner door. 'Open up! It's alright.

Dr Ludendorff sent me. I'm police. Don't worry, the good kind. I'm here to help.'

Footsteps crept up to the other side. A quiet voice said, 'What do you want?'

'We need to talk.'

'About what?'

'The missing baby.'

No response, but I heard low, hoarse breathing through the keyhole. The key turned in the lock and the door slid open, just a crack.

'Ludendorff sent you?' He peeped out. 'You shouldn't be here.'

'It won't take long.'

'It's dangerous.'

'Yeah, well.' I pushed against the door, catching him by surprise. The man fell backwards, and I was in the room before he could react. A small office filled with filing cabinets beneath a dusty skylight. There were no potted plants and no pictures in here.

'This isn't permitted.' He picked himself up.

'Relax. I don't care what you're up to. I'm not here to shut you down.'

'What then?'

'Let me see.' I pulled open a drawer in the nearest cabinet, but he jumped in front and blocked me.

'No!'

'Alright.' I showed him my police badge. 'Let's do it the hard way.'

'Listen… I'm just a secretary. This is an office. Nothing gets done here. I process the paperwork, that's all. I pass files from one hand to another. I've nothing to do with the rest of it.'

'Rest of what?'

'You already know, you said as much. The babies.'

'Tell me anyway.'

'Tell what?'

I pushed the badge into his flabby cheek. 'Don't play stupid. Tell me about the babies. We can do it here, or down at the station.'

'It's all above board, in the Reich at least. And Danzig is practically part of the Reich now. In days, they say. Perhaps tonight.'

'Tell me about the babies.'

'We… they… they find the blonde ones, the ones with blue eyes. The pure blood. Problem is, sometimes the pure blood are born to Polish mothers. I don't know how, I'm not a scientist. Perhaps those women had German ancestors and never knew it. Who can figure? Like I said, I just do the paperwork.'

'You find blue-eyed babies. Then what?'

'Well, you know… we collect them together. Take care of them. They're important. The Führer cares deeply about the future.'

'But these are Poles, you said, not Germans.'

'Polish mothers, yeah, but these babies are blonde, blue eyes. What should I say? I don't understand anything. We collect the babies together. We find German foster parents for them.'

'And the real parents?'

He blinked. 'I don't know anything about that.'

'Let me see.' I released him and looked through the filing cabinet. I pulled out a handful of papers, but it was all codes, numbers, meaningless. I showed him the first document. 'What does this mean? Translate it for me.'

'It's a baby. The date of birth, the weight, height. Everything.'

'And where is she? Where do they take the babies?'

'A kind of depot. I guess. I've never been there. Like I said, I just handle the paperwork…'

'I'm looking for this kid.' I put my hand to my pocket and realised that I'd torn up the birth certificate and left it in Dr Ludendorff's bin. 'Hold on.' I took out the newspaper and flicked through the pages which were slightly damp from the rain. 'Here.' I showed him the story of the amber dealer and his wife.

'What?' The look on this prick's face… like I was a maniac.

'This baby was adopted from here. Just a few weeks ago. Her name's Anna. The family is famous in Danzig, some rich amber dealer. You must know something. Where is she? Show me her file.'

'Shit.' The man sighed as he pulled out a drawer. 'I could lose my job. In this economy. I've got a wife and kids of my own. Think about that.'

He pulled out a file and I snatched it from him. Inside was another copy of the birth certificate, a list of measurements, and a photograph of the baby attached with a paper clip. I stared numbly at her.

'Happy now?' the man said.

'You people stole this child off her parents and gave her to somebody else.'

'I told you; I just handle the paperwork.'

'Paperwork?' Something snapped in my overwrought brain. I grabbed him by the neck, slamming him into the side of the cabinet. 'Say that again. "Paperwork." You're pathetic. "It's just the paperwork, just the paperwork."'

'Get off me! Don't hurt me.' He squirmed in my fists, helpless, unresisting, a worm.

'You're the ones who'll burn the world. You do the paperwork and imagine you're not guilty. You make excuses, sign the documents, look the other way.'

He shook his head but couldn't meet my eye. 'Come on, pal, life's complicated. We're not children anymore.'

'Shut up.' I punched him in the nose, he slumped back. *Admit it, Tal; you enjoy it. You like the feeling of power. You're worse than this scumbag in a suit.* I released him. 'And the kid's real parents, what about them?'

'They're just Poles. What do you care? These babies will have a better life. They'll be raised as Germans. They'll be educated, civilised. They'll enjoy all the privileges of the Reich.'

'And the parents will…' I swallowed down the desire to headbutt him.

'The parents will be better off too. You know what it's like for Poles. They're poor, illiterate. Catholic. They have too many children and they starve to death; they can't feed them all. They have to work so hard. It's better this way. Better for the children and for the parents…'

'You people are sick.'

'The Reich has such beautiful plans for the future. The German race–'

'Look at this picture now.' I pushed the photograph of the amber dealer and his wife into his face. 'Recognise these people? Did you give them that baby? Look at the baby. Was she stolen from some Polish mother?'

He pushed the newspaper away. 'Yes! Yes! Alright? That's a rich family. He's a jeweller, important. The baby was born to a harbour prostitute. Her dad was some rancid janitor. Now the kid has the chance to grow up in a nice house. Christ, they even have a butler. All the amber she could ever dream of. She had blue eyes, pretty. The picture's black-and-white, it doesn't show. She's happy now, her future's secure. Is that wrong?'

'These people are dead. Murdered.' I folded the paper and stuffed it back in my pocket. 'Found them in the dirt in an old warehouse in the shipyards. No amount of amber is worth a damn, and nobody's secure. Those Nazis you love so much, they're not going to save us. They're going to set fire to everything. All these files, all this paper's going to burn. And those "rancid janitors" you hate, the "harbour prostitutes", they'll eat us alive.'

'I… I just…'

'Give me that.' I snatched Anna's file and tucked it under my arm.

The man said nothing. I couldn't bear to be inside there anymore, but as I was running out, almost colliding with the door, I stopped and turned on him one more time. 'You got children, pal? You got a wife? Kids at home? You'd better get them out of Danzig while you can. You'll watch what happens to them with your eyelids pried open.'

'You're insane.'

'No, I've just seen how it ends.'

37

I was out of breath and weak and couldn't stop running. If I just didn't stop moving, the world might hold together, the collapse might be kept at bay a little longer. But I hadn't eaten anything, I hadn't slept, all that sustained me was a kind of moral frenzy. I burst through the entrance of the police station. A crowd of complainants blocked the desk, shouting and swearing. I pushed them away. Granma smoked. I pulled some stranger's hand off my shoulder. Two armed guards watched the crowd with amusement and said nothing.

'We're closed,' Granma said. 'Come back later.'

'I need to speak to Schechter. Is he in?'

'He was drinking beer in the canteen, last I heard.'

As I went running through the dark corridor, she called after me. 'Slow down, Tal. You'll slip.'

* * *

The deputy was reading a newspaper with his feet up on the table. A few other officers scattered around the canteen drank beers and tittered about something. They stopped when I came in.

'Why are you running, Detective?' Schechter lowered his newspaper. 'You're all sweaty. What's with you? I heard about your little scene in the cafe. Roman lodged a complaint. You'll be under investigation–'

'Look at this.' I took out the files from the adoption agency and laid them on the table in front of him. 'About the case.'

'What case?'

'The cop killer... This is the direction we need to focus on. It's connected to a kind of adoption agency. They take blue-eyed babies from Polish mothers–'

'Wait a minute. Slow down. What case are you talking about?'

'The manhunt. Call your men back. There's a new lead. Somebody killed this amber dealer' – I took out the newspaper, now damp and crumpled, and set it beside the files – 'and stole his baby.'

'Wait, wait, wait. You're talking a mile a minute. What amber dealer? What baby?'

The other officers eyed the newspaper with stifled grins as I smoothed the creases. I tried to remember what it all meant, how it fit together, why it had seemed so important.

'The murderer. First, he killed Gerhard, and took his uniform. He used the uniform to get into the house of the amber dealer. He stole their baby, who had been adopted via this Nazi child agency.'

Schechter blinked. 'We already found Gerhard's killer. The suspect is in custody.'

'What? Who?'

'I don't know. Some drifter, worked on and off at the shipyards. Roman brought him in. You can ask Roman if you want. Or don't. If you'll take my advice, you'll forget about this one. Nasty business, dead cops. It's closed now.'

'And the baby?'

'What baby?'

'The amber dealer and his wife. They had a child. It's missing.'

'That's not in the report that I read.'

'Can I see that report?'

He stared. 'No.'

'But–'

'Drop it.' He took his feet off the table and sat forwards. 'Tal, didn't anybody tell you? You've got a new assignment. You stay on the nightshift. There's a case over in Langfuhr, somebody's pissing on doorsteps at night.' He started to laugh at this and had to compose himself. 'Go use your famous powers of deduction to solve that one. Perhaps they'll write another newspaper article about you.'

'That job's below my rank.'

'Things have changed.'

'I'm the best detective on this force. Everyone knows it.'

'Bullshit. You were pals with Henrik. He protected you while you ran about, talking down to the rest of us, treating us like dirt. You always thought you were better. Nobody protects you now. If I were you, I'd find another job. In the meantime, you rustle up that midnight piss artist. Now go on, get lost.'

* * *

I found Roman drinking coffee outside the holding cells.

'I want to speak to your prisoner.'

Roman swallowed down the dregs of his cup. 'Tal. What are you doing here? I lodged a complaint against you. If I were you…'

I stared him down. 'I've been investigating Gerhard's death. They say you were working on a special operation with him. You were the last one who saw him.'

Roman shrugged. 'Could be. Well, you can relax anyway. We've got the killer behind bars. He signed his confession already.'

'I need to speak to him.'

'Not possible.'

'I have rank. I'm chief investigator.'

'So what? The case is closed. The paperwork just needs to be typed up.'

'I have another case I'm investigating. Your suspect is connected.'

'Which case?' A hint of doubt showed in his eyes.

'There's a missing child.'

'Missing child?' He blinked. 'First I heard about it.'

'Bernie was working on it before he died. Could be a connection. I need to speak to your suspect.'

Roman shrugged. 'You can try.'

'What does that mean?'

'He doesn't like to talk. It was hard work getting a confession out of him.'

* * *

The suspect cowered back in the corner of his cell and didn't look up when I went inside.

'Hey. Need to talk to you.'

He slumped back in the corner where the dank brick walls met. It was an empty chamber, nothing but a hole to shit in.

I took a step closer into the chill. 'Hey, I'm talking to you.'

The man showed no sign of hearing. He might have been asleep or drunk. Roman chuckled in the doorway behind me. 'Told you.'

'Do me a favour, leave me alone in here a minute.'

Roman whistled. 'Can't do that, Tal. This man's a cop killer. He's dangerous.'

'Don't act the fool. You beat this guy half to death. I can see it from here. He's not a threat to anyone. Leave me alone with him if you don't want an internal complaint filed. Police brutality.'

'I'm warning you, Tal. That's the kind of attitude that makes you enemies around here. Henrik can't protect you anymore. You'll wind up–'

'Just get out.'

I shoved him back. For a moment he resisted, our eyes locked. Behind us, the suspect let out a long, high-pitched moan of anguish, and a sob like despair.

'Alright,' Roman said. 'Five minutes.'

He stepped out and closed the door. As soon as I heard the key turn on the other side, I hurried over to the suspect, and raised his head to the meagre light.

'Are you OK? Can you talk?'

The man groaned. Both of his eyes were sealed behind a welter of purple bruising. A seam of blood showed through his eyelashes. When I tried to lift him, he let out a mutilated scream. Both his arms were broken; they dangled uselessly from the joints.

'I'm sorry.' I let him slide back down into the corner. 'I'm sorry. I'm different to the men who did this. I want to help. Understand?'

The man only moaned.

'Can you speak?'

He dribbled and cowered back, pushing his spine into the corner as if he wanted to disappear there. I grabbed his head. 'Listen to me. Can you speak?'

He shook his head.

'No?' I pulled out my torch. 'Open your mouth.' When he didn't respond, I tilted his mouth back, prised his swollen jaw open, and shone my torch inside. The back of the throat was a mess of burned tissue.

'What the hell? Did they pour acid down your throat? Or what? Something burning?'

The man jerked away from my hands and leaned his head back against the wall with a whimper.

'How tall are you?' I heard myself say. It must have sounded like a ridiculous question, and maybe it was.

The man seemed to weep.

'Sorry. It's going to hurt a moment, but it's necessary. I want to help you, but you have to trust me.'

I grabbed him by the shoulders and pulled him up. The howl he let out was agonising, it tore at the stone walls and found no release.

'Shush. Easy now. Easy. How tall are you? Shit, you're shorter than I am. What? 165cm… Stand up straight, let me see. No, you're short. Too short.'

I let him slide back down the wall into his agonised, bunched-up tangle.

'Alright, stay there. Don't sign any pieces of paper, no matter what they tell you. They're lying. They've got no proof. They can't keep you here. You understand? Try to stay calm. I'll get you out.'

He whined as I crossed the cell and banged on the door. In the momentary stillness, I feared to be trapped in there, but the lock shifted on the other side. The door opened.

Roman smiled. 'Told you he wasn't a talker.'

'That man's not your killer.' I pushed past him.

Behind me, Roman locked the door as I hurried away down the corridor. He shouted after me. 'What are you talking about?'

'It's not him.'

I turned the corner and headed to the stairs, desperate to get out of that freezing basement.

Roman caught up with me. 'I'm warning you, Tal, keep your nose out of my case. Don't fuck things up.'

'The killer is tall, over 185cm. That man in there, he's like Napoleon.'

'What are you talking about, *tall*? How would you know how tall the killer is?'

'From the uniform he wore. I told you, I've been working the case. I was working it before you. I've got evidence.'

'Bullshit. You're just trying to fuck things up because you hate the rest of us. You hate Danzig.'

'Stop bluffing. You arrested an innocent man and tortured him into a confession. That's a crime. I'll end your career. Your Nazi patrons won't lift a finger to save you. Public opinion matters to them, they won't like this.'

Roman tried to grin but could only snarl; his sharp teeth showed through pulled-back lips. 'That man signed his confession. And the confession was detailed. There's a whole web of Polish underground activity in Danzig. We'll sweep them up in a net. We'll clean this city overnight and make it pure again. Don't try to stand in our way.'

I pressed my forehead into his. 'Let that man go. When I find the real killer, you'll be finished. You'll be thrown in a cell.'

'You're the one who's finished. You're already finished, you just don't know it yet. You know what else was in that confession? Corrupt police, working with the Poles. Won't be difficult to drag you into an identity parade and finger you for guilty.'

'Just try it.'

'You're so blind, it's disgusting. The only reason you weren't shot in the back already is because this is a brotherhood. But you'd never stand shoulder to shoulder with your brothers. You make me sick.' He shook his head and went back down the stairs into the dark.

* * *

I ran up to my office, only wanting to sit alone in the quiet for a moment, but it wasn't empty. I saw a human shape in the dark and flicked on the light switch. The intern kid blinked his eyes and looked back.

'Sorry,' he said.

'What are you doing here?'

'I didn't know where to go. I couldn't stay at home. I can't bear it.'

'For God's sake. Alright, you want to help? Do me a favour. Write up a file for me. I'd do it, but I have to find a killer and there's no time.'

'What killer?'

'See this?' I took out the documents from the adoption agency. 'I need you to write it up. Do you know how to write up a file?'

'No.'

'Granma can help you. Just put it all together in a folder. Put my name on it. I'll sign it for you. Here' – I grabbed a blank form and signed the bottom – 'there. It's official now. Then when it's all together, you take it to Granma, and she'll put it in the right pigeonhole. OK?'

He stared at the blank form. 'But what am I supposed to write?'

'There's an agency. They steal babies from Polish mothers and give them to German foster families. This file is for a baby who belonged to murder victims in a case I'm working. The details of the kid are listed here. Even her picture. This is the family.' I took out my newspaper and tore out the page with the amber dealer. 'Add this to the file. Take their names from the story. Put them in the form. They're the victims.'

He took the torn page and sniffed it. 'These are the parents?'

'They're the foster parents. Real parents unknown. A Polish prostitute, I was told, but that's not reliable. You got all that?'

'Not really.'

'Good. It's like a story. You like stories, don't you? Think of it as a story and write it all down. Make half of it up if you like, just make sure the baby and the adoption agency are in there.'

He stared at the paper. I ran out.

'Wait…' He called after me. I just kept running.

38

Gdańsk, Polish People's Republic

1961

The Fourth Rune

The cell was plain, bare brick walls, a concrete floor stained with blood and shit. The only furniture was a plank of wood and a bucket. There was no window. This is what hell looks like. It's not the burning pit that people imagine, nothing like the lurid fantasies of Hieronymus Bosch, which are too colourful and too diverse. The communist version of hell was devoid of anything, it was a space for boredom where emptiness could expand infinitely, mixed with terror. The two intertwined, fed, and played off one another. The mind palls at the lack of detail, imagination starts to slip into crevices, the worst kinds of terrors present themselves, all the tortures hidden in bare walls, while nothing happens. What agonies are being prepared for you? And yet, as the hours pass in monotony, even fear gives way to emptiness.

It was dark in the cell. The only light came through a crack beneath the door. There must have been a light fixture in the ceiling before, but there was nothing now, just a hole and the loose end of a wire. The sense of time begins to fade. How long has it been? Two hours? Ten minutes? A full day? A week? As the thread of duration weakens, so your sense of self gives way. You can no longer be sure of anything. Who you were before you came in here feels no more substantial than the residue of a dream. How did you never notice that before? The accusations of your persecutors are the only real thing. It must all be true, everything they claim. You really are this fictive being, this personified guilt.

There were rumours around Gdańsk, whispers about the torture chambers, the places where disappeared people wandered in hell. But Anna was a police officer, she wasn't supposed to believe in slanders against communism. The State was good, it took care of its workers. Such rumours were only propaganda from the West, machinations of capitalism. The enemies would never rest until Gdańsk was taken from Poland and attached to West Germany. Or so they said. In this bare room, this dead end, no idea seemed impossible. There was only a locked door and her worst imaginings on the other side.

Mind over matter. Divide up the time. Keep a record of the days. She had to keep the story of her life straight, to remember who she was. She would have to tell it to herself, from the beginning, without missing anything. Keep active, push-ups, star jumps, she could maintain a full regime; she might end up fitter than she'd been in the outside world. She'd need food though. So far, she hadn't even received water. She felt faint. Best not to think about it. Keep hold of something. Keep believing you'll get out of this.

She lay down on the plank and tried to imagine that it might become comfortable with use. It was hard and rough, prickly with splinters. No. This was impossible. She'd lose her mind quickly. She needed a plan, but she had nothing, they hadn't left her with a single possession of her own. All she had were these plain overalls and socks. It was freezing, a stone basement. She didn't even have a blanket to keep warm. She'd have to play along with her jailers as best she could, try to win their trust. She might get access to a blanket that way, if nothing else.

* * *

The interview room of the prison was too bright after the cell. She closed her eyes and shielded her face from the bare bulb overhead. Sitting opposite, the Inspector wore the same silver-grey suit. He wore dark sunglasses to hide his eyes, or to protect them from the unshielded light.

He opened his file. 'Name?'

'You know my name. We've done this before.'

The room was narrow, painted white, with a concrete floor. A two-way mirror was set into the wall on the left; anybody might be watching. Anna was handcuffed to the table.

'Name?' He repeated himself patiently; he could play this game all day.

'Nowak. Anna Nowak. Detective, Gdańsk, Central Precinct.'

'Do you know why you're in here, Comrade Nowak?'

She opened her eyes a fraction, letting the light in. 'I haven't been given anything to eat or drink in twenty-four hours. That's a contravention of my human rights.'

'Do you presume to dictate terms to us?' he said, but as he glanced at the mirror, for a moment, unease showed beneath the act.

'I've always been a loyal servant of the State. I know the rules.'

'Conspirators always do know the rules.'

'What conspiracy?'

'That's what you're going to tell us.'

She could only stall, play the moments out one by one. 'My record speaks for itself.'

'Indeed. I've been looking closely into your records, Comrade.'

'I'm a committed Marxist. I'm one of the organisers of the reading group at work. I wrote an article about socialism for the newspaper. Ask anyone at the station, I read everything by Karl Marx. I never missed a reading session. Between that and work, I wouldn't have time for a conspiracy.'

The Inspector sighed. 'Why did you never marry, Comrade Nowak?'

'Excuse me?'

'A single woman, among so many suitable men.'

'I'm married to the job.'

He smiled beneath the sunglasses, just for a moment. 'Perhaps the detective's sarcasm puts off potential suitors.'

'If I promise to get married, will you let me out of here?'

'All this is only preliminary. Our methodology is to build a character portrait of the accused. Conspiracy works inwardly, like a poison. Outward behaviour can be misleading. Nobody can read the most inward part of another's soul, nobody except us. We seek out the clues that others miss. It may seem negligible to you, but I assure you, such casual matters are invaluable to our work.'

'Fine. What else would you like to know about my personal life? I could tell you about my breakfast routine…'

'It would be better if you told us about your parents.'

'What?' A chill passed through her starving frame. The thought of her parents didn't belong in this place. 'What's there to tell? Jakub Nowak, a ship worker. Lena Nowak, another ship worker. Both deceased. It's a common enough story, anyone in Gdańsk could tell the same.'

'Yes, except that Jakub and Lena Nowak were not your real parents.'

'What did you say?' She stared into the dark sunglasses and saw a wild woman, hatred, fury, vengeance reflected. She swiped at his face with her free hand. 'Take those things off!'

'Comrade!' He ducked away.

From the way he glanced at the mirror, she knew she had given herself away. She slumped back against the metal chair.

'A violent reaction.' He straightened the glasses. 'Is this topic stressful to you?'

'You're a liar. Everything down here's a lie. All this, it's a fake, the whole thing. I bet you're not even a real inspector.'

'I have the paperwork here. Would you like to see it?'

He picked up a briefcase from the floor and set it on the table. Anna watched as he flicked through some files and drew out a sheet of paper.

'This is the registration document. You were officially adopted by the Nowaks at the age of three.'

'You're insane.' She tore at the handcuffs that held her to the table and twisted around to face the mirror. 'You people are sick! You're monsters!' But there was nothing in the mirror, of course, except a crazy woman.

The Inspector waited for her to stop. 'If you're ready, I'll continue.'

'Whatever. It doesn't matter anyway.'

'But it does. This discovery is just the start. Our understanding is beginning to grow. We knew there was a German plot to take control of Gdańsk, but we had no idea how they planned to go about it. Now we learn there are German children who grew up in Polish families. What orders were you given?'

'Orders? What are you talking about?'

'How many children were hidden among Polish families? We need to know all the others that you're in contact with.'

Anna turned to the mirror, she was calm now, her voice was measured. 'Whoever's on the other side, listen to me. I won't talk to this man. He's a psychopath. Get him away from me before I scratch his eyes out. I want to speak to Roman, my superintendent. You get him in here, you sit him down opposite me, or I won't say another word.'

'But, Comrade…' The Inspector smoothed his papers.

She ignored him, addressing the mirror. 'Take me back to my cell now. I've heard enough. This interview is terminated.'

39

Somehow, she did manage to fall asleep on the old wooden plank. She dreamt of the dig site, and at its heart, the black surface of the bog where everything sank. She was knee-deep in viscous shadow; she took a step forward and was swallowed up to the waist. Gloop. She dug her nails into her palms, biting down a spurt of panic. Something moved in the dark. She jumped back and sought the wall, a hard surface to back against. Footsteps outside in the corridor gave shape to the emptiness, a picture of this place, a hint of its dimensions. She stopped breathing to listen, every fibre tautened, and caught a sound so soft it might have been a ghost. With an intense, exhausting concentration of will, she held her teeth from chattering together. The footsteps receded. Something clanged, but further away. Everything went still.

She waited a moment then crept to the door. Her fingertips explored its cold metal. Against the floor she found a scrap of paper poking through the gap. She felt further, will power used up, teeth rattling too loud, and found something else, something small, metal, a paper clip.

In the sliver of light beneath the door, she managed to read the note:

> KILL YOURSELF NOW, WHILE YOU HAVE THE CHANCE

With what…? She turned the paper clip and tested its edge. Of course, down here, it might be the most valuable commodity, a way out. If the self-inflicted cuts didn't finish you, blood poisoning would. She closed her eyes and the darkness, returning, was purified. As if nothing ever existed, ever would. The only flaw in the design was her wavering consciousness that explored the absence, negating it. The "negation of a negation" that Marx described. Yes, remove yourself, this stain on non-being, and let the darkness be complete.

A fine ligament held her back. *I have the paperwork right here… Would you like to see it? This is the registration document. You were officially adopted by the Nowaks at the age of three…* She stifled a scream. How could the State torture her like this, after all her dedication? For years she'd studied the arcane texts of socialism. She'd led the reading group with care. Sure, she'd broken rules, had kept up with smugglers and shipyard spies, but this was Gdańsk, and work demanded it. Everyone cut corners and looked the other way; that was just how things got done. Arrest her, if need be, charge her for her errors, the contraband drugs, and the prohibited books, she wasn't ashamed of what she'd done. But this… to deny her the memory of her dead parents. It was too cruel. They wanted to tear away her sense of self, her living substance.

In the freezing morning, the sound of her parents waking, the little apartment coming to life; her mother lighting the fire, her father dressing. An enchantment inside of which, all was safe, all was love. The best days, when Dad took her to the shipyards with him, and the other workers made a fuss of her, called her their angel, set her up in the unfinished boats. She had always known she'd work by the water when she grew up, she just didn't know it would be like this.

If she wasn't a child of the shipyards, then who was she? A question that pressed urgently, but she was too tired, too hungry and thirsty, she couldn't begin to touch it. She leaned back against the wall and gripped the clip. If she wasn't herself, there might be comfort in being nobody. Just this emptiness. They wanted to deprive her of daylight until she couldn't tell the interstices apart, until there was no longer inside or outside, just a scream in the void. No exit, no friend, not even logic to save her.

She tested the point of the paper clip: blunt, thin. It would cut the skin, but not easily. The consolation of a sharp knife was denied to her; the clip would take hard, concentrated effort. She traced the veins of her wrist with its edge and wondered.

In the dark, the only resource left was witchcraft. The others didn't believe in magic and couldn't understand it. She might have lived the same way if she had never ended up in this place, but she saw it now, the power of enchantment for human beings who live in the unknown. She knew a rune for daylight. Carved into a surface, the symbol offered protection and power to its user. Light. Where to put it? Somewhere her captors might not find it, but she would feel its presence.

She pulled down her overalls and prodded the skin between her shoulder and chest. Soft, yielding. She gritted her teeth and pressed the point of the clip inside. Deep, deeper. All the way. The first incision was like a pinprick, not too bad, but drawing a straight line was a different matter. She dragged the dirty metal through her flesh. In the dark, nothing to guide her, she felt her way slowly, following the picture in her imagination. Blood bubbled from the incision, and she bit her lip, trying to keep the line straight, trying to visualise the shape. It was slow work. Seeping blood made the skin slippery, it was hot on her fingers. She wiped it away and started the next line, a diagonal, crossing bar. Every millimetre was labour, but she wouldn't be stopped. Slowly, inevitably, the rune entered her.

ᛞ

40

Danzig, the Free City

Hours before the start of WWII

The carillon played. I was caught beneath an old tree behind the Long Market and could only lean against the trunk. Memory emptied. Who am I? This strange lullaby played in my veins tautened to breaking point, it sang of the past and the future. Darkness was falling, the streets were full of workers headed home. They would take shelter behind locked doors and closed curtains.

I sank into one of the dingy underground bars where the sailors disappear when pay runs low. I took a sip of beer and looked for solace, but this place was full of mirrors. Dirty and smudged, cracked in places, reflecting the dim light down here. I found a spot in the corner, as far away from the door as possible, and tried to forget my loneliness. Everything reminded me of it, the smell of tar and stale suds, and sleeplessness.

I took out the ragged newspaper I'd carried across the city and set it on the damp table. I sipped beer and leafed through the pages. I loved to investigate; once I allowed myself to sink into a trance, the world fell away with all its humiliations and rejection. I closed my eyes and sought him, a killer, in the wilderness of crooked streets that I knew more intimately inside than any map could show. His footsteps were just up ahead. I sensed that he slowed, wanting me to catch up; he desired to be chased. The card he'd sent to me; because it must have been him who sent it:

> DEAR BELOVED,
> I CANNOT WAIT FOR US TO BE TOGETHER.
> DON'T FORGET ME, YOUR TRUE HEART.

And why me? He must have seen my name in the newspaper, the detective who'd solved "the case of the year". How did I know this? I felt it. Over the years, when I managed to reach that trance state, I would reach over in moments and touch the killer's mind. Some membrane was broken, and I looked out through their eyes. If it was a game, I was losing, and he was disappointed in me. I needed to pick up his trail again before he found somebody else to play with. I sipped my beer and turned the page. Printed words danced in the copper light. In a different city, in a different world, these pictures, these stories all diverged. Alternate histories and futures swam in front of my eyes. I had to focus on what was real. Just a small side column of text, without a picture:

> POLICE OFFICER WINS SWIMMING GALA
> Local police officer Gerhard Kaymer claimed first place at the Danzig charity swimming gala this weekend. He credits his superior sportsmanship to a diet of oats and the teachings of Adolf Hitler.

I saw him laid out in an X, naked, the swimmer, and put the newspaper down. All I could remember for a moment was the smell of the murder scene. Three of us in the same newspaper: my story, the amber dealer, and Gerhard. Was that a link? I raced through the pages, skimming headlines. So many potential victims in here. Politicians, sport stars, actors, talented school kids, visiting dignitaries.

Say that it's true, just say. If the killer found his targets in the newspaper, who would he target next? I leafed. I closed my eyes and became the killer. Which person would I choose? What was the system? Eyes closed, I turned the pages, seeing them in my mind, the blur of names and photographs, the politicians and actors… It might be something to do with their names, or it could be more simple, more emotionless, the numbers of the pages. Perhaps the killer opened the newspaper at random. Ordinary people wouldn't understand that, but a detective knows: chance has its own logic.

I approached the bar and showed my badge. 'Do you have a phone I could use?'

'Police?' The woman ducked back. 'Hey, leave us in peace here. We don't hurt nobody.'

'I just need to use your phone for a moment.'

'Everyone knows, you police have been through the city like a plague, dragging people out of their beds. Smashing up homes. Take what you want but leave me in peace. Want a bottle of vodka? Here you go. On the house. Take it and good luck to you. Goodbye. This job is all I have.'

'Keep your vodka. All I want is to call someone on your phone. It'll only take a minute.'

'Whatever.' Keeping her distance, she set the phone on the counter, and backed away.

The first page of the newspaper was a story about the Polish ambassador. It seemed unlikely, but I rang through to the operator, gave my credentials, and got the number.

A man's voice spoke in Polish. 'We're closed.'

'I just wanted to know, is the ambassador alright?'

'What?'

'Is he OK? He's healthy, in good shape?'

'I'm going to hang up.'

'I'm police. It's probably nothing, I just need to know nothing happened to the ambassador.'

'Why would anything happen?'

'When did you last see him?'

'Ten minutes ago. But–'

'That's fine. Thank you.' I hung up.

The woman behind the bar stared at me. 'What kind of police are you?'

'The good kind.'

She set a beer in front of me. The other main stories in the paper were about the international situation, not Danzig. I flipped to the next page, a story about a panda in the zoo, and disregarded it. Opinion pieces followed, about "the Jewish question"; I never knew it was a question. The next page was, "ATROCITIES AGAINST GERMANS IN POLAND". This was pointless. I turned another page and saw "THE CASE OF THE YEAR". My picture. I felt nauseous and couldn't look at it. I was about to give up when I turned another page; the headline caught my eye.

LOCAL PRIEST CELEBRATES NINETIETH BIRTHDAY

I stared at the picture, but in his dark robes, the priest was just ink. I closed my eyes and became the killer. *It's me, the murderer. Who am I? I find my victims in the newspaper… I hunt them down… I take their clothes.* Why? Something to do with clothes. Uniforms perhaps… Gerhard wore a uniform, but the dead woman, what did she wear? Her clothes hadn't been recovered. The priest wore a kind of uniform, vestments, a symbol of sanctity. I picked up the phone and rang the operator, who queried if I knew what time it was, before putting me through to the church office. The phone rang out with no answer.

41

It was dark when I arrived at the church. Its arched roof billowed like a black sail over the street. The front door was locked. I made my way around to the priest's residence on the other side of the building, in a little square. There was no sound or movement back here, but I followed a flicker of light and crept forward, terrified like a child who wakes up far from their bed at night. I peered through a small window. The curtains were drawn, but light showed through a gap. I pushed on the front door and it creaked inwards. At the sound, I held my breath and stayed motionless on the threshold; nothing responded inside. What was I supposed to do? I couldn't just enter a priest's home without permission. I knocked on the door and heard the sound echo through the opening. Something moved, a footfall in the concealed hallway. I knocked again.

'Hello? Father? Are you awake? I'm sorry to disturb you at this hour.'

Nobody replied, but I heard footsteps scurry away inside.

'Hello?' I pushed the door all the way open, but still hesitated to enter. 'Father? Are you there?'

It was dark. I peered into the gloom and made out shadowy outlines of furniture. Light showed through the frame of a door at the end of a far wall. I heard a crash of wood or metal as something heavy clattered onto the floor.

'Father? Are you alright? Did you fall?'

The reverberations ceased. Silence filled the interior where my eyes adjusted, picking out a grandfather clock and a coat rack against the near wall.

'Father, please don't be afraid. I'm going to come in now.' I took a step further inside, feeling my way, and brushed a mirror hung by the entrance.

A voice came from the end of the hall. 'Who is that? What do you want?'

'I need to speak to you, Father.'

'I'm busy now. Come back later.'

'I heard a crash.' I followed the sound of the voice.

'Oh, that was just… I knocked over an ornament. It's nothing.'

'Can I speak with you for a moment, Father?'

I crept further along the hall until I reached the closed door, and the gap of light beneath. Somebody was just on the other side of the panel; I heard their hoarse breathing.

'Who are you?' they said.

'I'm nobody. A believer. I wanted your advice on a spiritual matter.'

'Come back tomorrow, we're closed.'

That seemed like an odd way for a priest to speak. The voice was raspy and weak, with a fluted, high-pitched edge, almost girlish. But then the priest was ninety, according to the newspaper. Strange things happen as you get older.

'Could I just see you for a moment? Then I'll leave.'

'Why?'

'I need your blessing. Bless me, Father, please. You don't know how dearly I need it.'

I'd be in trouble at the station if this priest made a formal complaint, I was already close to a suspension or worse.

The hoarse breathing stopped on the other side of the door as he calculated. 'A blessing. That's all? And then you'll leave?'

'I promise.'

'Very well.'

I heard a whisper behind the door, and a floorboard creaked as he shifted his feet.

'It's done,' he said.

'Thank you…'

'Please leave now, before I call the police.' The hoarse breaths grew faster, his voice more high-pitched.

'That won't be necessary, Father.'

'I'm going to step away from the door now,' he said. 'There's a phone in here. I'm going to pick up the receiver now. Please leave.'

Forehead pressed against the door, I hesitated. If I'd ever been a religious man, I might have been able to tell if this scene was real or false, but I had no idea. Maybe he really was a priest.

'You're still there…' he whispered.

'I'm leaving, I'm leaving.' Saying so made the decision for me. I stepped back from the door and was about to turn away. 'Goodbye, Father. I'll leave you in peace.' I checked back once and saw something, or thought I saw, beneath the door, lit up where the electric light showed. Was that…? I knelt and smelled it before my eyes could register the sight of blood trickling through the crack into the hall. Thick, dark, a puddle of rich shadow leaking out.

'Is that?'

Footsteps sprinted away on the other side. I pushed against the door and felt it give, but only partially.

'Father! Father! Are you there?'

Something fell to the floor and smashed. A gust of wind blew through. A window slammed. I laid my shoulder against the door and managed to heave it open just a foot or two. I squeezed through the gap and had to shield my eyes at the electric light. I caught fragments of a lounge, with a settee and a coffee table, various ornaments, religious paintings, a crucifix on the wall. Too many details in a whirl of flashes. I slumped against the wall next to a body that lay on the floor on the other side of the door. Naked, and so old, his flesh was shrivelled and stained with liver spots. Blood leaked out of his neck and mouth, turning the rough folds of skin glossy.

'Father?'

I listened for a breath and found none. I checked his dead pulse. By his side, a pile of clothes soaked up blood like a flannel. I picked up a cream-coloured blouse, and a string of pearls, expensive, a little flashy, belonging to a woman of class if not of taste. I let them drop to the floor in frustration. I'd picked up the trail and lost it again. There was a window across the opposite side of the room. A bloody handprint caught on the lace curtains. The wind came howling through the room, disturbing the fragments of shattered vases, when I pushed the window open.

'Ah shit.'

I crawled out into the cold and let myself topple down the outside of the window onto a flagged courtyard. I caught my head on the ground and lay still. The wind blew fresh with puddles on stone. The garden was empty.

42

Was it hours later? The priest's house was cordoned off. I lay in the corner while a medic bandaged my head. I watched as the body was bagged and taken away.

Lang came and knelt beside me. 'Go home, Tal. You've done enough here. Get some sleep.'

'There's no time for sleep.' I tried to get up, but the medic pushed me down.

'Don't move,' she said. 'I'm almost done.'

'Where's the deputy?' I asked Lang. 'He should be here, he's in charge.'

Lang looked away. 'Schechter's busy. Something big's going on. I don't know what. Me, I try to keep my head down. You could learn a thing or two.'

'The killer's out there. There'll be more deaths. That suspect Roman dragged in was a stitch-up job. You see that, don't you?'

Lang stared at the drying blood beneath his boots. 'Shit. I don't see anything. I do my job. I come into work in the morning, do what I'm told, go home at night and rest. I'm not like you. I'm not the kind who can afford to doubt. I need to know I'm on the right side.'

He looked lost. Without the others to back him up, to enforce conformity, he forgot why he was supposed to hate me. Or perhaps he just felt embarrassed to speak in front of the medic, who was a young woman.

She got up. 'Those bandages should hold. Don't go diving through any hedges.'

'Thank you.'

'You need to go to the hospital for a concussion check.'

'No time.'

'That's what they always say.' She picked up her bag. 'Don't blame me when you crash.'

Behind her, the forensics team hauled the body bag out of the door.

Lang stood up as well. 'That's that then.'

'A priest died.'

'He wasn't one of ours, was he? Not a Lutheran…'

'He was Catholic. What difference does it make?'

'You know what the Poles are like. They kill each other for fun.'

'Do you know what the difference is between Lutheran and Catholic?'

Lang scratched his head. 'I'm not much of a church person, truth be told.'

'Alright. Look.' I drew the increasingly dishevelled newspaper from my pocket.

He wrinkled his nose. 'Smells like an old beer mat.'

'I'll show you how I figured it out.'

'Save it for the journalists. Another "case of the year". I'm not interested.'

'It's important. Before he kills again. Look.' I showed him the story about the priest's ninetieth birthday. 'See? That's our victim.'

'OK…'

'Now, here's Gerhard.' I flicked through to the page about the swimming gala. 'See?'

'Tal, I need to get back to the station.'

'But there's more. Look… all the victims are in this newspaper. Here.' Leafing through the dog-eared pages, I couldn't find the jeweller, and remembered that I'd torn the page out and left it with the intern kid. 'There's more…'

'I get it. You think the killer finds his victims in this newspaper.'

'Go down to the station. Tell the others. Look in the archive. Find as many copies of this edition as you can. Set up a team. Check every person who's named in the newspaper.'

'Come on, Tal. It's just a coincidence.'

'No. It's–'

'You heard what the medic said, you got a bang on the head. You're not clear.'

'No. I'm–'

'Go to sleep, Tal. Get some rest.'

Forensics were gone. There was nobody left.

'Lang, listen–'

'No. You listen.' He glanced over his shoulder, even though we were alone, then crouched down next to me. 'I'll do you a favour,' he whispered. 'Because you're a good cop. You may be an arrogant prick who thinks he's smarter than the rest of us, but you care about the job. You always did. I'll tell you one thing: there's a list. Your name is on it. Find somewhere to lay low. They say the war's about to start. Tonight. Get out of Danzig if you can.'

'Lang, please…'

'Goodbye, Tal.'

He flipped the light switch off as he exited.

43

Gdańsk, Polish People's Republic

1961

The Fifth Rune

In dream she came to the black bog, but she wasn't afraid this time. She took off all her clothes and left them in a pile among the reeds. She dipped one toe in the liquid and shivered as it broke the surface. Her foot plunged into icy, dense viscosity. Now the other foot. She let herself sink until the black ooze sucked her in. Waist-deep, she knew no impatience. She sought the bottom of the bog with her feet and couldn't find it. She slipped down, waggling her toes, submerged up to the neck now. She closed her eyes and went under.

And woke to jagged pain. She clutched her shoulder and for a moment couldn't remember what ached. She must have slept too long, her limbs were heavy, her eyelids stuck together. Her fingers moved under the thin fabric of the overalls and found a crust of dried blood. The rune carved into her skin.

ᛞ

'Comrade Nowak, wake up…'

What kind of a name was that? In an instant the horror came back, and she struck out, screaming. Hands grabbed at her flailing wrists. She forced her eyes to come unglued.

'Get up.' The Inspector knelt in front of her. Electric light through the open door brought back the freezing confines.

'Leave me alone.' She rolled away and winced in pain at the raw place between her shoulder and chest. The whole shoulder ached.

He picked up the bloodied paper clip. 'What did you do?'

'It doesn't matter. I won't…'

'It's alright. I came to get you out. Come on, stand up.' He took her hand and pulled. She gritted her teeth in pain as he dragged her to her feet.

'I won't play.' She shivered in the cold, hugging the thin overalls to her skin.

'We'll get you something to eat. We're letting you out.'

'No.' She pushed him away. 'It's a trick. I won't confess to things I never did.'

'Relax. We know it wasn't you. You're being released.'

'I don't believe you. Why? How?'

'You were right about the dead woman. She's been identified. Gosia Svoboda, an archaeologist. There's a manhunt for her fiancé, he's on the run. You were right. The bureau wants to extend its apologies to you.'

'What are you talking about…?'

'There's news. Another killing. It happened while you were in here. We know it can't have been you. We need your help, Comrade Nowak. There's a killer on the loose. They left another one of those symbols. You're the only one who was onto them.' He reached into his pocket, causing her to flinch, but it wasn't a knife he took out, it was a slip of paper. 'What does this mean, Detective? Can you help us?'

'Is this real? You're not playing with me?' She took the slip of paper and stared. 'I recognise it, sure. It was in the old book of runes, but I don't remember what it meant.'

'Detective, there's a killer in Gdańsk using Nazi symbolism. We need all the help we can get. We want you. You're the one who figured out the runes. You're the one who identified Svoboda.'

'Just like that, you'd let me out?'

'First, you'll sign some documents. You'll agree to never talk to anyone about what you saw in this place. The State needs its security measures. I know it's hard, but the Republic is young, we face many threats from the inside and outside. It's–'

'I'll sign your documents, but I want something in return.'

'Don't push your luck, Nowak.'

'I want to visit the archive. I need to see the old German police records.'

'That's asking a lot.'

'Get me one hour in the archive. I'll go alone. I won't take anything, and I won't make copies. It's for the investigation. These killings go back to Danzig, I'm certain.'

'Danzig doesn't exist. It never did. There was only Gdańsk, always, and it was always Polish.'

'I don't care what you call it. Just get me in the archive.'

He shook his head. 'I'll see what I can do.'

* * *

It wasn't a dream or even a trick; she was outside in daylight. In the passenger seat of Roman's car, she held a flask of tea in one hand and flipped through the pages of her book of runes that the jailers had returned to her.

'The rune means "god". I don't know what kind of god, or which. But that's what it means.'

Roman glanced in the mirror. He shook his head. 'They don't mean anything at all. This madman's playing with us. What does he want?'

'There are twenty-four runes in this book. Let's hope he doesn't intend to do all of them.'

'He won't get away. The police are on high alert across the country. Security has been heightened at the borders.'

Anna closed the book. She let her gaze drift over the passing buildings through the window as Roman drove. 'I don't think he intends to get away. If he's leaving a trail, it's because he wants to be followed.'

'But why?'

'That's what we have to figure out.'

'And this man, this "Doc" you spoke with. The fiancé of the dead prostitute–'

'Gosia was an archaeologist.'

'Whatever. Do you think it could be him?'

'Doc has a motive, of sorts, for one of the murders. But no connection to the others. I don't know. I doubt it. We have to piece things together.'

They drove in silence for a few moments. 'We don't have much time,' Roman said eventually. 'This case has become dangerous. The latest victim was important, high up. I'll be replaced, and so will you, if we don't make progress. And there'll be nobody to get us out of that dungeon where you've been.'

'The answer is in the archive. All this links back to German Danzig somehow. The Inspector said he'd arrange something.'

'Forget it.' Roman stared at the road as he steered.

'What are you so afraid of? I'm free now, aren't I? My name's been cleared.'

'Don't be ridiculous. Those people, the secret ones, they never let anybody out of their cells once they're down there. Innocence or guilt is irrelevant.'

'And yet, I'm here, aren't I?'

'If they let you out, it was to follow you, to see where you go. If they suspect you of belonging to some conspiracy, they'll track your movements, your conversations, they'll use you to bring down the whole plot, and everyone involved with it.'

'But there is no plot.'

'That's what scares me.'

44

The victim lived in a spacious dacha in the seaside resort of Sopot, just down the coast from Gdańsk, overlooking a beach of white sand. The water withdrew into a pewter horizon. The front gate to an ivy-covered wall was sealed off and two officers stood guard over the crime scene. Their faces were haunted.

'Come on, they're waiting for us inside.' Roman patted one of the officers on the back, as if in consolation, as he pushed through the gate.

Anna stopped for a moment to watch the torn rags of cloud. She could lose herself in the sky. Her parents had never been real; she had to turn away, put a hand to the wall, something solid.

'Nowak! Come on.'

She hurried through the gate and caught up with the superintendent along a narrow path of stones set into a well-kept lawn. Looking up, she saw wooden balconies set over wide French windows. A holiday home for somebody important. Before the War, it might have been a banker who lived here, but now? Most likely some apparatchik.

They passed through glass doors into an elegant foyer. Flowers in vases sat along the wall beneath a sweeping mirror where the staircase curved out of view. Even though she knew that wealth still existed in the People's

Republic, where all citizens were equal, it was still shocking to see it with her own eyes. The kind of bourgeois disconnection that Karl Marx had witnessed and recorded in his works. It was difficult to grasp how such beachside luxury could coexist with the life of the shipyards, just along the coast.

'Careful where you step.' Roman indicated bloody footprints crossing the floor.

Anna knelt and looked closer. 'A man's boot. He's tall…'

'Leave it. Let forensics do their job.'

From the top of the staircase, somebody shouted down. 'Superintendent?'

'I got delayed. The detective is with me.'

'Upstairs, Comrades, upstairs.'

'I'm too old for this.' Roman set off up the staircase, holding the banister, his knees clicking as he bent them.

Halfway up, Anna smelled blood, mixed with some chemical trace. 'Alcohol?'

Roman sniffed. 'I can't smell anything anymore. Polyps in the nose, doctor said.'

At the top step, she hesitated. Blood was cast along the near wall like the imprint of a bird taking flight. It was gestural, expressionist. The drying scar of the rune under her shirt throbbed as she fingered the scab.

'Are you alright?' Roman said.

'I don't know. I hardly ate. I couldn't sleep in that place.'

'It's almost over now. Just look inside, and we can go home.'

The smell was like a barrier. She held her breath and pushed through into a bedroom at the end of the corridor. It was dazzling inside, the bleak seascape poured in through long floor-to-ceiling windows. Anna blinked and rubbed her eyes, trying to understand, but it didn't make sense. The forensics staff stood back at the side of the room for them, but Roman didn't cross the threshold.

'Detective.' He motioned for her to go first.

It was only when her eyes comprehended the naked man hung upside down, that the picture began to organise itself. A chandelier had been torn down, spilling decorative glass all over the floor so that the light was reflected from clashing angles like a scattered puzzle. The body hung from the hook in the ceiling where the fixture had been removed. She crouched and looked into the dead man's wide eyes.

'Looks like his neck was severed,' she said. 'But where's the blood? It should have drained down here underneath him…'

'We think there was a bucket set there to collect it,' one of the forensics team said. 'It spilled along the wall, as you see here, either on purpose or by chance.'

'Who was he?'

'Stanislaw Wozniak. Director of the Pomeranian Broadcasting Station. In charge of all radio output in the region. An influential man.'

'Sure. I've heard of him.'

'His record in the Party was spotless. Fought in the People's Army during the liberation of Poland. Was present at the Lublin Committee when the first post-war government was set up.'

What were they talking about? The clouds on the sea horizon outside had turned violet and pink. She gazed with thirst. She had been too deep underground.

'Are you alright, Detective?'

'I can't stay inside here.'

Daubed in blood on the wall above the bed, she saw the symbol:

ᚨ

45

At the station, a conference room was set aside for what was now recognised as a serial killer case. Anna laid out the clues on an evidence board: photographs, newspaper cuttings, maps. The superintendent watched, alongside the bunched officers brought in to help.

'There are three confirmed victims so far. Gosia Svoboda, an archaeologist.' She tapped at the photograph on the board. 'Found in an ash tree just outside Gdańsk. Cause of death: drowning. Here we have our lost colleague, Piotr Zielinski, known to all of you.'

Nobody spoke. She continued, 'Found in an apartment downtown. Cause of death: drowning. And here we have the latest victim, discovered this morning, Stanislaw Wozniak, director of the Pomeranian Broadcasting Station. Found dead in his home by the beach in Sopot. Cause of death: severed artery in the neck. All three bodies coincided with the discovery of what have been identified as Germanic runes.'

She stuck slips of paper with the runes next to each of the victims. 'This mark, found carved into the tree behind Gosia Svoboda, is believed to represent the harvest. This one, supposedly meaning "journey", was found by myself, stuck under the windscreen wiper of the car where Zielinski was last seen…'

Somebody coughed. 'Found by you?'

'Isn't that a bit odd?' Agent Sikorski said.

'What do you mean?'

'What, it was just there, in your car? No explanation?'

'I drove down to the shipyards with Zielinski. We were investigating the killing of Gosia Svoboda, who hadn't been identified at that point.'

'Wrongly supposed to be a prostitute,' Roman inserted.

'Right. We split up at the shipyards. When I came back to the car, Zielinski wasn't there. He never came back.'

'Strange,' Sikorski said.

Roman stared at him. 'Do you have a point you'd like to make?'

'No. Thank you. I just wanted to clarify.'

'Consider it clarified.' She turned her back on them. 'The final rune means "god", it was found written in blood on the wall of Wozniak's dacha.'

An officer put her hand up. 'And these runes? What do we know about them?'

'Not much. The dig where Svoboda worked is a Bronze Age burial site. During the wartime occupation, the Nazis hoped to find evidence of an ancient Germanic settlement in Poland to justify the annexation of our territory. But they didn't find what they were looking for.'

One of the men frowned. 'All the Germans are gone, aren't they?'

Mutterings around the room, suspicions, doubts.

Roman cleared his throat. 'The runes are an unknown part of the investigation. We'll look into them. But that's not the primary goal. It's the murders I want you to focus on. Comrade Nowak, tell us about the murders.'

The other officers shifted their eyes to her, alone at the front of the room. With their arms folded, their heads askance, she sensed their distrust. She tried to remember what she'd planned to say. Somebody coughed. A chair leg scratched the floor.

She raised her voice. 'The question is, what connects these three victims? As far as we know, they never met. They weren't related. They never crossed paths. To point out the obvious, one was a woman, the other two were men. One worked in law enforcement, one in academia, one in radio.'

Someone grunted at that word, but at a look from Roman they fell silent. A few of the others made eye contact across the room and glanced away, a message that Anna was excluded from. For a moment, she thought she couldn't understand, but of course, those daily group sessions at the radio, the long, tedious broadcasts… they hated it. An alternative vision of Gdańsk: the others only showed conformity in public. When they were alone, they must decry all this, Anna included – she was part of it, she was the only one who believed in communism. Or did Roman believe? She tried to read his scarred face, but his eyes were dead. No, Roman didn't believe in anything from their world. It was the past, a different reality that hung about him like an aura. Somebody coughed. The others stared. Why was she standing there in front of them all? Who was she? On the board, a photograph of a dead woman hung from a tree.

'Alright.' She cleared her throat. 'If we can figure out what these victims have in common, we might be able to anticipate the killer's next target. We might save a life.' She looked around the hostile faces. 'Does anybody have any ideas?'

A few people sighed. They scratched their heads.

'Division of labour.' Roman stood. 'I'm going to break you up into three groups. The first will look into Gosia Svoboda, the archaeologist. Interview friends, relatives, colleagues, neighbours. Dig up anything you can. Look for a link to the other victims. The second group will look into Zielinski; the third into Wozniak, the radio man.'

'And me,' Anna said. 'I need to see the archive of the old Danzig police force.'

Whispers died, the others glanced from her face to Roman's, to see his reaction.

'That's not possible.'

'I made a deal with the Inspector when they let me out of the cell. I just got confirmation on the phone before we came in here.'

Roman's face contorted with some repressed emotion. 'Let's discuss this in private, Comrade,' he muttered. 'The rest of you, get to work. Now.'

* * *

Seated in a squad car behind the station, Anna watched as the superintendent searched in the glove compartment, behind the mirror, under the dashboard, beneath the seats.

'What are you looking for?'

He slumped back in his seat. 'Alright. I don't think it's bugged.'

'Why would they…?'

'Anna, I'm pleading with you. Don't look in that archive.'

'It's just paper. What are you afraid of?'

'You don't understand. You were too young during the War. Do you even remember any of it?'

'Only flashes. The shipyards. Uniforms. A woman crying. The sea. I vaguely remember a giant ship in the night. But I don't know what's a real memory and what's just a dream.'

'Anna. I saw this city burn. I saw everybody die. I was one of the only survivors. If you knew me then, you'd understand, I didn't deserve to make it out alive. I was like a feral dog in those days. I should've been put down. For some reason, I was spared. I don't imagine there's a God behind all this. But something spared me, call it blind chance. The things I saw. The fire. The things that happened to women. The good people who suffered. I never managed to blot it out. It shouldn't have been me who survived. But here I am. I can't let Gdańsk burn again. I won't let you…'

'It's not going to burn. I just want to see a few files. What's the big deal?'

'There are Germans in those files. If people started to make connections… If they got it into their heads to claim

Gdańsk… There'd be another war. They can never, we'd never let them have Gdańsk… It's our jewel.'

Anna studied his grizzled face and hardly recognised him. A tortured boy showed through the craggy scar tissue and white stubble. She raised a hand as if to console him but couldn't bring herself to touch him.

She clutched her bag instead. 'It's alright, Comrade. Trust me. I'd never do anything to hurt the city. I'm going to the archive now. I'll let you know what I find out. Probably nothing.'

He didn't reply as she climbed out slowly. She peered back inside before closing the door behind her. Roman just stared through the windshield at a past invisible to her. Unimaginable. She almost smelled the burning.

46

From the outside it was an abandoned warehouse, moss growing out of crumbling brick, the metal shutters rusted into place. But as soon as she passed through an unmarked side entrance, Anna found herself in a modern office. Bright lights hung from the high ceiling over clean, white walls, partitioned desks, and separated rooms behind glass. The walls were lined with filing cabinets. Hard metal, surfaces, nothing to dampen sound; the place echoed with quiet footsteps and whispers, expansive hollowness. A guard checked her ID again, patted her down, and took her bag.

'I need that,' she said.

'You can collect it on the way out.' He put it aside and spoke into a phone. 'She's here.'

'Can I at least keep the German dictionary? I need it.'

He sighed, took out the dictionary, leafed through the pages, shook it upside down, and handed it over.

'I need a pen and paper as well.'

'You'll be given those.'

A door opened in the white wall to one side and the Inspector came out, wearing sunglasses despite being indoors.

'Follow me, Comrade.'

She wondered if this was a mistake. A glance back at the entrance showed no escape; the doorman barred her path backwards.

The Inspector stopped, a few feet ahead, realising that she still hesitated. 'It's alright, Detective. There's nothing to fear in here, except boredom.'

It was too late anyway, she hurried after him. Looking around the space, like those old workshops where her father once built ships, she saw a few lonely figures cross the emptiness. Women in suits carried files, went through doors, reappeared behind glass. She felt safer. It was just paper in the end. She followed the Inspector through a door set into a white-painted cubicle.

'Sit down, please.'

She pulled out a metal chair across the other side of an empty table. A bare bulb fizzed overhead.

He tried to smile. 'I'm sorry about what happened, Comrade. The State sometimes finds itself obliged to take measures that are distasteful; in extreme circumstances, when national security is at stake. It's a burden of our job. Not only the pain we must inflict, but the duty of secrecy.' He leaned forwards. 'It's better for the public not to know what goes on in such places.'

'Isn't it worse that they hear rumours instead? Whispers about torture, wild imaginings…'

'Our Republic is a work in progress. We inherited a world of rubble. The War was devastating.'

'I know. I was there.'

'While we labour to rebuild from the ruins, we're beset by enemies. In West Germany, they're agitating to take Gdańsk and Wrocław back.'

He stopped; the word "back" had been a slip. Staring into the shades, Anna couldn't tell if it was deliberate.

'Inspector, I've always been a loyal servant of the State. It saddens me that you feel the need to justify–'

'We acknowledge your loyalty. You were tested, in the cells, and you stayed strong, you proved yourself. Since being released, you haven't described anything you saw to anybody. You don't need to be told that the State must keep its secrets.'

'Is that what it was, a "test"?'

'And you passed. You wouldn't be in this archive otherwise. It's a privilege only granted to the trusted inner circles. You're a servant of the Republic.'

'OK… Where's this going, Inspector? I came here to consult some files for an ongoing murder investigation.'

'And you will, Comrade, you will. But in addition, we've reviewed your records. It's been decided.'

In the silence, she couldn't resist a glance at the door, it had no lock. She could still run out of here.

The Inspector caught her eyes. 'You don't say anything?'

'What should I…?'

'We're offering you a promotion. We need such servants for the secret police.'

'I never applied for the secret police.'

'Nobody applies. Candidates are handpicked, and only after lengthy observation. We've watched you for a while now. Your reading groups have been observed, your writings in the newspaper, and of course, your record as a police officer. The Republic is under threat, more than you realise. There are secret enemies among us. Who can we trust? Even the police are corrupted. Western influences seek to bring down communism. It's up to the self-sacrifice of a chosen few–'

'You're offering me a job in the secret police?'

'In a sense, you've already accepted. Else you wouldn't be in here.' He gestured to the door, the typewriters and the files that orbited in the echoey space like a constellation.

'Are you saying that I can't look at the files I need, if I don't accept?'

'There'll be a probation period, naturally. For you to decide if this job is really for you, and for us to make up our own minds.'

'And if I say no…?'

'It's never happened before. You'd be the first. Comrade, there are perks to advancement in the service of the State.'

'I know. I saw Wozniak's home this morning… Luxury. Most people couldn't imagine…'

'And he was merely an administrator for the radio.'

'He's also dead.'

'Think about our conversation. You can see the files now.' He stood up. 'An agent will assist you. You only have clearance for specific files. If you try to look at anything else… well, you understand. And, it goes without saying, nothing can be taken outside.'

* * *

The archive turned out to be even bigger than she had supposed; there was a downstairs. Anna followed the agent down a set of stone steps into an icy basement. She hadn't learned her name. Lights hung from the brickwork in a low ceiling as they walked a concrete hall past closed doors. Halfway along, the agent stopped.

'It's this one.' The nameless agent took out a key and opened the door marked "29". 'The records of the old police force were brought here not long after the liberation of the city. Some of the files were lost, unfortunately.'

She turned on a light to reveal a narrow room, like a cell – no window, no furniture, just row after row of filing cabinets.

'It's freezing,' Anna said.

'There's supposed to be a portable heater. I'll find it.'

'Smells musty. I guess nobody came in here for a while.'

'As far as I know, you're the first.'

Left alone for a moment, Anna moved between the cabinets, checking the labels on the drawers. The simple German words carried a hint of transgression:

1934 – LANGFUHR.

'Here it is.' The agent came back carrying a small electric heater that she plugged in by the side of the door.

'Thanks. You can leave me. I'll let you know when I'm finished, so you can lock up.'

'I can't do that. Visitors aren't allowed to be left unsupervised.'

'OK…'

'But I can help you, I've been trained to use the archive. The system can be tricky if you're new to it. What are you looking for?'

'It's a special investigation, I can't discuss it.'

'Very well. I suppose you can speak German?'

'Err…' Anna held up the German-Polish dictionary. 'I brought this.'

'I can translate. It's part of my job. I had to learn four languages.'

Anna looked at her: youngish, what – late twenties? It was difficult to estimate today, the War had left a legacy of injuries, trauma, and depression; nobody appeared young. Her blonde hair was tied back in a knot; she wore no makeup. Her suit looked like a man's but she had sewn it up by hand in places. Sensing herself judged, the agent straightened, but she didn't back down, didn't lower her cold blue eyes. Could she be dangerous?

Anna decided to trust her. 'Sure, you can help. We're looking for information about murders. There's a possible serial killer in the city; I'd like to see if there's anything like that in the old German records.'

'Why in the German records?'

'These crimes are connected by a kind of symbol. I'll show you…' She looked for her things and remembered it had all been taken from her. 'Do you have pen and paper?'

'Of course.' The agent looked in her bag and took out a file and a pencil case. She handed over a sheet of paper.

'It's something like this…' Drawing from memory, Anna sketched out the three runes. 'Sort of. They're runes; at least, that's the working theory. Symbols from old German mythology.'

'I know what runes are.' There was a touch of naivety in her petulance; she didn't realise the danger of familiarity with Nazism, or she didn't care. Anna started to like her.

'Good. Let's just start by digging through, looking for murders.'

'But where should we start?'

'How about the shipyards?'

'OK. This way.' The agent went to the right-hand side of the room, where several filing cabinets were set against the wall. 'Each one is for a different year. When do you want to look?'

'Not too far back. The killer's still active. What are the latest records we have?'

'Everything from the thirties, more or less. A lot of stuff from the forties was lost. During the War, you can imagine…'

'Alright, start with 1939. Let's take a drawer each, hey?'

A glint showed in the agent's eyes, a faint curve of the lip, as she pulled the first drawer out and set it down on the ground. She had that curiosity of the best cops, that perversity, almost like voyeurism.

Anna decided to push her luck. 'Do you think we could get something to eat or drink? I just got out of prison.'

The agent looked at her like she was a celebrity. 'I'll call upstairs, see if they can send something down.'

* * *

For hours they dug through the files, pulling down one drawer after another. Crime scene photos, mugshots, maps; like plunging into a collective dream. The photographs fascinated her, odd items recorded from forgotten investigations, a shoe, an earring, a pot of basil, a toy car. Paraphernalia of crime abstracted from life, just a shoe now, not even the shoe itself, an index card for a lost piece of evidence. There must have been a warehouse containing all this junk, but it would have burned down like the rest of the city. Old shoes and dolls catch fire easily and leave nothing behind.

There was a history buried here, another world that persisted only on paper. She studied maps, diagrams, traced streets she'd known since childhood, revealed here with different names: Holy Spirit Street was the Heilige-Geist-Gasse, the Green Gate was the Koggentor, the Long Market was the Langer Markt… the bend of the river, the Motława, was the Mottlau. She flipped through pages of such words seeking a trace of her parents, but they were gone of course, in any language, in any reality. They never existed.

'I've got something,' the agent said.

'What?' Anna broke from a trance of old townhouses that no longer stood even in memory, the former occupiers lost.

'There was a series of murders in 1939. They–'

'Let me see.' She jumped up and went over to where the agent was seated against the wall, surrounded by boxes and files.

'Here.'

It was a thick dossier, barely held together by string. Somebody had written in red letters on the front, "DANZIG POLICE KILLER". A few official stamps were marked below that, and at the bottom of the cover, an inscrutable signature.

'This stamp says "solved".' The secretary pointed. 'I can't read the others.'

'Alright, alright.' She carried the dossier over to an empty patch on the floor and started laying out the individual files, yellowing paper covers containing reams of loose sheets. She opened the first one and skimmed through, but the details came too quickly, too disconnected. There were photographs of dead bodies, piles of clothes, rooms, among typed pages in German.

'Help me with this,' Anna said. 'What does that say?'

The agent sat on the floor beside her and took the first file from her hand. 'A police officer was killed…'

'It fits our case, a murdered police officer.'

In a haze of excitement, they laid out the pages of the first file: photographs of the body, naked, laid out in a loose star shape.

'I'm going to need to take copies of these,' Anna said.

'That's not permitted.'

'Alright, we'll do it the slow way.' She glanced up to check the time, but there was no clock down here. She took a piece of paper and started sketching out a picture of the crime scene from the photograph.

'Does it fit?' the agent said.

'Not exactly. Our victim was drowned. There's no mention of a rune here either. But maybe…' She flicked through the pages. Half of them were blocked out with black ink. 'It's all gone. Here there should be a photograph, but it's missing. Here there should be a description of evidence, but it's redacted. Most of the file is like this. Is there anything else?'

The agent shook her head. 'That's all.'

'What's the name of the investigating detective?' Anna flipped the pages. 'Tal. Johann, Tal. Do me a favour, take a look through the other documents, see if you can find a file on him. Danzig Police Force, Chief Investigator, Johann Tal.'

The agent leafed through the file and squinted at the corner of a page. 'Tal. What kind of name is that? Is it German?'

'I don't know, I've never heard it before.'

'There's an index of police officers in the archive. Hold on.' The agent got up and crossed the room. 'The Gestapo kept tabs on their own people. Our archivists found a whole cache of their internal investigations.' She pulled open a drawer and dug through some files. 'Tal, Tal… Not this one.' She closed the drawer and pulled out the one beneath. 'Tal, Tal… where are you?'

Anna looked over her shoulder. 'Do they keep files like this for us? Don't answer; I know they do.'

'Here.' The agent pulled out a drawer.

'Let me.' Her hands shook as she grabbed it, wanting the pleasure of reading for herself. But she needed the agent. After this was over, she was going to take up German classes, if she could.

Tal. A small, square photograph in black and white showed a man's face. Wide, round eyes stared out, dark irises that called for life, as if the picture had only just been taken.

'Who was he?' She flicked through the pages, but there were no other photographs; it was mostly typewritten sheets of notes in German, redacted in parts. Digressions unwinding into meaninglessness.

'Can I?' The agent took the file and leafed through. 'It's about his work record, his personality… his ethnicity. Jeez. Somebody researched his family tree…' She brought the paper closer to her eyes. 'It says, "Grandparents on mother's side, German. On father's side, unknown. Surname may be derived from Hebrew (meaning "dew"), or of German/Scandinavian origin ("valley"). Exhibits degenerate tendencies."' She looked up. '"Degenerate tendencies"?'

'OK, that's useless. Is there anything–'

'Here's his last case file. Something about an adoption agency.' She drew out an old scrap that must have been torn from a newspaper. 'Something about an amber dealer and his wife. Their baby… It seems like nothing. No mention of a rune. Not even a murder. It's a birth announcement. Why would this be in the file?'

Anna took the torn page and stared at the photograph. The ink was faded, the paper lined with wrinkles. 'What else?'

'Here's a birth certificate. With a photo. It's a baby.'

Anna glanced. Her heart fell; this was all nothing. History turned out to be just an endless repetition of trivial shit. It was just as well the future blotted out the past, or we'd all drown in mundanity.

The agent flipped a page. 'It says here something about adoption. Wait. What? They took babies from Polish mothers. Gave them to German foster parents. But the text's practically illegible.'

'Let me see.' She glanced over the file, but it all ran together, lines and lines of data. Nothing.

'He died. This Tal.'

So many documents, so much wasted paper, a city that no longer existed, a world that had never been.

The agent read aloud. '"Killed in line of duty. 1939." It's signed by another officer. Roman somebody or other. I can't decipher his surname.'

'Roman?' Anna jumped. She took the file and stared at the signature. 'Schneider, I think it says. Roman Schneider.'

The woman shrugged. 'Does that mean anything to you?'

'No. I mean, there's a Roman in our police. He's old enough. He was around back then. But his name's Roman Krawiec. It's nothing. I guess. There's nothing here. It's just paper in the end.'

'Schneider means "tailor" in German. Krawiec? That's the same name translated into Polish…'

Time swelled; the walls beat like a heart. 'Wait. Let me see that file again, with the baby–'

Before she could finish, a man in a suit knocked and stuck his head through the door.

'Comrade Nowak? There's a phone call for you.'

'For me? Nobody knows I'm here.'

'It's upstairs. Please hurry, phone bills are expensive.'

'But–'

'They've arrested a suspect. They need you to come right away. "Now," they said.'

47

The archaeologist was almost unrecognisable. His eyes were bruised, one swollen over so that he could not open it, his lip was gashed, several of his teeth missing, a clump of hair had been torn out. Handcuffed to the other side of the desk, he drooled and lolled like he was about to pass out. Anna turned to the two-way mirror with a question in her face, but whoever was on the other side couldn't respond.

'Doc, it's me. Are you alright?'

His head dropped forwards onto the desk with a thud.

'For Christ's sake.' She got up and opened the door and shouted into the hall. 'The suspect's unconscious. I need a doctor.'

Nobody responded. In the cold corridor, there was only a guard stationed by the door, who gazed at the wall as if he hadn't heard. She ran past him to the observation room, on the other side of the two-way mirror, but it was locked. She banged on the panel.

'Hey! Let me in.'

Nothing. She continued around a bend in the corridor and skipped up a short staircase to the canteen. She filled a cup of water and made some tea from a lukewarm kettle. On the way out, she noticed a first aid kit by the door, and grabbed that too. It had never been opened; the bandages and iodine inside were unused.

Back in the interrogation room, she pulled Doc up in his seat, and smoothed the hair back out of his face.

'Hey, wake up.'

He made a gurgling sound.

'It's me, Nowak. Wake up. Talk to me.'

His one usable eye opened a crack in the purple flesh, to reveal a ball soaked in blood. He groaned. 'Pl… pl…'

'Here, drink some water.'

She held the edge of the cup to his cut lips and tipped it gently, just a few drops. He swallowed drily.

'Good, that's good. Drink it down.' Supporting his head, she poured more water into his mouth, until it flowed down his chin.

He swallowed and retched but didn't throw up.

'OK, now drink some tea, it'll revive you.'

His one eye closed over, and he slumped back, apparently unconscious.

'Hey, wake up. Don't take a nap.'

A trail of drool dropped from his bottom lip. Anna jumped up and banged on the two-way mirror.

'Roman! Are you in there?' She slammed with her fists. 'Hey! Who's in there?'

Behind her, the door to the interrogation cell opened. The Inspector stuck his head inside. 'Stop fussing, Detective.'

'What are you doing down here?'

'It's our case now. It already spread too far. The police show themselves to be incompetent. We'll take things over from here.'

Between them at the table, the prisoner coughed and spat blood, mumbling in his sleep.

'What did you do to him?' Anna said. 'He's half dead.'

'We interrogated him, that's all. He has vital information. The nation is vulnerable, Detective, you know that. Extract his confession, while you have the chance. If you can't, we'll find someone who will.'

'Why me?'

'He requested you. He promised he'd speak if it was to you. Of course, we could have made him speak anyway, but it was decided to play along. Let's see what he wants to tell you.'

'He can't say anything; he needs a doctor.'

'Don't be childish. He's just pretending. He wants to confess, Detective, the guilty always do. Open the door, they walk through joyfully.'

'And if he's not guilty?'

'If he wasn't guilty, he wouldn't be seated there, on the other side of the table.' The Inspector glanced at his watch. 'Time is running out. We have to act before anybody else gets killed. Before this rot spreads. You have fifteen minutes to get what we want.'

'Or what?'

The Inspector ducked out and slammed the door behind him. Anna banged with her fist. 'Hey! I'm talking to you! Open this goddamn door.'

She stopped with her fist raised to bang again; what was she doing? She'd end up back in an underground cell in the pitch black. Anything but that, she'd slit her wrists first. The rune on her chest itched and throbbed. She pulled her chair around next to the prisoner.

'Miro, Miro.' She lifted his head and patted him on the cheek. 'You have to wake up. It's important. Your life depends on it.'

His eye didn't open, but something like a smile showed at the edges of his damaged lips. He tried to speak.

'What did you say?' Anna leaned close into his face until her ear brushed his mouth.

'It's you…' he whispered.

'Alright, enough games. Drink this tea.'

He shook his head.

'Don't make me pour it down your throat.' She brought the cup to his face, but when she tipped in a mouthful of tea, he spat it out. 'For Christ's sake, Doc. I'm the only friend you've got in here. You requested to speak to me. Why?'

He shook his head.

'Tell me why, or I'm leaving.'

His one eye opened, wider now. 'Why do you think? Those men beat the shit out of me. They would've killed me.'

'So, you are awake. Drink the tea.'

'I don't want it.'

'I said drink the fucking tea. It might be the last cup you ever get. I've been in the cells, I know what it's like.'

He lifted the arm that wasn't handcuffed to the desk and held it up high so she could see. The wrist was broken, the fingers hung limp. She felt tears well and swallowed them down.

'Alright. I'll do it,' he said.

She brought the cup to his lips and was relieved when he drank, all of it, deep, thirsty gulps. The empty cup dropped from her fingers.

He let his head tip back. 'Happy now?'

'They are watching us behind that mirror. You need to give me something, if you want to save yourself.'

'What's the point? They already crippled me. They already told me, "Nothing I say makes any difference". I asked for a lawyer, they laughed in my face and broke my arm. They explained it clearly; I'm already guilty. Gosia's dead. I'm the last one who saw her. I have a motive; they know I was arguing with her. And they caught me at the border. They say I was trying to get across to the West. That's an admission of guilt, they say. I'm fucked, aren't I?'

'Why did you try to cross the border?'

'Wouldn't you? As soon as you said she was murdered, I knew I'd be accused.'

'There is justice in the People's Republic. The Law works for the people.'

He spat blood on the floor. 'You believe that? You're as insane as the others. I asked to speak to you because I thought you were different.'

'No. You asked to speak to me because I'm a woman; you thought I couldn't punch as hard. But you're wrong. I know how to hurt.'

'Fuck it then. There's no hope.'

'Did you kill Gosia?'

'I loved her!' The table rattled as he shook his handcuffed arm.

'Lovers kill each other. Happens all the time.'

'I didn't kill her, alright? But it makes no difference. They already told me I'll hang.'

'It does make a difference. If somebody else killed her, we have to find that other person. Find the real culprit, and you'll be innocent. Right?'

He closed his eyes. She heard him swallow painfully. 'Another person. But who?'

'Listen, somebody killed Gosia. You knew her better than anyone; who could have done it? And why?'

'I… I don't know… I…'

'What about the other guy from the dig site?'

'What, Miro? No. He's a baby, he could hardly talk to a woman, let alone touch one. And besides, he's my best friend.'

'Alright, so who else?'

Doc strained, gritting his teeth, the handcuff rattling on the table. 'I don't know. I can't think. Maybe if I could get out of here, I could see things clearly. Everything's blurred. I can't even believe she's really dead. I try to believe it. I know that she must be, or I wouldn't be in here. But I can't believe it. I can't.'

'Calm down. Think. Try to concentrate. We don't have much time. If you can't give me a suspect before I leave this room, there won't be anything I can do to help you.'

His wrecked hand moved from the table and brushed her arm. 'You're the detective. You'll find the suspect. It's your job, isn't it? You're smart, you found us at the dig site… you… what were you doing there? Why did you come to the site at all?'

'The… I don't know.' She stopped. 'Why did I?'

Behind her back, the door rattled as somebody knocked. 'Time's up, Nowak! Come out now.'

Doc jerked upright in his chair, suddenly wide awake. 'No! Don't leave me.'

She called over her shoulder, 'Just a minute!'

'Please. Those men… they'll kill me. You can't leave me with them.'

'Doc, you have to give me something. Give me a suspect.'

'Please… I can't go back to that dark room. I'll die…'

The door swung open. The Inspector stepped into the light. 'Time's up.'

'No!' Doc pulled back on his chair at the sight of him, pulling the handcuffs until they chafed his wrist. 'Not with him!'

'Inspector, we're making progress,' Anna said. 'The suspect cooperates with me. Give us a little longer.'

The Inspector laughed. 'Cooperates? He's playing you, and you let yourself be played like a whore. Look at him, he's desperate enough to do anything, to say anything. They're all like that, these bourgeois intellectuals. Decadent, Western types.'

'I'm not,' Doc blubbered. 'I swear, I'm a loyal socialist. I did everything they asked, at the dig site, it's all been approved, proper, dialectical methods. That's why it took so long.'

'Shut your mouth. Don't talk about what you don't understand.'

Anna closed her eyes. 'I can't think. Stop shouting, both of you. I need to think. The suspect, there is a suspect.' Her eyes blinked open. 'The engineer, from the dig site. He knew about the runes. What was his name?'

'What engineer?' Doc said. 'There was no engineer. There was just the three of us. Me, Gosia, and the other Miro.'

'No. There was a fourth. A man there, he gave me directions. Long grey hair, dungarees… A big dent in his head…'

'I don't know who that is.'

'We're wasting time.' The Inspector pushed past her. 'Stand up.' Doc pulled back as far as he could, as the handcuff was removed from his wrist. 'Don't try anything.'

'There was another man at the site.' Anna watched. 'Think. Who was he?'

'Please, help me, please.' Doc burst into tears.

'Shut up.' The Inspector pulled his arm back.

'Please…' His words became incoherent as he begged, and now screamed as his broken arm was twisted around his back and handcuffed to the other.

'Stop crying,' Anna said. 'Think. Who was the man? Who was he?'

Grimacing with pain, Doc allowed himself to be pushed forwards. The chair clattered as they stumbled towards the door. He screwed his face with a final effort of concentration. 'There was one day… Gosia said she spoke to some old weirdo… That's all she said. "A weirdo." I went to look around but couldn't find anyone. I told her she was paranoid. Do you think…?'

'He's making it up,' the Inspector said. 'You encourage him, Detective. Stop giving false hope. When a man's desperate enough, he'll grab at anything.'

'I… I…' Doc broke into tears as he was propelled out of the room.

Anna ran after them. 'Is there anything else? This man… did you see anything? Hear anything?'

'Let it go, Detective.' The Inspector pushed her back with his free hand, as he kept a grip on the handcuffs. 'This case is closed. Good riddance to it.'

48

She ran out of the building before anybody could query her. In the driver's seat of the car, she let out a scream and sank back against the leather and breathed. She turned the key in the ignition. Pulling out of the carpark, she glanced up at the windows as they caught the grey light but couldn't see anybody watching. Somebody always watched. She switched gears and accelerated down the street. She left the city behind. In a dream, she crossed the new tarmac highway, the pylons, the telephone wires lined with starlings. Doc might already be dead. Her parents were not real. Documents, birth certificates. A child. A dead police detective with an odd name. *Tal.* A handful of amber, petrified tree sap, washed up on the Baltic coast. Her mind wandered through shifting clues and lost its way, but the car drove straight.

An hour later she was back at the burnt-out wasteland. A weight in her stomach – circular return, repeated mistakes. She parked and retraced her path to the row of wrecked buildings, only one of which appeared to be inhabited. Like last time, a set of dirty footprints snaked out from beneath the door and faded into the scrag.

'Hello?' She banged on the door.

Inside, wind curled and sighed. The same old woman called out, 'Go away.'

'Police. Open up.'

Skittish feet ran through the flimsy walls.

'Open up, before I knock this door down.'

The house went still. Anna tried the door, but it was locked. The upstairs windows were clouded behind shreds of curtain, while the front window downstairs was boarded up.

She banged on the door. 'Open up! Police. I'm warning you.'

Nothing. There was a side alley between this house and the abandoned building next door, overgrown with weeds and dank with moss.

'Fuck it.' She took two steps back and threw herself into the door, shoulder first. The flimsy panel shook and bent inwards, almost giving way. The scarred rune on her chest screamed. She stepped back to charge again, but a voice from inside the hovel called out.

'Alright, alright. Don't break my door, for God's sake. The place is already falling apart.'

'Let me in then.'

A key turned in the lock, and the door slid inwards. The old woman looked out of inky must, blinking into the daylight. 'You, again. What do you want?'

'The man. Where is he?'

'What man?'

'Don't play games. The old guy with the overalls. Calls himself an engineer. Got a big dent in his skull, like someone smacked him over the head with a chair.'

'I don't know what you're talking about.'

Anna pointed at the dirt beneath her boots. 'Those are his footprints. Too big to be yours, you're like a mouse.'

The woman looked at the prints that led across her threshold and faded into the wasteland. She shook her head. 'I don't know who–'

'Fine. I'll look around and find him myself.' She stepped forwards as the woman propped herself behind the door, blocking her way.

'You can't!'

'If he's not here, what are you hiding? I just want to see. If you're alone, I'll leave and never come back.'

'This is my home. You can't just–'

'It's alright, Izabela,' a man's voice said from behind her. 'Let the officer in. I'll talk to her.'

'What?' Fear showed in the woman's eyes as she looked back over her shoulder into the dark.

'It's alright, I said. Let her in.'

'They'll take you away from me. I won't let them.'

Anna almost smiled. 'I'm not here to take anybody away. I just want to talk.'

The door opened with a breath of overgrown hair, mouldy furniture, rotting boards. The man came out of the darkness.

'It is you,' Anna said. 'You're the engineer. We spoke at the dig site.'

'What do you want, Detective?' He shoved Izabela away as she pawed at his side. 'Get off me, woman. Go back inside, make some tea. Let us talk.'

'But it's not safe…'

'Go and make tea, go on.'

Izabela glanced hatefully at Anna before she disappeared into the dark. When she was gone, the man stepped out into the daylight, shielding his eyes, and closed the door behind him.

'What do you want?' he said.

'Last time we spoke, you told me you worked at the dig site. An engineer, you said. That was a lie. I spoke to the archaeologists. They never heard of you.'

'I *am* an engineer. I know far more about the burial sites than those so-called scientists. I would've helped them gladly, and for free, but they swore at me, kicked me away any time I got close. They want it all for themselves. They're the liars, not me.'

'Liars, why?'

'They want to prove the site is Polish. The government pays them to do it. But it's not Polish.'

'You think it's German?'

'I used to think so. Now I know, it's much older than Germany or Poland. The people who lived here, they disappeared long before Germans or Poles existed.'

Anna felt the presence of the black bog like an emanation hidden beyond the crooked trees where the crows watched.

'Alright, listen, I'm not here to talk archaeology. A woman from the dig site was murdered.'

'And you think it was me. Because I have this dent in my head. I look like a monster. I get it. But why would I kill her? I've got a good life here. Izabela takes care of me. I study what's under the black water. The world leaves me in peace. I don't ask for more.'

'There have been ritual killings. Runes. You're the only one who knows what the runes mean. You're the one who's fascinated with all this stuff.'

'Doesn't make me a killer.'

'Do you have them tattooed on you?'

'What?'

'The runes. I was given a description of a possible suspect; his chest was covered in rune tattoos.'

'Lady, I'm sorry to disappoint you, but I'm not the one you're looking for.'

'Take off your shirt then. Show me.'

'Why should I?'

'Because if you don't, I'll take you down to the station and throw you in a cell for refusing to cooperate.'

'You're all alone out here, Detective. I'm bigger. I could catch you first, drown you in the bog.'

She stepped back instinctively, but the engineer made no move towards her. He grinned.

'My colleagues know I'm here,' she said. 'If I don't come back, they'll look for me.'

'Maybe so, maybe not.'

He lifted his arms, and she flinched, grabbing for the gun in her pocket, but he didn't approach. He pulled his shirt up over his head to reveal a scrawny chest, rib bones poking through translucent skin, a tangle of white hair, and no tattoos.

She let out a rush of breath. 'Christ. You could have done that right away and saved the unpleasantness.'

'I'm not obliged to take off my shirt for anyone else. If I do it, I do it as a favour.'

'You say you know about the dig site, you say you know more than the scientists do…'

'What does it matter, if nobody believes me? I don't have their fancy pieces of paper, their fancy qualifications. I never went to university.'

She studied his blank face. 'Alright. I believe you.'

'You do? Why?'

'Because I need help. Those scientists were no use. One ran away, the other won't tell me anything. The other's dead. Maybe you can tell me what they couldn't.'

'Tell you what?'

'Who is the killer? Who else knows about the runes? There can't be more than a handful of people in all of Poland who understand them. The Germans are gone. Who else knows about Germanic runes and ritual practices? Christ, we found a girl hanging from an ash tree. It's time to end this.'

'From an ash tree?' He rubbed his grizzled chin. Milky thoughts coiled in his eyes; maybe he really was an engineer, of a kind. 'An ash tree. Maybe…'

'Maybe what?'

'There was a man.'

'Which man?'

'I spent time in a mental institution. Many times, over the years. I made some mistakes, committed some sins. In the court, their experts said I wasn't sane. As if they were qualified to judge. They're all insane now, with their communism, their so-called equality.'

'Careful now, I could arrest you for that.'

'And what do you think would happen? They'd find me "insane" again and send me back to the madhouse. Of course they would, since communism is a science, in their minds, and this world is the inevitable outcome of historical forces that are crystal clear, if you're sane enough to understand them. By such measures, everyone's insane. You as well.'

'You were about to tell me about a man.'

'*Him.* Now he was special. He was different. I shared a cell with him in a terrible place. The walls are filled with screaming. It never ends. If you weren't insane before you went inside, you'd end up crazy in that place, believe me, lady, *you* would end up crazy too. The noises at night. I'll never forget.'

'Who was this man?'

'He told me his life. What a story. That man had lived, truly lived, in a way most humans never dream of. His personality was all broken up like a kaleidoscope. He was mad, of course, but the kaleidoscope gave him gifts; he lived so intensely. He'd been many people. You understand what that means, Detective? Most of us can only be one person, we're stuck that way our whole miserable lives. But he, he'd been many. And he'd seen the extremes. He'd known murder, torture, rape, ecstasy… dread… love… mystery… loneliness… I never knew a man with so many dreams bottled up in his brain.'

'And the runes…?'

'It was me who taught him. We were perfect for each other. He needed a teacher, but nobody could ever get close. I needed a listener, but nobody ever paid attention to me. They all thought I was crazy. Well, he was like a sponge. I taught him. I taught him everything, and he listened carefully. He drank it up like a man dying of thirst.'

'You taught him about the runes?'

'He knew a kind of magic, this man. He had his own ways. He told me he could become another person. I thought he was just talk at first, but I saw him do it. He watched the others at the madhouse, and he'd become them. He could become anyone he wanted. It was incredible. He'd move just like them, he'd sound just like them. He had magic, I tell you. But he was unstable, he couldn't control it.'

'Unstable?'

'No matter how many times he changed identity, he could never find what he was looking for. In the cells, he stopped wearing clothes. Just walked around naked until they strapped him into a jumpsuit. He said he used to believe in clothes, but he gave up; they didn't work.'

'What does that mean, clothes "didn't work"?'

'He used to take people's clothes, as if he could put on their lives. But he couldn't. Things went wrong. Christ, he hurt people, he killed people. He'd raped and maimed. It couldn't carry on; he'd end up hung. He gave up clothes. So, I taught him the runes.'

'Taught him, how?'

'I showed him, you don't have to kill or steal. The runes are powerful. If you carve one into a rock, or into a tree, or into skin, it enchants that place. There are all kinds of gifts. I taught him how to draw them, and what they all mean.'

'And the tattoos?'

'He tattooed himself in the madhouse. Wanted to have the whole dictionary of runes at his fingertips. He carved each one into his chest as soon as he'd mastered it.'

'Runes on the chest. This could be him. This could be the man I'm looking for. What's his name?'

'He's had many names. Said he can't remember the first. But the name he's called by, in his dreams, he said, is *Danzig*.'

The word fluttered like a sail at sea. Crows took flight. Clouds so complex, and never still, you could stare into them for hours.

'*Danzig*.' She dragged her eyes from the sky. 'That's not much help. I need a name I can look up in a directory, an address book. A first name and a surname.'

The engineer grinned. 'That is his name in the address book. He gave it to them at the hospital. They wrote it in their register. First name, Danzig. Surname, Danzig.'

'Danzig, Danzig. Are you fucking with me?'

'You'll find weirder things than that in the madhouse. But what's he done? Do you really think he might have killed? That's not how I taught him. He promised to stop all that. When he left the madhouse, he said he'd be sane now. He had the runes, he said, and… Christ. You don't think he could really… he couldn't… He told me, all he wanted was to find out who he was. He was looking for something, or for someone. He thought he could find his way back, and he'd be happy then… but he… I told him, to hurt people is a sin. I told him that. I can picture him, like he was standing in front of me now, how he nodded and smiled and said he'd never hurt. But that wasn't him, was it? He was playing another role. He always was.'

49

She drove back to the city through pouring rain. At the mental hospital, the woman on reception looked up lazily from a newspaper.

'He called himself *what*?'

'He called himself Danzig, Danzig.' Suddenly this seemed ridiculous. But she'd started now. 'He was a resident here a year or so ago, I was told.'

'That's before my time. His name was *Danzig*?' The woman looked again, with scepticism, at the police badge Anna held out. 'Wait here, I'll ask someone.'

Probably she should have spoken to Roman and the others before coming here, but her colleagues hated her, she saw it now. All the time and effort she'd put into studying the works of Marx and Engels had only made her despised. The Inspector's offer of a job with the secret police ran through her mind. A new beginning. Perhaps a place where she could belong, perhaps a place… But before she could complete the thought, a tall, skinny man with long white hair came through the rear door. 'You're looking for Danzig?'

'He was a patient of yours?'

'You'd better come into my office.'

* * *

The office was more like a cell. Bare brick, a metal desk and folding chairs by a window that overlooked a grey courtyard. A few lonely figures stood about outside, motionless in the rain.

'Found it.' Dr Baginski pulled out a file. 'One of the more interesting patients to come through here. People used to think his name was a prank, but he was earnest. I won his trust like that, by taking him seriously. He would pretend to be someone else. Every time he had an interview with me, he'd act as if he was one of the other patients. And he played them perfectly. He was a born mimic. He might have become an actor if he hadn't been, well, if he hadn't ended up in here. The only way to progress with him was to play along. Once I learnt that, I made the breakthrough. God, it was creepy the way he mimed, his voice sounded exactly like theirs, he could recreate every little gesture, the way they walked or moved or even just sat down.'

'And you let him free?'

'Had to. We have no resources. Can't keep people inside long unless someone pays for them. Most of the patients in here have family paying the bill. Danzig had nobody.'

'So, he walked out of here, just like that?'

'The only question I'm asked to determine is, can this patient take care of themselves out in the world? Can they feed themselves? Can they move around? Can they communicate? Danzig did all these things. I showed him how he could use his special powers. If he was ever stuck, he could just think about a different person and pretend to be them. What would they do in that situation? How would they act? And it worked. A remarkable case. If I had the time and the resources, I might have written a study about him. The scientific community would be fascinated. But there is no real science in Poland these days, not unless it's "dialectical".'

'We have reason to believe that Danzig has been killing people.'

'Well, he had no record of violence here. The main thing I remember about Danzig is he refused to wear clothes.'

'I was told by another inmate he'd killed people before he came here.'

'That's impossible.'

'Why?'

Baginski leaned forward across the desk. 'You see, he's like a child really. That's why he plays these parts, he never grew up. To become an adult is to discover who we are. He was never able to do that. He's an innocent really, just a baby.'

'But children can be dangerous, can't they? They can be cruel and selfish. If you put a child into a man's body, he could hurt people. Don't you think?'

'Well… when you put it like that. Maybe. But why would he?'

'Recognise these?' Anna flipped through the pages of her notebook to the runes and slid it across the table.

'Runes. But that was a different patient. Strange man. History of cranial trauma. You could see the deformation in his skull. Quite interesting in his own way. He was obsessed with the runes. He believed they were magic.'

'He taught Danzig how to use them.'

'I do recall something like that, but it was harmless. In fact, I remember thinking it was good for Danzig to make a friend.'

'There have been several murders in Gdańsk using these runes. Ritualistic killings.'

'And you think it was Danzig? That's… I don't believe it.'

'Maybe he's innocent, but I need to talk to him. Do you have an address? Do you know where he went after he left here?'

'All patients have to leave an address. But most don't stay at that place for long. I'll find it for you. Detective, if your fears are true, I hope you won't think it's any fault of our work here at the hospital. We do the best we can. We're understaffed, and well, the War left a lot of broken people. We can't fix everybody…'

'I don't care what you do. There are inspectors for that. My job is to solve crimes. I need to find a killer before they murder again.'

'Of course, of course. Anything we can help with, it's all at your disposal… Only, Detective, if we could keep the hospital out of the news reports. It's not our fault…'

50

She found the building, a half-ruined tenement where the branches of an old sycamore twisted out of broken windows. She shouldn't go inside alone. But the others at the station; she didn't want to work with any of them. She couldn't trust anybody, and this was her case; she'd got this far alone, she'd solve it alone and not share the glory. Fuck it. She went through a hole in the wall into a hollow filled with rain and burrs. The sunken walls seemed deserted, but a cat in the shadows spied her.

'Hey…' she whispered. The cat disappeared.

Through doorways she passed abandoned, dilapidated flats. The usable furniture had been looted long ago. It stunk like a compost heap. In the courtyard, the tree trunk was carved with graffiti and all kinds of symbols. Among them, a rune. She recognised it from the book, the rune that meant "yew tree":

ᛇ

Now she really should call for backup. Why didn't she? Across the other side of the tree, she found a working staircase. Something mewled. She shone her torch beneath the stairs into a trellis, a locked basement. Several mangy kittens were transfixed by the light. A mother cat hissed.

'Sorry.' She turned off the torch and took out her gun. She crept up the stairs.

The rain poured down through a crack in the ceiling; filtered through old rafters, the water tasted mildewy. Through the broken doors of the first-floor landing, cats stared, curious, distant, bored, from a realm where humans didn't exist and didn't matter. She ignored them and ran up to the next floor. Like stepping through a mirror, she turned off the landing and found a neat corridor, old-fashioned floral wallpaper, preserved as if nothing had ever happened in this building; as if there had never been a war. Plant pots, a swept floor, pictures on the wall showed galleons at sea. She hesitated and looked back. A few stray cats watched from the stairwell beneath.

She stepped out of the rain under a stretch of undamaged ceiling and passed closed doors with numbers, just like a regular tenement. The cats watched through the banisters but didn't follow. She still heard the rain lashing the stairwell as she hurried along this secret hall. 7B was the last door. She knocked and stepped back, wiping rain from her hair. She knocked again. Of course, nobody would respond, this place was like a dream and even in dreams, we know what's possible and impossible. She knocked again. It was too late to go back. She tried the handle and felt it turn. The door opened inwards into darkness. A chemical smell like formaldehyde. She was terrified.

She took one step across the threshold. 'Hello?'

Nothing. She took out her torch and closed the door carefully behind her. The sound of the rain from the stairwell was muffled. On the back of the door a symbol was painted:

ᛟ

She gasped and clapped her hand over her mouth. Nothing stirred at the sound. It was dead in here. From her memory of the book of runes, this symbol meant something like "possession" or "property".

'Hello? Is anybody there?' She took out her pistol and moved deeper into the shadow, the vinegary scent of this place.

A door at the end of the hall creaked when she pushed. Light leaked in through a crack in the curtains against the far wall to show a kind of living room, only there was nothing in it, no furniture, no decoration. Bare walls covered in rune designs, some she recognised from the book, but there were too many to take in.

She tried another door to the left and the smell of blood hit her. She raised her weapon and entered a bedroom with a small bed, a wardrobe, and a desk. More runes on the wall, and other details, pictures, cuttings. The floor was covered in clothes, as if somebody had discarded outfit after outfit, robes, uniforms, cloaks, all shapes and sizes; getting ready for a party and finding nothing to wear. She knelt and lifted a shirt to the weak light that filtered through the curtains. Blood. There were rips in the material where a knife or scissors had rent it.

She should get out of here. Now. She needed backup. But the clues were tantalising, and there was no sign of the killer. She let the material drop from her hand and just listened. In the silence of the building, the rain played on the windows like a carillon. She pulled the curtains open and let light shine over the mess. Something on the wall above the desk caught her eye, among the hand-drawn runes and the bits of paper stuck together. Photographs. She pulled the desk back from the wall so that she could look closer.

Newspaper cuttings, scraps of notepaper, and photographs. Amateurish, blurred. A few pictures showed a little girl, others showed a youth in her early teens, then an adolescent. At first, she assumed they were different, but there was a resemblance between them, something in the girl's serious face, her pointed jaw and strong nose. A presentiment crawled across her skin. She checked another picture and knew the girl. Another. *It was herself.* Time annulled the spaces. This picture might have been taken last week: she wore her police uniform, staring away into a grey sky, unawares that a hidden camera caught her.

Were they all her? She glanced back through the younger images, but they were taken from a distance. She could hardly remember early childhood at all, some block in her mind sealed it off. But these pictures, the young teen – she peered closer… yes, they were taken at the shipyards. She recognised bits of building, some of the workers in the background. Like staring through a forbidden window into the past. She had never had her picture taken when she was young, nobody around her growing up possessed such technology. Somehow, all of this was connected to herself, it must stretch back, back into the gaps in her memory. The shadows. She was guilty, in a way she couldn't explain. It was all her fault, it had to be. Who was she?

Who are you? Who are you?

51

Danzig, the Free City

Hours before the start of WWII

I knocked. Another door, another plea. Frau Grubach's sausage dog yapped and pawed on the other side. The landlady opened right away as if she'd been hiding inside, peeping out, watching for intruders. Dried tear tracks stained her hollow cheeks.

'Oh, Herr Tal. Is it true what they say?'

The dog ran out and jumped at my leg. 'Frau Grubach, it's an emergency. I need to use your phone.'

'It's true then. It's war.' She was so distracted she didn't seem to notice the dog's crazy barking.

'Not yet…'

I pushed past the landlady and her dog. She watched from the door as I went over to her phone on a little coffee table by the wall and picked it up. Running beside me, the little dog didn't stop jumping and pawing.

'What'll I do?' she said.

'Don't worry. You'll be alright. You're a good citizen. You keep this house clean and tidy.' I patted the dog and rubbed his floppy ears; he stopped barking.

'That's what I tell my tenants. And you'll speak up for me, won't you? A good police officer…'

'I can't help anyone.' I held the receiver to my ear and dialled, I was put through to Border Security.

'What happened?' Frau Grubach looked back from the front door, but I waved her to be quiet. 'Who are you calling?'

In my ear, a crackling voice spoke. 'Border Security Office. What is the purpose of your call?'

'This is Chief Inspector Johann Tal, Danzig Police Force, central branch. I'm ringing about a case.'

'Which case?'

'A party of Jews was detained at the border. Faulty documents.'

'What name?'

'Vogelsang, Esther. She was accompanied by her parents, grandparents, some children…'

'Wait there.' The voice went away into a cloud of interference.

Frau Grubach's fingernails tapped on the back of the door. She studied me with obsession. I motioned for her to be quiet; she stared at my waving hand.

The voice returned. 'Herr Tal…?'

'Yes?'

'The Vogelsang family was never detained. They crossed the border and continued with their journey.'

My heart must have been squeezed so tight, it released now in a gush of relief that was almost painful. 'Oh, thank you. Thank you.' I sank against the wall with the receiver clutched in my hands.

Frau Grubach watched. 'Oh, Herr Tal, you're crying…'

'I'm alright. Actually, I'm happy.'

'The war…?'

'I don't know. I don't know anything.' I tried to get up from the wall and couldn't.

Somewhere, in a foreign country, unknown, the family of refugees made their way to whatever future awaited them. They would never return, and I was glad. But the man with the mirror over his face, he was the one who'd told me they were detained. Who was he?

'Herr Tal, you're strange. But I don't judge.' The look on the landlady's face shifted. 'Did you go upstairs to your room? Did you speak to them?'

'What?'

A chill came through the gap beneath the bottom of the front door. I still clung to the phone receiver.

'I almost forgot,' she said. 'I've been in such a fog all day, with the news. The rumours. Everyone says the war already started…'

'You said you forgot something, what was it?'

'What? Oh. Some men came to see you. They said they'd wait. I showed them to your room. As far as I know, they're still up there.'

'Some men?' Through a patina of tears, I saw her hunched over me. 'Men? What men?'

'They said they were colleagues of yours.'

'Wearing uniforms?'

'No. They were all dressed in black.'

I dried my eyes and looked at the ceiling. 'And they're up there now?'

'Oh yes, they said they'd wait. I offered them a cup of tea. Very polite young men.'

'I have to leave.'

I crept to the door and glanced out through the peephole. The landing was empty, but the building shivered. The foot of the staircase was submerged in shadow, the upper floor hidden from view.

'Herr Tal…'

'Shush.' I crept out into the hall.

Halfway across, I caught my breath as a door opened upstairs. I glanced up the stairwell and saw nobody. All of myself was up there, in the bedroom I'd rented for years. My photographs, my clothes, my gramophone; without my totems, I was nobody. Frau Grubach watched me from her doorway as I crept to the foot of the stairs and peered up through the spiral of banisters. Her eyes widened as she perceived my fear. I backed away from the stairs. The floorboards winced as I tiptoed to the front door. It creaked open, too loud on its hinges. I heard Frau Grubach close her door. I was alone. Outside, I breathed. In the street, the gentle rain, I glanced up, but the curtains were shut in my window. I put up my collar and left all my belongings behind, I'd never go back for them.

Free. Just like any passing stranger in Danzig, and what could be more beautiful? The leaves of the trees were red and ochre. I crossed town and found the car, where I'd abandoned it. The intern kid was gone. It was better this way, even if it was painful to know I'd be alone until the end now. Seated behind the wheel, I took out the bedraggled newspaper and leafed through its pages. I hardly needed to look at them anymore; I knew the headlines off by heart:

> REICH'S AMBASSADOR PRAISES DANZIG SPIRIT
>
> DANZIG DETECTIVE SOLVES "CASE OF THE YEAR"
>
> POLISH FORCES MOBILISE ALONG BORDER
>
> LOCAL PRIEST CELEBRATES NINETIETH BIRTHDAY
>
> TROPICAL DISEASE IDENTIFIED AT SHIPYARDS
>
> DANZIG'S FIRST COUPLE ANNOUNCE BIRTH OF DAUGHTER

But that page was missing. I'd torn it out and left it with the intern to file away; perhaps someone would find it one day and understand. I flipped the remaining pages and let my eyes wander over the creases, seeking the one detail I'd missed. The clue that would solve the case, save my job and Henrik's and bring down Roman along with Schechter and all his cronies.

The problem wasn't a lack of clues, rather an excess. The sentences seemed to grow, possibilities branched. Here was a story about a school play; how many human beings were involved in that? Teachers, pupils, the families of the pupils… Here was a story about a football match; how many players, coaches, supporters? A whole world crept and whispered between the lines of the *Danziger Neueste Nachrichten*, nobody could take responsibility for so many lives.

'Where are you?' I mumbled. 'Where are you?'

I turned back to the front page. *Start again.* I stared at the banner headline, not even words anymore, just blocky shapes in black ink. It was no longer about any particular story; the question was, why this newspaper, why this particular edition, this date. But even that was just numbers. I began to work my way through the pages once again. The columns blurred; I had to shake my head and rub my eyes. There was nothing here, I'd never find a killer this way. I was about to put the newspaper down when a word on the penultimate page caught my eye, a single word: "BURIAL".

> BURIAL HELD TODAY FOR LOVING MOTHER
> Susanna Winter… mother of one… well-loved organist at local church… buried today in Danzig… friends and family in attendance…

The grainy photograph was like a window, black dots of mourners against a white block: the evangelical Christuskirche in the district of New Scotland, where I grew up. The past shimmered and disappeared around a bend in the smoky air. I turned the key in the ignition.

52

New Scotland. I probed the past; this terrain of menial workers and migrants had never been my beat on the police force, but I grew up here, back when Danzig was a kind of heaven. As a child, wandering in springtime, even the ugliest streets here hid glamour behind their curtains. I crossed the park just like a summer night of my teens, the old willow caught in a net of streetlights, silhouetted against the sky, and gone just as quickly, dissolved into nothingness. I swallowed a deep draught of the suburban air, grass and river, the industry that was not so far away. I used to sleepwalk as a child, searching for something in the dark. Sometimes through the wall of dream, I caught my mother's voice, soft enough that it didn't wake me, loving enough, trusted, that she could soothe me.

What are you doing out here, child, so far from your bed?

In the morning, I'd wake and remember, and wonder if I'd only dreamt it. On the other side of the park, I felt tears well in my eyes. A hint of infancy, that I couldn't pin down, and didn't want to. The house where I grew up was just around the corner, but I turned and hurried in the opposite direction without looking back at that ulcer in time.

Deeper into Old Scotland. The building was beat-up and appeared deserted, its inhabitants might have all been at work. A door flapped on its hinges in the wind. I found the flat that had belonged to the deceased at the end of the second floor. A sign said, "For Let". I knocked and listened to the sound of my fist fade, swallowed up by emptiness on the other side of the wood. I tried the handle and was relieved when it didn't open.

A door down the hall opened and an elderly lady looked out. 'Didn't you hear the news? She's gone.'

'Oh.' I took a step towards her, slowly, not wanting to frighten her away. 'Actually, it was the son I was looking for.'

'What do you want with that one?' She narrowed the opening of her doorway, looking out with just the side of her face. 'You one of them social worker types? You all did a bad job there, if you don't mind me saying.'

'I don't mind at all. Actually, I'm police. I wonder if I could talk to you for a moment?'

'What about? Why, was there something fishy about the business? They said she fell and hit her head. It happens, she used to fall over a lot. Sort of scatter-brained, she was. Well, you can understand it. With everything…'

'That's what interests me. Could I ask you a few questions?'

'I dunno… it's not done around here, to talk with police.' She glanced over my shoulder, but the corridor was motionless.

'Don't worry, you're not a suspect. There's nothing to be afraid of. Truth be told, it's not her death I'm investigating. It's a different case altogether, happened outside the city a few days ago.'

She didn't reply, but she didn't close the door either. She stared and seemed to see somebody else in my place. 'I've seen you before, haven't I?'

'I don't think so…'

'But where was it?' She stared and wondered.

'Perhaps we could talk inside,' I tried. 'Just a chat, with a cup of tea?'

'Oh, it's a cup of tea you want. You'd better come in then.'

* * *

I'd worried she wouldn't want to open up, but Frau Goldschmidt loved to talk. We sat down in her tidy kitchen that seemed to be without food but smelled of dough and God; my mother might have just stepped out of the door, only she'd been dead for years. The old walls with their faded yellow wallpaper didn't recognise the mourning I'd done or tried to do.

'It all started when her husband left. He was no good. Everyone knew it, but she loved him. What can you say? Love's like that, for the young at least. And she was pretty, for a time. They are the ones who catch it worst. But I never thought she'd end up with his type, a wanderer he was. Came in off the ships from Lord knows where, with his strange accent like a mix of every language on the docks.'

In her melodic voice, her triviality, her white hair that was neatly combed, she seemed to be describing my own parents and all that had taken place, all that had been lost, before I was born. I held onto the cup tightly; it might fall and shatter against the floor.

'Him, I'll never forget,' she continued. 'Tattoos of strange birds, weird animals you couldn't dream of. Said he'd seen them in Australia. The man was mad. Everyone knew he'd disappear again, a man like that can't stay away from sea. But she was in love, and that was that. No lover was ever afraid to ruin their lives.'

'Wait a moment.' I took out my notepad and pen. 'So, this man…'

It might have been my father. How long ago had he sailed away and left us? My mother never recovered. She pored over out-of-date newspapers that other people threw away and looked for references to Australia or America. Anywhere that wasn't here. That's when I'd decided to become a detective; I'd find my dad. Maybe then, she'd stop crying at night when she thought I was asleep.

'It's not about him, not really,' Frau Goldschmidt said. 'He was only around for a while before he disappeared. She never took another lover, never even tried. She kept saying he'd come back, he'd promised. "He'd only gone down to the harbour to make a little money to bring back," she said. We felt sorry for her. She started to go crazy after that. Or maybe not, maybe she was already crazy. Maybe that's how she ended up this way in the first place.'

'Crazy?' I made a note. 'In what way?'

'I'm getting ahead of myself, aren't I? Typical me. Around here, they say "talking to Frau Goldschmidt is like trying to untangle a ball of string". Forgive me, Officer.'

'It's fine. You're doing fine, continue, please.'

'Would you like some more tea?'

'No, that's enough, thank you.'

'You're just being polite.' She got up to refill my cup.

'Really, Frau Goldschmidt, if I drink any more, I won't sleep. I already stay up half the night with this job.'

She sat down. 'I'm sorry, I'm wasting your time, aren't I? I just get so little chance to speak nowadays. All my children died, and their father, for what he was worth.'

'I'm sorry to hear that.'

'Don't be. Somebody has to be the last alive. Their job is to remember. It's a hard task, but I'd rather it was me, to save the rest of them from having to do it. But here I'm wandering again.'

'I understand. I'm the last alive of my family too.'

'I could tell right away.' She patted me on the knee. 'Someone has to remember. It shows in the eyes.'

'So, you were telling me about…'

'Well, people started to talk. We're all terrible gossips in this tenement, but what else is there to do? There's no food, nothing works. Oh gosh, I shouldn't say that, should I? You won't arrest me…'

'You can say anything you like. I only want to know about the deceased woman and her son.'

'Well, she went crazy, didn't she? It started when the boy was tiny. She dressed him up strange. She seemed to think he was somebody else.'

'What do you mean?'

'Sometimes, the way she talked, she seemed to think that little boy was her brother, who'd been dead twenty years, drowned in a shipwreck. She'd ask him about all the places he'd seen in his sailing, and she'd tell him all the family news that he'd missed. Sometimes she even got angry with him about things that happened years ago, arguments from when she was just a little girl in the tenement. But the boy was a new-born baby. Then it got worse. She talked to him like he was her long-dead mother. Used to chat about the old times, old neighbours, old places that had been pulled down.'

'That is strange. So, this boy…'

'He grew up confused, you can imagine. She found all kinds of clothes for him, hand-me-downs, and rags, and dressed him up like a doll. Sometimes he was a brother, sometimes a mother, sometimes an old friend, sometimes – who knows? – an old lover, she bantered with him like a flirt. Most of all, she dressed him like a little sailor.'

'Clothes…' I moved my pen but didn't write anything.

'Poor boy didn't know who he was. He'd knock on my door sometimes and call me mother. I'd tell him, "I'm not your mother, little one." It got worse as he grew older. Maybe she was angry with him because he wasn't who she wanted. She'd beat him, scream at him, throw him out the door. She called him all kinds of names. He never knew what to do to make her happy. How could he? But he tried, he tried to be all these people. You could see he was struggling, he used to sit in the hall and cry. Then he got older, he became aggressive. People in the building were scared of him.'

I made a note. 'Why?'

'Ask them yourself. He'd knock on your door and start an argument like you were somebody else, like he'd knocked on the wrong door by accident. He'd scream and shout and headbutt the walls until his forehead bled.'

'And where is he now?'

'God, did he do something? Is he in trouble?' Her eyes shone with excitement.

'Please, Frau Goldschmidt, this is important. When did you last see him?'

'Of course, you can't say anything. Police confidentiality, I understand. You can rely on me.'

'When did you last see him?'

'Well, it must have been at the funeral. He hasn't been back here since. I knocked on the door once or twice to see if he needed anything, but nobody answered. Then that sign appeared on the door, "For Let". The landlords around here don't waste any time. As soon as she was in the ground, they put the flat up.'

'Where is the landlord? Do they live in this building?'

'No, but one of the neighbours does jobs for him. She can talk to you. She has a key to the flat in case people want to view it.'

I jumped up. 'Is she home? Let's go talk to her.'

* * *

After another half hour of chit-chat, the neighbour agreed to show me around the flat as a potential renter. It was musty and cramped inside. There was only one bedroom, the mother and son must have shared it, next to a kitchen with peeling wallpaper and bloodstains in places where the boy had apparently headbutted the wall. I stroked the grainy, dark traces that crumbled away under my fingertips.

'He was a strange boy,' the neighbour said.

'I can relate.' I took out a sample envelope and brushed some of the crumbled blood off the wall.

'What are you doing? Are you one of them government inspectors? I have to tell the landlord. I'm not supposed to let people in here if they're not real tenants.'

'I'm a police officer.'

'Oh God. What did I do? Herr Schubert will kill me.'

'Relax. It's nothing to do with your employer. It's not about the flat. I'm here investigating a separate case. It's the boy I'm interested in.'

'Well, why didn't you say so?'

'I was worried you wouldn't let me in.'

'That boy's always been trouble. I said so since he was a toddler.'

I walked past her into the kitchen. The smell of the place hit me, almost knocked me down. The past surged too strongly, close to the surface, almost bursting. I held onto the edge of the dining table, which was covered in a checked cloth just like in my mother's kitchen. 'What is that smell?'

In the doorway, the neighbour sniffed. 'That's dill. See…'

I looked at the windowsill where she pointed: a row of little pots with dwindling plants.

'Oh, she used to put dill in everything. It was a curse. I tried to tell her there are other herbs, but that was the only one she wanted. She said it reminded her of some river when she was a kid…'

The neighbour kept on talking but I no longer paid attention. On a corkboard attached to the wall above the table, my eyes wandered over rows of faded postcards. Jakarta. Calcutta. Sydney. Cape Town. In the middle, a yellowing slip was stuck face down among the pictures of islands and foreign ports. In sloping letters in blue ink, I read:

> DEAR BELOVED,
> I CANNOT WAIT FOR US TO BE TOGETHER.
> DON'T FORGET ME, YOUR TRUE HEART.

I pulled it off the board and looked closer. The postage stamp in the corner was from Hong Kong. I felt all the distances of the world contract and densify, disappear.

53

Was it enough? I raced across town to Henrik's house. I had a killer, I just didn't know where to find him. His method became clear: he impersonated others and used disguises to reach his victims. Something about uniforms appealed to him, and he found his victims in the newspaper that had written up his mother's funeral. He was unstable, and he'd be difficult to track if his identity continued to change. In the sky, where the stars were flooded out by blinking streetlights, I sought his name. Who are you? How long before you kill again?

I parked outside Henrik's house. Running up the driveway I noticed all the lights were turned off. Another blackout perhaps. In the gloom, the building receded from reality. It was only when I came up to the door that I saw it was ajar. Dread played in the tissues of my belly. I knocked and held my breath. A breeze stirred inside.

'Henrik…? Are you there?'

The building wept silently. I pushed open the door and flashed my torch across the hall, picking out the piled suitcases I'd seen last time. As if only a moment had elapsed, and everything inverted. I stepped inside, and the smell hit me. The tang of life that bubbles under human skin.

'Henrik? Henrik?'

My torchlight darted across the floor and walls as I sought him, trembling, the beam wavered through the dark…

'Henrik? It's me, Tal…'

…and found a shoe. My old boss lay thrown forwards across the opening of the living room. One shoe had fallen off. I crawled over, holding my breath.

'Are you OK? Can you hear me?'

The wisp of light found a slick hole in the back of his head. I touched his blood, and it was still hot, still oozing. A seed of mad hope throttled me as I turned Henrik over and slapped his face.

'Are you alright? Wake up! Wake up!'

But his pulse was dead. I laid him down gently and couldn't quite believe the body was empty. Further along in the living room I found his wife, seated in an armchair, a gun wound in the middle of her face. Her fingers gripped the edges of her seat. The heat of the blood leaked into the stupefied stillness of this room, these walls they'd decorated, the fancy furniture they'd accumulated. I was paralysed. My mind tried to move and couldn't, it didn't want to, it didn't want to know that this was my fault. I was the one who'd brought the camera film to Henrik and convinced him to make a phone call. I ran back to his corpse and rifled through his pockets. The film was gone.

I emptied his wallet on the floor, spilling coins and keys. I sifted through the cards and notes – identity papers for a man who no longer existed, a photograph of his wife, a spare button – and pulled out the tickets. Tickets for a boat leaving tonight, as if anybody could ever leave Danzig. Barely conscious of what I was doing, I stuffed them in my pocket and let the wallet drop.

My mistakes were poisonous, they spread to loved ones and their relatives. Henrik was a family man. It was wrong to involve him in this. Those who work the night shift should stay alone, keep the innocent, the daytime, free of knowledge. A family man… he had children. Now I was nauseous. I raced up the old wooden staircase, holding my breath. In the dark of the upstairs landing, I found a light and switched it on. Too bright. Blinking, shielding my eyes, I stumbled through half-open doors and found a children's bedroom.

'Are you in here?' I flicked the light on.

The bed was made but it was empty. I checked underneath and only found a discarded teddy bear. I pulled open the wardrobe. Two small children looked back at me, just their faces showing behind a pile of clothes. They gripped each other tightly.

* * *

The carillon was playing as I rushed across the Long Market. I stopped in the rain a moment, trying to remember where I was going. Every time I hear this melody it's like the first time. Alien, music-box chimes, neither sad nor happy. I shook it away and ran to the cafe. It was closed. Through the window, I saw Daria finishing her shift. She didn't look up from the table she wiped. I went inside and winced at the jingle of the bell over the door.

'Daria–'

'Get lost, Tal, I'm busy.'

'That's what everyone says. Daria, listen.' I stepped closer, causing her to flinch. She really hated me.

'I'll scream, I swear.' She backed away.

'The war's about to start. It's starting in Danzig.'

'Think I don't know? I work in a cafe. Every rumour comes through here.'

'The rumours are true. The police force is gearing up to help the invaders. There's an army hidden in the city, they're just waiting for the signal.'

She shrugged. 'Nazis drink tea and coffee too. The world will always need cafes.'

'There won't be any buildings left standing. Everything's going to burn.'

'Oh, that's right. I remember now, your visions. Your prophecies of the end…'

'There's a boat leaving tonight.'

She straightened, rubbing a twinge in her side, and looked at me. Shock showed in her eyes as she noticed now the two small children who clung together just behind my back. Like she'd seen a new reality. 'Your dreams…' she said.

'I need you to take these children. There's a boat leaving Danzig. It's the last chance. Anyone who doesn't get out now, will never get out.'

'Hah! A boat, he says. You were always a dreamer, Tal. And where does this boat sail to?'

'New York.'

She scoffed. 'If you came here to make fun of me, you're wasting your time. There's nothing left to mock. I'm a wreck. We all are.' But her voice softened, she looked at the kids, couldn't stop looking.

'It's not a joke.' I took out the tickets and showed her. 'Here. Take this one. The children have their own. Meet me at the harbour. The wharf is on the ticket. The ship is called the *Humboldt*. You don't have to talk to me on the boat or ever again. Just get on it. That's all.'

'You're not real, Tal. You're a ghost. Find somebody else to haunt.'

'I have to leave these kids with you now.'

'What?'

'I have a case to solve. It might just save us all. Might just avert a war. But I can't take two small children with me. You look after them. Get them on that boat. Please, Daria. They're just children.'

She stared and found no words to say. The silent children left my side and went to her, they grabbed the edges of her apron. She looked at them with shocked, tender eyes.

I laid the ticket down on the wiped table. 'I'm leaving this here. Do what you want with it. If I can solve the case, I'll find you on the boat. Otherwise…'

54

The silent streets were strangled with tension. Dazed passers-by stared into nothingness and hurried along. I heard the anxiety in their faces like a screamed plea: where was safe? Where could they keep their children sheltered? As I drove towards the harbour, I passed a group of police and ducked my head down. In the rear-view mirror, I saw them drag some man out of a doorway, his dressing gown flapping in the breeze. They stuffed him into the back of a van, while his wife shouted at them from the doorstep. The round-ups were spreading. Plumes of black smoke showed on the horizon. In the next street, a gang dressed in black were smashing the windows of a shop. I didn't slow down, just kept moving forwards. There was nothing left for me in Danzig.

The traffic picked up as I neared the harbour. The roads were full of cars and pedestrians headed towards the sea. Did everyone know what was about to happen? The path up ahead was sealed off. Officers at a barrier checked the identity papers of the crowds trying to get through. I turned off into a side street. There was still time, still two hours until the ship was due to leave. A surfeit of freedom; a man could lose himself in two hours.

The creased newspaper lay on the passenger seat. My final possession. I scooped it up and flicked through the pages, one last read-through, one last chance to find the hidden detail that had eluded me. I already knew, of course, it was the one story that I'd paid no attention to. The mind works like that, it resists the truth.

> DANZIG DOCTOR IDENTIFIES TROPICAL DISEASE

The overseer at the shipyards had said …*my wife with some kind of tropical disease. Can you believe that? It comes from Madagascar…*

My eyes read the story with dull foreknowledge. Horror.

> Disease first recognised in Madagascar… Danzig specialist identified strain… Scientific community celebrates German breakthrough…

The killer couldn't control his imitations. Especially when he was face to face with the detective hunting him, he'd played the game, acting a part, pulling out quotations, miming, mixing characters like a sick clown. The harbour was close, and the ship that would take me away. If I ever left Danzig, I knew, I'd never return. But the boat wouldn't leave just yet. I turned the key in the ignition and felt alive again as the car pulled out from the kerb. The roads were emptier heading away from the harbour. I coasted quickly over to the outside of the shipyards, and this was all too easy. I had plenty of time, and a tank of petrol.

* * *

The shipyards. Where this started, the city's womb. I pushed my hat down and hurried into the wind through the giant metal gates. The heat flickered in my chest, the old glow, a mystery to be solved; it's what I was made for. But the glow didn't last. I had only turned one corner among the warehouses when cruel voices broke through the air in a burst of screams.

I ducked against the wall of a tool shed and peeked around the edge. Five police officers stared off against a group of workers toting tools, makeshift weapons. They aimed their guns, and the workers backed down but didn't run. The officers pinned one of them to the ground and cuffed him. They pulled him up, while a mob of the man's colleagues crowded around. I didn't recognise the officers. New men, from the day shift. One of them raised his pistol and fired it up into the air. The workers ducked down with hands over their ears.

The police headed towards me, dragging their prisoner. I dodged back out of view and ran around the other side of the tool shed. I found the first door and went through. Outside, the wind tore screams from their mouths and made them dance. I kept running.

A few buildings along, I entered the roar of the furnace. One of the workers mouthed something that I couldn't hear. The noise was unbearable. I poked my head out of the entrance and saw the police officers on the other side, headed out towards the front gates with their prisoner. One of them glanced back. Had he seen me? I didn't recognise him. Could he know who I was?

Another worker in the furnace shouted at me, words lost in the machinery. I peeked around the edge of the door, and the police were almost gone, shadows receding against the warehouses. It was a relief to get away from the furnace. I went back out into the wind and skipped around to the offices, looking for Kostek. He was one of the young union leaders in the yards. I'd worked with him before on a case. We'd learnt to trust one another. But the workers shuffled away from me, they scented a cop, they gripped wrenches. It was no use; there was no sign of Kostek, and nobody here would talk to me.

Back outside in the dark, I gazed in the direction of the harbour, wondering if the ship was there, the *Humboldt*, if such a thing really existed. A ship to carry us away. The brown river chugged and frothed as it always had through the centre of the shipyards. I retraced my path back to the other side of the complex, looking for the abandoned buildings where the dead amber dealer and his wife were found. It was quieter back here among the disused spaces. The yards were dying, more and more workers laid off, buildings left unused, scrap metal piled up among weeds.

I glanced at my watch, still an hour to spare, but the panic was rising in my blood. I found myself running. As I went racing around the corner of a crumbling brick outhouse, I almost collided with a young woman.

'Watch where you're going, moron.' She stopped, realising I was a cop.

'Could you help me?' I said.

'I'm busy.' She hurried away.

Keeping pace, I shouted into the wind, 'I'm looking for an overseer. He works nights…'

'There are no overseers here.' She ran off without looking back.

I checked my watch again, and found the numbers no longer made sense. This place was a labyrinth. It changed every time I left and came back. Despite a lifetime in Danzig, just when you think you know the city, it shifts. Warehouses and cranes towered over the altered walkways. My heart beat too hard against my ribs, and my thoughts swam, leaking back to childhood and all the nights of loneliness in between. The shipyards swarmed with running feet and shouts. A group of workers bustled past me, hardly noticing as I jumped out of the way. I caught a fragment of their conversation: police in the shipyards; workers rounded up, beaten, arrested; a new war starting. I lowered my hat into the gusts and trudged in the opposite direction. There was still time.

55

Beside the abandoned warehouse complex, where I'd seen the bodies, a little shed was set back out of the wind that wanted to rip my coat off. Inside, a wonky, rectangular table was set out with a deck of cards and some empty cups, a dirty ashtray, but there was nobody there.

'Hello?' I called out. 'Hello? Anybody?'

My voice echoed dully against the brick edifices that tightened around me, and I didn't recognise it. On the other side of the shed, I entered a vacant lot with a huge pile of scrap metal. Was it the same as the other night? It had to be. This was the warehouse.

'Hello? Anybody?'

I found the metal door and put my ear to it. Chambers within chambers, resonant with dripping water, decay, and emptiness. Tangled winds cried inside. I checked my watch and felt a dull premonition of my own desire to see the end. A ship's sail on the skyline, but there was no skyline here, just edifices of brick that blocked the sky. *Leave now, run while you can.* I listened again. There was something else, a tiny, quivering resistance against the shipyard's deeper background swell of groaning infrastructure. I gritted my teeth, pressed my ear to the freezing metal door, listened. A baby cried inside somewhere. A baby. I was sure, but the sound was muffled, it disappeared, swallowed by wind.

I checked over my shoulder, nobody around, ran back to the little shed where nobody had disturbed the deck of cards or the cups, or the dirty ashtray. I rifled through the drawers of a dresser against the wooden wall and found a set of keys. They jangled in my hand as I ran back to the warehouse. When I listened at the door, I couldn't catch the sound of the baby anymore. Was it just the wind I'd heard?

The door was stiff and noisy on its rusted hinges as it opened, and I found myself back in the throbbing corridor. The stairway to my right led down to the murder scene, but I headed left, splashing through copper-coloured puddles. I stopped to listen after every few steps, trying to hear the baby. The deeper I pressed, the more the emptiness echoed, a web of dripping, clanking, scurrying decay. I turned a corner and entered a wide storage area beneath a leaking ceiling high above. Deserted crates, pallets and other rubbish lay mouldering, brown and red beneath a soft layer of brick dust.

The baby's wail was nearby. I ran through puddles and rotten garbage chasing the sound that wavered like breeze, disappearing, surging, calling. At the end of the storage area, a low doorway led to a short staircase and an antechamber blocked with pallets. The baby was crying through an opening just on the other side. I clambered through soggy bits of wood, trying to stay quiet, but acoustics played games in here – a drop of water sounded too loud, a falling metal chain was swallowed by silence. I ran up the stairs and stopped outside the door. On the other side, the baby's wailing was vivid, so clear, it cut through brick and concrete. I heard Danzig herself call out. I drew my pistol and opened the door.

The room stunk of human waste. Through a crack in the wall, a diagonal slash of light revealed dirty clothes scattered over the floor. A body lay face down in a black-red patch of dried blood in their midst. The X-shaped splay of his limbs held my eyes; I dragged them away. At the back of the room, a man cradled a baby. I saw that he wore the priest's vestments, smeared with blood. He seemed ancient, slumped in his chair. The dim light caught on an oval mirror that he held over his face.

'You came,' he said. 'I waited for you. I didn't think you'd understand.'

I recognised the voice that had whispered through the door at the priest's home.

'The love note. Yeah, I got it.' I stepped closer, slowly, not wanting to spook him.

'It's real then, all of this,' he said.

'The murders you committed? Yes, it's real. Drop the mirror. It's not needed; I know who you are.'

'Are you sure?'

'I've been to your house. I know all about you.' I tried to see him, caught between shadow and a shaft of light, as he sat up, tall, strong, despite his ancient voice.

'But are you sure? I thought I knew, once. I killed a man. I thought, now it's real. I dug my fingertips into his flesh to make sure, but even when I was elbow-deep, I still didn't know. The sounds he made when I gutted him, so intense, but all I could think was, is this real? It felt less real, not more.'

'I need to take the baby.'

'But then… you came.' His voice shifted, sounding younger. Echoes of the old priest faded. 'You're the only one who understood.'

'It's my job.'

'Do you know how it feels, Detective, to look in a mirror and see nothing?'

'I don't look in the mirror if I can help it.'

'You should. If you knew what a privilege it was, you'd want to see your reflection, you'd want to check, just to be certain it hadn't gone.'

'You do have a reflection. Everyone does.'

'How can we believe in what we can't see?' He let the mirror fall.

I watched as he straightened, trying to see his face. He tilted his head, rotated his shoulder blades like a swimmer preparing to dive into the water from the top board. He got up from the chair, and he was tall, he loomed over me.

I held the gun steady. 'That's a question for a priest, not a cop.'

When he spoke, it was like hearing a recording of my own voice. '"That's a question for a priest, not a cop."'

'Don't do that.' I stepped back.

'"Don't do that."' His body became a reflection of mine. He mirrored every gesture. His face in the dim light had become my own, the set of his jaw, the way he squinted, it was a pantomime of myself. He was more Tal than I was. He took a step towards me.

'Don't be afraid.'

I held my ground. 'Give me the baby; she's no use to you.'

'Oh, that's what you want.' He looked down at her as he rocked her, her crying softened now to a low complaint. 'And I thought you came here for me…' He took a step closer; I saw he held a knife against the baby's throat. 'You should be careful, Detective. No sudden moves. This knife could slip.'

'She's innocent. It's a sin to harm a child.'

'I don't want to harm her. I want to be her, more than anything. To be a baby. Nobody. Loved. To be free of the poison. But I couldn't do it. I couldn't find a way to take her. She was the only one I couldn't enter. Then I thought, what if I waited? I could raise her, be like a mother. I'll wait until she grows up, and I'll become her then. But babies are noisy. They're demanding. Selfish.'

'Give her to me, I'll see she gets looked after.'

'You'd take her from me? And I'll be lost.' His voice shifted, softened, sharpened its pitch. He sounded like a woman now. 'She's all I have; I'm her mother. Everyone else deserted me. I'd rather die than give her up.'

'That's not you. It's your mother talking.'

'How would you know?'

'My mother was the same.'

'You think you know everything, with your gun. I'd like to see you without it.' The voice was flirtatious, mocking. 'Put the gun down, or I'll slit her throat.'

I searched for something I could exchange. With my free hand, I fished in my jacket pocket and pulled out the boat ticket. For a moment, I thought of Daria, the ocean, a white sail.

'There's another way,' I said.

'Oh, what a clever one. I knew he'd help. He'd come up with a clever idea, for little old me.'

I felt like a little boy faced with an insane old lady, and I was terrified.

'There's a ship leaving the harbour, soon. Less than an hour. It's the last one. War will start tonight, everyone says. The German troops are already here, hidden among us.

They're just waiting until dark. If you get on that ship you can escape. Out there, there's a whole world. You could become anyone. Be anybody you like.'

'And the nice young man would give that ticket to me? Something so precious…'

'In exchange for the baby.'

He looked down at the child, cooed and fussed her without removing the knife from her throat. The baby went quiet. It was uncanny, the man's body language, his whole mode of movement and being, every gesture was transformed into something else. It was hard to believe that I wasn't watching somebody's grandmother playing with a child.

And then a man spoke. His voice was deep and hostile. 'You'd trick me of course. You don't care about me at all. You'd take the baby and throw me in jail.'

'I just want a solution.'

'You'd really make a deal with me?'

'Take it or leave it. The ship is leaving soon.'

He thought this over. When he spoke again, his voice was reedy like a teenage boy's. 'Give me your gun then.'

'What?'

'Slide it along the floor.'

'I can't do that.'

He shrugged. 'I'll keep the baby then.'

I glanced at the pistol in my hand. Without it, I could no longer pretend to be police. I laid the gun on the concrete floor and slid it across. The boy, for it really was a boy, grabbed it up with childish curiosity. He pointed it at me, laughed, waved it in the air, testing the feeling.

'Careful with that,' I said.

The gun was aimed at my chest. 'And now the boat ticket. Slowly. No tricks.'

'And you'll give me the baby?'

He thought a moment too long. In the quiet, dim footsteps clattered somewhere in the building. Voices. There was somebody else, moving, coming towards us.

His eyes widened. 'Who's that?' The end of the gun jerked up towards my eyes. 'Who did you bring?'

'I came alone. But there are police everywhere. I told you, a war's about to start.'

Fear and curiosity showed in his adolescent's face, but his eyes were older. 'A war.'

'Hurry. Let's do this now and get out. Is there another exit?'

'There's a back door, if you know the way.'

'Here.' I held out the ticket, my free hand open, signalling calm. I stepped forward and placed it on the ground. 'There you go.'

'Get away!' He waved the gun.

Behind my back, deeper in the belly of the warehouse, something clanged. Indistinct voices shouted back and forth. Two or three strangers, coming closer.

'Let me see…' He crawled forwards and snatched up the ticket with his free hand. The baby complained. I watched him stare at the stump of paper, as if he couldn't understand.

'It's real,' I said. 'It's valid. All the information's there. The name of the ship, the quay, the time.'

In the room behind me, footsteps splashed among gritty puddles, broken rafters, and chains.

'We'll see.' He kept the gun pointed at me, as he laid the baby down on the ground. She grumbled with discomfort or protest but didn't cry.

'That's good,' I said. 'Easy now. You go first, I'll follow. Those men–'

'No. You'll stay here.' He raised the gun.

'What are you–'

I dived back as he fired. The bullet caught my shoulder and knocked me down. Numb. In a cloud of red, I was blind, deaf. When I managed to breathe, the killer was gone. I tried to move my left arm, but it was like it wasn't there; not even pain, just nothing.

Shouts broke out, nearby, roused by the gunshot, they called into the echoing architecture. Feet crashed through broken industry. I tried to move, and the pain sent bolts of agony that scattered from my shoulder, paralysing my lower body. The baby, left alone on the dirty floor, began to cry.

'Shush, shush.' Perhaps the desire to soothe her calmed my own nervous system. I managed to crawl forwards, swallowing down a scream as my limp arm swung and caught on the ground.

From back in the stairwell outside, a voice shouted. 'See anything?'

'There's a door.'

'Careful. They have guns.'

I scooped up the baby and scurried ahead, almost blind with the pain that came in waves through my neck. I found a door in the dark at the end of the chamber and pushed through into a branching corridor where the killer had disappeared.

Just behind me, a voice called, 'What the fuck? This place…'

Another voice. 'There's a body. Who is that?'

'Some docker…?'

The third voice I recognised as Roman. 'Tal's nearby. He was here. He came this way. Find him. Quickly now.'

I heard their feet move through the mess of dirty clothes and bloody traces. I pushed ahead, gasping for air. It was almost too dark to see. There was an exit back here somewhere.

Voices carried along the stone floors. 'He's nearby. He must be.'

I found a door and went through it, too urgent to think or to check, but this was not the exit. In the shadow, I made out the contours of a little office with a desk and some filing cabinets. A dead end. The men were in the corridor just outside.

'Has to be a back way out,' Roman shouted. 'Shit. Hurry up, come on, don't let him get away.'

Nowhere to hide in this bare room, I pressed against the wall behind the door. My one arm held the baby to my chest, pinpricks of sorrow coursing through its fibres, while the other hung limp. Babies are surprisingly heavy. I felt my grip weakening, and clutched her tight against my chest, cold. She sank into my bloodstained shirt. I rocked her but didn't dare to shush her when she gurgled and coughed. Footsteps stopped outside.

'Did you hear something?'

'There's a door here.'

Further back. 'What is it?'

A man stepped into the room. I held the baby as tightly as I could manage. My arm weakened and sagged. I couldn't even rock her. I only stared into her blue eyes and tried to smile, I tried to gather all the pain in my body together, like a message, to show her somehow, I wouldn't let anything happen. Her tiny fingers knitted the air.

'Some kind of office,' the man said.

I smelled his sweat.

'Hey,' Roman shouted from further along the corridor, 'there's an exit here.'

The man hurried back out of the room. I heard his feet running away, and still didn't dare move. I could only rock the child, as best I could. The voices shrank. A metal door banged. The wind outside blew the rest away. I didn't move. My clothes stuck to the wall with blood. The baby started to cry.

'Shush, shush. It's OK. They've gone now. Let's just stay hidden here.'

The crying intensified. It was incredible how loud such a small thing could scream. The hollow chambers of the warehouse amplified and echoed the sound like a machine that taps sorrow. I tore myself from the wall and set off running through the building, in the opposite direction from the men who had just left. I sought a hidden, deep place, where all our noise would be buried. She screamed and screamed as we crossed the wide storeroom full of empty pallets. My spine rattled with pain as I held her.

'Shush, shush.'

On the other side of the hall, I found myself back in the stairwell, heading towards the front entrance. The wind blew through with a taste of the sea: escape. If I could just sneak out there and find a way back to my car. I didn't ask for anything more. But the baby wouldn't stop screaming, and there was no muffled surface in here to deaden the sound. I heard voices out front. Trapped. I turned too fast, trying to get back into the middle of the warehouse, I caught my ankle and felt it twist. With one arm holding the baby, and the other hanging uselessly, I couldn't protect myself, I couldn't balance; I fell into a pile of old crates, sending them clattering.

Voices filled the entrance. Feet came running over concrete. I couldn't right myself to stand up. I only held the baby tightly as she screamed.

'You.' Kostek stood over me. 'Get up.'

'They shot me. I can't move my arm.'

Three other men gathered behind their boss. 'Should we chuck him in the water?'

'What's he got there?'

'Wait,' I said. 'Wait. I'm on your side. I came here to help.'

'Like shit,' Kostek said. 'Cops are all over the shipyards dragging my men into vans.'

'I'm not with them. I'm working alone.'

'What are you doing here then?'

'This baby.' I tried to hold her out but could not. 'She's Polish. They stole her from her parents. They're looking for kids with blonde hair and blue eyes, for the Reich.'

'Revolting.' One of the men spat at me. 'Let's kill this scumbag now before his pals come back.'

'I only want to help,' I said. 'Here. Take her. Take her from me. I can't carry her anymore. My arm's wrecked.'

Kostek crouched and took the baby. 'She's Polish?'

'You have to keep her safe. If they find her, they'll take her away. She'll be raised a Nazi. She'll never find out she was Polish. Her name is Anna.'

'What happened to your arm?'

'They shot me. My pals, as you call them.'

'Why?' He rocked the baby and she started to quieten down.

The other men leaned over, staring at her. Their anger softened.

'The war starts now,' I said. 'They're rounding up internal enemies. That includes me. I never fit in.'

'You'd better get out of here then. Cops are everywhere.'

* * *

I hobbled through the shipyards, clutching my wounded arm, but I was dizzy. When I looked back, a trail of blood stretched back in spattered drops. I knew then, I would never escape this place. I staggered on, my movements reduced to a crooked stumble between the endless warehouses. If I could just survive until morning, I might be able to find a place to hide. Pull the bullet out of my shoulder, wrap it up. Wait to see what tomorrow's light disclosed. I dreamed as I hunched forwards, I already thought I was there, sitting in my car, and had to open my eyes: I was still in the shipyards.

Bent, almost doubled, I held onto the railings by the side of the water and pulled myself along. Danzig had never smelled so intense. The wind tasted of life itself, I wanted to gulp it down, but it was always just gone. Shouts and screams played in the distance, but the background world was fading out. I dragged myself forward along the railings.

At some point, I must have wandered into a trance. I heard Daria's laugh. She was on the ship. She looked back into a storm of spray as they pulled out from the harbour, and she told me again, *you always wanted to be alone. You'll stay alone forever now.* And I could only laugh as the churning foam of the boat splashed my face with chilling, beautiful ice. My mother's hand guided me deftly as I sleepwalked. *What are you doing out of bed, child? It's late…*

'Tal,' a voice called from outside the dream. 'Tal. Didn't you hear the news?'

My one good hand clutched the metal railing. I turned around, wincing, to see Roman, flanked by two men in black overalls. I didn't recognise them.

'What do you want?' I said.

'We were looking for you.'

'I'm dying. Look. Happy now? I've been shot. Let me die in peace.'

Roman laughed. 'You could never do anything straight. I wouldn't trust you to deliver a letter. I certainly don't trust you to die.'

'Why do you hate me?'

He laughed again. 'That's the question.'

'I'm sorry…' I mumbled.

'Sorry, why?'

He thought I was talking to him; he didn't realise I'd slipped back into the beautiful trance. I called to Daria. 'I'm sorry. I really did try…' But she wouldn't look back at me from the prow of the boat where she stared out into the future.

'He sounds sad,' one of the other men said.

'Tal was always confused.' Roman grabbed my wounded shoulder, sending excesses of pain in a crippling, unfolding mesh through my spine. I lost my grip on the railing and fell to the ground. I tried to beg but couldn't make any other sound than a dog's whimper.

'It's alright.' He knelt beside me and stroked my hair. 'Hush now. The nightmare is over. After all these years. Decades of ruin. Germany will have her revenge. Danzig will be saved; we'll be returned to the Fatherland. We're too strong now. Nothing will stand in our way. The rest of the world will shake. The Poles will be crushed. In the future, they'll never know there was a place called Poland.'

'Roman…' My dying hand tried to grab his collar but failed. 'Don't… You… I've seen the end. It's all going to burn, all this. You have to prevent it…'

He couldn't hear me; my voice shrivelled until nothing remained. He sniffed the wind. 'Sleep now. It's all taken care of. The Führer foresees every detail. Parasites must be eradicated. That means you, Tal. I'm sorry.'

When I tried to speak, I only let out a splutter of clotted blood.

'Some people are just born wrong. It's not their fault.' He turned to his cronies. 'Help me lift him.'

Hands caught at my feet and wrists. They splayed and spread apart all the agony I folded, trying to keep it as tightly hunched together as possible. Now it came loose. My arm was almost torn from the socket. I floated in air and plummeted. Too heavy. Somebody, somewhere far away, was laughing at a clown show. I crashed into the water. Danzig rushed in through my nose and mouth, finding no resistance. I filled up with the freezing current, mud, oil, barnacles and seaweed, scrap metal, old rope, brick, herring, seagull shit. The tang of blood. I fell into a place with no bottom, no resistance. To sink forever.

56

Gdańsk, Polish People's Republic

1961

The Last Rune

Outside the shipyard gates, a crowd of workers faced off against police. Nothing made sense anymore. If they knew, if they could understand, what childhood meant among these warehouses… but the past was dead. Nothing was true; the memory of her parents, just actors playing a role. She was adopted, the child of a murder. Everything came back to murder in the end. The cranes and the muddy water didn't recognise her. It had all been a kind of game. Anna pushed through a line of her colleagues who fingered the triggers of their weapons but made no move. What did these people want? Why did they hate each other? Who were they?

'What's happening?' she shouted over the raucous chants of the protestors.

Lukasz grimaced. 'What else? Troublemakers trying to ruin communism. Western sabotage. The cells will be full tonight. Whole lot of overtime and paperwork for everyone.'

The words made no sense, nor did his rictus sneer. On the other side of the street, the protestors, fifty-strong, hunched in the cold, blocking the entrance to the shipyards and her childhood.

'I need to get through,' she said.

'Why?'

'A case. I need to get inside.'

'Forget it. You can't go through here.' He pointed at the barrels and piled crates, the bonfires that blocked the entrance. 'You'd need a tractor.'

'I'll find another way.'

'Hey,' Lukasz shouted after her as she withdrew, 'you have contacts in the shipyards. You could put in a good word. Tell them to stop throwing rotten fish at us. We're just doing our jobs.'

* * *

She had always hated heights. When they were kids, wartime orphans of the shipyards, they used to climb the fence. It seemed easier at that time. She found a section of fence out of the way, unobserved, and tucked the ends of her trousers into her socks. The metal wires rattled as she started up. The first part was easy, but the fence wavered and shook in the wind as she came to the top. The metal dug into her fingers as she clung on. From up here, the green cranes and the brick warehouses were motionless, nobody was working, they had all joined the strike.

Eyes closed, she pivoted at the top of the trembling fence as it rattled like a tambourine, reached one leg over to the other side, and scrambled for purchase in the links. Exposed, she balanced in the wind. She smelled its hard, metal kernel. Childhood feels endless from the inside. For years she'd played with the other kids in the ruins and never felt any sense of the catastrophe that had destroyed all this, that still haunted the adults. How carefully those traumatised survivors must have shielded her from the truth. Even now, her memory resisted, she saw it as the industrial playground she once explored with nameless friends, a gang of ragged children. But it had always been war debris. The past was just a fairy tale.

The jagged edges at the top of the fence drew blood from her palms as she held on tight, brought the other leg around, found a foothold. She was on the other side now. She could almost believe she was just nine years old, nothing had happened yet, nothing ever would. She let go and dropped to the ground.

* * *

Kostek was smoking behind the main warehouse, warming his hands at a barrel with a fire inside. Some of the other workers tried to push her away, but she called over their shoulders.

'Hey! Let me through. I need to talk to your boss.'

Kostek threw down his cigarette. 'What are you doing here? You should be out front with your cronies, beating the proletariat over the head.'

'I want answers.' She tried to slip through to him, but the others blocked her path.

'Tried to tell her.' A tall man in overalls towered over her. 'She wouldn't listen. Real stubborn.'

'She's a cop.' Another just like him spat on the floor. 'Needs to learn, the rules are different here, even for police.'

The first man pulled at her shoulder sending scratching pain through the carved rune in her chest. 'Just because she's a woman, she thinks we wouldn't touch her…'

'Get off me.'

She squared herself to him, stood tall, refusing to back down. He grinned at that.

Kostek glowered. 'Let her be. I know the detective. Let's hear what she has to say.'

The men huddled around, mumbling, eyeing her.

'Not with them,' she said. 'Just me and you.'

'Shit.' Kostek shook his head. 'You're a pain in the ass. Alright, the rest of you. Give me a minute alone with the detective.'

They grunted and cursed but they backed down. They went out slowly. One man glanced back at his boss as he left. 'We're being strangled here. This isn't time to be soft.'

Kostek didn't look. 'Gimme five minutes.' When they were alone, he sighed and turned to her. 'Anna, you can't come here–'

She cut him off. 'I need to know the truth. About the past. What really happened.'

'What "past"?'

'I was adopted. I found the documents at the archive. You've known me my whole life. How did I end up in the shipyards? Why do I have these black holes in my memory? Something bad happened. I feel it. There's a kind of poison that leaks out sometimes at night.'

'Is that what this is about? I thought you came to stop the strike.'

'Strike all you want. I don't care.'

'Anna…' He studied her face like she was a stranger. 'You were a baby during the War. Times were hard for everyone. Lot of folks died. We've all got gaps in our memories… Nobody likes to talk about the things that happened.'

'Don't try to fob me off. You know something. You've always known. Even as a kid, I could tell. There was something you kept from me, to protect me. I don't know what, but I'm old enough now. I need to know.'

'What happened? Why are you doing this? Did something…?'

'Look at this.' She took out the photograph from the wall of the killer's home. 'Recognise this?'

'I'm not the kind for pictures.'

'Just look at it.'

'Christ's sake.' Blankness gave way to surprise as he glanced at the image. 'It's you. That's you when you were little. Shit. That's me in the background. It's outside the furnace. I had hair then…'

'This belongs to a murderer. And there are more. All kinds of photographs.'

'I don't understand.'

'Somebody was watching me the whole time, here in the shipyards. They took pictures, they gathered evidence. Who?'

'Anna–'

'Don't bullshit me. I need to know.'

He opened his mouth but said nothing. He took out a cigarette. 'I'm sorry, Anna. It was to protect you, we kept things secret. I never intended this… I had no idea.'

'Kept what secret?'

'All I know is, it was a cop who brought you to the shipyards. Just as the War was starting. Soldiers everywhere. The Nazis moved in fast, took control of the city. Easy as falling asleep. This cop came. He was one of the good ones. I knew him, vaguely. I knew he was alright. He had an unusual name, don't remember what.'

'Tal.'

He exhaled acrid smoke, Russian brand. 'There you go. The past comes back, no matter what. It's like the tide. Funny thing, I'll never forget it. In the middle of all that chaos, we found him holding a baby.'

'Why?'

'I laughed at first. The shipyards aren't an orphanage. He said, "She's Polish. Her parents are dead. If the authorities find her, they'll raise her as a Nazi. They're looking for blonde-haired kids. She'll grow up without ever knowing she was Polish."'

'Blonde hair…'

'That was a thing back then. Blonde hair mattered for some reason. Anyway, times were urgent. There was no time to think. It's all a blur. I don't remember. Somehow, I took that baby and hid her. We raised you ourselves, everyone on the shipyards did. Later on, when things settled down, I found out about a Polish couple who wanted a child. They adopted you. We agreed you should never learn the truth. We'd let you think they were your real parents. Why should the young grow up as sad as we did? Let youth have a chance. Let the future… They did good, raised you well, before the communists got rid of them.'

'"Got rid of them…?" They died in a car crash.'

'Did they? Some things are best left alone. You're a cop now. You're part of the system.'

'I'm just me. What happened to my parents?'

His face turned bleak. 'They were trade union leaders. They had to go.'

She tried to resist. 'The People's Republic supports the unions, it's what it was created for.'

'Open your goddamn eyes, Anna. They hate us because their own teachings make the unions important. If they crush the unions, they prove it's all a lie. All this, "The Workers' State". They have to keep the unions quiet, compliant, in order to not give up control.'

'I don't believe it.'

'Believe what you want. Your colleagues are out there now arresting us.'

'And my parents, or my foster parents, I guess. You think the communists killed them?'

'I have no idea. Those days were chaos. If you survived from one day to the next you thanked God. People got real religious.'

'I need to use your phone.'

* * *

From Kostek's office, Anna called the police station and was put through to Roman.

'Detective? Where the hell are you?'

'It's the case. I discovered something. It's big…'

'What?'

Somebody was shouting in the background. Roman muttered something away from the phone. When he came back, he was distant.

'There's no time, Detective,' he said. 'Listen carefully–'

'Roman, I found where the killer lives. Zielinski's killer. I've been in his room.'

'What? Wait a minute…'

Lunar gales blew through the connection; his voice distorted, faded.

'Roman? Are you there? There's more. Somehow, it's linked to me, and to the past. The killer. This guy has pictures of me in his room, pictures of the shipyards.'

'What pictures?'

'I've been digging. Something happened during the War. I think the same killer was at work back then. He killed my parents. There was a cop who brought me to the shipyards.'

'A cop? This is crazy. Anna…'

'But this cop was involved in something. He's the one who found out who the killer was. If we can discover what happened to him, we can break the case open. His name was Tal.'

Static, electronic wind.

'Slow down, Anna, this is too much.'

'Johann Tal. I saw his record at the archive. He's the key.'

Silence at the other end of the line. Distant voices shouted. She pushed the receiver against her ear. 'Hello? Are you still there? Roman?'

His tone was changed when it returned. Mechanical. 'You've been in the killer's room?'

'Yeah. He–'

'But where is he?'

'I don't know. He wasn't there.'

'And where are you now?'

'At the shipyards. I wanted to find out about–'

'What's the killer's address? I'll meet you there. Come right away. And come alone. Don't tell anybody else.'

'Alone…?'

'There are things going on, Anna. I can't talk on the phone. There are things happening. It's not safe. I'll meet you there. I'll leave right away. What's the address?'

57

A feral cat stared back at her from inside the front entrance of the old tenement. Roman's car was parked on the pavement. He must be waiting upstairs. How long had he been here? Breathing heavily, Anna hurried through the building. Her feet echoed in the courtyard where tree roots broke the slabs. The ground floor was filled with cats. Where before just a few intrepid strays spied out of their hiding places, now they all came out, waiting for something. The door was closed at the killer's flat. She pushed through without stopping to think, and it was only as she crossed the dark hall that she remembered and stopped to listen. A soft sound, textured, as of material being folded.

'Superintendent?' she called; her voice was just a croak.

Through the door, his familiar voice from the station sounded out of place, strange. 'Anna? You're here. Where were you?'

She hadn't known how tense she was; her shoulders slumped with relief. 'I was at the shipyards. The strike… So many people… I couldn't get out.' She pushed open the door to find Roman seated on the edge of the bed, rummaging in the loose clothes that covered the floorboards.

'He didn't come back…' she said.

'What?' Roman looked up from the bed as if unsure where he was.

'The killer.'

'I've been here ten minutes. He won't come back, not if he's smart. Killers change their hiding places.' Roman seemed distracted; his voice absentminded, his eyes lost in an old shirt that he picked up and rubbed between finger and thumb.

'Did you see the pictures?' She grabbed a handful of photographs from the desk. Too rushed, panicky, she dropped one to the floor. Bending down she saw it: a little girl climbing the fence of the shipyards, her face hidden in a cloud of windblown hair.

A click behind her back. She spun around. Roman held a gun to her neck.

'I'm sorry, Anna.'

'What are you doing?'

'You dug too deep. I told you to stop, but you don't listen. You never will.'

'I don't understand. Can I…' She reached out.

'No!' Roman screamed. The gun shook in his grip. 'Stay down there!'

'I… I just wanted to solve the case…'

'Some secrets need to stay buried. For everyone's sake.'

'Roman Schneider. That's you, isn't it…' She couldn't take her eyes off the end of the gun as she turned slowly to face it. A simple, blunt finality. But her mind didn't care. At root, she was still the little shipyard orphan, and everything was just a game. Nobody died, only in make-believe. Rooms like this one didn't really exist.

'A burden I live with,' Roman said. 'I was a witness when it all burned. The things I know. They need to be forgotten. The country's raw. It needs to move forwards without these memories, this weight. This pain. But you, you can't stop digging around in the dirt.'

'And the truth–'

'Is irrelevant. We'll never be free if we can't forget. Your detective, Tal. He's one of those secrets. So are you.'

'I was only–'

'You wanted to find out about your parents, your childhood. I know. That's what makes you dangerous. I always knew it. I was there in the shipyards… You should've gone to one of the Reich's orphanages, but I let the workers keep you. Never dreamed you'd become a cop. I kept an eye on you. I hoped you'd be satisfied with your life and leave the past alone. Let it go. But you couldn't let it go, and you never will. You'll always dig. You'll dig and you'll dig until you find out something you'll wish you never knew.'

'I just want–'

'You can't have what you want! Nobody can. The secret police are crawling all over us, Christ, they've bugged the station. They bugged my own home. I found it last night in the bedside lamp. By my fucking bed. What do they think they'll hear?'

'Roman, I can help you. I'm not your enemy… you know I've always been loyal…'

'You're only loyal to the past.' He raised the gun to her forehead. 'You're another secret that needs to be buried. It's my job to be the one who buries. And me, I'll spend my years sweating somebody might dig you up. This city, it's like a curse. You can't put your foot down without stepping on a grave.'

'Please…' It wasn't her voice. Just a girl, a dirty-faced kid alone in a ruined city. 'Please…'

'I'm sorry.' The gun shook in his hand.

A voice through the shut door said, '*Roman*.'

His swollen eyes held hers, just terror, the rest had fallen away. 'Did you tell somebody else?'

She tried to speak but could only shake her head as a cry burst and broke from her chest. 'No…'

'Roman.' The voice was old, dewed with loss. 'We should talk.'

'Stay back!' He swung the gun around towards the door. 'Stay back. Who are you?'

'I just wanted to talk. Two old-timers from Danzig. It's lonely when you have nobody to talk with about the past.'

'What past?'

'You remember. The old days, before everything was lost. When the streets were lined with runes. Every house was a different pastel shade. Do you remember the carillon?'

'Who are you? What do you want?' Flecks of spittle clung to the edges of his lips.

The door opened, slowly, creaking. A man in the dark of the hall held back. Anna squinted into the shadow, but he wore a black trench coat and a dark grey fedora. A stray cat twined about his legs.

'Hello, Roman. Aren't you glad to see me?' His face was concealed beneath the low brim of his hat. He breathed heavily as if with exhaustion. The cat stared.

'Who?' Roman jumped up. He held the rattling gun in both hands and couldn't keep it steady. Craning his neck, he peered into the dark. '*Tal*…? Is that you?'

He spoke in German. A spell broke in thin air. Anna had never heard that language at the station, she had never imagined Roman was capable of it. He sounded like a different person altogether, a wholly new personality.

The stranger replied in German. 'Funny how you recognise a man, even after twenty years. Was it in your dreams you saw me again?'

The German cadences lilted like an old folk song. Anna only half understood, eavesdropping on two ghosts, words and phrases snatched from the past.

'You were dead, Tal. You're still dead.'

'One thing I don't understand. Could you always speak Polish? Back when the police were beating up Poles, closing their businesses, confiscating their belongings… could you speak Polish all along? Or did you learn it after the Soviets came?'

Roman snarled like a sick animal. 'You need to die.' He raised the gun. 'You need to be gone, like you never lived.'

'No!' Anna jumped on him.

The bullet blew past her ear, deafening, and blasted the wall. In the hiss of soundlessness, Roman threw her to the ground. His contorted jaws appeared to scream, but she heard nothing above the whistle inside her skull. In whirling deafness, she lost sense of forwards, backwards, up, or down. She crawled and didn't know where. She felt a hand on her back and twisted around. Roman stared with one eye, sharp teeth bared, and she braced herself. He'd kill her. But he dropped limp. Clothes on a washing line as the breeze passes out of them. He crumpled to the ground. Anna might have screamed. The man in the trench coat knelt over Roman and felt his pulse. She was deaf, and she studied his slow lips set into a grizzled white beard, weathered skin.

'He's gone. He's gone now.'

58

'Twenty years ago,' Tal said, 'I chased a killer. Strange thing, I found him in a newspaper. The *Danziger Neueste Nachrichten*, it doesn't exist anymore. One day, they ran an obituary about a woman. Her son was sick. He didn't know who he was. He kept that edition of the paper and read it over and over until he knew every page. All his victims were inside.'

'But why?' Anna kept pace as he strode ahead.

He was old, with a white beard, and he limped as he moved, but he was fast. Determined. He didn't slow down as he pressed through quiet streets; most of the city's people were either at the shipyards to watch the strikes or hiding indoors from the coming reprisals. Blood in the air.

'Where are we going? Hold on a minute. Tell me.'

He didn't stop. 'My theory is, with his struggle for identity, the people in the newspaper had a kind of reality, because they were written about. They were recorded there in black and white, it made them official.'

'That's weird.'

'Isn't God's eye the same? I've had many years to ponder these things. God's eye sees everything and keeps record, it knows all our secret thoughts and actions. Who else, if not God? Without a witness, it's like we don't exist.'

'I'm happy to not exist, in that case.'

'Whatever the reason, he killed those people and took their clothes. The clothes were symbolic for him. He became those people, at least in part. He gained their powers. He killed a cop and gained the power of law and order. He killed a priest and gained morality. He killed a mother and gained love. Only, that didn't work, not quite the way he wanted.'

'He gave up clothes, I found out. In the mental hospital, he stopped wearing them, he said they didn't work.'

'He gave up clothes…'

'Now he kills an archaeologist on a dig site. What did he gain from that?'

'Power over history, and the runes.'

'OK. And now? What does he want?'

'He took you as a baby, but he wasn't able to become you. If he could only manage it, he'd gain the power of innocence. He might be able to cure himself and start over. A baby has no identity, it's pure in that way. He couldn't do it then, but he's stayed in the shadows and watched you grow. He's been patient. He's waited all these years. Now it's time. He thinks he can become you. An end to the cycle.'

'How do you know this? Hold on. Will you stop a minute? I'm police, you have to do what I say. You're not in charge here, I am.'

He kept on striding ahead. 'I watch from the shadows as well. I've seen the runes.'

'You followed my case?'

He scoffed. 'There were runes all over the city. You and your colleagues never found them; you didn't look. Drug addicts, homeless lunatics, prostitutes. Nobody cared. Nobody bothered to pay attention or to notice the runes.'

'That's not possible. If there were runes, somebody would've recorded them…'

'Nobody noticed. Nobody wanted to. German history in this city is forbidden. But I found them. It's been six months now. I've been building a case.'

Up ahead, the harbour rose in a chilling wind. Tal turned down the brim of his hat and plunged into the salt vapour.

'Wait a second.' Anna had to shout as the gust stole her voice. 'Let's say I believe you. You've been investigating on your own, which is illegal by the way. You really think you know where the killer is now?'

'Yes.'

'Where?'

'A lowlife drug dealer went missing months back. A scumbag who nobody missed, not even the addicts or the gangsters. Here.' He took out a notepad but didn't slow down as he flipped through the pages in a fierce wind. 'Do you know this one?'

ᚾ

She stared at the rune. 'Looks like a crucifix.'

'No. The bar is asymmetrical. It's the Elder Futhark symbol for "need". Addiction. He took the drug dealer; he's become him now.' Tal put the pad away.

'And this rune…'

'Was painted in the victim's blood on the wall of a flophouse. One of your colleagues scrubbed it off. Nobody cared.'

'I don't believe you.'

Tal shrugged. 'The dealer was a scumbag. He cut his products with rat poison. Nobody mourned him.'

'And this dealer…?'

'A few weeks ago, the rat poison drugs surfaced again. Underground, there are whispers, the dealer came back from the dead.'

'The killer took his identity.'

'He found a new role to play. It suits him for now. He changes from time to time. He enjoys playing different characters. But they don't last long for him. The act starts to erode, he has to find a new one.'

'And you think you know where–'

'It's here.' Tal stopped outside an abandoned warehouse. A monolith of brick and ragged gutters. 'This is it. This is the end.'

59

Anna flashed her torch through a hole in the wall into darkness. She tried to go forwards, but the world was spinning, she held onto a brick outcropping and sank. Tal grabbed her elbow.

'Are you OK?'

'Yeah. I'm fine. I just…' She took a step inside and tumbled to the ground. Space flooded in, like the sky turned inside out and she was falling upwards. She reached for anything to hold onto and couldn't find a thing.

'Wait a moment.' Tal knelt beside her. 'The gunshot knocked your balance. It was too close to your ear. You've got vertigo. Lie still for a second.'

'I'm alright, I'm alright.' She tried to get up and was pushed down by a crushing weight on her shoulders. She almost screamed.

'Wait, wait,' Tal said. 'I'll get some water.'

'I don't need water. I don't need anything.'

'You stay down here,' he said. 'I'll go up on my own and see what's there.'

She grabbed his wrist. 'Don't even think about it.'

'It's my case. I've been tracking him twenty years.'

He tried to get up from beside her, but Anna gripped his arm. 'No. I'm the detective. Legally speaking. You shouldn't be here at all. You don't have a badge. I should call the station for backup. Probably I should arrest you.'

'I'm a detective just as much as you are. It's not a job you can retire from. It stays with you until you die. Even afterwards, in my case.'

'I said, no. Just give me a moment. The dizziness is passing.' She winced and managed to sit upright, bracing for the sky to collapse, but there was no sky overhead, just the shadowy rafters of the warehouse. She blinked and rubbed her eyes, and the dizziness was gone. Still, she couldn't stand.

Tal crouched beside her. 'Be careful, it could come back.'

'I need to know something. You're the only one from the past who's still here. You met my real parents…?'

'I never met them.'

'But you must know something… Were they Polish or German?'

He hesitated. 'I heard they were Polish.'

'And what else? Can't you give me anything… a name? What job did they have?'

His eyes moved off to that oblique, diagonal space where the past resides. He thought a beat too long. 'I'm sorry, Anna,' he said. 'I don't know.'

'That's it then. I'll never find out. You were the last link.'

'Does it matter? I lost my parents too. Everyone does in the end.'

'I've been orphaned twice. My foster parents were killed; I hardly remember them. My real parents I don't even know their names. Who am I?'

'You're just you. That's enough.'

'I grew up on the shipyards, but I can't go back there. Cops aren't welcome. Worst thing is, I don't even belong at the police station. My colleagues hate me, so do my superiors. I tried to believe in communism, I gave it everything, studied the texts, puzzled it all out, but they threw me in a cell. I've seen the other side of it now. What's left? Who am I?'

Tal shook his head. 'When I was young, we argued all the time about who Gdańsk belonged to. Was it German, or Polish, or Kashubian, or what? The truth is different. A city doesn't belong to anyone. The street signs here used to all be in German, but they're in Polish now. It's easier than you think to redraw a map, to change a name.'

'Nothing's real then.'

'I didn't say that. The city belongs to whoever loves it. You may have been an orphan, but there were a thousand people on the shipyards who took care of you, in ways you never knew.'

'You were there the whole time…'

'Nothing lasts beyond a moment. Only memory remains. Who remembers? That's the question.'

'Alright, help me up.' She held his hand and let him drag her to her feet. 'I'm ready. Let's get this over with.'

60

The interior was hollow, porous with wind, dripping and mossy. Their footsteps echoed too loud beneath splintered rafters. At the end of a collapsed foyer, they found a metal stairway riveted into the bare brick. It spiralled into darkness, upwards and downwards. A patter of rain played through the shaft and scattered off the steps overhead. Anna peered over the edge of the railing and saw the red-painted steps disappear into a pit of black. From above it was brighter, a suggestion of the outside. The stairwell rattled and creaked, the rain drummed vague tunes off the metal steps.

'I'll go first,' Anna said.

The stairway rattled as they climbed through a shower of rain, notes of ivy, mould, brick, and dust. Cobweb. Just a touch of the sea. A stairway from a dream that leads nowhere, turning in place like a screw. At the third twist of the steps, a door was set into the wall. It was painted red and was just like the front door to somebody's house, except that there was no sign or number or any other kind of identifying mark, and it hung in the emptiness. Anna wiped the rain from her face. She tried the handle, and it gave, rusted, grinding. The door opened.

'Careful.' Tal breathed hoarsely as he came up behind her. He seemed older than she had thought, and weak. The stairwell shook against the wall.

She pushed and the door opened further. It was light inside. Somebody's home; stained floorboards, bare brick walls, tattered curtains, but still a home. An old picture of a sailing ship was stuck to the wall just inside, and a few overcoats hung from a rack. Rain danced on the windows. It was a large, self-contained space, with a grimy portable stove and a basin against one wall. On the other side, a living area was washed in grey light through two tall windows. A dog-eared sofa and a table occupied the centre of the space. At the opposite end, behind a folding partition, the edge of a bed poked out, with the sheets and duvet cover in disarray. A radio played, classical music with the volume turned low, but nobody seemed to be listening. There were signs of occupation: a full ashtray on a little table by the sofa, dirty dishes piled up by the sink. A faint chemical scent hung in the air.

She saw a closed door in the wall behind the stove. Nowhere else to go, she stepped into the middle of the room. Moving away from the door, she registered a camera set on a tripod to one side.

'See anybody?' Tal whispered.

'Shush.'

She stepped forwards, away from the camera, moving towards the far corner, trying to peek behind the partition, which was half folded inwards. She touched its edge and looked around. In a wide, makeshift bed, a mound was formed under the duvet cover, a human outline curled beneath. She stepped closer and stopped when a woman's voice said, 'What time is it?'

There was a moment in which she could have run away, but she didn't reply, didn't move.

A young woman sat up in the bed, stretched, and said, 'Is it yesterday or tomorrow?'

She didn't look like a drug dealer; her hair was blonde, and her skin was fresh, although pockmarked with acne. She looked feverish. What was she, sixteen? She squinted beneath the palm of one hand as if the light stung her eyes. She stared at Anna, trying to place her or to figure her.

'Are you OK?' Anna said.

'Just give me a minute.' She reached for a bedside table and took up a pack of cigarettes and a lighter.

'Take your time.' Anna glanced back at Tal, who was hidden from view behind the partition, but he only shrugged. She looked for the right words. 'Did anybody else come?'

The girl took a first, deep inhalation from the cigarette and in the twining smoke let her eyes go unfocused, as if she were alone. 'Where did you appear from?'

'I'm new,' Anna said.

'Jesus. You don't look the type. Are you sure you belong here? Things happen in this place, you know. You should get out while you can.'

'Maybe you should get out too.'

The girl laughed and it was like the laughter of a crone. 'Me? You don't know anything. Come here, look.'

Anna approached slowly, and suddenly she was a child at the edge of her mother's bed – enormous and rich with odours and bodily warmth – and the sleepy dishevelment of her mother contained the mystery of the whole future into which the child stood facing backwards in her ignorance. And yet, she couldn't bring back her mother's face; and that woman had never been her real mother anyway. Nothing was real. She stopped a foot away from the bedframe, but the girl beckoned with the hand that held the cigarette.

'Come on,' she said, 'come closer.' She reached under the far side of the bed and came up with a handful of syringes.

Anna flinched at the sight of them, and the girl laughed.

'What did you expect? The others come here for the orgasms; I come for the drugs, Comrade.' She pulled back the sleeve of her pyjama and there was a long trail of puncture marks.

Anna needed to get out. The needles rolled on the stained bedsheet. She wouldn't look at them. She reached into the memory of all the muttered conversation she had ever heard at the shipyards. 'Whatever you're into.'

'I haven't been sober since I set foot in here. I don't know what year it is anymore. Don't tell me. And he has the best stuff, Comrade, the best you'll ever taste, and no end to it.'

'Is that true?' Anna stared at the needles and couldn't help it.

'Oh, he's generous. He's a generous man.'

She wanted to ask, "Who is he?" But a single wrong word would expose her as an imposter. 'Yeah. I know what you mean.'

'Have you ever tried?'

'I smoke a little weed.'

The girl stared into nothingness with her dilated pupils. 'Come on then.' She patted the bare mattress beside her.

'Where is he now? I need to talk to him.'

'Why?'

'I have a message for him.'

'Fuck him, jeez. Let's chat a bit. I haven't talked to a woman in ages. I could tell you things.' The glazed madness in her eyes coalesced at the passing thought as she blew out smoke, turning hard. 'The secrets I know about this place.'

'Really?' Anna sat down on the edge of the bed.

The girl pulled herself up into a sitting position, arranging the pillows behind her back. 'What's your name?'

'Anna,' she answered automatically, before she could lie.

'Oh.' The girl nodded as if with recognition. 'I'm Lucie. You know it's funny, I still remember being a virgin, it only seems like yesterday. But I can't remember ever being off drugs, it's like they put it in my milk when I was a baby.' She tapped the long trail of ash from the end of her cigarette into a mug on the bedside table. For a few moments she just looked at the end of the cigarette, seeming to have forgotten already the stories she had offered.

'You were going to tell me,' Anna said.

'My ma was a kind of priest, isn't that funny? I never even knew women were allowed to be priests.'

'When did you last see him?'

'Wait.'

'What?'

Lucie didn't reply. Anna scanned the back of the partition; Tal was out of sight and silent on the other side. When Anna's gaze returned to her, Lucie stared back, a hint of hysteria dancing in one eye. From nowhere she asked, 'Do you really think I could get out of here?'

'Of course,' Anna said.

The girl only laughed, with surprising richness. 'Are you sure you're free to come and go?'

'Yes.'

'Maybe you could take a message for me to my ma, she might be worried about me.'

'I would be happy to.'

The girl lit up a second cigarette with the butt of the first one. 'Forget it. That old cunt already forgot who I am.'

Silence, and the girl's eyes went scratching anxiously around the dusty corners of the brick walls. Anna only wanted to leave, but she didn't. Incredibly, her tongue flexed, she said, 'I need to speak to him.'

Lucie tilted her head back to look up at the ceiling, as if listening for the sound of feet in the desiccated nests of the warehouse roof. She blew out a lazy trail of smoke. Back behind the partition, Tal took a step backwards. When Lucie looked down again her eyes were wild. 'Oh God, he's here, isn't he?'

Anna hesitated. 'It's just us. But I need to speak to him. Where is he?'

'He was supposed to… he said…'

'Go on…'

'Shush!' They froze, the girl's hand holding her in a passionate clasp. 'Is that him?'

'I can't hear anything.'

'Shush!'

In the silence, Anna scrutinised the girl's face, the way her eyes twisted from the partition to the floor, to the wall, drawing a map of all the hiding places of dread. She was about to say something, to try to reassure her that it was only silence and paranoia, but she hesitated: she did hear something. Movement within the building, a tremor passed through the floors and walls.

'Oh Jesus,' the girl whispered, 'oh Jesus, oh Jesus.'

'What is it? What's happening?'

Footsteps came up the stairs outside, but the auditory distortion of the room was confusing, Anna could not tell if they were near or far. She jumped up and skipped around the partition. Tal was gone; he must be hiding somewhere. She tiptoed to the front door. She pressed her ear against it: footsteps, the metal stairwell rattled. She felt a breath of presence and span around, stifling a scream, to find Lucie stood behind her, naked beneath the pyjama top, and unsteady on her feet. She held a syringe loosely in one hand. She grabbed at her, and Anna tried to pull her arms away, but there was no space to escape, pressed against the back of the door. The point of the syringe danced in the air.

'Please don't.'

'Who are you?' Lucie whispered.

'Nobody.'

The stairwell creaked. Footsteps rang so close they seemed to rise through the floor.

'I'm not stupid, bitch. You're police.'

'I swear…'

The footsteps stopped outside the door.

'Oh Christ.' Lucie dropped the needle. 'Come with me.'

She almost stumbled as she lunged, catching hold of Anna's forearm. Anna felt herself pulled with force – the girl was surprisingly strong – and let herself be dragged. She saw Tal crouched behind the sofa. He raised a finger to his lips.

Lucie dragged her to the door in the corner. 'She's inside.' Her voice was quiet, awestruck, as if she feared to wake a baby.

'OK.' Anna glanced back as the front door opened.

'Quick!'

They fell together into a dirty bathroom. The chemical smell flared in her nostrils as the door opened inwards. A light clicked on to show filthy, pale floor tiles, a cracked sink, a chipped mug with toothbrushes inside. The bathtub was full to the top with black liquid.

'What…?'

'Shush.' Lucie locked the door behind them.

Anna tried to say, 'What are you doing?' but no sound came out.

Footsteps crossed the room outside. A man's voice, deep, wretched, shouted, 'Lucie!'

Lucie pulled Anna down onto the floor that was wet with overflow from the bathtub.

'Help us,' Lucie whispered.

'I don't understand.' Panic welled up in the tight confines of the room, with its hard, tiled surfaces. 'What is that?' Anna pointed at the tub.

'It's her,' Lucie said, in a murmur. 'The actress. She's inside. Do you want to see?'

In the room outside, a deep voice shouted, 'Lucie? Where are you?'

Anna recoiled, springing to the door, her hands shaking, trying to grasp at the slippery handle. It half turned and then stopped and squirmed out of her grip.

On the other side of that door, the voice said, 'Lucie? Are you in there?'

Lucie backed against the wall, with the key in her hand. She seemed to disintegrate into dust motes, without losing the integrity of her terrified shape. Outside, a fist banged against the door. She reached out a hand.

Through the door, the man's voice shouted, 'Come out here.'

'Police.' Tal's voice. 'Turn around slowly.'

Funny, to hear his voice without seeing him, he didn't sound old at all. He sounded like a young man, strong, energetic.

'Police?' The man laughed.

Anna hissed at Lucie, 'Open this door. I need to…'

Lucie showed no sign of hearing her. She drooled, rocking back and forth against the tiled wall. 'I can't take it. I can't anymore. I'm going to climb in there as well.'

'Don't move!' Tal shouted outside. 'I'm warning you. Stand back.'

'Where is she?' the man said.

Their voices played off the hard brick walls like the inside of Anna's throbbing skull.

'Where is who?' Tal said. 'I came here alone.'

'I don't believe you.'

Anna clawed at Lucie's shoulder. 'Give me the key,' she whispered. 'I need to get out.'

Footsteps crossed the floor outside as if it were her ear canal. 'Tal. It's you, isn't it? It's really you. What are you doing here? You don't belong in the future.'

'Neither do you.'

'Yet here we are.'

'I chased you down here,' Tal said. 'I always chased you, always will. In the past life and in the future.'

'And you'll never catch me.'

'Do you imagine your runes protect you?'

The man laughed. Pinned against the inside of the door, Anna listened. Dread welled in her throat.

'You failed, Tal.'

'No, I won. You just don't see it yet.'

A gunshot pierced the air, breaking a scream in half. Crazy echoes bounced off the tiles. Lucie shrieked. She grabbed at Anna, ripping her shirt.

Anna couldn't move. Reduced to just an ear pressed against nothingness trying to know… 'Tal?' she screamed. 'Tal? Are you alright…?'

'Beloved.' The voice vibrated through the bathroom door against her ear. 'Your friend's dead. He already was, he just didn't realise until now. But it's over. Open up. Open, and find out what you always wanted.'

'Don't do it,' Lucie whispered. 'You don't know him. You don't know what he does.'

His fist banged on the wood. 'Open! Open! Now!'

'Go away!' Lucie shouted. 'I hate you.'

The fist hammered; the hinges rattled in the frame.

'Go away!' Lucie clutched Anna tightly. 'Leave us alone!'

The door beat with the shuddering impact of some large blunt object trying to break it open. It thudded in dreary, inevitable rhythm, and the door lurched on its hinges like a sick thing. Anna and Lucie curled together in the far corner, wedged between the toilet bowl and the tiled wall, watching the door's heart-like beating. Their arms wrapped around one another; damp clothes pressed together. Lucie moaned with stuttering sounds that almost formed words, while Anna stroked her hair, clumsily.

The knocking stopped. Anna couldn't move. She waited for the voice to speak again, but it was silent. There was no sound or intimation of movement through the door; everything waited. Anna turned to the girl, who sat hunched against the side of the stained, leaking bathtub.

'Can I have the key please, Lucie? I have to go home now.'

The girl shook her head, wordless. Beyond her terror, Anna became aware of haggard movement, something heavy was dragged across the floor, but it was faraway and brittle, like the residue of a dream.

Lucie whispered hotly in her ear, 'How can I escape? There's no way out.'

'Come with me, I'll help you.' She tried to extricate herself, but the girl held her so tightly. Her nails were ragged.

'No. That's what he wants. He always gets what he wants.'

'Can you give me the key, please…' She tried to stand and was pulled backwards, the girl's nails raking across her back. She tried to turn, and their two bodies twisted together, slipped on the wet floor, and fell sideways, entangled. They tumbled over the edge of the bath.

'No!' Anna's left arm disappeared up to the shoulder in the black liquid that frothed over her legs onto the tiles. 'Stop!'

Her hand slipped against eel-like skin beneath the water as she tried to right herself. Lucie's arms meshed with hers, pushing her deeper. Water sloshed over the edge, and a woman's face broke the surface. Adrenaline gave her strength. She pulled her arm free. Lucie slipped on the overflow as she came after her, falling onto the hard tiles with a scream. Footsteps ran across the boards outside. The door slammed. Something crashed. A gunshot rang out across the other side of the room. Lucie's teeth gnashed in the aftershock. Silence. A different footstep, slower. Somebody touched the door, but more softly than before.

'Anna…?' A different voice, somebody new.

In the fading whine of the gunshot, impossible sounds clawed through. She recognised the speaker.

'Kostek…? Is that…?'

'Anna! You're alright. What happened?'

'I… I don't know. Is Tal there…?'

'He's… I'm sorry, Anna. Tal's dead.'

She couldn't respond. Pressed against her shoulder Lucie held her breath so tightly, Anna felt her rib bones through the wet fabric pressed against her.

'Are you alright?' she whispered.

Lucie shook her head. Her cheeks were purple.

'Breathe out. Breathe out, he's gone.'

'It's OK now,' Kostek said from outside the door. 'He's dead. Jesus Christ. It's just as well I followed you over here.'

'I'm going to take the key now.' Gently, Anna prised at Lucie's fingers and pulled the key loose, while the girl sobbed against her. 'Shush. Good, alright. I'm going to stand up.'

'As soon as Tal told me, I knew you'd get in trouble. What were you thinking of?'

She put the key in the lock and turned it quickly, desperate to get out of that room. Only as the door opened, the words of the doctor from the sanatorium played in her mind. *God, it was creepy the way he could mimic another person, his voice sounded exactly like theirs, he could recreate every little gesture, the way they walked or moved or even just sat down.* She tried to stop the door, but it was too late. A powerful hand on the other side pushed inwards.

'You came. I called you, and you came.' The voice was still Kostek's, he even kept his left eye closed, and he hunched just the same way Kostek hunched, but it was not him. It was somebody else entirely. He was tall, bald, muscular, wearing a vest that revealed the scar tissue of ugly runes carved into the skin.

'Get out here, into the light.' He pulled her out of the bathroom, and he was so strong.

She tried to raise the gun in her free hand, but he punched her in the face and, as she recoiled, he swatted the weapon away. It bounced against the floor.

'No!'

'Let her go!' Lucie ran out of the bathroom and jumped on him, but he threw her aside with ease. She crashed into the wall, headfirst, and just lay there, a trickle of blood oozing from her nose.

'You killed her!' Anna writhed uselessly in his hands.

He stared for a moment at the girl's body. 'She was insane. I think she gave me a venereal disease.' The voice was changed again, neutral, without any accent, almost bored. 'Drugs are strange.'

Anna clawed at his thick, hairy knuckles. 'What do you want?'

'Shut up a minute.' He punched her in the face, a blow that sent her head snapping backwards.

She spat out a tooth, eyes closed to stop the spinning. 'Please.'

'What do I want? To be free. To stop the poison choking me. To become you.'

'That's impossible.'

'I've done it before. You'll see.' He pinned her down on the ground.

'Why me?' Splayed there, her loose arm stretched for the gun that was just out of reach on the floor.

'It has to be you.'

'Why?'

'It's the only way back. To the past, to the beginning, before all this. You're the link. The first time, everything went wrong, but now I know better.'

'You're insane.' Her fingers wriggled and strained and could not reach the gun.

'Insanity and logic have never been apart. The Nazis knew that. So do your communists.'

'The communists are nothing like the Nazis.'

One fist closed around her throat. 'And yet they have their runes. Your hammer and sickle, isn't that a rune? And a powerful one. They enslave millions with it. But I know better runes.'

'Danzig, please. It doesn't have to be–'

He slapped her face, spat in her eye. 'Don't say my name. You don't know what it means. You never saw Danzig.'

'What do you want?'

'You already know the answer.' He ripped the front of her shirt free from her body in a fistful of material, scattering buttons, and tore it away.

'No!' She writhed in his grip, kicking and punching at his side as hard as she could, but he didn't flinch.

'You feel it now.' His eyes were like foglamps. 'It's already started. You feel me becoming you.'

It was true: his voice became hers, his face shifted, trying out expressions, mirroring her terror.

He saw the recognition in her eyes and laughed. 'Yes. Now you feel it.'

'You'll never…' She gave up resisting, she had to conserve energy, but her body trembled uncontrollably. Sick with desperation, she glanced around for a strategy, and saw Tal's body, face down, in the corner in a dark mirror of blood. He had seemed so alive before, despite his brittle age, a source of will had played in his rich voice. *A city doesn't belong to anyone*, she heard him say in a fragment of memory where all was slow, infinite time. *You may have been an orphan, but there were a thousand people on the shipyards who took care of you, in ways you never knew.*

A blow to the face snapped her out of the fantasy.

'Give yourself to me.'

'No!'

'You already did.' He let out a groan of animal pleasure, eyes glazed with inner sensation. And then he stopped. 'What's that?'

The floor rattled as all her bones shook against it. She reached into nothingness.

'A rune…' He stroked the scabbed outline where she had carved the rune into her chest. Like a little boy, he wondered aloud. 'The rune of daylight.'

ᛞ

'How?' His face changed. Somebody else. Nobody. He stared in confusion. 'Who are you?'

Her fingers found the gun. All at once, she stopped trembling. She raised the gun to his forehead, and knew the answer.

'I'm Gdańsk.'

If you enjoyed this book, please let others know by leaving a quick review on Amazon. Also, if you spot anything untoward in the paperback, get in touch. We strive for the best quality and appreciate reader feedback.

editor@thebookfolks.com

www.thebookfolks.com

More fiction by the author

OUTCAST SISTER

London detective Eleanor Rose is lured back to her old city of Liverpool by Daniel, an ex-boyfriend and colleague who's in danger. It's against her better instincts, as she has no desire to confront her past. But when she gets there, he's nowhere to be found, and as she retraces his steps, Eleanor gets caught in a dark web of deceit, corruption and violence. Her half-sister, who never forgave her for leaving, seems involved too. Will their path cross? Will she find Daniel?

ROUGH SLEEPER

Eleanor Rose rejoins the force when a serial killer dubbed The Binman terrifies Liverpool. He is suffocating his victims with a refuse sack and discarding their bodies like trash. Her detective sister, Beth, is confined to hospital with a serious knife wound and a bad case of insomnia. Both are determined to catch the murderer. Will they prevail or succumb to the madness gripping the city?

FREE with Kindle Unlimited and available in paperback!

THE LONG DEAD
by John Dean

When a routine archaeological dig turns up bodies on the site of a WWII prisoner of war camp, it should be an open and shut case for detective John Blizzard. But forensics discover one of the deaths is more recent and the force have a murder investigation on their hands.

FREE with Kindle Unlimited and available in paperback!

Printed in Great Britain
by Amazon

43906825R00202